WOLVES AT THE DOOR

Happy Reading!

Thomas A. Chown

Thos A Chown

Pipers Willow, Inc.
www.PipersWillow.com

Happy dreams,

mrs. it me?

Reviews of *Wolves at the Door*

In his solid inaugural novel, *Wolves at the Door*, Tom Chown evinces an historian's eye and a storyteller's soul. His saga of Henry and Tamsen Devon's journey from the American frontier to the founding of the modern Midwest is one part history lesson, one part sociology primer, and one part action movie script. It's also a well-crafted study of the frontier family, something rarely attempted since Willa Cather's masterworks. The early descriptions of Henry's experience as a Jayhawker in 1860's "Bloody Kansas" are harrowing, and Chown describes the beauty, hardships, and spirituality of frontier Kansas in dead-on fashion. He constructs the novel in subtitled snippets, stories of everyday frontier lives. Henry Devon is an epic western character, forged by a savage world yet understanding how quickly it is all slipping away. His spiritual awakening while watching an Osage band hunt and kill a bull Buffalo is profound, providing a fine literary explanation of the historical respect and regret with which many settlers viewed the conquered and dispirited Indians. Inspired by his forebears, Chown's novel is a rich tapestry of accurate history, humor, folklore, and legend, expertly defining those who, in the last half of the 19th century, may well have been America's true "greatest generation."

— **Jon Chandler**

Author, singer/songwriter, and 1999 Western Writers of America Spur Award Winner for Best New Novel for *The Spanish Peaks*

Filled with a warm whimsy reminiscent of Mark Twain, *Wolves At The Door* is a well-researched slice of prairie life.

— **Richard D. Jensen**
Book reviewer for *Roundup* Magazine and author of *Tom Mix: The Most Famous Cowboy of the Movies.*

Acknowledgements

In any endeavor such as this book, the writer is not the only person responsible for the words scattered across the pages. There are always other people who help in so many ways. In my case, there are two such people. First is my cousin, Dr. Tom Reichert of St. Cloud, Minnesota. Tom not only provided terrific detailed research into the lives and times that this story involves, but he also gave me two other priceless ingredients: encouragement and enthusiasm. He and I have shared many hours of philosophizing about our common ancestry and wondering if it will be of interest to future generations. We hope so.

The other person I want to thank is my valued local editor and friend, Drollene Brown. Drollene offers the same encouragement mentioned above, but also has the courage to look me in the eye and say, "why on earth would you say it like that?" Any writer that has a competent person like Drollene to evaluate his efforts is blessed.

I am grateful for the support I have received from both of these kind souls.

WOLVES AT THE DOOR
by Thomas A. Chown
Copyright © 2007 by Thomas A. Chown

Published by:
Pipers Willow, Inc.
Sheridan, Wyoming

ISBN-13: 978-0-9787277-6-5 (Hardback)
ISBN-13: 978-0-9787277-5-8 (Paperback)
Library of Congress Control Number: 2007929038
Edited by Drollene P. Brown, Morriston, Florida.
Cover Design and Typeset by Jaspal S. Bisht, For more information, contact Aruna Enterprises by email at jpl@rediffmail.com
Printed in the United States of America.
All rights reserved. Printed in the United States of America. No part of this book may be reproduced or transmitted in any form or by any means, electronic or mechanical, including photocopying, recording or by any information storage and retrieval system, without written permission from the author, except for the inclusions of brief quotations in a review.

For more information, contact Pipers Willow, Inc., by email at piperswillow@gmail.com

Dedication

To all the real life folks the characters in this book represent. To us, this story is merely an entertaining fable. To them, it was their life.

Table of Contents

Part One

Bleeding Kansas—Life and Death in Bourbon County ... 1

Part Two

Wagons, Ho!—New Beginning in Kiowa ... 185

Part Three

On to La Junta—The Baton is Passed in Colorado ... 293

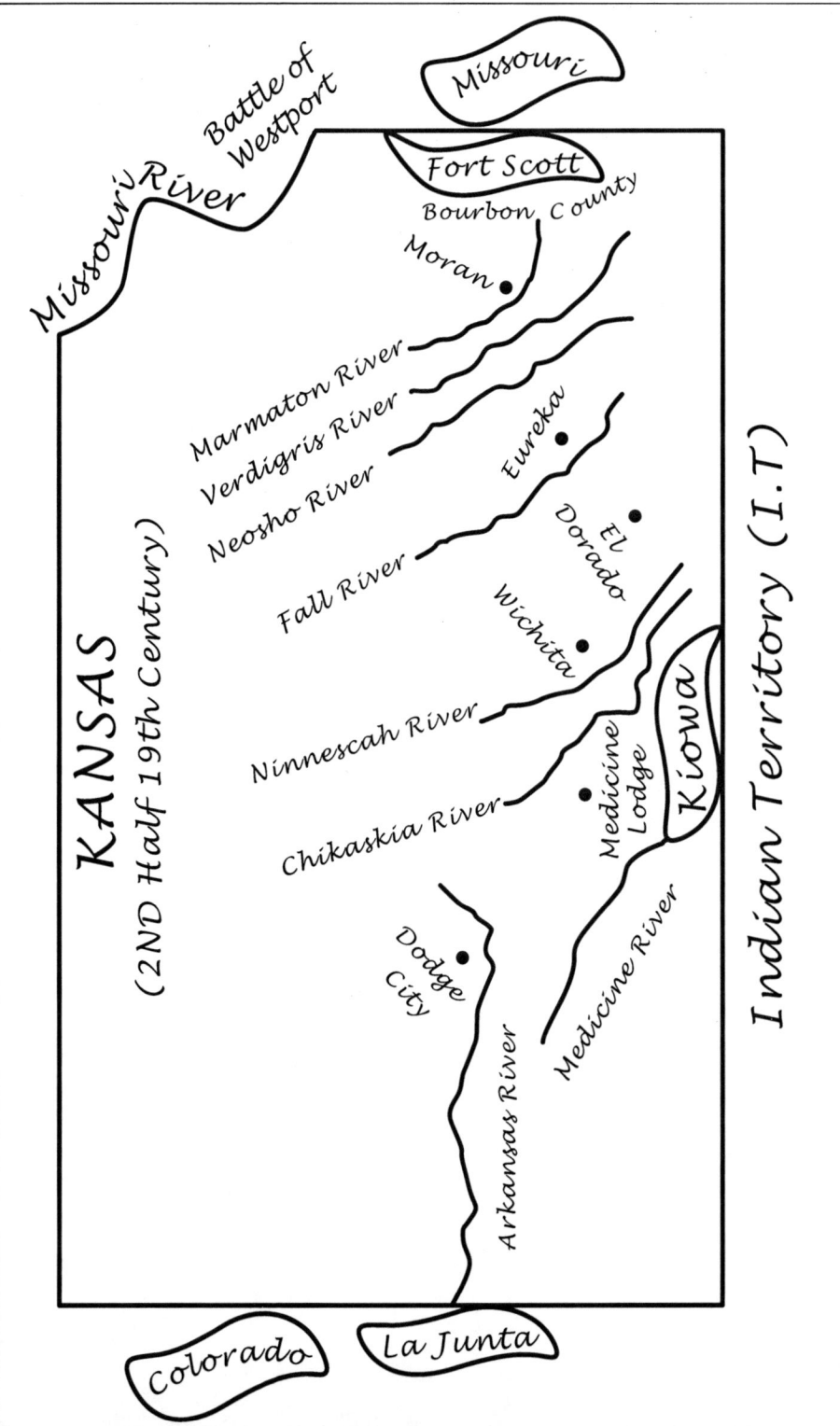

In cognizant appreciation
Of my people and your people
Who were here before us,
We peek at life standing on their shoulders.
We trod on dirt once fashioned by their footfalls.
They loved people, killed people, tried hard and died.
And along the way they made babies.
We are those babies.
Are we like them? Could we actually *be* them?
They may be gone some hundred years,
Yet little Johnny has Great Grandma's chin.
Although they were here so long ago,
Cousin Bill looks like the photo of Grandpa Jack.
Let's tell their stories as best we know how.
Let's always remember that they were here
On these very paths, breathing this same air.
Let's keep our own babies informed.

Prologue

October 23, 1864, dawned just like the day before it, and the day before that, cold and rainy. Henry Devon didn't mind harsh weather under normal conditions. He knew that every drop of rain that fell somehow added to the chances he and Tamsen could bring in a workable crop later. It had been a back breaking and probably futile effort to get a toe hold in the quarter section they were trying to prove up down in Bourbon County. At least it was futile for a lot of folks who finally decided that either no rain or too much rain, rattlesnakes, grasshoppers, diseased Texas longhorns and all other damnations along the Kansas/Missouri line made it futile. Hank dreamily cogitated on what that life was like, what a totally irksome bother the whole damn thing was, including the goddamn rain, or lack of it, up to about half a day ago.

As he hitched his corduroy collar as high as possible on his neck and tried to find at least one square foot of ground without a rock in it, his eyes and mind slowly refocused to where he currently was and what this coming day would bring. He was not in the little log cabin about to stir the fire so Tamsen and the children would stay warm. No, he was awakening to the scene he had dreaded, but must now deal with. Beside him in the little ravine just north of Brush Creek, just south of Westport, Missouri, he could barely make out the sodden looking hulks of his comrades in arms, Oliver Boutwell and Tommy Julion. Beyond them, either still snoring or

Wolves at the Door

wide-awake, lay the rest of Company D, Kansas State Militia's 6th Regiment. Kansas had only become a state three years earlier, and already here was its militia about to very literally kill or be killed by the invading Huns. Well, not exactly the Huns—worse! Those Confederate campfires across Brush Creek and on up the hill were mostly Jo Shelby's boys, the best cavalry in the Civil War, Confederate or Union. They were the best part of General Sterling Price's "Invasion Army."

"Jesus Christ, Boutwell," Tommy said, "do you mind rollin' over and pointing your breath toward Dixon? That puts any elephant fart I ever heard of to shame!"

Hank smiled. Tommy Julion had something funny to say no matter what. He could walk up and tell one of the boys his horse just got eaten by a pack of wolves and have the whole company howling by the way he said it.

"Go to hell, Tommy," replied Boutwell. "If you'd had to eat whatever vermin that was Cookie perked up for us last night, your breath'd be a little frisky, too! Oh, that's right, you did eat it. I guess that's why you're just a tad gamey yerself!"

These guys had a genuine and long standing fondness for each other. Regardless of where they originally hailed from, they were all Kansans now, having their homes in either Bourbon or Linn counties, down near Fort Scott. They all had known each other and had done their militia training, such as it was, together for a couple of years. Almost all were young farmers out of the Fort Scott or Mound City area. Colonel Charles Jennison, the great Jayhawker, was their inspiration,

Prologue

along with James Montgomery. Both were focused and fearless and ferocious men, especially the maniacal Jennison. All these guys were well seasoned as to the viciousness overwhelming the Kansas/Missouri border over the previous five years. The rebel bushwhackers, unofficial guerilla combatants, got the blue ribbon for being less than human satans, mainly due to the totally barbaric raid on Lawrence, Kansas, in 1863. They killed every adult man in town and a lot of very young boys, too. From Henry's view, the bushwhackers were the enemy, and he'd kill any of those bastards around those yonder campfires come sun up. In fact, he had killed three of them over the past seven months. Not as part of any official militia operations, but with Jennison's jayhawkers, the Union counterpart of the bushwhackers. He may have killed more than the three he knew about, depending on where some of his bullets ended up. But those three he really saw up close. Two were over in Missouri outside McGarvey's farmhouse in a retaliation raid one night the previous April. Jennison had taken some of his boys in after a mean bunch who had previously come across the state line and killed a Kansas farmer and his son right on the front porch of their farm house, and right in front of his missus. She went plain nuts. *The boy was only about twelve, and those devils shot him down*, thought Henry at the time. The wife just held onto her three-year-old girl and started wailing. Never stopped. All the women around were terrorized over what had been happening. They'd all seen butchery the likes of nothing those actual Huns ever thought about. The hatred

Wolves at the Door

that welled up was beyond all reason, and beyond fixing and forgetting. It was well past turning back the calendar.

When Henry killed the first two men it was an act in retaliation for the Kansas farm folks. Some of the boys knew these guys were part of those killings. They had big X's on their foreheads. They were lying low in the woods behind McGarvey's farmhouse over near Horton, Missouri, on the Osage River. The boys knew they were there and had surrounded the place. Henry had watched from behind a hill as those damn devils whooped and hollered over dinner in the farmhouse. Whether the McGarvey family had invited them in freely or were forced, Henry didn't know or care. These were the bushwhackers they had been seeking.

Henry's friends hadn't made of secret of what they were going to do. All fifteen rode up and called out the rebel guerillas. With no other options, the Missourians at least didn't hide behind the family. Henry thought they must have been enjoying the confidence of drink, or the dumb sonsabitches simply couldn't count. Must have thought fifteen and six were equal, because out they came, shotguns and revolvers blazing. One of the jayhawks, Ralph Sweeney, took a load to his face and was dead on his horse.

After that, Henry zoned into his own private war. He spotted a really dirty looking man with two big, solitary teeth. On reflex, Henry sent a pistol ball right into the man's forehead. No big mess, just a small hole like a bloodshot third eye. That eye stayed open, but the two original ones rolled back. He was instantly, Henry imagined, having

Prologue

dessert with his ancestors in a warm and fiery final destination. Without a blink, Henry caught more movement coming toward him from directly behind the now prostrate, two-toothed devil. Some detached spirit was by now operating Henry's body because, with no conscious command from Henry, his left arm swung up and very nicely unloaded both barrels of his shotgun. Henry was as surprised as the recipient of the buckshot seemed to be. A young boy, probably half Henry's age, maybe sixteen or seventeen, was stopped rigid. He would have been blown back onto the porch but for a support post behind him, holding him straight upright for a few seconds. Henry and the boy locked glares for what seemed to Henry like an eternity. The boy owned totally uncomprehending, clear, blue eyes. His momma must have adored him for that innocent countenance. For all purposes, he was dead at that point. He would have no more dealings on this earth, either with rebels or jayhawks. But he did manage to slide his gaze down from Henry's eyes, as did Henry, to the four-inch wide gaping hole in his stomach. The boy saw only red meat, death and oblivion. But from Henry's position, he wished he had gotten there before, not after, dinner. Henry had decided then and there that he would never again eat green peas.

The third life taken that Henry saw up close was unusual, or at least unplanned, and it led to confusion for Henry. Once again he was in the company of jayhawkers. He had never liked or even used the term *jayhawkers*.

Wolves at the Door

To Henry, these were mostly decent, God-loving farmers, with a few merchants and tradesmen from Fort Scott or Mound City thrown in. Good fathers, husbands, sons and brothers. He had to admit a few of them got a little enthusiastic over the killing of these slave-holding swine, but Henry himself figured the killing itself was righteous and justified.

On the occasion mentioned, a bunch of the boys had chased down several suspected bushwhackers and easily overwhelmed them. Shot them all point blank. David Biger jumped down on the one still alive and started stabbing him with a deer knife. The poor fellow was finally well dead, but to Henry's amazement Biger had kept at it. He carved up the man's chest and neck, and he got so worked up that he finally whittled through till the man's head was severed. This was the only time Henry had actually seen a head taken. He failed to laugh when Biger held the head aloft and proclaimed, "There boys, this ol' Reb's noggin done deserted his corpus delicti. But now we ain't got nothin' to hang him by."

Henry had nothing to do with it. In fact, he never even got off his horse. Never fired a shot in the whole episode. But he sure got a ringside view of the scene. The severed head instantly became an inanimate and impersonal object. To Henry, and apparently to his laughing and jeering companions, the head was now about five or ten pounds of pale meat, like a ball with hair on a school playground. One of the boys, Pinky Brillheart, actually gave it a little kick, more like a nudge, then picked it up and placed it in the crotch of a small tree.

Prologue

"You stay here, Shorty, and keep an eye out for more of us 'hawkers!'" Brillheart said.

A few fellas laughed. Henry didn't. He didn't feel good about this, didn't see the humor in it. He definitely thought what they were doing was a necessity, a godawful way to exist, but still a necessity. But some, not all or even many, of his associates seemed to revel in it. Henry couldn't quite grasp that. He didn't say anything, but the thought crossed his mind that the headless victim probably had been some loving gal's heart mate yesterday. Or maybe a little girl's daddy. Wouldn't that be something? What if little four-year-old Mariah could see that head in that tree? What if it was Henry's head in the tree and Mariah saw it?

Cut it out, thought Henry. *It's not my head, and Mariah isn't even here.* But he still thought, *wouldn't that be something?*

After that incident Henry realized that all these boys, in fact the boys on both sides, were forever changed. How could they not be? The time and place in which they were living was horrifically harsh. Maybe a Chicago, or Boston or Charleston man wouldn't have seen all this death. But out here on the western frontier death was one snakebite, or one cholera outbreak, or just one everyday accident away, every day. But not like this. Not all this killing. *Dyin' is one thing*, Henry had thought, *but killin' is another.*

He suspected every mother's son in his outfit had felt his heart grow rigid, just as he had. He knew Tamsen had brittled up inside to keep from just plain going crazy.

Wolves at the Door

Some of the women did go crazy. Lonny Zellweger's wife, Ursala, ran out two nights after burying their third child, six-year-old Sarah, and calmly walked into the Marmaton River. It was so shallow she had to hold rocks to stay under, but she did it. And others, quite a few others, just developed glassy stares and emulated the walking dead.

Henry and Tamsen wouldn't fall to that fate. He knew that. They both for whatever reason, either genetics or experience, were completely committed to each other, this place, this cause. Their very coming out to Kansas in 1858 was a leap of faith and courage and commitment.

Henry had been born in Sidbury, England, in 1832, but his father, Robert, took him as an infant to Canada in 1834. He grew up a farm boy there but came on into the USA through Chicago in 1849. Farm work through his teens and twenties had toughened him up. The abolitionist siren calling him to Bleeding Kansas and this sorry mess had steeled his backbone.

Or maybe abolition didn't have a thing to do with it. Free land certainly did. The Homestead Act of 1862 gave Henry, and most of these rascals beside him this rainy morning on Brush creek, their one shot at owning some land. Most everything was spoken for back east. The federal government, however, said *If you go out west and fill it in fast, before the goddamn slaveholders get there, all will be happiness in your heavenly western home.* They didn't mention the tornadoes, droughts, floods, grasshoppers, isolation, blizzards and Indians. All of that was acceptable for Henry and Tamsen, in that no place is perfect. What they

Prologue

really hadn't bargained for was the "Bleeding" part of Kansas. Boy, was it bleeding. The Uncivil War was going full steam on the Kansas/Missouri border well before a shot was fired at Fort Sumter. Henry and Tamsen had found themselves smack dab in the middle of unimaginable hatred and violence.

Like it or not, here they were. More specifically, here he was at Brush Creek.

"Hey, Hank, go see if Tim has those horses firmed up in the back. I think we're going out soon," Sgt. Hamilton said.

The regulars, although they always mildly belittled the militia for being unprofessional part-timers, showed a level of respect for the KSM 6th. They knew most of these Bourbon and Linn county boys had "seen the elephant," so to speak. The intensity of violence down on the state line had spared nobody. This particular militia was anything but untested. Col. Shelby's cavalry forces may have thought they were looking north that morning at some greenhorns who would cut and run when the first minié ball buzzed by. They were mistaken.

"Yeah, Tom, I'm on my way," Henry said to Sgt. Thomas Hamilton. No formality was given or expected in Company D. "I'll fill our group's canteens in the creek if any need fillin'." None did.

"All of you with the Enfield three-banders, fix bayonets now," Hamilton said. "This won't be a horsy ride. We'll be on foot, cheek to jowl with the sonsabitches. That goddamn

Wolves at the Door

lunkhead in gray over there is why you're not home curled up by the fire with your pretty little missus this miserable morning. I suggest the quicker we get over there and stick these bayonets up their sorry asses, the quicker we can tell old Abe we quit! Now re-check everything a last time. I know you've counted bullets and bayonets, but double tie shoelaces, take a piss, tighten your belt so your pants stay up. Leave your last letter with the horse holder if you're so inclined. And have your little chitchat with your Maker, again if you're so inclined."

Hamilton saw Henry approach. "Hank, good, you're back. All okay with the horses?" Seeing Henry nod, the sergeant continued. "Good. We're not going back to those horses, boys. As you know, some of us aren't coming back at all. But who the hell wants to live forever? You want to be an old man? Neither do I. All I want to do is live to be a little older than that sonovabitchin', gray-coated, lice-riddled, slave-holdin', piss ant of a mongrel dog over there havin' his nice buckwheat cakes with that esteemed southern gentleman, Mr. Shelby.

"Our first contact will be with Jackman's Cavalry and the fifth and sixth Missouri cavalries. Our friends on our right, Barker's battery, will open on 'em real soon. Our militia compadres of the tenth and nineteenth are on past Barker. When we move across Brush Creek, keep in order. Don't go mixin' with those other KSMs. And on the left, the Wisconsin and Colorado batteries should also have softened them up for you. They may be a little testy, though, if they don't like grape canister in their biscuits."

Prologue

Henry felt his stomach knot. Regardless of Hamilton's cavalier comments, several of the boys were vomiting. "Our Father, who art in heaven, hallowed be thy name," Henry said quietly to himself. The Lord's Prayer was the only prayer he knew. Henry normally wasn't a passionate believer, but now he figured, *Well, what the hell could it hurt?*

Many of the boys were likewise employed. Others were so casual you would have thought they were merely going to a barn raising.

"Hey, Campbell!" Sam Craig said. "Don't forget the two dollars you owe me from the card game last night. I want paid off tonight, and being shot through the heart today won't be no excuse to forfeit your just debt, you miserable bastard."

"Go to hell, Craig," returned Cambell. "You'll be a bloated pig by tonight, and I'll be down at your cabin keeping Maggie Ann all warm and cuddly!"

Others jeered across the creek at the Rebs. "Hey you cockeyed, lunatickin', dimwitted Johnnies. Better pucker up them assholes, 'cause this bayonet's just itchin' to jump up yer back door and look around!"

Then with a suddenness that jolted Henry to his toes, it started. As predicted, Barker's battery opened up on Shelby and Fagan's forces, mostly Missouri cavalry units. The Union forces were reasonably well equipped, particularly compared to the rebels, in every theater of the war and especially here at Westport. Price's army was largely a rag tag bunch of weaponless stragglers. The boys in blue had a distinct armament advantage over the Rebs because lots of

Wolves at the Door

Price's boys had only knives, pitchforks and old shotguns. But one thing they did have to their very great advantage was Col. Jo Shelby. He was a wealthy Tennessee hemp grower who was born to a patrician life and excelled at it. He had no business being a tough and wiley cavalry leader, but he was among the best in the war, either side.

For the South, probably only Bedford Forest of Tennessee outdid him for sheer audacity and battle tactics. Shelby had the unquestioned loyalty, respect and love of his Iron Brigade. Henry's KSM knew full well that regardless of the artillery advantage, probably three to one, and regardless of large numbers of underarmed men over there in Price's hordes, they still had Shelby right in front of them this morning of October 23, 1864.

"Go, Go now, boys!" yelled Sgt. Hamilton. "Keep it orderly, keep it slow and straight. They don't think much of us militiamen. They don't know us. Angle in on Wornall Road. Use Bent's house as our goal. Our eleventh cavalry and nineteenth KSM are pinching in from our right. Go! Join 'em and pinch up the hill. Go get Jackman! Go get Collins' battery! That's all they got. Go all the way down Wornall Road. Run those bastards to the end of the earth! Go, go, fire, load! Go, go, fire, load!" Then over the din of battle he again shrieked, "Go … go … fire … load!"

And that's what Henry did. This wasn't his profession, but it was his job today. He didn't know the ways of war, but he was a warrior today. It all became a blur. He had been coldly scared, maybe in a terrified stupor only minutes ago.

Prologue

No cogent thoughts, just a duty to perform that he could not shy away from. Now he was engaged.

Frank Banks had a quarter section two farms over from Henry down in Bourbon County. Now, oddly, Frank occupied the space two men down from Henry in their battle line. All were so engrossed in "Go, fire, load" that nobody was much aware of the personalities nearby. But in a glance over to keep correct space between himself and Jack Cross, who was beside him, Henry saw that Frank had been hit. Not really down, yet, but erratically stumbling forward.

They had just gotten a breeze of canister from Collins' battery that filled the air like a swarm of bees. All Henry had sensed was the wind-whooshed, whiney whistle of nuts, bolts and metal chards blow by. Not having been hit, he hadn't even cogitated on it until he saw Frank. How it had happened, Henry couldn't say. Frank must have presented himself in just such a way that a projectile in that canister stew neatly sliced off his right arm as he was leaning forward and his arm was pumping. For a split second, maybe before Frank even knew he'd been hit, his severed arm somersaulted right on up and nestled on his back, sort of like a long knapsack with fingers. And there it balanced for the two or three seconds it took for Frank to come off level plane and pitch forward. Henry knew he shouldn't stop, but he had to, if just for a moment. He lurched over to stop Frank's roll, right arm now eight feet back somewhere in the prairie grass. He noticed that Frank's coat and checkered shirt on his left side were shredded and

Wolves at the Door

turning red. Henry realized Frank had caught a lot more of the canister load than just an isolated piece at his arm. Frank was deadweight dead. He probably had been before he ever realized his arm was gone.

Go, go, fire, load. The words continued to reverberate in Henry's head as he regained his footing and slowly but surely proceeded toward his own fate.

Henry didn't have any profound thought on this as he caught up with his line. The only thing that passed his mind was he certainly couldn't tell Thelma what he'd seen. She'd know soon enough that her husband, Frank, had been killed, but Henry hoped she'd never have to visualize what he had just seen. No sense in worrying about it now. He, himself, might not be alive later to tell her anything anyway.

But he was. Henry Devon, KSM 6th Regiment, Company D, made it through the day without a nick. He was part of the Union forces who routed the Rebels, drove Gen. Price's wagon train on past Wornall Road, and then pursued the Rebs into darkness to oblivion.

The war on the border effectively ended that day. Westport would be referred to as the Gettysburg of the West for two reasons. One was the sheer number of warring participants, almost thirty thousand. Two, it was the Confederates' "high water mark" in the west. If they had won, the northern leadership would have been forced to deploy more forces out there, weakening its assault on Robert E. Lee's Army of Virginia. Henry's militia unit would have had to stay engaged indefinitely. The war

Prologue

would almost surely have strung out longer than April of 1865, and Appomattox would likely have come much later, if at all.

But Henry's war definitely ended that day. His unit followed along down the state line the next day as the rebel horde retreated in a panic. General Price was old, lame and fat. He had to be carried in a wagon-type ambulance. Shelby turned and counterattacked the pursuing Yankees to no avail.

When the Confederates reached Mine Creek they got bottled up in the mud and the steep bank beyond. Rather than discard all the booty they had pillaged along the way and skedaddle, they stupidly and greedily hung on to the treasures too long. It weighed them down. The final Union attack at Mine Creek, a large and very dramatic cavalry charge, finished them off for good.

Henry and company spent two miserable, rainy nights trying to sleep on horseback, being kept in reserve for Mine Creek. Seeing no action on October 25, they were released the next day to go home to Bourbon County to defend their home sites against vicious and enraged southern stragglers.

The local newspaper, *The Border Sentinel*, Friday morning, October 28, 1864, reported that General Field Order Number 2 had been issued from KSM 6th headquarters in Mound City on October 26. It read "The Sixth Regiment of Kansas State Militia is hereby honorably discharged from active service."

For Henry's nineteen days of actual service, he was paid a grand total of $19.94, $7.60 of which was for the use and the feeding of his horse. It was time to go home to Tamsen. Time to build a life for Libby, Bob and little Charlie. Time to live.

PART-1

I

Bleeding Kansas

Life and Death in Bourbon County

The last several days of October found Henry on horseback, plodding along, tired and slow. He was spent. He badly wanted to get home but was so physically and emotionally drained he could hardly spit. He just turned the horse to amble south. While horse and man made their way home, Henry casually observed the surroundings.

Almost treeless in 1865, Kansas was the beginning eastern edge of the Great American Plains. Tall lush grasses had covered the plains for eons and provided bountiful resources to sustain a myriad of wildlife. Be it fur or fowl, it could thrive in Kansas. Henry loved that about his chosen home state. The mightiest of mammals, both individually and in huge herds, was the American bison, the buffalo. Millions of them covered the Great Plains. They had originally been present in almost all the eastern states as well. But after centuries of depletion by the Indians, not to mention final ruination at the white man's hands, the big animals were all but totally gone east of the Mississippi River. Henry only occasionally saw buffalo, and never in the huge herds of thousands as in days gone by. But about a week after his return, he did witness an event involving buffalo that he would never forget.

Wolves at the Door

As Henry rested at the end of a furrow and gazed out upon a three-mile vista, he saw a small herd. Probably a dozen were grazing nonchalantly near the Marmaton River, lined with cottonwood trees, maybe a mile away. Bourbon County had been named after a county in Kentucky that some of its earliest settlers had hailed from, and Fort Scott was its first and busiest settlement. Fort Scott, established in 1847, was one of the eight federal military forts in Kansas, one of a few set up prior to Kansas statehood. It had originally served to protect and maintain the separation of white settlers and the Indian Territory (I.T.). The Indians west of the Mississippi were the Sac and the Fox in Iowa; Missouria in Missouri; and the Osage, Kansa, Kiowa and Cheyenne out through Kansas and into Colorado. The Devons had mostly seen Osage, primarily around the old fort in Fort Scott itself.

The immediate area Henry and Tamsen were homesteading around Fort Scott was more or less devoid of any Indian population, except for a few Osage. They, like many Plains Indian tribes, had originally been eastern indigenous people who, starting in the 1830s, had been peaceably or forcibly moved west. "Ol' Andy Jackson made sure the path was clear for us white settlers," Henry had explained to Tamsen when they first headed out to Kansas in '58. She had been greatly concerned about wild savages. In reality they hardly ever saw Indians, and those they did encounter turned out to be neither wild nor savage. And although more than 4,000 men, women and children died in this prolonged forced march—later called the "Trail of

Bleeding Kansas—Life and Death in Bourbon County

Tears"—Henry Devon didn't mind. Or more accurately, he didn't know. This epic migration took place gradually and out of sight of any one farmer. All Henry and Tamsen knew was that they didn't see much, if any, Indian suffering in their neck of the woods.

Lots of Osage came and went in Fort Scott itself. Not many were seen out in the newly partitioned quarter section that Henry was trying to prove up. That's why his attention had been caught by the scene unfolding before him down by the river on this bright November day. Only twice had he seen fairly large herds of fifty to a hundred animals, and those were in the far distance. But he did see small groups now and then. He had never killed one. His family largely survived on homegrown vegetables and grains, some beef and poultry, and a fair share of venison and wild fowl.

Killing a buffalo was not likely logistically, and cleaning one out for butchering was a Herculean job. Plus, they were way too big for one family to process and preserve.

But for the Osage, the buffalo was an animal made in heaven. First of all, animal and Indian were almost religiously joined at the hip. For hundreds of years the Osage and the buffalo had been connected. These people had originally been run down to the Mississippi Valley area by the war-like Iroquois from the Ohio River Valley. They had most likely seen and used buffalo in ancestral homelands.

Henry and Tamsen were only vaguely aware of this history. What they did know either came from small articles they chanced to read or comments overheard in Fort Scott

Wolves at the Door

mercantiles. Along the way west, past the Missouri River basin, the Osage had become dependant on the buffalo. Differing from the way the small Henry Devon family might go about it, the Osage approach to a buffalo kill was a well-choreographed event. Henry stood spellbound at what he was about to witness.

This herd had moved close enough to Henry that he could see individual beasts fairly well. His slightly elevated field position gave him a ringside seat to what was about to unfold.

The Osage people were a strikingly handsome and statuesque people. They held themselves to be a cut above all others. First, they were tall. At his own six-foot height, Henry was not accustomed to looking up to many people. But that was not the case when he saw Osage at Fort Scott. Many, if not most, were well over six feet and some between six and a half and seven feet. And they were cosmetically dramatic. The men shaved their heads and eyebrows but left a two-inch high scalp top knot about three inches wide from forehead to the back of the neck. Deerskin loincloth and leggings accompanied tattooed chests and arms for the warriors. Pierced ears allowed flamboyant earrings, and painted faces, arms and legs topped the whole thing off.

The likewise stately, longhaired women wore formfitting deerskin dresses and leggings. Their cinch belts were, by the 1860s, brightly colored with European dyed wool. And they too made aggressive use of bracelets, tattoos and earrings. All in all, these were an abundantly graceful and strikingly handsome people—both men and women.

Bleeding Kansas—Life and Death in Bourbon County

These were the people with whom Henry and Tamsen were familiar. These were the people they knew were always to some degree in their general vicinity. And Henry now saw four of these young, virile looking men slowly and unobtrusively edging closer to the small herd from the periphery.

He recognized one, Long Eyes, from seeing him in Fort Scott. *He must be an important warrior*, thought Henry, *or he wouldn't have been at a Fort Scott meeting.* Henry vaguely remembered he had seen Long Eyes when a big powwow between several tribal leaders and military men occurred after the Fort Humbolt/Verdigris River incident.

That was back in '63. It had involved some Confederate officers disguised in blue Union uniforms. The practice of impersonating Union soldiers infuriated true Union partisans. During the response of trying to capture these Rebels, the Union soldiers were joined by a large band of Osage. When cornered at the Verdigris River, the twenty-two Confederates tried to make a stand on a sandbar. Osage had killed, scalped and beheaded eighteen of them. The Union papers and grapevine had played up the Osage assistance to the Union cause, giving these Indians brief, appreciative accolades.

"At least they decapitated the right guys," Henry had commented to Tamsen.

He agreed with her that these beheadings, although inflicted on their mortal enemies, were beyond the pale of anything they ever expected to countenance. How ironic that Henry had been, to some degree, involved in the

Wolves at the Door

beheading of Dave Biger's victim. Henry never mentioned that to Tamsen, perhaps out of some unearned feeling of guilt. But he never really assigned great guilt to the Osage for this atrocious act, either. Some of his neighbors had attributed the beheadings to the savage nature of the Indians. Henry knew better. It was the nature of the times for all of them, red man or white man, union or rebel.

His thoughts returned to the scene he now beheld. Long Eyes and two companions slowly slid between one male buffalo and the main group. One of the three braves rode his mount to an almost flush position on the buffalo's right side. In the split second between the animal's notice of an encroachment at his flank and the expected reaction to it, Long Eyes was quartering the buffalo on his opposite rear flank. The timing of Long Eyes' approach was essential to attack when the animal's attention was ever so momentarily diverted. A second too soon or too late would give the prey full chance to react against either the young brave or against Long Eyes.

As it was, Long Eyes got right on him and loosed an arrow behind his shoulder, angled through a lung. Henry knew this must require both steeled nerves and practiced experience, and he felt certain Long Eyes had both. The animal bolted, swinging his head and horns in a furious rage. Left and right, he thrust an arc of lethal power that Henry knew could disembowel a horse or tear the leg right off a rider. Henry's own heart jumped, and his own breath faltered. But it was the heart and breath of this magnificent beast that gave evidence of its demise. The spewing blood

Bleeding Kansas—Life and Death in Bourbon County

poured forth throughout its bellowing exhalations, covering both its executioners and their horses in a misty, crimson veil.

Henry was dumbstruck. He knew this event had been played out hundreds of times right here in Bourbon County. He surmised this was not even a rare action for Long Eyes and his business associates. Their calm, measured assassination expertise proved that.

No sir, Henry thought. *This may not be a first time effort for Long Eyes, but it sure as hell is mine.* Henry was deeply moved by the almost solemn ceremony. The buffalo was giving of himself, giving his very being. And Long Eyes was taking out of necessity. Killing for fun or sport didn't exist with these Osage. Probably not with any Indian culture. Only white people would book train excursions throughout the west for "hunting" expeditions. Brave white easterners would take turns shooting buffalo with their Hawkins rifles from 500 feet away, off an elevated platform. They would be photographed with their "trophies" to show friends back home how courageous they were. They were blissfully ignorant of the courage and skill required to participate in what Henry was viewing.

As the buffalo internalized a full awareness of impending death, he gave one last terrifying swing of his horns. To the left, Long Eyes anticipated it and faded just out of range. But on the creature's return last gasp lunge to the right, the young brave didn't react quickly enough. The dying beast drove his horn toward rider and pony … and got the pony. With excited eyes as big as fists, the poor

Wolves at the Door

horse was ripped. This rider was no Long Eyes. He might be in future hunts, and this accident might even hasten his own capability. But today his failure to anticipate and react cost him the life of his noble pony. The horn drove through the horse's rising neck just under his throat. In the terrified buffalo's last act, he ripped the windpipe right out of the horse. Both went down amid a cacophony of wheezing, screaming and horrifying panic. The buffalo was dead in spirit, if not quite yet in fact. The horse was immersed, only seconds behind, in a state of incredulous bewilderment. And the young rider tumbled away in a scrambling, frantic effort to avoid being on the wrong longitude/latitude of several thousand pounds of fur, meat, bones, horns and guts.

Henry stood stock-still. It was as if he were watching a slow motion minidrama of the whole miasma of life. He was so stupefied he felt he was somewhere outside himself, witnessing truth from afar. He had never seen anything so captivating, so horrible, so wonderful. But now it was over. Both buffalo and horse were dead. Their creator had allowed them to perform their parts and exit the stage.

The young brave was shaking and weeping uncontrollably, fearing his judgment and punishment for failure. But Long Eyes issued no apparent judgment or punishment. He was too far away to be heard, but Henry could imagine the conversation, based on his own experience as a man. As Long Eyes dismounted and approached the boy, the man's very posture and gait foretold that no recrimination was coming. Henry intuitively knew the young lad was being told that this was a deadly business. That he would learn from this episode

Bleeding Kansas—Life and Death in Bourbon County

and that he should honor this buffalo for bravely bestowing the Osage with his entire being. That he should honor this dead pony for donating himself to the young brave's learning effort. That they would honor their Creator for letting them all, men and beasts, sway together in this eternal dance of life and death, which are surely one and the same thing. Or something like that.

Henry backed off the furrow, turned and headed to the cabin. He knew much more of interest would surely follow, but he felt so privileged to have seen what had already transpired, that to view more seemed sacrilegious. These people, he thought, were a different breed of human. They could be so cruel, so backward, so savage. Yet the almost surreal scene he had just seen suggested something different.

"I can't describe it as it was," he quietly told Tamsen at the table over supper that night. "I can tell what I saw, but I can't say what a strange reaction I had to it. It was like being there when you gave birth to Mary Mariah. And even as unexplainable, similar to the feeling at her grave last year. These red people, Tamsen, may be on this earth with the same problems we face. I mean, they certainly seem to be dancing to a different tune than we are, but are they?"

Henry took a deep breath. "Maybe they just want to breathe air, eat food, and drink water like we do. You and I want to get up tomorrow and work our own furrows. My heart almost tore in two when we put our little angel in that earth up behind the house. And God knows I surely know it was worse for you. Do you suppose that all these feelings and struggles and aspirations that we have, they do too?"

Wolves at the Door

Mary Mariah

Tamsen just sat there not knowing what to say. Every time either of them mentioned Mary Mariah, which they often did, Tamsen was aware of a palpable constriction in her chest. It had been just over a year since their firstborn had died. Nobody knew exactly from what. It happened on, of all days, New Year's Day. Mary Mariah was almost five years old, had curly blond, almost white hair, and deep-set blue eyes. Her most noticeable gift was the ability to energize a room with her unbridled laughter. She was Henry and Tamsen's first child and naturally the light of their lives. Then she died. It would have been easier if some obvious accident or illness had caused it. But like so many deaths out on the Kansas frontier, it just happened.

At Christmas she was deliriously happy with the little China doll Henry had bought in Fort Scott. It had belonged to a soldier and his wife who had a stillborn girl and were too heart-broken to look at the doll. Henry bought it and thought to himself, *how could anyone bear up under the sorrow of losing a pretty little girl and her pretty little doll.* He would soon find out.

Then on December 27, Mary Mariah got sick. No big pain, just listless. She was like a wild puppy one day and devoid of energy the next. She had started coughing and spitting up a little blood a few days later and simply didn't wake up the next morning, January 1.

Their 160-acre homestead was just five miles north of Devon, which was itself about ten miles northwest of Fort

Bleeding Kansas—Life and Death in Bourbon County

Scott. Never knowing if a cold or influenza was just that or something else, they couldn't go into Fort Scott every time somebody coughed. And neither the medical doctor at the fort, whom they didn't even know, nor old Doc Reardon in Fort Scott, could make a thirty-mile round trip on every sneeze either. The life Henry and Tamsen had chosen had left them pretty much on their own. It had now cost them dearly.

Devon, the little hamlet's name, had no connection to Henry other than somehow coincidentally stemming from Devonshire, England. Henry and Tamsen had met in Rockford, Illinois, near Rock County, where both sets of parents had recently moved. They, as many other young couples, were greatly influenced by the "Go west, young man, go west" sentiment being promulgated in New England. But instead of meaning the gold fields of 1849 California, it now meant Kansas. More specifically, Bleeding Kansas, for Henry and other homesteaders.

Lots of people, many of English or Irish ancestry, were pouring into Kansas, ostensibly for the noble cause of liberty, but realistically for free land. The Homestead Act meant that Henry and Tamsen, and many like them, could have a chance at a better, more independent life than might be available back east. And many ethnic groups stayed with their own kind. Thus, Henry assumed, Devon most likely had been named by people whose parents or grandparents hailed from that part of England. And the little cemetery on their quarter section was named Avondale, another English reference.

Wolves at the Door

That's where they had laid Mary Mariah. And Tamsen just couldn't get over the sight of that little wooden box down at the bottom of the grave. Or the muffled splat of cold dirt being gently dropped on it in the bitter freeze of that January day. *What a godawful way to start a new year, she had thought. Will 1864 be as black a year as Mary Mariah's death seems to auger?* Tamsen now knew, more than a year later, that like all years, it had been both terrible and hopeful. Little Mary was truly in that grave, but little Libby was at Tamsen's side. Elizabeth had been born in 1861, two years younger than Mary Mariah. She was now four and very sturdy, very healthy. Tamsen just knew that whatever had happened to Mary would not happen to Libby. Tamsen had a maternal instinct that Libby was a tough little survivor.

And Tamsen now knew that 1864 had included more border battles involving Henry. She had wept and trembled when he dutifully reported with the militia at Westport in October and had cried even harder with relief when she finally saw him walking his horse, Becky, up the hill coming home. He also was a tough survivor. They all were. God bless little Mary, but Tamsen and Henry and the rest of their children would make it. She just knew it. Henry was the most determined and dependable person she had ever met. And so was she. She knew that about herself. She wasn't going back to Illinois. Her parents, the McGinnises, had fought their way out through Pennsylvania and Kentucky, to Indiana, and then to Illinois. Americans were forever going west. Just as trees inherently grow north and water inherently flows south, Americans inherently seemed to go west.

"Henry," she murmured as they lay in bed that night, "I don't know what you saw out there today, but I can see it moved you tremendously. I've seen Long Eyes before in town. And like you, I assess him to be a man. A strong and purposeful man. And red, white, green or blue, I'm sure he does have the same color blood pumping through his heart as you do. I'm sure he wants the same right to live that we do."

Tamsen sighed and patted Henry's arm. "I can't guess what's in store for him, but I can tell you what's in store for you and me. We're going to raise this strong girl, Libby, and the boys, and maybe a few more along the way. Libby will live to be an old lady, Henry, I feel it in my bones. And we'll prove up this quarter section. Regardless of how many good folks cut and run and falter from the hardship, you and I won't. Somebody has to build the farms, towns and cities out here so our kids will have a safe and blessed America to grow in. That Bible you signed to me in 1858, we're gonna fill it up with babies' names. And as for Long Eyes? Let him handle himself and his people. I know he's capable. As for you, Henry, roll over into my arms and let's start making our future!"

Homesteaders

Henry and Tamsen progressed along the path Tamsen had foreseen. Their family grew while they got a toehold into ownership of their quarter section. Several years after the

Wolves at the Door

fact, in 1872, they applied for and got their patent deed, signed by President Ulysses S. Grant.

"Look at this Tamsen," said Henry, with beaming pride. "Our hard work, sweat and tears finally got us this piece of paper, signed by ol' Grant himself. I guess he appreciates me getting my hind quarters shot at back in Westport. Some day this here piece of papyrus will be hanging on some great grandson's wall as proof we were land barons. I can't believe we actually own all down that hill to the road. This cabin, those cows and horses, all of it."

A funny memory came back to Henry, and he grinned.

"What's amusing about it, Mr. Devon?" asked Tamsen.

"Oh, the mention of Westport and this cabin all in one sentence reminded me of the fireplace money incident."

A couple of months after the battle of October 1864, the militiamen had gotten paid. Even though they were officially mustered out by General Field Order Number 2 on October 26, it took a while to get paid. Cash was handed out at the next militia drill. Henry proudly accepted his pay, all $19.94 of it, taking it home to his cabin. Because life on these homesteads largely existed on self-sufficiency and barter, cash was in fairly short supply. And being mid-December of '64, Henry believed this windfall would be perfect for a merry Christmas. He had sat at the table in front of the fireplace, counting it out in piles.

"These dollars will buy us some sugar, salt and whatever else you think we need," Henry said to Tamsen. "The rest will buy both you and Libby new bonnets, then maybe something for Bob and Charlie."

Bleeding Kansas—Life and Death in Bourbon County

It was quite cold outside and a pretty lively fire, mostly fueled by cowpies, was roaring a few feet from the table. Little Libby was attempting to improve a snowman Henry had started for her right outside the cabin door. Only four at the time, she wasn't getting very far with it, and she was as cold as she cared to be. As she barged through the doorway with a bang, all nineteen dollars so neatly configured on the table instantly drafted into the fireplace. One whoosh and it was all charcoal and cinders up the chimney, thereby ensuring there would be much less Christmas joy than had been expected.

Henry was speechless, Tamsen stupefied, and Libby mostly befuddled. Bobby and Charlie kept playing, totally unperturbed, on the floor. Henry looked at Tamsen and she looked back. Both faces contorted in amazement, passed into agonizing comprehension, slid over to furious anger, backed down to bemused acceptance and finally broke wide open into uproarious laughter. Almost a year earlier they had buried Mary Mariah. They had borne the anguish and fear of battle. They had persevered through the natural obstacles of a year's worth of farming, and here they were. Nineteen dollars, truly almost all their cash on hand, had been a heaven sent bonus this Christmas time to ease their frustration and provide a little yuletide cheer. Now that "manna from heaven" had been consumed in what they both instantly regarded as the fiery furnace of hell. And all they could do was laugh.

"At least," Henry had said with a moan, "it's not as bad as what happened to Harvey Hickson. He told me he was

Wolves at the Door

counting his pay out in the side field on a stump. Jane called him in for supper and he left it laid out. Came back in thirty minutes and it was all gone! And I mean all ... even the ninety-four cents! Couldn't find it. Gone, not a farthing in sight! Harv told me he started accusing the kids, and then lit in on Jane."

Henry was guffawing, hardly able to continue. "When he realized they wouldn't have swiped it, he accused some invisible, wandering bunch of Osage. I mean the hard fought fortune had vanished into thin air." By this time Tamsen had buckled over with laughter, listening to Henry tell the tale.

"Then, the next afternoon, Harv goes to pick up an axe leaning against the fence rail, glances a couple of feet ahead of him at one of Florence's turds. It had a proud glint to it. Now Harvey always said that mule was worth her weight in gold, but he never dreamed she could actually poop gold coins." Henry was almost crying with hilarity now. "Before he could devise a plan to just tie ol' Florence to a tree, keep feeding her, and wait for a fortune to start roaring out her ass end, it dawned on him! That damned Missouri mule had snuck in through a slit in the fence, made quick work of the greenbacks and slickered down the doubloons for dessert. And I had assumed it was no lasting tragedy because Harv could merely retrieve the money, dust it off and be no worse for wear." Henry wiped the tears from his eyes as he finished the tale. "But no, says Harv, twenty-four hours of stomach sarsaparilla ate up those nineteen bills to where, first, you wouldn't want

Bleeding Kansas—Life and Death in Bourbon County

to touch 'em and, second, the value to a merchant would be a bit tarnished."

Gradually Henry and Tamsen calmed down. Full bore jocularity can be maintained only so long. "And think how lucky we are Tamsen," Henry had opined, "Harv and Jane, and you and I, we each at least have the ninety-four cents left. But yours and my money is clean money. By the time I tell everyone in Bourbon County about ol' Harv's misfortune he won't be able to spend the ninety-four cents anywhere. I'll have 'em all aware if they take it they'll be gettin' the shitty end of the stick."

And so it went for a few more years. By 1870, children Libby, Bobby and Charlie had been joined by John, Sadie and infant Frank. Just as Fort Scott had proceeded to legal incorporation in 1860 and Kansas became a free state in 1861, Bourbon County and its homestead settlers also inched their way along the path of progress. And so did the Devon family.

The military function of Fort Scott died and was resurrected. After Price's raid and the Civil War ended, the fort was abandoned and sold in 1865. Subsequently the railroads moved in to help push white settlements westward. By 1870, the number of homesteaders who had pushed west into southern Kansas and the old Cherokee neutral ground was enough to cause clashes. The military presence of Fort Scott was once again needed to keep peace. Not so much between settlers and Indians as between settlers and railroaders. The farmers wanted and needed unrestricted land, and the railroads needed right of way.

Wolves at the Door

Soldiers had been brought in to a reopened Fort Scott to help prevent bloodshed and violence between the two interests.

"When does it end, Henry?" said Tamsen. "When do we finally get to peacefully go about the labors of this farm and our family without persecution? Surely after the dark times of the war we should be left to prosper in peace."

"Tamsen, there is a bigger picture here," he responded. "The country is now put back together and to some degree free of civil strife. There is an explodin' energy that can't be bottled up. America is peopled by the industrious, the risk takers, those who can't let well enough alone. My vague recollection of my own family is that many stayed in England. Many of your McGinnises stayed in Ireland, although why, I don't know. Even here, many are content to stay in Indiana, Ohio, Pennsylvania and New England. But many also just can't do that."

Henry looked around their home and opened his arms wide. "Tamsen, we've got this little cabin and these 160 acres. It'll feed us and be a nice home regardless of the railroads. But I'm uneasy on it. Truth be told, I understand this railroad thing, and I almost back it myself. Look at Dan and Helen Smithfield. They are in their mid-fifties. They have what, two or three children? Dan's strong, but Helen's got a tremor. They are happy here. They've worked their hearts out just like us, but they're not far from being wore out. I, well, I can see their anger at railroad disturbance. But even for them, this country should just keep going and growing. Even staying right here, I think we all need each other."

Bleeding Kansas—Life and Death in Bourbon County

A fly landed on Henry's ear. Tamsen reached over and whisked it off.

"What if Dan and Helen do stay here? Nothin' wrong with that," Henry continued. "Maybe the railroads keep going, maybe all the way to the other ocean. Maybe up to Canada and down to Mexico. What if one of Dan's grandkids someday needs some special doctoring or he dies? Now I know this is an insane idea, but what if the special doctor a kid needs is in, say, Ohio? Or even harder to 'cipher, say a fella lives in California and the special doctor lives in Massachusetts? What if these railroad tracks were laid out the whole way, right over rivers and mountains and deserts? I know it's far fetched, but what if that doctor could get on a train in Boston and be in San Francisco to save that child in two weeks, or one week? I just feel something big is going on here. So big, the world has never seen or dreamed it."

He was agitated and she was exasperated. When Henry got all riled up like this she saw in him what she loved. He dominated the mundane in a way most folks could not. He could see and feel a future he had trouble articulating.

"Look, Tamsen, we are both still under forty, both still strong and healthy. Those trains aren't merely coming here to disrupt Bourbon County. To be factual, they aren't even particularly coming here. They're coming through here. Yes, they'll bring the hardware, furniture, clothing and whatall to Dan and Helen, but they're steamin' on farther west, up north and down south, to all the Dans and Helens.

He rose, circled the table twice and sat back down.

Wolves at the Door

"I can vaguely see a future where we ourselves are out there somewhere. I read all about Kansas City and Ellsworth and the cattle drives. These trains keep going west and those cowboys keep drivin' the longhorns out of Texas up to the railheads. That's going to keep happening farther and farther west. Fort Scott will stay here. It's not going to fall off the map. And Ellsworth will stay up there, too. But Ellsworth and Fort Scott will be followed by other towns springing up out there as the trains keep plodding west. I just have a feeling we should be out there helping to build one or two of those towns while we are still young and strong."

He finally stopped to breathe. There, he had said it. There, she had heard it. All she had said was couldn't they for once get a little peace and quiet right here. And up he pops with this whole pioneering plan. Well not really a plan, just a pie in the sky palaverment.

"What on God's earth are you talking about, Henry?" she said. "We've just got our five years in to prove up this place, and you want to move on? Did our mule kick you in the head? Bad enough Florence ate up all Harvey Hickson's money, now our Thelma went and kicked out your brains! These mules must be at war with us now. Bad enough we got to worry about the Rebs, the Osage, the grasshoppers and the weather. Now my poor burdened soul has to worry about attack by these mules? Git out of the cabin you bean-brained, numbskulled, frightful excuse of a farmer before I give you a real kick in the head that any mule would admire."

Bleeding Kansas—Life and Death in Bourbon County

With that she shoved him out the door, but she could hear him laughing as he walked down the hill toward Thelma. *God, I love that man,* she thought as she beheld her flock in various stages of eating, playing and napping. *Who knows, maybe he's right.* "John Enoch, you little pioneer, I know you're only four, but do you feel like movin' on?" she said. "Do you want to go with your pa and jump into this America building thing?" The bright-eyed little rascal looked up and smiled. She thought again, *God, I truly do love that man.*

John Enoch had been born March 2, 1866. Attesting not only to the love of Henry and Tamsen for each other in the marital way, but also to the virility and good health of them both, was the fact that Tamsen had given birth about every two years. At this point in 1870, Mary Mariah would have been eleven had she lived; Libby was nine, Bob was seven, Charlie six, John four, Sadie two and little Frank just a couple of months old. Tamsen had given birth to seven children and had lost but one. And though the loss of their first child, angelic Mary Mariah, had almost killed their spirit, both Henry and Tamsen knew they were ahead of the averages.

All they had to do to confirm that was look around. Almost all their neighbors had a higher death rate among their children. Just the deaths at birth alone were enough to cause fear to expectant parents—either death of the child or mother or both. Henry could think of three men who had lost their wives in childbirth and had no choice but to take the remaining youngsters back east to family homes so

Wolves at the Door

somebody could care for them. And even if the birth mother survived each delivery, losing three or four children along the way wasn't unusual.

But Tamsen had proven to not only be strong and resilient in pregnancy and childbirth herself but also to bear very durable offspring. She and Henry would keep Mary Mariah in their hearts and prayers to the day they died. She traveled through life with them in spirit and never a day passed they did not think of her. As any parent does who has lost a child, they said aloud to each other, "Mary would be ten today, wonder what she'd be like?" or in later years, "Mary would be twenty-one today, wouldn't she be beautiful?" or, "Lordy, Mary would be forty today, wonder how many children she'd have had?"

These musings most often were not tearful, but more likely warm and tender. The memory of Mary Mariah was intensely personal and truly private between Henry and Tamsen. None of their other kids, even Libby and Bob, had any memory of Mary. And to Henry and Tamsen, she really represented their own youth. She had been conceived and born in 1859 in Illinois, the only one of their children not born in Bourbon County, when they were both under thirty. Henry was twenty-seven and Tamsen twenty-six when they made their first child. So young, so passionate, so wide-eyed. All the other children had come along like clockwork to them. All conceived and born between arduous enterprises of plowing, planting, fence making, tool sharpening, baking, mending, doctoring and all the other backbreaking efforts required in keeping a pioneer homestead together.

Bleeding Kansas—Life and Death in Bourbon County

Only Mary lived forever in their hearts as a product of their unfettered, carefree, anticipatory youth. Her little marker in Avondale Cemetery up in the top corner of their farm was like a shrine to them. The wording, "Mary M. Devon, daughter of Henry D. and Tamsen E.," and so forth, told the basic details. But on occasion when Tamsen placed a small bouquet on her daughter's grave, her eyes fell only on the tiny foot marker, which simply read "MMD." It was so simple that it burned into her heart. *I know it can't last forever up here, she thought, but as long as it does last, maybe somebody will remember our angel.* And that's when she sometimes cried a little, if only to herself. She didn't mind because her strongly felt emotion merely substantiated Mary's existence. She hoped only that somebody would forever remember.

Thus Mary Mariah had established herself in death as the standout in Henry and Tamsen's union. Their other children commanded their love and attention on a daily basis. And being among the living, they were all proceeding in time's vibrant parade. None of them had stopped growing or developing on some certain date, but had kept progressing and expanding before their parents' eyes. John Enoch, at four, was the proverbial "apple of his father's eye." Bobby and Charlie, at ages seven and six, were so close they almost melded into one. They were only a year apart, closer in age than any of the others, almost like twins. They looked alike, talked alike, laughed alike and thought alike. They were so close they each occupied the position of the other's best friend. They loved their Pa and he loved them, but they, to some extent, didn't need him so much because they had each other.

Wolves at the Door

And Frank was only two months old, not even off Tamsen's breast. Not walking, not talking. He seemed only to exude action at both ends, neither of which really concerned Henry. At this stage, Frank was exclusively a "momma's boy."

So that left young John Enoch Devon. Henry was already beginning to think of him as "JED," but Tamsen insisted on John.

"That's what we wrote in the Bible, Henry," she stressed. "John, John Enoch. It's a good, strong name. Good for him now and good when he's a man."

And he was a strong little boy. Bred well, built well, behaved well, even misbehaved well.

"I don't know if that little jayhawker is any smarter than the rest of 'em," Henry told a friend, "but he is sure more devilish. I come in every noontime for dinner and hook my hat on the back rung of our rocker, and every day he sneaks over and hides it. Now keep in mind he's only four. I sit down at the table to eat and pretend I don't see him. He pretends I don't see him. Over he goes and hides the hat under the chair, behind the wood box, wherever. I make a big deal of finding it and scooping him up for a fake whupin', and he squeals and squeals and brightens the whole house. I sure do love 'em all, but that kid is somethin' special. He delights in every breath!" Henry said, beaming.

But as fate kept bringing people back to reality out here on the prairie, it wasn't to last.

Bleeding Kansas—Life and Death in Bourbon County

July Fourth in Fort Scott

There could be bad food, bad weather, bad accidents, sometimes bad doctorin' and too often bad people who now and then showed up. But so far springtime of 1870 hadn't been too bad. Brutal winter had passed, planting had gone as hoped with no major breakdowns, and summer loomed ahead. No terrible tragedies with family and friends, so everybody looked forward to the upcoming July Fourth celebration in Fort Scott. The fort was still going in 1870, and the little town itself had hung on through the fort's closing and reopening. It had many respectable families, mainly people operating the mercantiles. Every frontier town needed a butcher, a blacksmith, a haberdasher, a gunsmith and a grocer. But Fort Scott also had its share of bar rooms and bawdy houses. It still had activity as a stopping off place for drovers pushing longhorns out of Texas, even though the railheads were slowly inching west and would eventually give rise to Wichita and Dodge City. The old, established routes continued to be well used. The famous Chisholm Trail was somewhat of a generic term for all the cow trails from the 1860s through the 1890s. Although there actually was a Chisholm Trail, it was a catchall name that to many folks included the path to and through Fort Scott.

On this July Independence Day celebration, there would be strangers of all stripes holed up in Fort Scott. Local farm families going about normal trading were in town, as well as local small time ranchers trading cows, horses, mules and goats. Local merchants whipped up enthusiasm, which they hoped would result in patriotic sales. And out-of-towners, be they cowboys, gamblers, adventurers or drifters were there in abundance.

By noon of July 3, many of these disparate dignitaries were finished with business, full of orneriness and about half full of demon rum or whiskey. Benjamin Files' Livery Stable and Moses Boire's Blacksmith were still open and more or less would be throughout the celebration. But Billy Shannehan, the mason, and wagon maker Jack Bryant had closed up. So had shoemaker John Crow. Rubicam and Dilworth would close their hardware store at 4 P.M.

Not to imply that all the non-resident males in town that day were riffraff. The flotsam and jetsam had largely moved on when the war ended. And not to imply that every chance meeting of ex-bushwhacker and ex-jayhawker instantly erupted in renewed battle. A few ongoing open feuds continued, but most just smoldered. Many former enemies passed each other on Market Street with nary a glance. A few couldn't resist the offhanded insult, which either resulted in a fight, a laugh or a similar insult. In some cases, past enemies became fast friends. But just the sheer number of well imbibed men in town over this July Fourth celebration guaranteed somebody would act out their partisan resentment, or act out their liquor-fueled bravery, or act out some other attention-getting misbehavior.

It so happened the Devons chose to come into Fort Scott in their farm wagon, although it was not their only conveyance. Henry had managed to scrounge an old

Bleeding Kansas—Life and Death in Bourbon County

buckboard, and with some fairly serious cleaning, greasing and patching, it was quicker transportation than the bigger, more cumbersome wagon, which they were using out of practically today. Only two adults or an adult and one or two small children could fit into the smaller wagon. Henry really loved it. He had trued the wheels and greased the hubs to where it zipped right along with just him in it.

As he drove into town for this Independence Day, he reminisced about previous occasions when he had gone into Fort Scott alone in the buckboard. Twice he had chanced upon Dan Smithfield going the same way. The sight of each other without disapproving wives aboard was more than either could resist. It was literally off to the races. No matter that they both had old, fairly worn out buckboards, and old and fairly worn out horses. Neither man considered himself old or worn out. For Dan, the race was a brief, cheerful interlude away from Helen's growing health problems. For at least a few minutes Dan could step out of his struggles and act a boy. And for Henry, the situation was basically the same.

A man has to occasionally forget his everyday worries and just let 'er rip! Henry had thought as he and Dan neared the turnoff toward Devon, on the way to Fort Scott. It was only about a mile to the little stream bridge they considered the finish line, but at about two-thirds of the way there was a fairly sharp S curve that required a bit of negotiation. Flat out speed, then the curve, then a last burst to the finish. The first time they had raced, Henry beat Dan handily, and Henry figured the second race would end the same way.

Wolves at the Door

In the second race, coming from opposite directions, they both hit the Devon Road at the same instant, swung the corner and headed south. The race was on. No parlezvous was needed about the race or the rules. They both knew the only rule was he who goes across the little bridge first, wins. So off they went!

"Mornin', Dan," yelled Henry.

"Howdy, Hank," replied Dan. "I see yer still hangin' on to that octogenarian plow horse you bought as soon as he stepped off Noah's Ark!"

"Right you are, Mr. Smithfield," said Henry, "and I see your great granddaddy willed you the nag he used at Valley Forge!"

"Fine day for a spirited trot, don't you think, Hank?"

"Yes it is, Dan, but while you're palaverin' on about ancient history, don't let all this dust get in your eyes from my fine steed's rear shoes. Now you'll be pardonin' me, as I got some business just over that distant bridge and I'll be leavin' you to enjoy your morning walk!"

With that, Henry flicked the rawhide over Becky's ears just so she heard it and kicked in her pretty modest high gear. He would never strike her in any way, but he figured just a little audible snap would wake her up a bit.

Henry didn't know much about Dan's horse, but he was immediately certain it was not the same equine Dan had commanded in their last encounter. It was slightly taller, slightly leaner and much younger than he last remembered it. The light brown color was the same, but now being side by side, Henry detected an entirely different look in this horse's eyes. He smelled a rat.

Damn! This isn't that old plug Becky 'n' I whipped last time out, Henry thought. *This is a ringer he snuck in on me.*

"Why you miserable son of a bitch!" Henry yelled over the clatter of the race. "That isn't that old coyote that drug your buckboard before. When and where'd you get that war horse?"

Dan howled with glee as he shot by Henry. He laughed so hard he almost fell off the bench seat.

"No, No, Hank. You got it all wrong. This is still old Susie," he lied, "I just fed her a nice Kansas City steak and a little French wine last night and read her some of that purty English poetry this morning. I told her she'd have to do or die against that old glob of glue you've got. I guess she decided to do. Har, har, har, Hank. See you at the other side of the bridge. I'll wait, but try to get there by the end of the week!"

And in a blink he was way out ahead of Henry and quickly around the curve. Henry himself couldn't stop chuckling as he took Becky around the double curve and on over the bridge. When he arrived and coasted up to Dan's resting buckboard, there was Dan, boots off, lying down beside the small creek, feigning sleep.

"Oh, good morning, Hank. 'Scuse me while I wipe the sleeping bugs out of my eyes. I guess I've been here an hour or two!"

They were good friends, and Henry was glad Dan had managed to get a younger horse. They both needed and enjoyed the stolen man-to-man moments like this. But Dan needed it more, and Henry had been uplifted to know he could be a part of it.

Today, however, with his entire family in tow, was going to be a totally different affair. This July 3 trip in with Tamsen and the kids was a wagon plod, not a buckboard sprint. Libby, Bob and Charlie were in the back, in the wagon bed. Henry, Tamsen, John, Sadie and Frank sat up front. Always trying to combine all needed errands into one trip, they were heading in early on the third so they could get supplies. After that they would either see enough festivities and head home or decide to stay the night. Henry had brought a greased tarpaulin in case of rain. It was a white military tent side he had picked up when the fort closed up. He had rubbed grease into it as well as he could and kept it in a wooden box behind the bench seat. Several times it had kept supplies dry on a return trip from town.

"Well, Mother, looks like a perfect day for the trip in," Henry said to Tamsen. "With this weather, we'll get there in less than two hours. No sense in pushing it with the kids, though. Let's just enjoy being alive."

That's what their existence really flourished in, merely being alive. They both reveled in their love, their strength, their kids and their good fortune.

"And let's thank dear God, our Great Benefactor, for this day, Henry. Let's read from His Book while we ride. Children, listen now," Tamsen said. "Our Savior has given the little Devon family all we need. Let me read a couple of

Bleeding Kansas—Life and Death in Bourbon County

my favorite passages of our blessed Bible. We'll praise our Lord."

And put us all to sleep, mused Henry.

As the old wagon creaked along and Tamsen spoke the words, Henry daydreamed of what he really thought about religion. The scene surrounding him was his religion. The clean air and sunshine, the rolling hills and waving tall grass and, above all, his family right here in this wagon. And the good health and bright-eyed enthusiasm for life they all seemed to possess. That sufficed for Henry.

"'My soul is weary of my life; I will leave my complaint upon myself,' said Job to God. 'I will speak in the bitterness of my soul,'" Tamsen read.

Apparently Job wasn't having as good a day as Henry was. But that was all right with Henry. As Tamsen droned on, he settled into the rhythm of the creaking wagon and the glow of his own thoughts. *Strange,* he thought, *how so many folks are so comforted by "Thou knowest that I am not wicked; and there is none that can deliver out of thy hand."* Henry's overall approach to the afterlife was similar to his Monday thoughts about Friday: *It'll git here in its own good time and I'm not feared of it.* He didn't want to detract from his full enjoyment and best efforts toward today by worrying about tomorrow.

He couldn't understand all the preoccupation with "thou had poured me out as milk and curdled me like cheese." To him, the afterlife was a totally unknown blank space that no living man could correctly predict. And more so, he couldn't understand why some folks cared anyway. *What will come will come. Why obsess on it?* he wondered. Those who claimed they had the answer, be they Pope, priest, preacher or rabbi, usually were on some sort of payroll to pontificate. And he further wondered if such a leaning on all this Bible thumping wasn't a result of at least some trifle of cowardice.

Are people so afraid of living for today that they fabricate a whole illusion about tomorrow? he mused. *And why the doom and gloom preachin'? I came here from somewhere, and it's a right fine life. I guess God will put me in some good place later.*

But there was an incongruity. First, the thought about Christian heavenly concern resulting from cowardice sure didn't play out with Tamsen. She really believed, and she was about as far away from a coward as one could be. And second, he did actually believe in God, a Creator. He just thought the way all the pious numbskulls used God to their advantage was loony.

Somebody surely made all this, he allowed, as Becky's hooves plodded on, tossing up little clods of mud. *Obviously, there is great order in this world. Iffen not, water lilies would beget porcupines, rattlesnakes would bear butterflies, and some falling apples would go up!*

At that very moment Becky, without missing a beat in her cadence of locomotion, lifted her tail, unraveled her back door like a sock turning inside out and deposited a half dozen prairie muffins right before their eyes.

Bleeding Kansas—Life and Death in Bourbon County

"There, Tamsen, look at that. That's just what I've been cogitatin' on. If things weren't in order, Becky might have just slung out a coonskin cap instead of those darlin' road apples."

She interrupted her "thou hunteth me as a fierce lion" long enough to ask incredulously, "What in God's name are you thinking about, Henry? I'm reading the tale of Job from this Good Book, and you're somehow interpreting it to be a tale of horse turds? Shame on you, Henry. And in front of the children!"

He sheepishly smiled and thought to himself, *That's it. She's hit the nail on the head. That's what all this preachin', prevaricatin' and pious pontificatin' amount to. A big pile of horse turds!*

So the pleasant journey ended. Tamsen closed her beloved 1851 American Bible Society Book while Henry reeled himself in from his daydreaming. Libby, Bob and Charlie stopped pushing, shoving and arguing in the back. John Enoch sat beside his father and shyly gazed at the town before him. Little Sadie and infant Frank woke up from the sleep they always drifted into on a wagon ride.

Tragedy in Town

"You can take that goddamn son of a tanner and send him back to Illinois," bellowed a cowboy near the Devon wagon to another man still back in the saloon. Henry had no idea what the argument specifically was, but among these bar patrons in the Fort Scott saloons it was always the same.

Wolves at the Door

One way or the other, it always referred to the old North/South, Yank/Reb animosity. Since no armies or militias were still on the warpath, individual boozed up former adversaries were called upon to keep the arguments going. And now, with Ulysses Grant recently elected, there was fodder for the festering feuds.

"What's wrong with Grant?" came a voice from within.

"He's a helluva sight better'n that southern sympathizin' snake out of your damn Kentuck, Andy Johnson!" came the reply.

Most of these flare ups were liquor induced and mainly just smoke screens for some other resentment. A man down on his luck at the poker table, or a man recently jilted by a lady friend, or a man shortchanged at the cattle auction might take an accidental bump in a crowded saloon as a major offense.

There was a bit of a problem with a few of the ex-Rebs. Most just sucked up the South's defeat, rejoined the American tapestry, and went about their business. But some confederate soldiers had such resentment in their hearts, and some bushwhackers had lived so long in isolation, they simply couldn't rejoin civilized society. Jo Shelby himself came back into the American mainstream, ending up as U.S. Marshal in Independence, Missouri, but many just couldn't readjust. A lot of ex-Rebels ended up wandering down into Texas and pushing cows up the trails. These men were fairly content as long as they were leading lonely and undisturbed lives on the prairies, but they could get greatly agitated in a cattle town by some liquored up former bluebelly.

Bleeding Kansas—Life and Death in Bourbon County

That's what was happening here. If nothing else, Henry could tell the accent from inside the saloon was a Yankee's—Ohio, Pennsylvania, he couldn't tell, but somewhere up north and slightly back east. And this young buckaroo standing beside Henry and his family was clearly a product of rural Georgia or Louisiana, or some such southern backwater. Henry wasn't too good at deciphering the many southern accents. They fell into two categories to him. If he could understand them at all, they were from a city—Atlanta, New Orleans, Shreveport, or so. If he could hardly make out a word they were saying and they sounded as though they had a mouthful of grits, they were rural. This cowpoke, Henry figured, was from somewhere back in the puckerbrush and would be best left alone.

"C'mon Tamsen, let's move it along. Get the kids out of the wagon before this gets ugly," Henry instructed.

"Listen to me you blue-coated, blue-eyed bag of wind Dutchman, at least Johnson was better'n that goddamn weasel Lincoln. Old Abe, good ol' Honest Abe, my ass. Hear! Hear! A cheer for Mr. Booth! Thank the Lord his bullet had a vote," barked the cowboy.

Out the saloon doors strode a large, blond man with a huge yellow mustache. And he was furious. "No, you listen to me, General Lee," he shouted. "I'm sick of you bad tempered cowbums drifting into this town and terrorizin' the good folks. And if you can't see the difference between our President Grant and your slow-witted Johnson, I feel sorry for ya. But when you speak ill of Mr. Lincoln, that won't do. I don't care how drunk either you or I may be, I can't let that stand."

Wolves at the Door

"Uh oh," said Henry. "This is going to get bad quick."

He hastily pushed Libby and Charlie, who were already out of the wagon, behind it. Almost in the same motion he reached up and grabbed Bob by the arm and almost threw him over the side of the wagon.

"Darn it, Pa, what'd you go and do that for?" Bob yelped. At the same time Tamsen, who was still holding half asleep Frank and dragging an uncomprehending Sadie by her shoulder, managed to get them both sheltered behind the wagon.

"Oh, I'm very rattled you blue pig. I'm so scared I'm—"

At that instant the Union drunk had his '61 Colt revolver out and was pointing it at the Reb drunk. All the kids were behind the wagon with Tamsen and Henry, all except John Enoch. Henry quickly reached up to the bench seat and yanked John sideways facing him. As he strained to lift him,

Bam, Bam, Bam, Bam, Bam.

Henry hoisted John down to the ground in a heap. They were all in a heap. Henry didn't have a gun, and the thought wasn't occurring to him to use one anyway. He was in total shock and confusion. Silence. Now after a bunch of shots, he didn't know how many he had heard, he heard nothing. For what seemed like minutes but was only seconds, they all lay completely still. Slowly Henry got up and inched to where he could peek over the wagon. The southern man was writhing on the ground, with blood pooling in front of his chest. The northern man was sitting wide-eyed and motionless on the wooden steps in front of the saloon, as

Bleeding Kansas—Life and Death in Bourbon County

though he had calmly sat down and was looking at someone across Market Street.

In this severe setting Henry could see that the man's eyes really were quite blue, as his enemy had so rudely pointed out. By the small hole just above the man's left temple and the bigger hole above his right temple, Henry knew the man's last thought was wedged somewhere in between. Looking at the several men standing close by on either side of the two combatants, all with smoking pistols and rifles poised, Henry wondered, *Who shot who?*

Jesus Christ he thought, *that's more lead than I've ever seen in the air in so small a space since Westport.* And then he remembered. He had a whole family just several feet away from this melee. How could this have happened right at their feet? If they hadn't been able to tumble off the far side of the wagon what might have happened? He peered again at the fight scene. The writhing Reb had quit writhing. He wouldn't be cowboying any more. He was dead. The other shooters, whoever they were, disappeared into the crowd. The townspeople slowly advanced toward the two corpses. The piano music from within the saloon resumed. And Henry snapped back to the reality of his sequestered family huddled on the ground.

"Everybody OK?" he anxiously said.

"I think so," answered Tamsen as she stood dusting herself off. "Kids? Libby, John, Bobby, everybody all right?"

All of them arose timidly and looked curiously at their father. All except John Enoch. They were expecting some

Wolves at the Door

kind of answer from Henry explaining the scene they had just witnessed. They weren't quite old enough for blatant swearing yet, but both Libby and Bob were thinking along the lines of, *Jesus Kee-rist, what in the hell was that all about?* As they all gazed at each other in a state of quizzical disbelief, Tamsen noticed John on the ground.

"All right, get up John, it's all over now," she said. "We're safe. Sure as the dickens shook up, but safe."

John didn't move. He looked at her and tried to speak, but only garbled noise came out.

"C'mon, John Enoch, what's wrong with you, can't you get up?" Libby said.

John Enoch lay still, all crumpled up with a look of confusion turning to fear on his face.

"C'mon, son," said Henry, "you're just scared and shaken. We're all OK and so are you. No bullets could have made it through the horse or wagon. Nobody was shot, including you. Just must of got your wind knocked out falling from the seat. Give it a minute and you'll be fine."

"Can't move, trying, legs, arms, can't, uhh," stammered little John.

"Oh, oh no, dear Jesus," said Tamsen, "what's that Henry?"

Henry followed her terror filled gaze down to the dead center of John's back, just a few inches below his neck. A one-inch wide piece of jagged splinter protruded out about another inch.

Bleeding Kansas—Life and Death in Bourbon County

"Oh my God," said Henry, "oh my God. Don't move John, lie still." It was an unnecessary instruction. John couldn't move anything below his neck. He could barely speak, and could breathe only haltingly.

"What happened, Pa, what's wrong?" Bob asked.

As Tamsen knelt down to cradle John, Henry shot up and yelled, "Help! Help!, A doctor! We need a doctor!" No response. "Please, is a doctor in town? Please, my boy's bad hurt. We need a doctor!"

"There is one, actually two, if they're in town," a voice rang out. And before anything else was said a tall scruffy looking white haired man came walking rapidly up Market Street.

"I'm here. I'm a doctor at the fort. What's the problem?" said Dr. L.M. Timmonds.

"So am I, a doctor," added J.S. Redfield, "office down the street. What's goin' on?"

"My boy, here. My boy's stuck with this wood. I don't know what it is or where it come from. Please, oh God, please help," Tamsen wailed.

Simultaneously the men knelt by John.

"Hello, Lawrence," said Redfield.

"Mornin', J.S., what we got here?" said Timmonds. "Straighten out slowly if you can, son."

Nothing.

"All right," Timmonds said gently, "then we'll try to very carefully straighten your legs and roll you over onto your stomach."

Wolves at the Door

As they did this, Dr. Redfield, a portly, balding man, glanced around as if looking for something. "Lawrence, I saw this shootout from down the street. He couldn't have been hit with a bullet where he was lying, but I'm sure he was the last one off the wagon just when the shooting started. I don't think he was shot, but I'll bet this wood splintered off somewhere a bullet did hit."

Henry looked around and, sure enough, a freshly ripped strip right along the wagon side where John had been standing was apparent. Henry looked more closely and saw a very clear piece of wood grain had been abruptly torn asunder. He glanced down at the one inch visibly sticking out of John's back. The grain matched. Henry shuddered. Dr. Redfield stood up and examined the wound in the wagon.

Redfield shook his head in sorrow. "It's terrible to say, sir, but as we can see by the fresh scar on that board, this splinter is more than four inches long and widens to almost two inches. I believe it has severed, or nearly severed, your boy's spine. I am so sorry."

Nobody spoke. Tamsen felt light headed and could feel herself drifting up through the clouds. She closed her eyes and bowed her head. She tightly held Henry's arm for support. Then she knelt, almost fell, beside John and placed her other hand on his small shoulder.

"Oh, John, my John Enoch, my little boy," and her chest and shoulders began heaving with the sobs she tried to stifle lest he see them.

As Henry gently took his arm away from her, Timmonds knelt by Tamsen to steady her. Henry walked to

Bleeding Kansas—Life and Death in Bourbon County

the other side of the wagon. Bobby looked under the wagon and spotted the lower pant of his pa's legs. Splattering on his boots was a downfall of yellowy, brownish liquid. Henry was vomiting.

How could this happen? Henry thought. *We were just comin' in for a nice day. Tamsen was just talkin' to God, or Job, or someone in that damn book. I was just thanking our lucky stars for our good life. What is this? Please God, not again. First our little Mary. Now don't take this boy from me, you awful son of a bitch. If you got to have more blood, take me, dammit. How can you ask a man to give up his son?* The irony of making that statement to God briefly crossed Henry's awareness. *No, enough of this,* he thought. *John ain't dead yet, or is he?*

He rushed back around the wagon and faced the doctors. "What now? What can we do? Can we take it out? Can we move him to a bed? Will he live? Will he be paralyzed?"

"I truly don't know," said Dr. Timmonds. "I defer to any opinion Dr. Redfield may venture, but I'd prefer to discuss it out of earshot of your missus and kids."

"No! said Tamsen. "That will not happen." She looked toward several kindly looking ladies standing nearby. "Miss … miss … somebody? Will someone look after these my other children for a short while?"

"I'd be happy to, ma'am," said a sympathetic looking older lady. "Don't give a care. I live right there in that yellow house across the street. They'll be over there with me. You do what you must do." Whereupon she rounded up the Devon children and departed.

Wolves at the Door

"Look, I agree with Dr. Timmonds," said Redfield. "It's impossible to know the nerve damage. If that entire splinter is in there, which we can't know, it is very, very bad. I think we must move him to a stable setting. I suggest my office just down the street. It's too far to Dr. Timmonds' office at the fort. Do you agree, Lawrence?"

Timmonds nodded. "As to a course of action, I truly don't know. If the stick stays in, well, it can't stay in. If we try to remove it, who knows what results? For the moment let's slide a blanket under him, hold it taut and gently move him over there to my office."

As six men accomplished that task, Henry and Tamsen sadly conversed. "What do we do now, Henry?" inquired Tamsen as they followed the little procession toward Redfield's office.

"Let's see what these fellows come up with. This is ... this is ... it's just awful, Tamsen. I can't believe it! And I don't think there's any other doctors anywhere near. Ol' Doc Reardon died awhile back. Maybe up in Kansas City, but that's way too far to help John now. It's **awful**."

Tamsen merely nodded, unable to think of **words** any better to express her horror and bewilderment.

After the boy had been laid out on a cot in Dr. Redfield's examining room, both doctors took a look at the splinter. Timmonds, in his practice at Fort Scott, had dealt with somewhat similar impalements from several accidents and a few arrows. But with arrows, he knew what the other end

Bleeding Kansas—Life and Death in Bourbon County

looked like. If the projectile head was in soft tissue, he had on occasion just run it on through, cut it off, removed the shaft and dressed the wound.

In a few cases when he didn't know what the business end of an arrow was impacting, it was much more of a risk to do that. He couldn't run it through, so he usually cut around the entry canal as needed, enough to back out the projectile head. Both of these had fairly good results, until the victim later died of infection anyway.

"This, I must confess, mystifies me," Timmonds said. "Since we don't know what contact that wood has already made with the spinal cord, we don't know what nerves are already cut, or about to be, by the slightest movement. Again, J.S., if you have any better feeling of certainty than I do, I'm all ears. But I almost think our best choice right now is to wait. Maybe in a day or so it'll become more clear what paralysis remains. Maybe he'll get some motion back overnight that may indicate this is not as precarious a situation as we thought. What do you think?"

"Lawrence, I've never seen anything like this. I surely deliver many more babies than you, but this is way out of my experience. I humbly, hopefully and totally defer to your judgment."

With that, Dr. J.S. Redfield officially turned over the authority on this to his friend and colleague, Dr. Lawrence Timmonds.

"All right, folks, let me explain." Timmonds took a deep breath. "You heard what I just said. It is really a guess,

Wolves at the Door

which we hope may become more clear with a slight passage of time. But to be brutally honest, we don't have much time. He has to breathe, which he is doing now very laboriously. He will have to eliminate, and we don't have any idea how that's been affected. He'll have to receive nourishment and water."

The doctor looked from Tamsen to Henry, allowing his gaze to stay on the father. It was too painful to look into the mother's eyes. "That splinter will set up an infection in a while. And the angle it has entered, as you can see, leads directly through or around his spine to his heart or lung. I'd rather cut my arm off than have to speak to you this way, but that's where we are."

John Enoch lay still. If he was conscious he didn't manifest it. If he heard the conversation, they didn't know. Henry stood, head bowed, in a trance.

Tamsen took a very deep breath. "Doctors, both of you, I thank you from the bottom of my heart for your obvious care and concern for this, my fine boy. Our fine boy. He is in the same God's hands that put you two men here at this time and place. I want you to know that we appreciate your best council, especially you, Dr. Timmonds, but we do not hold you responsible for John's life. I so strongly believe in God's mercy and wisdom that I can abide His will."

Henry heard all this, happy and grateful to hide in Tamsen's faith. He couldn't share it, but he was glad she had it.

Tamsen went on. "You have said wait, so let's wait. John Enoch seems unconscious, but comfortable. Henry, if

Bleeding Kansas—Life and Death in Bourbon County

Dr. Redfield doesn't object, maybe one of us can stay with John, maybe sleep on that davenport. The other can stay with the children at that kind lady's home."

"That is Mrs. Scofield," Redfield informed them. "I'm sure she would welcome you."

Tamsen nodded. "Fine, then." She looked at her husband. "Henry, I'd like to stay with John right now. Do you mind going over to watch over the others?"

"That's fine, dear. I'll round 'em up and settle them in for tonight. Maybe Mrs. Scofield can suggest a supper or dinner place. The kids'll be hungry. I'll bring something over for you. We'll have to keep our strength up."

As he departed he realized what a remarkable woman Tamsen was. He couldn't fathom how she must have felt on losing Mary Mariah. Or how she stayed afloat. And now this. She seemed to disappear for a while in grief and terror, and then return from wherever she went with a calmness of spirit and a steeled purpose.

Where do they make women like her? he wondered, *and how did I deserve her?*

They let almost three days pass. John faded in and out of delirium. He didn't seem to register much pain or awareness. Tamsen, with the help of both doctors, managed to ease him over a tiny bit, enough to give him a few spoonfuls of broth. He swallowed some out of reflex, but most of it dribbled down his cheek. Also out of involuntary reflex he urinated a small amount.

"We are losing this battle," she announced on the morning of July 6. "Something else must be done."

Wolves at the Door

The two doctors exchanged pensive glances and looked at the floor. Henry had just walked in and asked what was going on.

"Henry," said Tamsen, "we can't just stand here and do nothing. He clearly is not improving. He is withering away. Even if we fail, we must act, and act now!"

He knew she was right but was powerless to instruct the doctors. "I can't, Tamsen, I just …" and he lowered his face into his hands and wept.

Tamsen turned to the doctors. "Dr. Timmonds, since you have had more experience with this kind of injury, I think you should try to remove the splinter. Yes, please remove it now," she said.

"Ma'am," he answered, "I am fearful of that course of action, but I agree it must be done. This isn't working. Although removing it may be fatal, so will doing nothing. I hate this more than I can say. I would give anything if a well trained Boston or Philadelphia surgeon could be here in my shoes. But I'll do it. With your and Mr. Devon's permission and Dr. Redfield's concurrence, I'll try my best."

They all nodded.

After preparing both himself and John, Timmonds placed his well-scrubbed hand on the protruding splinter. Other than very slight and irregular breaths, young John showed no outward signs of life. The doctor gently but firmly pulled on the wood. No give. Again he pulled but added a little twist as well. Very slight movement.

Bleeding Kansas—Life and Death in Bourbon County

He stepped back and wiped perspiration from his forehead with his shirtsleeve.

"I felt a bit of movement, but it doesn't feel like it can be finessed out. And I can't push it forward. Actually, I could try to push it ahead just a little, then give it a slow twist and see if it will back out."

He did and it did. Some jagged edge on it must have been acting like a barb on a fishhook, catching up and not allowing retrieval. By pushing just a small distance forward and twisting, the rough edge cleared and smoothly backed out.

"There it is," he said as he held the offending splinter up for all to see.

"Good Lord," said Redfield. "That thing is much sharper than I imagined. No wonder it dug so deep."

John deeply exhaled, producing a gurgling sound.

"Now, we just wait. I can't believe no serious damage was done. We must all hope for the best," continued Dr. Timmonds, "but you must be prepared for what may follow. He may never wake up, or he may awake totally and permanently without use of arms and legs. I fear the worst. We again must resign ourselves to a waiting game."

Tamsen and Henry stepped outside to breathe. They were both strung out to the point of exhaustion.

"You sit there on that bench, Henry, and rest a bit. I'm going over to Mrs. Scofield's and visit the children. God knows the older ones must be frantic over all this. Get me if

Wolves at the Door

anything happens. I'll be back at noontime with a food basket. God bless her. Mrs. Scofield has been sent to us by angels."

Henry just nodded and sat down. He was in a daze.

Two more days went by. By the evening of the eighth, John's breathing was increasingly labored. They had turned him over on his back, thinking with the splinter out he'd rest easier. But he wasn't resting easy. Whatever had happened in his frail little chest had clearly impacted his lungs. And absolutely no movement had returned to his limbs. He was a dying little boy, and Tamsen knew it.

"Henry, come over here. Doctors, would you please leave the room?"

Both doctors instinctively realized what she was about to do. Both solemnly nodded, both hugged her, and both left.

"Henry, we've got to release our boy now," she said.

"Huh, what do you mean?"

"Come hold my hand, Henry. I love you, and I know you are anguishing. And John knows it, too. He's staying with us to abate our pain. But God wants him now."

Henry knew but didn't want to acknowledge her intent. He almost fell down with frantic grief. He listened as his wife spoke to their boy.

"John, John Enoch. You can hear us. I know you can hear us with either your ears or your heart. We are both here, son. Your loving ma and pa. We'll be with you, son. We're holding your hands and won't let go till we hand you over to Jesus."

Bleeding Kansas—Life and Death in Bourbon County

Her voice was sad but firm. Henry was now kneeling by the bed, violently sobbing.

"You go now, boy. Go whenever you want. Jesus will take real good care of you. We've loved you so much. And you've been such a good boy." Now she broke. Her voice choked but she remained upright. "You go, son. We'll never forget you. We love you. You go to Jesus, son."

They both were spent. They had cried themselves out. About an hour later Dr. Redfield's wall clock struck twelve times. Midnight. Not meaning to, they had both drifted off to sleep as they leaned against the cot. The clock startled Tamsen awake. They were both still holding John's small hands. She saw Henry looking peaceful in his sleep. She looked at John's face. He was almost smiling. No more labored breathing. Not a single crease of discomfort on his countenance. An angelic look of total acceptance.

"Henry, Henry. Wake up you wonderful man," she said as she gently shook his shoulder.

"Wha—what is it?" he mumbled.

"Henry, our little boy is gone. He's flown right out of here like a sweet bird, Henry. Thank God he isn't hurt no more. You took good care of him always, Henry. You were the best pa he could've had on this earth. And Jesus took him home."

Henry's eyes filled and his shoulders shook. Tamsen gently released John's cold hand and strongly embraced her husband.

"You'll see him again, Father. You 'n' me will hold him again in our arms someday. Now c'mon, get up. We got to tell the kids. You know we have five strong and blessed children across the street. They're waiting for us and we have to go to them. C'mon, c'mon."

A Little Girl's Impression

Libby looked at the fresh-cut gravestone and read the words aloud. "John E, son of Henry and Mary Devon, died July 9, 1870, aged four years, four months and seven days." How could that be? Where was Johnny? At nine, Libby was a little more aware of the solemnity of the event than Bobby, at seven. But she wondered how little Johnny could be in this hole up behind the cabin. Mary Mariah had always been here, as though she lived here or something. Libby thought she remembered Mary but wasn't sure. Was Mary the girl she thought she remembered or was that the girl she vaguely knew from a neighbor family that had moved away? All very confusing. But now this was John Enoch. She really had known him. He was her four-year-old brother. She cried when Ma and Pa said John had died. And Bobby cried. Charlie just looked blank and Sadie and Frank wanted something to eat. On the way home from Fort Scott, Sadie had kept asking "Where Yahn? Where Yahn?" unaware that John was stretched out in that oddly shaped crate in the back of the wagon.

Then there had been the burial up here. Her parents had wept hard, as had neighbor ladies and a few men. That

Bleeding Kansas—Life and Death in Bourbon County

really disarmed her. She didn't ever remember seeing Pa cry, and rarely Ma. Both she and Bobby had been startled at other grownups' standing there bawling. But Charlie had paid more attention to the butterflies swarming all over the pretty orange wild flowers in full bloom. His father finally had to grab him sternly by the arm and tell him to be quiet and stand still.

During the burial, Henry had again drifted between his own thoughts and the preacher's blather.

"The Lord made not this covenant with our Father but with us, even we who are alive here today," the preacher had droned.

Wonder why this had to happen. Was it my fault for subjecting our family to possible danger? Henry wondered.

"I clothe the heavens with blackness, and I make sackcloth their covering," said the preacher.

How could I know those two yahoos would come out, guns blazin'? Is this country too full of hate to prevent this? Could it, will it happen again? pondered Henry.

"The Lord God hath opened mine ear, and I was not rebellious," thundered the preacher.

Rebellious is the right word, thought Henry. *What does this Bible thumping blowhard know about rebellion? Those goddamn Rebels shot at me, not him. And that goddamn rebel cowboy got my son killed, not his. I wish he would wind it up, shut his pie hole and go home!* thought Henry.

But that had been more than a month ago, and Libby had no idea what her father had been thinking. She stood now, looking down at the newly installed grave marker. There was Johnny, and there to her right was Mary Mariah. *Why were they down in the ground? Were they going to come out? Were they all, Ma and Pa and the kids all going to be put down under ground someday?* All very confusing.

Good Lord, Woman!

"Tamsen, it's been five years since we buried John Enoch. Been eleven years since Mary Mariah. I want to ask you somethin'," said Henry. "Remember our discussion back then about movin' on further west? 'Bout new towns and cheaper land?"

"I don't remember no discussing. I remember you talking and me listening. Not really what you might call discussing!"

He smiled. "OK, but you do remember. Well, let's go over it again, and this time we'll discuss. Back then, I guess I was motivated by bad feelin's after the war and all. And sure, by Mary's death and, of course, John Enoch. But I heard somethin' in town last week made me think on it again. Do you want to talk about it?"

"Sure, Henry," she agreed, "in fact I've been wonderin' how long it'd take you to revisit the subject. Shoot!"

"Well, I still feel as I did back then that this railroad thing is driving this country's future farther and farther west. I remember telling you how wonderful it would be for

Bleeding Kansas—Life and Death in Bourbon County

some eastern doctor to be able to get quickly to some child out west. I had no idea that child would end up being our John. But what an example! Who knows if the right surgeon could've gotten here in time, even ten or twenty years from now, on the trains? But you see what I mean. They're starting to tie this whole country together so everybody's connected to everybody, and it's just gonna keep on happenin'." He paused to take a breath, aware he was getting all worked up again.

"I heard of a settlement down on the I.T. near Cherokee lands, near Oklahoma territory, bein' started up. Name is Kiowa, after that tribe, I reckon. You hear of Medicine Lodge? The Medicine River? It's out there. Well, some of the town folks and a few farm families like us is gettin' up a group to head out there together. They're goin' in a wagon train with a couple of men who've been there and know the way. "Land is cheaper out there, and there can't be as much leftover smolderin' war anger. These fellas puttin' it together say since practically everyone already there or going there is new to the area, there's little or no rancor among 'em. I've thought deep on it, Tamsen, and I'm sure I truly have no hate left in my heart for anyone. I don't give a damn if its Rebel or Yank, white, black, Mex or Injun, I think we all just want to be left alone to live our lives as we see fit. I'm even hearin' the railroads are hirin' Chinamen cause they'll do work others won't."

Henry stretched and pulled off one of his boots. "My point is it's a helluva big space from here on out, and I think we should make a clean bust of it here and join in the fun.

Wolves at the Door

We did good here in Bourbon County. We been here over fifteen years, and we've done real good. We carved out our quarter section and proved it up. We did our share in the war. We had a passel of kids and, even though we'd be leavin' two up on the hill, we'd be takin' six with us. We've had our youth here, Tamsen, but we're not too old to make a new start. I know we're both past forty now, but I swear we're healthier than any other couple in the county. Maybe we just both come from good stock, but I think we got about as much left in us as is behind us. What do you think?"

"Well, Mr. Devon, what I think is I'm not too sure I want to traipse off even farther into the wild west with some pathetic farmer who can't even count. That's what I think!" she replied.

"Whadya mean I can't count? Count what?"

"Yer kids, that's what. You can't even count yer own children we'd be totin' along on the trip. You're right about leavin' our little Mary and Johnny here, but its seven, not six, we'd have to cram into a wagon."

"Are you tetched in the head woman?" he said. "Can't even count yer own covey. You got Libby 'n' Bob, Charlie 'n' Sadie, and Frank 'n' baby Olive. That's three pair, six. Can't you ... Oh, no! Not again!" He sputtered as Tamsen just sat there grinning at him. "Don't tell me, Lord have mercy," he said in a fit of exasperation.

"The Lord will have mercy in His own time, Henry, but you could help Him along if you could keep that little pony of yours locked up in the barn a bit more often!" She smiled.

Bleeding Kansas—Life and Death in Bourbon County

"We've got another little Devon due in the fall, which I guess proves you are absolutely keerect, Mr. Romeo. We are apparently still young and healthy. Some might even call us feisty." She was glowing.

"Good Lord, woman!" he said when he caught his breath. "If you're gonna keep foalin' till you're eighty we damn near have to widen our range just to accommodate our own herd. But that's great, Tamsen. It's a true wonderment. Well, if you're all right with a new adventure, let's have this here baby in autumn of '76, and soon as yer up to it, we'll head on out to Kiowa. We'll throw in with whatever group that might be going thataway then. God Almighty, I can't believe it! Another child, at forty-two years old. You just get me all worked up. But we'll do it. We got three boys and three girls, so this 'un'll be sort of a tiebreaker. But we will sure as hell do it."

Henry sighed and removed his other boot, then tossed it playfully at Tamsen. "You go easy now. We'll get by spring and summer and sometime in maybe September or October we'll add to the clan. For the last time, I sure as hell hope. But we'll do it. That'll give me time to get this place ready to sell. Shouldn't be hard, 'cause plenty of folks is streamin' out here to enjoy the fruits of our hard work. It'll also give me time to line up our ducks in Kiowa. It's brand new, Tamsen, probably not even a town yet. And it'll be hard just like this was. But we'll be in at the beginnin'. It will be an adventure. We'll take our six, excuse me, seven little varmints to Kiowa, and we'll help build a town. We'll help build America!"

Wolves at the Door

Barkin' at the Moon

"September 17, Tamsen. You sure didn't miss it by much. We said September October, and the seventeenth is about as September October as you can get." Henry beamed as he looked at his infant son. "Yessir, young fella, here it is September 17, 1876. You showed up right on schedule didn't you? He's stout, Mother. You really did a good one this time. Solid little cuss."

"My Lordy, Henry, you'd think you were describing a keg of nails. I'd prefer we referred to our newborn son as, well, princely rather than cussedly."

"Princely?" Henry exclaimed. "Princely? I never thought of no kid of ours as exactly princely. But I'll tell you what. If you think he's so princely, I'll go along with it. What'll we name this young bird?"

"Now there you go again, Henry. Young bird indeed! Why not name him Partridge, or Mr. Pheasant, or Ornery Owl? He's no bird, Henry."

They basked in the glow of knowing how well things had turned out this happy day. The other children had remained healthy and grown faster than prairie flowers in May. Little Ollie was three, up and running. This new baby boy, they both felt, would be their last child.

"Tamsen, this is a wonderful day. That Maker you pray to so much must be hearing you," Henry said as he sat on the edge of their rope bed. He held the little boy on his lap, cradling him with his left arm. He held Tamsen's

Bleeding Kansas—Life and Death in Bourbon County

hand in his right hand. "Look at 'im. He is princely. Listen, we'd kinda settled on Thomas if he had a pecker—which I'd still appreciate if it's OK with you. I've known several Toms and liked them all. Especially Sergeant Tom Hamilton. But for the middle name, what's some prince's name? You know that royal stuff better'n me."

"How about Albert?" she suggested. "After Prince Albert. He's been dead quite awhile now, but he was Queen Victoria's husband, and I've always loved her."

"Yea, I also vaguely remember he was her cousin, too. Isn't there something in that Bible of yours about fraternizing a little too close to the home fires?"

"Oh pshaw, Henry. That don't mean a thing. Besides, he's the only prince I can think of. Let's make him Thomas Albert, Thomas Albert Devon! A rather princely name for a rather princely fellow."

"Then that's it," said Henry as he threw open the cabin door and stepped out on the small plank stoop. "Attention world! May I please have your attention? You folks back in England and over in Russia! You darkies down in Africa! All you Injuns north, south and west of here! And even you micks in Ireland, not to mention all the ships at sea. A new force to be reckoned with has just poked his little bald head into this here cabin. His name is Mr. Thomas Albert Devon, and he is somehow connected to our mournful Queen Victoria herself! Therefore you must all treat him with the respect due royalty, which he is," Henry resonantly announced.

Wolves at the Door

Bobby and Frank were only a few feet from Henry. The other kids were either scattered around the yard or in the cabin. They all looked at Henry with inquisitive eyes, then looked at their mother for some explanation.

"Don't fret," exclaimed Charlie, "he just ate some of that loco weed. He'll be barkin' at the moon by tonight!" They all grinned as Henry got his second wind.

"No sir, I am not loco. I am seriously announcing the arrival of this young whelp as a special child. He is named Thomas Albert, and you may call him Tom, or Tommy. I, however, plan to call him Caboose, 'cause he sure as hell better be the last car on this here train!"

"Henry!" gasped Tamsen. "What has gotten into you? Get in here this very minute. Please God don't let anyone hear you or they'll come and cart you off. And don't you dare call him Caboose or I'll snatch you bald headed, which I've noticed you're getting a pretty good head start on all by yourself. He is Thomas. They'll all call him Tom."

She stroked the little boys head as she now held him to her exposed breast. "He's my Tommy, my boy, my baby boy. And he'll live a long life. They all will, Henry. We've had our sorrow back with Mariah and Johnny. No more, never again. We'll take all these with us to our dying days, I'm sure. And if I live to be eighty, which I will, this darling little cherub will always be my baby boy."

Bleeding Kansas—Life and Death in Bourbon County

Let's Git!

A little more than a year later, in February 1878, Tamsen and Henry and all the children sat in the cabin enjoying the fireplace. It was Sunday, mid-afternoon. The warmth was wonderful but the feeling of togetherness even better. Their crop of vegetables had been good for the last several years. Some pork and beef was salted, cured and hanging in an outbuilding. Two horses, one mule and an ox had died in the previous year, but Henry found good, younger replacements. They were comfortably stabled out in the lean-to. Tamsen had just served up one of her better meals. They didn't get a lot of beef, and what they got they used sparingly. Same with pork. Today they had enjoyed rabbit stew, beans and okra and of all blessed things, apple pie. They could truly say, "Our cup runneth over." Tamsen had made the pie using apples she had preserved in the fall, presenting it to her family as a mid-winter cure for the doldrums.

"Holy Hezekialla, Mother," Henry said, nearly swooning with pleasure, "that was about as good as heavenly nectar, slidin' over my taster."

Tamsen rolled her eyes. "First of all, Father, thank you. Second of all, there is no Hezekialla or whatever you said. There was a Hezekiah, but you weren't even close. Third of all, I don't think I'd be bringing up 'heavenly' nectar if I didn't know any more about heaven than you seem to know. Blaspheming like that may just jeopardize any chances you have at another piece of pie!"

Wolves at the Door

"Well, now, I am genuinely hurt by that remark, Tamsen. Hezekiah? Hez to Kiah? Here's to Kiowa! You see, the good Lord just went out of his way to give us divine guidance in the form of an apple pie dispute. Don't you get it? Here's to Kiowa! He's telling us it's time to pack it in here and head on out to Kiowa. And the way he brought us to see his guidance means Kiowa must literally and truly be God's country."

The kids all looked up and shook their heads in cadence with their mother. "What're you talkin' about Pa?" asked Bob. "What's Kiowa?"

"Well, son, glad you asked. Kiowa is a beautiful about-to-be town a few hundred miles west of here, down on the I.T. Oklahoma border. Its rivers flow with milk and honey, and delicious corn fritters grow wild on the trees!"

"Really, Pa?" asked an excited Sadie. "Corn fritters on the trees?"

"You betcha, punkin. And they have a law saying all mothers have to serve apple pie to their children for every meal!"

"Really, Dad? Are you kidding?" Frank asked.

"Yes indeed they do, son. Only allowed exception is if the kid would rather have peach pie."

"Henry, wha—God Almighty!" said Tamsen.

"Hush, woman!" he playfully interrupted as he held his arm out straight, palm facing her. "You hush now. We've been jawin' on this for five years or so. It's time we had a democratic family vote on the matter. Everybody who wants to stay here and shovel out the same stalls, mend the same fence and plow the same rows we done a thousand times, jump in the fire. Everyone who wants to move to Kiowa for all that milk and honey and fritters raise your hand."

All the hands except Tamsen's and baby Tommy's shot up.

"There, the Kiowa team has it. The vote's in, we move to Kiowa!" he said. "How 'bout it, Mother. Don't you want to go with us?"

Her arm slowly rose as she reluctantly agreed.

Everyone laughed, cheered and hoorahed. "Yahoo, yahoo," yelled Charlie. Henry glanced down at little Tommy on the floor, totally unaware of the whole episode. All he knew was that everyone was clearly excited about something. As he toddled over to a chair, he slowly extended his arm upward to steady his balance.

"Well I'll be hornswoggled, kids. Look at that. Mr. Thomas Albert Devon is throwing in with us too! See his arm go up? He just voted, Tamsen! Hot damn, it's unanimous! Let's git!"

None Too Bright

Henry had already confided in several friends his intention to head out to Kiowa in the spring or early summer of 1878. It all depended on his ability to talk Tamsen into the venture, which he had now done. And on his ability to sell the Bourbon County quarter section, which he hadn't done. There was no question that he himself was ready for the next adventure, but he did feel a pang of sentiment about the farm. Not only because of the backbreaking effort they all had put into it, but also because, well, that was President U. S. Grant's signature right there on that deed. He kind of hated to give that up.

But no matter, they were all fired up and ready to go. Even Tamsen. "Tell me more about all that milk and honey, Henry, or anything else you know about Kiowa. You do know something don't you? Anything? Like exactly how far is it, meaning how long a wagon ride will it really be? Don't forget that when you and I steamboated up the Missouri back in '60 there was only little Mariah. No horses, oxen, pigs, chickens, furniture or other stuff. That was a delightful and easy trip. Even the wagon ride down from Westport was easy on the military road. This won't be such a walk in the park, Henry."

"I know that, Mother. I also know we were still in our mid-twenties back then and full of piss and vinegar. This trip will, of course, be much harder. Libby's married, and it's a godsend to have Jim Dwyer on board. He's strong and bright and as welcome as any of our own sons. With them plus our other six it'll of course be a much bigger effort than our coming out from Illinois. But really, except for Tom and maybe Ollie, all the others can more or less carry their own pail. In fact, Charlie and Bob are practically growed up men. Bob's a bit of a numbskull, but that's neither here nor there."

Bleeding Kansas—Life and Death in Bourbon County

"You're too hard on him, Henry. He's just an unruly fifteen-year-old boy. What was you like at fifteen?"

"More responsible than he is, but let's not get going on that. His craziness reminds me a lot of your cockeyed brother Ned back in Illinois."

She glared. "As you said, sir, let's not get going on that."

"Speaking of Libby and James," he continued, "his folks are anxious to go, too. With them and the MacNaughtens, LeClercs, Stamlers, Traisleys and Deteaus, we'll have a pretty good group. And Boney Korzack will be out of jail by then. They'll be anxious to get out of here, too."

"That bunch you just mentioned is a little questionable don't you think? Just about all of 'em have a pretty close relationship with John Barleycorn don't they?"

"Look, Tamsen, we're not perfect either." He laughed. "Yes, they could be viewed from afar as a tribe of dullards, drunks and horse thieves, but they're our friends. Let's face it, they wouldn't be so all fired ready to leave if all was paradise here. I know Tim Deteau don't have enough sense to pour piss out of a boot, but what the hell, they're all here! And all ready, willing and able. Beggars can't be choosers, ya know. And besides, this will be at the fastest a two-week, more'n likely a month-long escapade. We will need a bunch of tough and dependable friends at our side if we meet trouble. And they're all that, even if none of 'em is too bright."

Wolves at the Door

"Well, you can sure say that again, Henry, or they wouldn't be settin' out on this harebrained Kioway skedaddle. And that includes the dimwitted likes of you'n me, Mr. Devon."

"All right," he said. "As to your question of how long, what I am told is, it depends on who you get to guide you. We need to git us a good wagon master. We can't do that here in Fort Scott, but we can up on the ol' trail, the Santa Fe. If we grope our way out to Humbolt and follow the Neosha River up to Council Grove, we can pick up someone to guide us on out to Great Bend and then head straight south to Medicine Lodge. That's just twenty or thirty miles above Kiowa. All in all, I'm told that's about 300 miles, give or take. At maybe twenty miles a day, that'd be the two weeks I mentioned. But that's with no breakdowns, no accidents, no creek risin's or washouts, no Injun problems, and travelin' every day. No days of rest and no bad weather. Which of course ain't gonna' happen. That's why I said a month or more."

Tamsen could not hide the dismay she felt. "Lordy, that really scares me. Well, it doesn't really scare me, it just sorta gets my attention. And all that with young children aboard. Sounds kinda scary doesn't it, Henry, or is it just me?"

"No, Mother. It's not just you. I'm pretty sober about it, too. So are the other folks I've discussed it with. Look, people get discouraged on these trips. Even on well established trails like the Santa Fe, or the California, the

Bleeding Kansas—Life and Death in Bourbon County

Mormon or the Oregon, people die. It can possibly be fairly easy if everything goes perfect. But it don't." He leaned back and massaged the back of his neck. At age forty-five, Henry was beginning to notice a few aches and stiffness when he stopped moving. To combat the pains he simply rarely stopped moving.

"People get sick, animals get wore out, wagons tip over and all kinds of other damnations happen," he said. "It ain't easy. It would be likely, or at least not unlikely, that a few of these friends going with us may not get to Kiowa alive. But we can sure do all in our power to plan it out right. Actually though, Mother, we'd all be crazy if we weren't a little scared. That's what keeps us alert and ready."

"Henry, is there any ol' argument that will ever make you turn back on an idea once you set your mind to it? How 'bout a stampede of elephants? How 'bout mosquitoes the size of buzzards the whole way? How 'bout man-eating crocodiles in every creek 'tween here and Kioway? Do we turn back then?"

"No, ma'am. Not unless one of 'em up and eats you. 'Cause unless I lose you, we're ploddin' on!" he said as he swooped her toward him for a kiss.

"Good Lord, Henry. What's got into you? You think you're still twenty-five?"

"Only when I look at you, my dear, only when I look at you!"

He Ain't No Fisherman

Henry stood beside the splitting stump on the south side of the cabin. It was mid-March. This had been a pretty harsh winter, and everyone was looking forward to spring. Trees not being in abundance, Henry had drug a few downed branches up from the creek to cut for firewood. He hoped for spring but knew more cold weather lay ahead.

"Hello the cabin!" someone shouted from down the south slope. "Yahoo, Henry, is that you? It's me, Jack Marchant."

"How do, Jack, c'mon up. Good to see you. What're you doing out in our neck of the woods?" Henry asked as he laid aside the ax, glad for a respite.

"Hello, Hank." Jack was puffing after the walk up the slow incline. "Beautiful day, ain't it? You and Tamsen have a great spread here, course you both busted your humps provin' it up. I know that."

"That we did, Jack, that we did. So what brings you all the way out here from Fort Scott?"

"Land, Henry, land. More specifically, your land. This here farm. Word has it you folks and several other families is settin' out for new horizons. Kiowa, is it? Can't say I ever heard of that."

"You will, Jack, but yep, you got it right. We hope to go this summer. What's your interest in our farm here?"

"Not mine, Henry. But an old friend of mine from back east, name of Messer, is interested in building a life out here. They're young folks. I knew his father. Couple of kids, two or three. Real nice man and real pretty, good wife. Netty, I think. Would you be interested in sellin' out?

"Well, Jack, I'd like to say maybe or it depends, but you know as well as me that we can't head out till this place is pretty well spoken for. What'll he pay?"

"I don't know, Henry. I imagine the going rate for a quarter out here must be several hundred dollars. Why don't you let me ask back in Fort Scott and I'll arrange it? He's just as open and fair a fellow as you are. At least his daddy was, and I'm sure he is, too. I told him what you and Tamsen had carved out of this sod, and he's all for it. I'm sure we can work something out fair to you both."

"That's fine, Jack. That'll help us settle on a departin' date. All that's holding us up now will be trying to get a wagon master up on the Santa Fe."

"Why you going all the way up there, Hank?" said Marchant. "Isn't Kiowa down on the Oklahoma line? Down at the I.T.?"

"Yep, it is, but I don't know any other way to safely go. Tamsen and all the other ladies like the comfort of goin' on a well-trod road. I do, too. Maybe it's a 'misery loves company' thing."

"Hank, I wouldn't say anything, but I know a man who somewhat regularly travels to Dodge City and back. That place is growing with the cow runs up to the railroad. It'll be the next Wichita real quick. He takes a few supply goods wagons out from Fort Scott on a regular basis. Knows it pretty well, he claims. A direct shot out to your area must save almost half the time … just a thought."

Henry tapped the ax gently against the stump. "Half the trip? Are you sure, Jack?"

"Well, no Henry. I ain't sure it's half. But you know Council Grove, if that's where yer going, is way north. Why not talk to him and see what he says? What can you lose?"

Henry swung the ax purposefully into the cutting stump, imbedding it into the wood to prevent rust. "C'mon up to the house, Jack. Tamsen would like to hear about this."

When they entered the cabin Tamsen was just finishing cleaning up after the mid-day meal. "Well hello, Jack. I thought I heard an extra voice outside."

"Mother," Henry said, "Jack has an interesting suggestion on a possible short cut to Kiowa."

"Well, not so much a suggestion as just an observation, ma'am. You all are proposing going way out of your way, going well north to hook up with the main trail traffic. Which I understand. I was just tellin' Henry 'bout a man I know, name's Ken Littrell, who seems pretty adept at carvin' out his own wagon trails all over out there. I know he goes often and has guided several groups like yours to both Wichita and even Dodge City. Don't know what arrangements he makes, but he sure talks like he knows what he's doin'."

"How do you know him, Jack, and maybe better yet, how well do you know him?" Tamsen asked.

"Well, I don't know him real well, but I can tell you one thing, he's a liar," Marchant said with a deadpan look on his face.

"A liar, Jack! What do you mean he's a liar? That doesn't sound good!" said a concerned Tamsen.

"Well, I'm afraid the circumstances under which we met guarantee him to be a colossal prevaricator. See, I met Ken on a fishing expedition down on the Marmaton one Sunday with our mutual friend Slim Sterrett. Since I actually saw him fishing, I know he is a so-called fisherman. And as a fisherman, he is by definition, a liar," mused Marchant. "But if it makes you feel any better, I'll reverse my opinion a little. All that afternoon he didn't catch a single fish. All the rest of us did, but not him. So I guess in all fairness, he can't be a liar, cause I one hundred percent guarantee you that ol' Ken Littrell sure as hell ain't no fisherman!"

The Big Meeting

Three weeks later Henry, along with Traisley, Deteau and Stamler, went in Henry's buckboard to meet with Ken Littrell in Fort Scott. They crammed into the wagon, got an early start and were in town quickly. They also met up with Boney Korzack, who had just been released from the jail.

"Good morning, gentlemen," said Littrell after being introduced to one and all. "I understand from Mr. Marchant you all plan to permanently move out to Kiowa. I haven't been there, but I've been to Medicine Lodge three times. Once alone, twice transporting folks like yourselves."

Wolves at the Door

"Really?" said a blinking Korzack, still adjusting his eyes to full daylight. He was the only non-farmer in the group. He did general construction work in Bourbon County and had been hired by a farmer up near Dayton to dig a pond. The idea was to coordinate a windmill pump to fill a small pool for cattle to drink and cool off in. The farmer accused Korzack of not only shoddy workmanship but overcharging as well. Plus, Korzack had missed his promised deadline last summer resulting in the death of several cows from thirst.

The farmer claimed Korzack was a lousy pond builder. The judge and jury unfairly agreed, and he got thirty days in the Fort Scott lock up, plus a twenty-five-dollar fine. His fury at this was his reason for wanting to move. He stated to anyone who would listen that he and his voluptuous Swedish wife, Inga, were leaving their miserable town and they could all kiss his behind. Henry thought to himself that most of the men would probably rather kiss Inga's behind.

Traisley, Deteau and Stamler intently listened as Littrell outlined his plan to knock off at least two weeks of travel time. He himself had to be out again to Dodge City to deliver some barbed wire by mid to late summer. At least well prior to snowfall. He would be glad at the price of $100 per family to guide them, not only out to the area, but down to Medicine Lodge as well. They would have to bring all their own supplies. He would be providing only directions, guidance and general tips to avoid problems.

Bleeding Kansas—Life and Death in Bourbon County

"Ain't this here shortcut sort of like what the Donners tried back in '49? And look what it got them," said Tim Deteau, proudly showing off his keen sense of history.

"Yes, Mr. Dingo, it is vaguely like the Donner party's route. Different only in there is no snow and no mountains and plus, we leave in May. And in that I'm not only telling you of this more direct route, I'm actually taking you there myself. But you are, in a sense, correct in that all of the horses we use will have four feet, just like the Donners' horses," said Littrell.

"Deteau, the name's Deteau, not Dingo. But your points are well taken." Tim said with a chuckle.

"Let me ask you something, Mr. Littrell," said Frank Stamler. "What about emergencies along the way? I'm a farmer like these men and pretty good at avoiding accidents before they happen. But what about normal medical emergencies? My one boy had a ruptured appendix three years ago, and it killed him. We know what happened to two of Henry's kids. These things happening here are bad enough, but what do we do out there? Even not the dying kind. Say one of us gets a terrible toothache. Like one tooth's stuck under another. That can be so painfully miserable, you jest can't go on. Whadda we do then?"

"You're right, Mr. Steamer. I, of course, can't possibly give a satisfactory answer in cases like your poor boy, or Henry's kids. Those occasions must have been awful," Littrell said as they were finishing up a late breakfast in the Big Bonnet Hotel. "But those, you certainly would agree, are calamitous events. They're acts of God. Nobody can predict or avoid events like those. But a more normal event like your dental example is a good question. Let me ask you, do you know Dr. Coston, the dentist right over on South Main Street, Mr. Steamer? I think it's Dr. Whalen Coston."

"No I don't, and it's Stamler, not Steamer," said Frank, a bit miffed.

"Well my Lord, I'm so sorry," said Littrell. "I usually do better on names. But it don't matter if it's Dr. Coston or any other dentist. They're all the same. I maintain there ain't nothing any of those tooth pulling purveyors of pain can do by charging you a whole lot of money, Mr. Stamler, that your average blacksmith can't do with a bottle of whiskey and a good stout pair of tongs! Do you agree? And what galls me is they run around like they was a real doctor. Don't you agree Mr. Stamler?"

"Well, yes, I guess I do. Guess I'd have to allow I never met a dentist I didn't think should be shot at sunrise ... or right after he worked on me!"

Littrell stood. "Fellas, I'm about out of time today. Quite frankly, I'd like to be of service to you and your families. I'm sure I could shorten your trip, make it more enjoyable, and not give up a bit of safety doing it. But just as frankly I respectfully don't care one way or t'other. I'm going anyway. If you choose to throw in with me, let me know as soon as possible so we can coordinate arrangements."

"Ken ... OK to call you Ken, Mr. Littrell?" asked Daniel Traisley, a pig farmer.

Bleeding Kansas—Life and Death in Bourbon County

Littrell nodded.

"Let me ask you this, Ken. Going off on our own like you propose, what recourse do we have if you mislead us? Or provisioning ourselves, what recourse do we have against some Fort Scott merchant or supplier back here if we are somehow wronged, but we're then way out to hell 'n' gone? I read years ago all the passengers on some English ship trying to find the Northwest Passage went nuts and died due to lead poisoning. I remember the captain's name was Franklin. They went to the lowest bidder for their canned food, and the supplier sealed the cans with lead that leached into the food and poisoned them all. Of course they were dead, but what recourse would we have in some similar mishap, going out on our own like you suggest?"

"Jesus Christ, Mr. Trotsky, are you all paranoid? You think these Fort Scott folks are going to solder your long johns up with lead? You think I'm going to lead you all into an Apache war party? I realize Fort Scott has too many goddamn lawyers and you must have been talkin' to the miserable sonsabitches. Recourse this and recourse that. I'm getting' a little nervous myself at the prospect of hauling you all to the promised land for fear you're gonna sue me if a mosquito bites you. I have no idea what to tell you if everything doesn't turn out perfect, Trotsky. I'm sure it won't. But can we agree right now the goddamn lawyers have bollixed it up for us all, and can we agree not to let one of those cantankerous bastards west of the Verdigris River?" Littrell was fuming.

Wolves at the Door

"Yes, Ken, we can. And it's Traisley, not Trotsky. I'm Danny Traisley. I raise pigs about three miles past Henry's place. And I'm embarrassed to say I see your point. I guess I just read or hear things that some lawyer somewhere says just to get us all riled at each other. Tell you what. Soon as I get to Kioway, I'll run for some office on the platform of hanging by the neck until dead any goddamn lawyer caught anyplace in the whole state of Kansas. We'll ship 'em all to Injun territory, how's that?"

Everybody laughed and the meeting broke up. All agreed to speak with their families and the others not present that day. On the way back home before nightfall, Henry said to the others, "Boys, I don't know about you all, but I think that's our man. He sounds confident and has a good sense of humor, and I think he knows his stuff."

"So did the Donners' guide," said Deteau.

"Just don't get a toothache," said Stamler.

"Who cares, if he leads us astray we'll just sue his sorry ass," said Traisley.

"What's with all this goddamn suing?" griped Korzack, still smarting from his one-month sojourn in the Fort Scott pokey.

Tighter 'n Orange On A Pumpkin

About two weeks after the Fort Scott meeting, Jack Marchant showed up with a letter from the Messers offering to buy the farm for $500 and asking Henry to leave anything the Devons couldn't use themselves or didn't have room to take. By now Henry had learned that Kiowa was cattle country, not farm produce country. They wouldn't have a use for the seed stock and cultivator implements they had used in Bourbon County. He was happy to leave whatever he knew the Messers would put to good use, especially since the lighter the Devons could travel, the better.

"Do you think five hundred is fair, Father?" asked Tamsen. "Almost seems high!"

"It's hard to figure. It's not just the land. They'd have to scrounge up timber if this ol' log house wasn't here. And I'm sure Jack told 'em about the outbuildings and the fencing, and we got the windmill, too. That'd cost 'em more than just the acreage. Plus it took a lot of blood, sweat and tears to bust up this sod. That'd kill most people like it almost killed us. Yeah, I guess five hundred is about right. I trust Jack on that. And you know what, Tamsen, I'll bet five hundred is a drop in the bucket to what this quarter will be worth someday. Five hundred dollars. Hell, I'll bet it'll be worth five thousand dollars someday!"

"Oh sure," she said, "and that'll be the same day we go for a stroll on the moon!"

"Another thing to consider is the Messers is a bird in the hand. There may not be another bird come by too soon," said Henry as he looked at Marchant. "I suppose the best person to sell something to is the guy who wants to buy it. I can live with this if Messer can. What do you want out of this, Jack?"

Wolves at the Door

"Oh, I dunno, Hank. How does ten or twenty dollars sound? And I notice you got two scythes out there. How 'bout I take one of them?"

"You take the scythe, Jack, and twenty dollars. You've been a good friend. We wouldn't have found a buyer without you. Here, let us sign that agreement. Give the Messers our best wishes. We've loved this place and know they will, too."

As Henry finished signing, Tamsen, who had been gazing out the doorway toward the little Avondale cemetery, turned and took Marchant's hand in both of hers.

"Jack, have you actually met Mrs. Messer?"

"Why, yes, of course, ma'am. Why do you ask?"

"Is she a good woman, Jack, a really good Christian woman? Does she seem to really love and care for her children?"

Jack Marchant looked quizzically at Henry and back at Tamsen. "Why yes, Tamsen. I'm sure she is a really fine woman. She seems to me to draw admiration from all. They both do."

"Jack, Henry knows I'm all for this move to Kioway. The whole world knows I love Henry, and wherever he sets his cap to go, me 'n' the kids go. But I must tell you, Jack, I'm not takin' all my children with me. Two of 'em's up on that hill and will be forever. Please tell Mrs. Messer I'd be real beholdin' to her to look after them two every now and then. If she could pluck the weeds off our sweet babies' graves ever so often. And maybe put a few wildflowers on

Bleeding Kansas—Life and Death in Bourbon County

'em in spring and summer. When we leave here for Kioway I know I'll never be back. Will you ask her for me, Jack?"

"She's a fine young woman, ma'am, and yes, of course I'll ask her. I know she'll treat them and honor them like they was her own. And don't you forget, I'll be by here occasionally to check on the Messers, and I promise I'll look in on your dear children myself. Don't you worry none about that," assured Marchant.

As Henry walked Jack down the hill toward his buggy they agreed the Messers could move in anytime after June 1. "We'll probably be on our way well before then, but I'm sure that'll be time enough to get our belongings out, Jack. I've talked to the others. There's eight, possibly ten families agreed to head out on June 1 or before, maybe even May 1, dependin' on everybody gettin' sold out or leased out and provisioned up. Your man Littrell has a strange humor and demeanor, but I feel good about him."

"What exactly are you taking, Hank?" asked Marchant as he stepped up into his buggy.

"Our clothing and necessaries. Tamsen plans to leave a few items like the table 'n' chairs for Mrs. Messer. I made those and I'll just make new ones out there. We'll take our bed in the wagon if it fits. I'll take any useful equipment I can tie on, over or under the wagon. Did I tell you I was gettin' a new road wagon down at Page's in town?"

"No, you didn't, but Page did. He says several of your party is either having new ones made or gettin' used rigs from him."

Wolves at the Door

"Yes, I know. Red LeClerc and Cob MacNaughten are good friends and both gettin' new ones. We've bought a right nice used one, but they're both gettin' new. I laughed when I reminded Cob about his wife's last episode with a wagon. You hear about that? Not a road wagon, but she cajoled him into buying her some fancy little buggy. Something like yours, here, but imported! Can you believe that? I can't remember, Italy or France. No, Germany I think. Or maybe England. Yeah, I think it was made in England. Some rich land dealer up in Kansas City or Independence had brought it out. Seems his wife didn't like the upholstery color or somethin' and wouldn't use it. The guy got furious and sold it to Cob MacNaughten at half price. That's the only way he'll buy anything y'know. Tighter than orange on a pumpkin!"

Henry took a few breaths and continued. "So Cob brings it home and presents it to his missus. Married over his head, ya know. She's real buxom, and sweet as she can be. But apparently not a wagon mechanic. Just for the fun of it, he puts her in charge of axle maintenance. All she has to do is dab a little axle grease on once a month to keep it rollin' smooth as silk. But beside the grease bucket in his shed is a bucket of sand-laced piney tar which some folks out here use in winter on the wheel rims to catch a little traction. Ain't worth a damn but MacNaughten had tried it once and gave up on the idea. Unfortunately, he did not throw the stuff away. So there was that bucket, right beside the grease bucket."

Henry was gleeful as he continued. "Well, now you can see this coming can't you? Out she comes, the buxom but not mechanical Mrs. MacNaughten, exactly thirty days after taking possession of this fine chariot, and applies the 'grease.' Then she uses the buggy a few times and thinks it's getting a little sluggish. She suggests she and Cob take it all the way to Fort Scott for an outing to kinda limber it up a tad."

Henry was doubled up he was laughing so hard, and he could hardly finish the story. Marchant was just waiting for what he knew was coming.

"Off they go trottin' down the road," Henry continued. "You know that bridge over the creek past the curve?"

"Yes, I know it well, Hank."

"Well, just as they hit the incline up the bridge, zingo!, Both hubs saw through the axle simultaneous. The wagon bed and seat take a drop and, as MacNaughten goes sailing out, he sees both wheels shootin' ahead on their own. The buggy, cause they had just come out of a turn onto the bridge, was listing a bit to the starboard side, is that right or left? Anyway, to the right. Ol' MacNaughten just sails right over the short railing into the creek. But as the seat bed and his missus hit the bridge deck, she careens on over the left side and into the creek."

Both Henry and Marchant were laughing hard. Henry began wheezing and Marchant broke wind with a loud bang.

"Jesus Christ, Jack, get a hold on yer inner workin's," Henry complained. "At least let me finish the story afore you start shootin' at me!" That remark sent them into new gales of laughter.

Wolves at the Door

"All right, Jack, you OK? Not gonna fart again are you? All right, so there they are, both in the drink, when a wagonload of Aganbrights come by. You know them, out a mile past the Colby place. Ol' man Aganbright and all four sons. They stop and survey the situation. To their right is his excellency, Mr. MacNaughten, snortin', fumin', splashin' and cussin' to beat the band. On their left is the beautiful Mrs. MacNaughten, obviously a damsel in distress. Without any hesitation they all jump from their wagon and plod into the water to save poor Mrs. MacNaughten. I did mention, didn't I, she's quite buxom?"

The story wound down, and after a couple more were told, Henry and Jack shook hands and bade each other farewell. They thanked each other for the farm sale and wished each other the best of luck.

Finally, Jack said, "Well, Hank, that's about it. Guess I'll mosey on back to town. When I hear your departure date, maybe my missus and I will see you all off. I know lots of folks ride along with the trains for a day or so if they know folks in 'em. Anyway, I hope to see you again, Hank, I sure do."

"I do too, Jack. Thanks again for all your help. You take care now!" Henry said as Marchant clucked for his horse to move on. The buggy rolled on down the road and out of sight, while Henry wondered how many old friends like Jack they'd never see again.

Bleeding Kansas—Life and Death in Bourbon County

Roundup Day

May 10, 1878, was the day chosen for the included families to join together at the outskirts of Fort Scott. The Moran Road just north of Fort Scott had been a kicking off spot for other such groups. It cut a little south, following the Marmaton River, and then curved up on a northerly path to Moran, about twenty miles due west of Fort Scott.

Henry and Tamsen had come in two days earlier to pick up and outfit their wagon from H.L. Page & Co. at Number 1 Market Square. Horace Page was one of the most reliable wagon dealers in the area. He just happened to have had one on hand Tamsen really liked, at the right price. Tamsen liked the colors, a vibrant green bed with red trim and wheels. And the seating was a broad padded bench seat forward with a small step seat on each side that could possibly work for Ollie or Tommy. The older kids could walk or ride a horse. Henry liked the slightly higher bed and wagon bow, thinking it might keep them drier when they were fording rivers.

He had decided on a span of four mules and two oxen. The oxen would be alternated in and out, resting a pair of mules when needed. They already had two mules and one ox, so Henry had arranged for the others to be at Page's on the day prior to hookup.

They also had two horses, one cow and their younger dog, Raisin, with them. They left a 10-year-old terrier named Dog with Marchant to give to the Messers. Dog had spent his life on the farm and was too old for the trip. They thought the Messers could use him.

Wolves at the Door

Raisin was a piece of artistry. He was of some ancient, totally unknown conglomeration of dogdom. Curly black fur all over except a lighter brown patch of slightly straighter fur on his back. He had a severe underbite and an all around good disposition, aside from being a little horny at all times. Henry enjoyed having Raisin follow him up and down each furrow at planting time.

One day when he was planting, Henry had picked up a flattened and well dried cow pie. To get it away from where he was presently planting, he absentmindedly gave it a pretty good toss. The thing happened to catch a breeze just right and off it sailed, like a flat stone skipped on a calm surface. That's all it took. Ol' Raisin shot after it as though he had been fired from a slingshot. As the bovine biscuit skimmed through the stratosphere on gossamer wings, Raisin zeroed in on it like a homing pigeon to its roost. It took a slight dip to the left, then caught an updraft to about six feet off the ground. Raisin the Wonder Dog was born at that minute. Up he leaped and intercepted that flatulated flying disk right out of thin air. What a vision of grace and poise he had been, proudly strutting back to Henry with that malodorous meadow muffin between his teeth!

Henry felt it just wouldn't be right to leave a talented pup like that behind, so he made him a small platform surrounded by a four-inch rim. Its cover was a slanted roof plank that was mounted on the bow just ahead of the bench seat and behind the tongue. Raisin soon became adept at hopping up on the bow and then the platform. He could

Bleeding Kansas—Life and Death in Bourbon County

walk along and inspect this new world or ride in his covered nest, whichever he desired. As he learned by the end of the first or second day out, he could bejabber the bejesus out of the mules with total impunity from his protected platform. Life was always good for Raisin.

"Why did you name him Raisin?" Littrell asked as he stopped for a moment to watch Henry load his wagon.

"Cause he's always raisin' his leg, Ken. And a word of warning 'fore we start off, keep the women, be they human, horse, cow or sheep, padlocked at all times. He's a devilish little swordsman."

They both laughed and continued their separate tasks. Henry and Tamsen had ordered all the food such as beans, flour, canned fruit, oats and pickles that they could carry and had it pretty well stowed away—some in the larger watertight box on the back of the bed, some in smaller side compartments, and some little items in inside cubby holes. Whoever first owned this road wagon had done a good job of putting some kind of box, shelf, hook or hammock wherever possible. It would look majestic sailing across the Kansas prairie under its white canvas duck cover. Henry had his trusty old oilcloth stowed in the rear box.

"Mother, I believe we're set. God, what a trip this will be! I've read a few accounts from folks who did these trails in the '50s and '60s. We'll have it easier than them, I hope. The kids will remember it forever, 'cept for Ollie and Tom."

Tamsen took her own final inventory and concluded they were so stocked up she feared the mules couldn't budge the

Wolves at the Door

wagon. Nevertheless, she asked, "Do you think we need more sugar, or salt, Father? Or do you think we got too much?"

"Look, Tamsen, let's just go with what we got now. It's just a guess as to what we have too much or little of."

Just then Littrell walked his mare by them and interrupted. "You two are having the same consternation of all the others. Mrs. Korzack has loaded in her spinet from 'Sveden' and won't part with it. Red LeClerc has pool cues and balls. Claims he will ship his old table to Kiowa by rail later. Unbelievable. And your little dog is bad enough, but Cob MacNaughten has two, not one, but two, German Shepherds the size of elephants loaded in his wagon. They eat and shit like elephants, too! Oh, sorry Mrs. Devon."

Littrell, although almost always prone to keeping on an even keel, was getting a little piqued. "I told you all the two most needed things was wood 'n' water. It'll get right cold at night, and we all need water. You got plenty? For your family and animals?"

No, they didn't. Neither did the others. "Can't we get it along the way, Ken?" said Henry.

"Well, hell yes or hell no, Hank! We either stumble on it or we don't. But if it's no, we're in a troublesome shape!"

Henry and Tamsen procured what extra water they could, but Henry figured the water barrel on the back beside the cargo box would suffice. After all, they'd be running along the Marmaton and then the Neosho for well over a week. As to firewood, they'd simply pick it up at each night's campsite.

Bleeding Kansas—Life and Death in Bourbon County

"Hey, Hank," Dan Traisley yelled from his wagon, "you got any extra space in your rig for some extra stuff of ours?"

Henry walked over to Traisley's wagon, getting more exercised over this space quandary by the minute. "What 'extra stuff,' Danny? Is it important?"

Dan looked both ways and then peeked inside his wagon to make sure Zill wasn't within earshot. "It's her dresses, Hank. We got about a dozen special made dresses. Ya know, she's a bit sturdy!"

Henry thought to himself, *Yeah, a bit sturdy, like two axe handles across her stern!* But he actually answered, "What do you mean, Danny, by special dresses?"

"Fer chrissakes, Hank, if she hears me ... Look, you know goddamn well my sweet little titmouse goes about two-fifty on the scale at the granary. We've had Harold Brown at his tailor shop rig out a dozen dresses for Zilly over the years. She can get only about nine of 'em in our box. They cost too much to leave 'em behind, and we probably can't get them duplicated in Kiowa. Can you help me out, as a friend?"

"Danny," Hank said, trying to curtail his mirth, "'as a friend' has nothin' to do with it. I'll admit, Zill is a well-rounded, corn-fed, fine figure of a woman who possibly does make the creeks rise when she jumps in, but I'm afraid that falls under the category of your problem. We have no more space, anyway."

Henry had to turn away to prevent a big guffaw, but he still heard Danny Traisley muttering, "Goddamn that woman. She eats fifteen biscuits at a sitting and then has to have Omar the tent maker rig her out."

Tamsen strolled over to the Dwyer wagon. "Mornin' folks, you all pretty well set? How about you, Mr. Dwyer?"

"I think so, Mrs. Devon, but we may have a little problem. Jim wants to go in their own wagon so's he and your Libby can have a parcel of privacy, if you get my drift. Whadya think?"

Henry walked up and said, "I overheard, and I see his point. I guess she's not 'our' Libby anymore. She is rightfully 'his' Libby. Mr. Dwyer, why don't you and I solve this problem for them? Why don't we each throw in half and buy them rail fare out to Medicine Lodge? Maybe they can delay from here enough to arrive out there about when we show up. We can probably telegraph back when we're almost there. Being newlyweds, they don't got nothin' to carry to Kiowa anyway. We could buy 'em a small wagon for the trip with us, but doesn't the railroad make more sense?"

"I see your point, Mr. Devon." Harlan Dwyer said with a wink. "I think we all forget sometimes what it was like to be twenty years old and new married. I fully agree, and if Jim and Libby go along with it, I'd like to furnish train fare myself. We know they didn't get any honeymoon, so to speak. They can stay the two or three weeks right here in a Fort Scott hotel, picnic in daytime and, well, whatever at night, and then follow out when we summon 'em. The missus and I would like to provide all that, with your permission. We really should have provided something earlier."

Henry and Tamsen made an opinion then and there that would last them the rest of their lives. Gretta and Harlan Dwyer were good, straightforward people whom they henceforth were proud to call friends and family. Libby and Jim, of course, jumped at the idea of having some private time. Jim, openly with enthusiasm, Libby, a little more coy. They unpacked their sparse belongings from both wagons, transferred them into a Market Street hotel, and now fell into the camp of well-wishers.

Danny Traisley, upon witnessing Libby's bags being removed from the Devon wagon said, "Psst, Hank, that change anything 'bout Zill's dresses?"

Last Chance Saloon

May 11, 1878, was the last day any of these folks would ever spend in Fort Scott, Bourbon County, Kansas. A makeshift hotel of sorts had sprung up when it became obvious the final gathering spot for departing wagon trains was also a gathering spot for the many well-wishers. The owners of the Last Chance, a not so good eatery and hotel, found the situation quite lucrative. The night before roundup, the Last Chance was always crowded with travelers and their friends. The establishment's main feature was its bar, which had a formidable sign over the backdrop that spelled out, in empty Bourbon whiskey bottles, "Go west, young man, go west!"

The night before this departure was—as with others like it—rife with stories of old times and queries about coming adventures, all punctuated with well-oiled and tearful promises. "Go gettum, Podner," or, "We'll never forget you, Sweetie," or the good-humored, "Good riddance, Lefty. It'll be good to have an honest poker game around here now!" Finally, all interested parties bedded down, either in and around their rigs or in the hotel. Not much sleep was had waiting for sunrise.

"Wake up, Mother," ordered Henry. "Time to wake the kids, get breakfast and line up. This is the day. Hallelujah!"

"Don't have to wake up if yer not sleepin', Henry. I haven't seen a wink go by all night. Can't stop runnin' every bit of this here plan by my mind. What have we forgot? What'll go wrong? Are we plain loco for doin' this?"

"Last minute jitters, dear. We're past the point of no return. C'mon, kids, shake a leg. Bob, poke Frank and the others. Dress warm, stow those blankets, use that privy across the field. You and Charlie tend to the animals. I'll help you boys with that in a minute. Sadie, you help 'em, too. Get a move on. We gotta be ready to roll at eight sharp. Frank, get with Ollie and, Ollie, what're you crying about?"

"Frank kicked me. I was sound asleep and he kicked me ... hard, too!" she blubbered.

"I did not, Pa!" Frank said emphatically. "I jest woke her like you said."

"My Lord, Tamsen, will you please get this passel of jayhawks of yours under control. We got serious gettin' goin' tasks to do, and we can't have this caterwaullin'."

She glanced at Henry and rolled her eyes. "Good boy, Tommy. At two years old you're already better at behavin' than any of your brothers or sisters, and a good lick smarter than your own father." With that she lifted young Thomas out of his blanket, helped him get his shoes on and headed over to the outhouse with him.

"See that, girls. Take a good look," said Charlie. "That'll be your last visit to an outhouse for awhile. You'll be poopin' in a hole in the ground for the next month."

"You hush your mouth, Charlie," demanded an absolutely appalled ten-year-old Sadie. "Somebody's gonna hear you, and I'll just die of mortification" (a word she had only recently learned and appreciated an opportunity to try out).

Charlie smirked and headed out to help untie the animals.

Littrell had advised everyone to start out with mules if they had them and switch in oxen later. He thought the early stages would be pretty easy going, a good time to break in the mules. The Devons yoked up the four mules, which Tamsen had named Matthew, Mark, Luke and John.

"Those names will give us confidence. They'll always lead us on the straight and narrow path," she had explained.

Henry was going to suggest Grant, Sherman, Lincoln and Rosecrans, but he deferred to her judgment.

"You never know, Father, those Union names could cause a fight somewhere along the trail."

Why not name 'em Grant and Sherman, and Lee and Stonewall, and let 'em fight it out among themselves? Henry thought.

Wolves at the Door

"How 'bout the oxen, dear? Would you like Fire and Brimstone?" he asked. "Or we could name 'em Numb and Skull, after your brother." She just glared. They had settled on Burr and Bon to remind themselves where they had come from.

The next hour went smoothly for the Devon family. In fact, it had all been coordinated pretty well the days and weeks before. Nobody had any major hitches. Libby and Jim Dwyer couldn't wait for everyone to depart so they could make a beeline for their newly acquired hotel room. They would barely surface during the following ten days.

Hooz Deteau, the giant of a son belonging to Tim and Jane Deteau, had overbarleyed the night before, gotten in a tiff at the Last Chance Saloon and been knocked in the head with a shovel. He was just coming to at sun up. He said he had really enjoyed his bon voyage party, then he threw up and passed out till about noon the next day.

Red and Deborah LeClerc, usually romantic hand-holders, had gotten into an argument at dinner at the Last Chance. Deborah accused Red of gawking at the dancing girls. "His eyes bugged out so much and for so long I was afeared he'd catch 'em alongside the hat rack and snap 'em right off. Then I'd be headin' out on this fiasco with a blind man!" she said.

"Jesus, Mary and Joseph, dear, just 'cause I admire the cows don't mean I got plans to milk 'em. Simmer down, will ya?" he had said. They didn't speak for two days, which is tough bouncing along at a snail's pace, shoulder to shoulder in a wagon.

Bleeding Kansas—Life and Death in Bourbon County

Cob and Dagmar MacNaughten were plugging along like a well-oiled machine, which was a cause for concern given her history of oiling machines. They had gotten loaded up quickly, due to ample help from the Aganbright brothers.

The Stamlers were trimmed out, tied down and raring to depart. Frank had been totally ready since five A.M. and was getting mildly annoyed by his wife, Wallace, who was visiting around with last minute goodbyes.

"Would you please get in the damn wagon, Walli," Frank said. "Gettin' you to shut up and settle down is like pullin' teeth."

"Teeth, teeth, more with the teeth," she said. "Always the damn teeth."

Dan and Zilly Traisley were right behind the Devons in line. As Littrell held everyone in place and trotted up and down the line for a last look see, Dan hopped down and approached Henry, who was making a last adjustment of a strap on the rear cargo box.

"Just thought you'd like to know, Hank," he whispered. "Got the problem of Zill's dresses solved. I wedged two of 'em in on a cross support under the wagon. The last one I quietly traded off to ol' Shoots the Dog of the Osage family just outside Fort Scott. He said it's big enough to be a tent for his three younger children. And his lady loved the color. But you gotta do me a favor, Hank. As we're rollin' by their village, if you look over and see a bright green side tent, with yellow stripes and orangey lookin' flowers

Wolves at the Door

runnin' all over it, give me a heads up. Fact, if you could cause some diversion out the other way it'd help. If Zilly sees one of her dresses coverin' up practically the whole Osage nation ... well, it ain't gonna be purty!"

The last of their cohesive group were Inga and Boney Korzack. Boney's actual name was Bonaparte. His father named him after the great French general, thinking the great man had been a giant among men. Little did he know the real Bonaparte could run full speed under a toadstool standing straight up. And with the local Bonaparte growing to about six and a half feet, the whole rationale behind the name seemed to lose something. So his father went to calling him Boney and saying it was because he was so thin.

Anyway, still smarting from being jailed over his pond digging business, as the wagons creaked into motion and everyone else called out "Farewell, friends" and "Goodbye, comrades", Boney yelled out "Go to hell, you yahoos" and "Kiss my bony arse, you ungrateful scallywags."

All in all, this great cavalcade began like many before it. It was peopled by folks sad to leave and happy to leave, full of confidence and stricken with fear, well prepared and at wits' end. They were a conglomeration of middle-age men and women, their children and animals, heading into a world they did not know. It wasn't as totally unknown and unexplored as it had been to the groups preceding them by twenty or thirty years. But, it was still a giant leap of faith requiring a lot of courage, and a little bit of insanity.

"Head 'em up!"—Ken Littrell paused before he bellowed-"and Roll 'em out!"

Bleeding Kansas—Life and Death in Bourbon County

Are We There Yet?

Camp that night was pitched at Union Town, barely fifteen miles due west of Fort Scott. As Littrell had suspected, even after a fairly on-time start, the procession was somewhat slow and jerky. Several stops were necessary because of improperly arranged teams. The mules, oxen and horses did all right, but they had to be readjusted until proper cinching fell into place. Then a considerable amount of stopping to rest occurred, or stopping to eat or to go out behind a bush. No actual equipment breakdown happened because the road was relatively smooth and level. And the pace was slow. Folks yahooed back and forth, exuberant with their big adventure.

And another thing. Practically nobody they had bid farewell to stayed farewelled. Most of them rode right along with the wagon train the whole day, all the way to Union Town. Many ladies hopped on the rigs and rode with their pioneering friends, helping with suggestions on how to rearrange everything in the wagon. At day's end, about five o'clock, the original crew of forty-six people tallied almost twice that number. The wagons were circled as protection against the "savage" Osage, even though there hadn't been a savage Indian of any stripe around those parts in more than a dozen years, if ever. All the tagalongs gave more advice, broke out their fiddles and graciously proceeded to eat and drink up at least a week's worth of provisions. About two-thirds of them left at dark for the moonlit buggy ride back to Fort Scott. The rest stayed the night drinking, singing, dancing and swapping stories. Almost all finally left by noon the next day. The original group, who now felt worse than they had the previous morning, hitched up for day number two.

"Holy Moses, Ken," Henry said to Littrell, "why'd you let us do that? These people just put us back a week by the time most of us recoup."

"What did you think was gonna happen, Hank? Besides, I've seen those second 'last roundups' happen every time. People can't say a real goodbye all in one shot. But it's probably over now. Let's at least get to Moran today, its about ten miles."

As they bounced along, still on the fairly well established road, right beside the Marmaton, the little entourage looked idyllic. The shallow stream gurgled over a sand bottom and provided animals and humans with both drink and scenery.

"The water is so clear, Father. Look, you can see several fish right off that sandbar. It's beautiful, Henry. I wish Libby and Jim were here to see this. I was surprised they didn't come out with the others yesterday, although I know they don't have a buggy, yet. Still, they must have been lonely last night back at the hotel, all alone with nothing to do!"

"Yes, dear, I'm sure they were sad," Henry said. *Yes, dear, and I'm sure they shook the building down,* Henry thought.

As they circled up after the second day in Moran, a well-earned, feel-good fatigue was pervasive around

Bleeding Kansas—Life and Death in Bourbon County

the campfires. Red and Deborah LeClerc were again holding hands. Hooz Deteau had awakened with no idea how they had all gotten out to Moran and no memory of well-wishers either the first or second day.

Bob and Charlie were immediately off to roam around camp. Sadie and Olive gave Tamsen some token assistance in cleaning up supper dishes. Henry held Tommy on his knee, bouncing him up and down. He then followed with his familiar "Rocky horsy, rocky horsy, Mulberry Town, witchy watchy, itchy autchey, all fall down!!" as he gently dropped a squealing Tommy through his knees.

"Pa," asked Frank, "are we almost there yet?"

The Real Beginning

Day three, May 14, was the day at least a modicum of reality descended on the group. The morning sun made enough appearance to generate some optimism and cheer, but by noon it had vanished. Ken Littrell informed each family that Humboldt, about seventeen or eighteen miles away, was that day's target. They would be exchanging one river, the Marmaton, for another, the Neosho.

And while the previous week had been rather warm, a noticeable drop in temperature began to settle in throughout the day. As it clouded up and began to chill, so did spirits.

"Brrr, Mother," said Sadie as she and Tamsen cuddled together under a blanket. They were riding beside Henry on the front bench.

"I know, sweetie, spring's a comin', but it hasn't showed up quite yet, has it?"

"Those clouds are really dark, and they're widening out all in front of us," said Henry. "I'm sure we got us a good Nor'wester comin'. That's fine, though, better'n stifling heat in August."

The party held up briefly at noontime, partly to have dinner and partly to check their cold weather gear.

"It may get pretty windy on into afternoon, folks," Littrell warned. "Might be a good idea for you all to take another look see at your canvas tiedowns. And double check your team hitches. Easier to do it now than if something goes astray in a full gale." Just as he was about to mention the possibility of rain, the first few drops fell. "Everyone listen up! It's a comin' on us pretty quick. My guess is it'll hit hard and furious for a while and then settle into an all day drizzle. Let's just button up right here and ride out the first part."

Which is what they did. "My Lord," said Tamsen to nobody in particular, "it must be down to forty degrees and we was wadin' barefoot in the river yesterday. Amazin'!"

"No different here as at home, Mother," Henry said, " 'cept you ain't got no cozy cabin and roarin' fire to nestle up to."

They quickly stowed any exposed items and formed a cocoon inside the canvas cover. Since the storm was coming head on to them, Henry secured the flap up front and left the rear flap open. Everyone cuddled in except Bob and

Charlie, who had been riding Betsy and Biscuit. The boys liked to ride atop the two walking horses and visit from family to family. They were almost to an age, especially Bob, at which the last place they wanted to be was with their own family. By the time they had demonstrated their toughness and imperviousness to the weather, they were soaked to the skin. When they finally returned to the wagon shivering to beat all, Tamsen hauled them up.

"Look at you two nitwits, soaked through. You'll catch your death, strip out of those wet clothes now," she demanded of Bob, who entered first.

"But, Ma, there's no private place to undress with all you in here!" pleaded Bob as Sadie smirked.

"I said now, junior," Tamsen demanded further. And when her octave level reached a certain plateau, everyone knew speed was of the essence in obeying her commands.

"Yes'm," caved Bob as he stripped naked in front of all.

"What is that little worm?" Sadie asked through almost sadistic mirth as she pointed at Bob's privates. "It looks like a little grasshopper done smuggled hisself aboard this ship!"

"You hush up, sister," Tamsen said as Bob turned a dark magenta with embarrassment.

"That's none of your business," he hollered while disappearing under a blanket.

"And you better show some respect, Sadie, 'cause without that little six-shooter of Bob's, you may never get to be an auntie," Henry cautioned.

"Father!" Tamsen said with a chuckle. "I've a mind to wash your mouth out with soap."

"What six-shooter, Pa?" asked an oblivious Frank.

"Sadie's an auntie, Ma? I don't get it," said Ollie.

"Hey, Charlie," Sadie said to a wet and confused Charlie who was just now climbing into the back of the wagon. "C'mon in an' show us your grasshopper!"

"What? What in all tarnation are you all talkin' about?" Charlie asked, seeing that everyone in his family was for some strange reason busting a gut trying not to laugh. He couldn't help wondering where Bob had gone to.

The heavy downpour lasted about an hour, then as predicted let up to a constant, cold drizzle the rest of the day. Every family had gotten through with no bad leaks or other disasters and just settled into a slower procession than before.

Henry handed the reins to a now dry-clothed Bob and hopped off to go visit with Danny Traisley.

"You all do OK? That was a humdinger of a storm wasn't it?" he inquired of Dan.

"Yeah, we're fine. Zilly isn't feelin' too chipper and she's stretched out in the wagon," he said as Henry glanced back to the wagon bed.

"Uh, Danny, what color dresses did you store up under the axle?"

"Red , one was solid red up top with red and green stripe of a skirt. Why'd you ask?"

"And the other?"

"Pale yellow, whole dress, why?"

"Well, iffen you'll slowly turn your head out to the side here so as not to disturb Zill, you'll notice that one of Korzack's lead mules looks right pretty in pale yellow!"

"What the hell?" Traisley started coughing, his eyes bugging out and his jaw quivering. "How the … ? Oh my God, Hank, I'm a dead man. How on earth could that've happened? I stowed 'em up under good and tight. How did that damned mule get Zilly's dress on?"

"I don't know, but I can guess. I'll bet Zilly laying down right above the axle caused the bed to sag, no offense Dan, and opened up yer little hideaway a bit. The dress hung down, the mud chunks flipped up, and eventually jostled it out. That'd be my guess."

As Dan glanced into the inside wagon to stealthily check on Zill, a few beads of perspiration slipped down his forehead from under his beaver hat. Zilly fidgeted her nose and kept snoring.

"Then how did Korzack's mule slip into that dress, Hank?" asked a terrified Traisley.

"Well, he of course ain't actually wearin' the dress, Dan. He probably leaned down and grasped it in his teeth as he walked by. Damn mules'll eat anything, you know, including military pay, but that's a whole 'nother story. I'll bet Korzack's mule tried to scoop it up and somehow tossed it over his head. Maybe the wind caught it and splayed it out like it was meant to be there. Wonder what color bonnet would go good with it?"

Wolves at the Door

"Jesus Christ, Hank, will you shut up? If Zill wakes up and sees that, there'll be hell to pay!"

Just about then in the Korzack's wagon, things began to stir. Boney had procured an old Army blanket and wrapped it around his voluptuous Inga. They had both been comfortably jostling along on the front bench and in time had dozed off. Their mule team just kept plodding along in the procession. A small bump caused Boney to start awake. He glanced ahead and noticed Henry and Danny staring back his way. Then he noticed, about half way between them and him, was one of his lead mules, apparently wearing a yellow dress!

Thinking he might still be asleep and dreaming, he nudged Inga. As she barely opened her eyes and peeked out from the blanket, he quietly asked, "Inga, do you see what I think I see? Do you see our mule wearing a dress? A yellow dress?

"Yes, Sveetheart," Inga sleepily answered, "I do. And I don't think it looks good. Pale pink vould be more becoming!" She closed her eyes and drifted back to sleep.

This kind of phenomenon had happened before with his voluptuous Swedish beauty, and Boney had learned to pass off a comment like this as an 'Ingaism'."

Meanwhile, at Danny's urgent request, Henry stood in place as the Korzack mule strode by, whereupon he plucked the offending garment off its head, shoulders and back. He casually meandered off to the side of the road, deposited the muddy dress behind a large prickly pear and scampered back to his own wagon. As he was passing by the Traisley wagon, Zill was just relocating to an upright position on the bench seat. Henry winked at Dan, who mouthed back, "I, owe, you, BIG!"

"Everything all right while I napped, dear?" Zill inquired.

"Yes, my love. All is well. And our rolling home on the range is ever so slightly lighter!" And nobody was the wiser.

The third day ended without further incident. It got progressively colder and by nightfall was down to the low to mid 30s. They did in fact make Humboldt and camped beside the Neosho. The general mood of the entourage was quieter and more somber than after the first two days. Everyone was cold, and a lot had wet clothes and blankets to deal with. Those who fit inside the wagons spent a more comfortable night than those trying to sleep under soggy blankets on hard ground underneath the wagons.

"Good night, Ma and Pa," muttered Bob, trying to find a reasonably level spot on the ground. "Uh, how many more days of this?" he asked.

"Maybe a month, son, go to sleep!"

Quick Stop in Humboldt

Day four, May 15, dawned really cold, frost on everything, ice on water buckets. All the animals were exhaling frosty breath blasts resembling locomotive smoke stacks.

"Good grief, Henry," exclaimed Tamsen, "isn't it mid-May? Did I miss somethin' and we're still back in March?"

Wolves at the Door

"No, Mother, these last cold snaps can be as bad as the winter ones. But it'll warm up quick today. Wait 'n' see."

"Well, I guess I'll agree to wait around 'n' see, if you insist. Otherwise I was going to take the noontime magic carpet up to Chicago, have a fancy dinner and go see a play! But if you'd rather we all wait around here, we'll abide by your wishes." She chuckled and he smiled.

"That a girl, it'll warm up."

And it did. By noon it was a bright blue day and warm enough to shed the blankets. Littrell suggested to all that today might be a good time to delay a bit, maybe even stay over a second night. Everyone agreed. They were tired and would like a chance to hang out whatever needed to dry, then start the next day with a good second wind.

In making the rounds, Henry detected a more serious sense of purpose in each family. Young Hooz Deteau was now clear headed and enthusiastically helping his folks where needed. He even lent himself out to the other families where his strength and agility would be appreciated. Walli Stamler went to each of the other women to offer a hand in hanging out clothing, refilling water barrels and rearranging food supplies.

Since they were camped on the river and just barely out of Humboldt, water was easy to get, and ample supply stocks could be purchased. By noontime, everyone felt so chipper almost the entire group walked less than a mile into town for mid-day dinner.

"Well, this is far enough for me," said Boney Korzack.

"All I wanted was to rid myself of those weasels back in Fort Scott. Whadya say we just stake ourselves right here in Humboldt, Inga?" he kidded.

"Ya, ya, Boney. Veed be happy to stay right in this pretty town and not go anyvhere," she agreed, laughing.

"Not us, folks," piped Red LeClerc as he shoveled two more pieces of fried chicken off onto his plate. "Deb and I are in for the long haul! Like those 'forty-niners, but our motto is 'Kioway or bust!'"

Each family settled into its own quiet dinner conversation, with an occasional comment being lobbed back and forth.

"Hey, Ken, where to next after Humboldt? What's yer plan?" Tim Deteau shouted.

"I dunno, Tim. I knew how to get this far but I'm kinda drawin' a blank from here. I suppose we either pass on down to Mexico City or double back on up to Boston. What do y'all want to do?"

Zill Traisley flicked a spoonful of mashed potatoes at Littrell as protest, but immediately regretted having let that amount of food get away and vowed not to part with anymore.

"Actually, friends, let's wind up this here good meal and head back to camp. My thought is if everybody is stored up, rested up, dried out and well-fed, why not get a few miles behind us yet today?" suggested the guide. "It's a nice day, warm enough, and the road is pretty dry. As you'll all find out, that isn't always the case, yesterday being an example."

"You're right, Ken," responded MacNaughten.

Wolves at the Door

"We're in," agreed Harlan and Gretta Dwyer. "We still have at least six hours of sunlight. Let's get on the road."

Everybody hurrahed.

"Now listen up, everyone," Littrell added. "Before we head out, which by the way I think is right thinkin', let me say my plan. This here spot is where we sorta head off on our own tack. You all have seen the heavier ruts in the road we walked in on. That road goes north, then northwest, along the Neosho up to Burlington. Then on to Emporia. Those wagons going to Council Grove, them's the people settin' out on the Santa Fe, or going to California, or Oregon. Majority folks pass this way'll be going that way. We ain't."

He looked into the eyes of one traveler after the other. "The reason you all signed on with me was to go a more straight shot down to Medicine Lodge, then to Kiowa. Well, this is our jumpin' off spot. Our road sometimes won't really be a road at all. Maybe just a vague path 'tween little villages. And we may go days without see'n another group. I just want you all clear on our intent. Everybody all OK on that?"

"I guess I speak for us all, Ken," Henry said as he glanced from table to table. "I believe all of us understood your previous explanations, and I think everyone here wants to proceed. Do you all agree?"

"Hear, hear!" said Cob.

"Let's do it!" Red yelled.

"What're we waitin' fer?" asked Hooz.

Bleeding Kansas—Life and Death in Bourbon County

A Fartin' Team

Day five, May 16, found the group about ten miles west of Humboldt camped on open prairie. They arose to warming weather, coffee on the fire, and breakfast smells permeating camp. The girls and mothers were settling into established duties for starting off each day. The boys and fathers took care of any necessary repairs as well as feeding, watering and hitching up the teams. Oats were kept on board for the horses, but they all grazed bountifully on the undulating grasses.

"Look at that, Pa," Charlie said as he pointed just off to their right. "There's more kinds of grass out here than I've ever seen. Must be six or eight kinds of grasses and plants right there where we're lookin' at."

"It's great grazin' country, Charlie. It sure is that." Henry said. "And those holy mules we got, they'll eat anything. I think even the prickly pear. I heard every one of these animals flatulate several times yesterday, son. That shows they're all well and abundantly fed."

Tamsen looked quizzically at Henry as he continued, "Which just underscores the importance of what I'm about to tell you, Charlie. It's good advice for your whole life, and it is this. 'A fartin' team will never tire, a fartin' man's the man to hire.' Don't ever forget that, son."

Charlie ran off laughing to tell the others. Tamsen just rolled her eyes and thought, *What chance do these poor kids have?* Tamsen spent about half her life rolling her eyes at Henry.

Wolves at the Door

Days five, six and seven were all about the same. The party plodded on over the uncharted plain. The two major anticipated events coming up involved the crossing of two rivers. The first was the Verdigris. As they approached it, maybe sixty miles or so out of Fort Scott, they all remembered tales of the Osage massacre there in 1863. Most of the kids weren't even born then, but the story was still vivid to them. The scalpings and beheadings played right into the hands of the older children in scaring the pants off of the younger ones.

"Cut their heads right off," claimed Bob.

"And sucked the brains right out of those Rebels," added Charlie. "It was awful, 'cept they was on Pa's side, so's it was all right. Them Injuns cut 'em all up in little pieces and ate 'em," the two older boys explained to Frank and Olive. "Right here on this river," said Charlie. "When we cross over look real close, cause all their bones is still in the shallows. Last train through, a little girl—about your age, Ollie—got grabbed by a dead Rebel. Reached up from the water, all bony 'n' all, and grabbed her right out of her wagon. Held her under till she went limp. Afore she actually died he pulled her up and ate her, head, heart, shoes 'n' all. It was awful, they say. Being a skeleton, you could see the little girl all chewed up in a blob right in the dead Reb's stomach. Ain't that right, Bob?"

"Shore is, brother," Bob said as Olive shrieked and started to shake. They were having a field day because neither Henry nor Tamsen was within earshot. "Another one too, brother, happened a week before that. Those same Osages, they're totally savage you know, caught a little six-year-old white boy as he was peein' out behind a grass clump. Cut his weenie right off and put it on a bony fish hook, caught a whopper fish with it," Bob grinned as Frank sweated and squirmed.

"No, he didn't," pleaded Frank. "You're joshin' us, Bob ... aren't you?"

"Quite the contrary mister, and those Osages are still around here, too. Their ancient grounds is right here on this here Verdigris River. Folks say those Injuns know they can't do much about big white people, so they lay in wait for little white kids, 'bout your ages. Iffen you go out to poop or take a stroll, they'll get ya. They's all out in those grass clumps waitin' to spring on little kids. I'm just warnin' you!"

Henry and Tamsen returned. Bob and Charlie remembered they had business elsewhere and skedaddled. Frank and Ollie just huddled in the back of the wagon and didn't move. Ollie kept her legs lifted off the floor and away from any cracks. Frank held his crotch tightly. Neither said a word, just sat there bugeyed.

"Why're you two hidin' in there on this glorious day? Go on out and play," Tamsen said as Henry took back the reins from Sadie.

Neither kid moved. Ollie kept looking intently at the floor, while Frank just shook his head slowly and kept a firm grip on his manhood.

"Gw'on, git. We're only a mile from the Verdigris. It's your last chance to stretch your legs 'fore we head into the water."

Both children gulped, shook their heads and didn't move.

"What in all tarnation is up with you two? You better go on out behind a bush while we're movin' slow. Don't neither of you have to pee or anything afore we get to the river?"

Neither kid moved an inch, not even a twitch.

"You know, Father, you 'n' I has got some very strange children. Specially those two little cusses there in the back."

And even more 'specially those two trouble makin' sons of yours, thought Sadie as she climbed down from the bench. She had, of course, heard the entire "Injun" warnings from Bob and Charlie while she was up front filling in for her father. But she was enjoying it too much to tattle.

Nice 'n' Easy

The crossing on May 19, their eighth day out, was approached with some foreboding. When the group had crossed over the Neosho back in Humboldt, they had still been in the company of civilization. Many trains had preceded them and no problems were expected or experienced. The Verdigris, however, was encountered in the isolation of their chosen route. Others had crossed it, but not a solitary wagon, horse or person was on hand when they approached it. Ken Littrell halted the parade at the east bank of the river.

"Folks, let's hold up a minute and discuss this. As you see, this looks like an easy ford. By appearance, it's a level and shallow bottom. Hooz, why don't you and some other boys on

Bleeding Kansas—Life and Death in Bourbon County

horseback just walk 'em across in this line. Start here, maybe ride three or four abreast about twenty feet apart, on over to that biggest cottonwood, that one blacked by lightnin'. Maybe zig zag a little on the way back. It's good conditions, but we don't want to stumble into any quicksand."

As Hooz and LeClerc's son Reg, nicknamed Knothead, along with the two older Devon boys sauntered off across the stream, Ken continued. "It isn't too full right this minute. I'm guessing it's only two or three feet at the most. Anybody don't want your kids or dogs to get wet, load 'em on up. Just talk gentle to the teams and single stock. Can't be a hundred yards across right here. As soon as the boys check it out we'll go."

"Have 'em look for skeletons, Ma," begged Ollie, who was hunkered under a blanket on a chest well above the wagon floorboards. Frank didn't say anything. He was too busy keeping a sharp eye out for savages.

"All looks and feels good," said Hooz Deteau, returning to the shoreline. "Knothead found a little patch of soft sand just downstream about two thirds over, but it's not in our path 'less we get real cockeyed."

"OK, folks," Littrell said, "you heard the man! Stay in this here order, nobody passes nor veers out. Hooz, you just ride ahead of your folks and head on in. Let's get it goin', nice and easy."

And so it went. They crossed in less than half an hour. Nice gentle slope in and similar exit on the west side.

"How easy can a crossing be?" Dagmar MacNaughten said to her husband, Cob. "Makes you wonder about all these tall tales of difficulties. Heck, you had a much tougher time getting our buggy over the bridge and 'cross the creek back home."

He ignored her and hoped these wagon axles had ample grease.

Day eight ended about fifteen miles past the Verdigris and about two miles short of the Fall River. It had been a pleasant day, and everyone went to sleep quite content.

"Pa," whispered Bob, looking up from the ground toward the bottom of the wagon, "you think tomorrow will go as easy over the Fall?"

"I sure hope so, son. It's really clouding up, and I suspect we'll get some rain. At least it's not as cold as a few days ago," he said as the first drops began to hit.

And Little Tommy Said

May 20, the ninth day, arrived with a whole new dimension. Again, the temperature dropped and the rain started, but with much more fury than the previous storm. Even with both flaps tied down, the wind was so ferocious it drove the rain sideways, right through the canvas. Everything inside not in a water tight box got soaked. Henry managed to get the oiled tarp out of the storage box, and the whole family huddled under it inside the wagon.

The outside canvas, although soaked, did at least cut the wind velocity inside and allowed the family to remain fairly dry. They even let Raisin under the tarp with them. The only real discomfort was that with them all crammed together there was no room to change positions, much less stretch out. And it never let up all day. The outside animals had to be miserable, but they just stood stoically, tied to the wagon.

"Lordy, Father, this is unbearable. It must be goin' on suppertime, but we can't get a thing out and couldn't start a fire anyway. And did you see any firewood around here last night? We used up what we had, so when this hullabaloo stops we gotta get more," Tamsen said.

"Darn it, Frank, quick kicking me," Ollie complained.

"I'm not kicking her, Pa, I'm just trying to change my legs. They hurt."

Little Tom, who was just over a year old, had surprised everyone with his good behavior but now started to say hello.

"Waaaa, waaaa," he shrieked in protest of this uncomfortable state of affairs. "Waaaaaaaaa."

"Holy buckwheat, Mother, that boy could break glass with that voice. What the devil is wrong with him?" Henry asked.

"What's wrong? What's wrong? Oh nothing. We all's just wadded up in this nice spacious abode in the pourin' rain and howlin' wind, cold, wet and miserable. But no problem 'cause it's only been about ten hours of this, with no food and no let up in sight. Other 'n' that, he's in fine fettle!"

"Well, you don't have to be so all fired huffy about it," he meekly mumbled, hoping she wouldn't remember this was all his idea.

Nothing Else Can Go Wrong

Days ten and eleven went on with the same miserable conditions. It rained a little, then it rained a lot. Then it rained with very little wind, then it rained with a driving wind. In short, this weather system had just parked right on top of this merry little group and never let up for going onto three days.

Finally on the 12th day of this cavalcade, May 23, the rain stopped ... and turned to hail! Tamsen had barely been able to round up enough dry food to keep body and soul together. Littrell came by each wagon once or twice a day inquiring about everyone and exchanging food or necessities when possible.

"We're gettin' by Ken, barely. Gettin' low on water, and no wood. Tried to graze the animals but not much out there. Our oats is gone."

As they spoke, the hail began to sting Littrell. "M'God, Ken, this is turning into a dang frozen artillery. Git in here, quick," Henry said as he moved over so the guide could jump in. No time to tether his horse. "I swear, I never saw nothin' like this before. How's everyone else doin'?"

"'Bout like you all, pretty bad. I guess we didn't expect to be holed up for three days barely able to get vittles or get out of these wagons." The hail started hitting like bullets. "Jesus, Hank, will you look at that?"

"Pa, whichever ox this is back off this side is really jerkin'. Either Bon or Burr, don't know, but he's pullin' and cryin' out," Sadie said.

"Same over here, Pa. They's all jerkin' up and down like they's gonna pull the wagon apart," Charlie added.

All of a sudden the hail drove the livestock into a fearsome frenzy, all tethered to the wagon and bolting in different directions. The precarious predicament quickly became obvious. Little Tommy's piercing cries were drowned out by the cacophony of pounding hail, shrieking animals and screaming kids.

"Lord help us! Father, do something," Tamsen wailed.

Henry wasn't sure which Father she was imploring but assumed she meant him. He and Ken looked at each other and, with no discussion, both drew knives and jumped out the front flap.

"Cut 'em all loose, Ken," Henry bellowed, barely audible in the howling hail. "You get 'em up here and I'll take the rear."

Barely able to see six feet ahead and in a state of stinging pain from the bombarding pellets, both men forged ahead. All the animals, especially the horses, were in near panic. One by one the two men slit the lines tethering the horses, mules and oxen. They knew it might be hard to round them up again, but at least the immediate danger of an overturned wagon had passed. Their task complete, they

Wolves at the Door

leaped up and back into the wagon. Miraculously, the outer canvas held. The hail bounced off with a fury, but Henry saw only a few holes where the hail had penetrated.

Thank God for new canvas, he thought. *I just hope everyone else's held together.* They didn't even try to converse over the devilish whine of wind and rat-a-tat of hail. Tamsen, in fact all of them, were absolutely astonished at the ferocity of this event.

Finally after about forty minutes the hail abruptly stopped and the wind abated. Littrell knew he had to take stock of the others so he left on foot. Tamsen asked if everybody was all right, and they were. Badly shaken up, but all right.

"What time is it, Henry?" she asked.

"I don't know. Don't know where my pocket watch is, maybe out in the mud. It's gettin' dark, but it's dark in this storm anyway. Seems like it's goin' on night. I just don't know. Let's try to round up a little food. We got anything dry left?"

They bedded down somewhat shellshocked. The tarp had kept them at least merely cold and damp rather then cold and soaked. As Tamsen rooted around for food and hoped morning would vastly improve their situation, Henry thought to himself, *What the devil have I gotten my family into? Is this the dumbest thing I've ever done?*

"Hey, Pa," Bob said. "I just thunk up a poem."

"Thought," Tamsen said, "not thunk."

"Yeah, here it is, Pa. "Oh what turrible weather this awful howling is, First it blew, and then it snew, and then by gosh it frizz!"

They all chuckled and then laughed pretty hard out loud. *God damn,* Henry thought, *after all this we're still together and still laughing. That must mean it's over. I guess nothing else could possibly go wrong.*

"Phew, Ma," Ollie said with a disgusted look on her face, "the baby just pooped his pants."

"Well, Holy moly, so did Raisin!" Bob said. "Looky right there on your pillow, Ma!" Mercifully, the day ended.

Eureka!

The beat up wagon train slowly crept forward to the east bank of the Fall River. It was the morning of the thirteenth day, May 24, and a beautiful day it was. About two inches of hail covered the frozen muddy road, but it would soon melt off.

"That was a real humdinger, wasn't it, Tim?" Harlan Dwyer said to Deteau.

"I'll say. You and yours fare it OK?" was the response.

The Dwyers had five children with them. Son James was, of course, still back in Fort Scott with Libby. Those two had undoubtedly just had a much more comfortable night than either of their families had experienced.

"Yes. I believe the worst is over. Looks like a real nice day shapin' up. A good breakfast would really help," Harlan answered.

The plan Littrell had suggested was for everyone to round up their animals, inch forward on up to the river and take stock of the situation. Preferably over a hot meal.

Wolves at the Door

"Man, we took a ferocious beatin', Ken," Cob MacNaughten said. "Day or two to dry out and recoup sounds good."

"Same here." "Us too." "Count us in." These were the replies from some. But others responded in an opposite way: "No, let's git going!" "Why wait?" "That river is gonna rise."

Henry was ambivalent. "I realize a warm, relaxed day or so to dry everything would really help," he told Tamsen, "but they're right. We've already lost a couple of days to this damn rain. But then again, some of 'em has to repair a lot of canvas and other stuff."

"Look, folks, there's good reasoning on both sides, but we stay," Littrell said. "We absolutely have to dry the clothes, blankets and food supplies. No sense going on half baked. And another thing is these animals. The mules and oxen don't normally mind bad weather, but they really got whacked. And the horses is even more skittish. We're lucky as hell we didn't lose a few of 'em. No, we gotta stay right here along the river for long enough to get a second wind. Let the kids run around and blow off a little steam. Get your sodden stuff hung out to dry. It's gonna warm up soon today, probably mid-sixties by noon."

Ken Littrell had been down this path before, both literally and figuratively. He knew this recent storm was not predictable, but neither was it unprecedented. From his own experience as well as conversations with other guides, he knew to expect the unexpected. He felt a little sense of dishonesty for not spelling out these discomforts more clearly to everyone before they signed on. But he knew if he had, a lot of them would have balked at the endeavor. He continued with that thought in mind.

"We might could very well endure more storms, unforeseen accidents, or worse. We need to take our rest where possible and keep all bodies and beasts in good shape. Eureka is right up river, a half mile. After all repairs are made, why don't we walk in and get ourselves a good meal. We'll take a couple of wagons and load in more oats, 'cause grazin' may thin out. We can get more firewood at the railroad. We'll be pickin' up cow patties in a few days, 'cause firewood will get real scarce. We mighten' also fill water barrels at the train tank if anyone needs it."

Nobody did, because the rivers and rain had kept plenty of water on hand. But the nice hot meals and chance to resupply while everything dried out back at camp really helped. That day ended on a note of rising spirits. Even Raisin felt perky enough to chase a rabbit out from under a sage bush. Didn't catch it, but he did notice it had unusually long ears.

The Price of Hesitation

Everyone arose on May 25, the fourteenth day, feeling one hundred percent better. Bedding was dry, food was restocked and about a dozen small fish had been caught in the river by the older kids. Littrell, who seemed to like fishing, tried but was once again was skunked. The only lasting problem resulting from the storm was the death of one of Korzack's mules. All the stock had been shelled hard by hail, and this one just gave up the ghost. It was the same one who had tried on Zill Traisley's dress.

"Serves it right for dressin' up so audaciously," Inga said to Zilly, who stood there with an uncomprehending look on her face. Dan pulled his portly wife aside quickly before an explanation became required.

"What did she—"

"Don't you pay her no never mind," Dan interrupted. "You know she marches to a different drummer. No sense eggin' her on."

The respite had panned out, and those wanting the delay were vindicated. Now, however, the price of hesitation was about to be exacted.

"Jesus, Red, look at that river," MacNaughten remarked to LeClerc. "Weren't that just a nice peaceable stream when we climbed into our blankets last night? It must be better 'n four or five feet deep now, and look at that current!"

As is the case in the Great Plains, normally dry creek beds can quickly become full and flowing if rain falls upstream. And actual rivers can become frightening torrents. The Fall was ordinarily not a "mighty Mississippi," but it wasn't a dry creek, either. And due to several days of rain, both near Eureka and farther north, it was showing its dander. Cob was right. It did have several feet of water gushing through it.

"How long will this last, Ken?" Wallace Stamler asked.

"Don't know, Walli, depends how much rain fell on upwards of here. Maybe a few hours or maybe a few days. And no telegraph goin' that away, nobody to ask. But we can't move on it yet, that's for sure."

"Damn it," Harlan Dwyer said. "I knew we should've crossed yesterday. Now this, damn the luck!"

"Well don't be in such an all fired hurry, Father," said Gretta rather meekly. Her normal reticence usually led her to defer to her husband's opinions. She now, however, had an uneasy feeling about this river. "Let's just wait it out 'til Mr. Littrell thinks it's safe."

"We'll wait for several hours, but soon as it's down a couple of feet I say let's go," he said with obvious irritation. "We're already several days behind. Jim and Libby are going to be expecting word from us and will get worried if we delay much longer."

Through the course of the day the deluge barely backed off. By about one o'clock the rushing water had dropped a foot, and by three o'clock, another foot. Then it remained fairly steady.

"This may not drop much more if the ground up north is really saturated. Even worse, it may go back up if any more rain falls tonight," Dwyer said to Henry. "Whadya you think, Mr. Devon?"

The two of them were the only two men in the party still calling each other Mister. Littrell could only figure it stemmed from some formality involving the marriage of their children.

"Well, Mr. Dwyer, I guess I don't rightly know or much care, give or take a day or so either way."

"Well we do, dammit," Cob MacNaughten said. Red LeClerc agreed, saying, "We bought these new wagons with raised floor beds just for an occasion like this. With all respect to you, Hank, and any others who want to lag back till the river drops, we want to go. In fact, we're gonna go," Red added, not in a confrontational tone, just stating a fact. "You agree, Cob?"

MacNaughten nodded. "We'll cross over and you'll see where we made it. Just follow on over. It'll take us an hour to head in, plow on through it, and roll on up the west bank. By then, it'll probably have dropped another six inches to a foot. At least we'll be over. We won't make much distance the rest of the day, but this damn delay will be behind us and tomorrow we can put in a long day to gain back some lost time."

"We're in," said Harlan, adding, "let's tie everything down and get goin'."

She Wore A Yellow Ribbon

By just after 4:30 P.M. on May 25, the MacNaughten, LeClerc and Dwyer families were all loaded, tied firm and heading into the Fall River. Ken Littrell just didn't know how to respond. He knew it was unsafe, but he figured you can't lie back and wait for perfect conditions or you'll never get there. True in life, and true in this journey. He was beginning to wish he hadn't signed on with this bunch.

Bleeding Kansas—Life and Death in Bourbon County

As he had previously allowed, bad things can and do happen on these emigrations, but he was beginning to have a bad feeling about this one. These three wanted to force it. They were grown men, they could see the river, and they could speak for their families.

"All right, Ken," Red said, "we're ready."

Ken looked at them, lowered his head, put the heels of his palms over his eyes and ran his hands down his cheeks. He sat on his horse like a general on a stone statue. He wished he was astride a stone horse, but he wasn't. He gently clucked and his mount eased into the rushing water.

"Y'all come up behind me, and don't lag. Lead wagon, you LeClerc, you keep a close eye on me. I'm gonna pole along. Don't want no drop offs and don't want no quicksand. You other two, don't veer an inch. Stay right behind LeClerc. Keep all your tethered animals right tight. And if you lose one, if he strays, don't stop, don't hesitate and don't send no rider after him. You hear me? Don't nobody separate from your wagon no how!" he commanded. They all nodded. "OK, let's go."

The remaining families stayed on the sandbar, eyes glued to Littrell. He slowly inched his way into the turbulent water, poling with a ten-foot long, two-inch thick branch. At about twenty yards out he stopped his mount and began poling rapidly in a circle to his right. At the fifth thrust down, the poll all but disappeared. It would have were it not for his firm grasp, along with the rawhide line with which he had attached it to his wrist.

Wolves at the Door

"Hold up!" he screamed as he shot his left hand into the air. "Quicksand!" He backed up, came about ten feet farther north and slowly tried again. As he proceeded to ease forward, poling as he went, he signaled with his left arm to come on ahead.

Red LeClerc, as well as the others, had made the decision to use oxen if they had them. They were stronger than the horses and taller than the mules. Plus, they weren't terribly excitable and would, the men hoped, just plow on through.

"Keep it movin'!" Littrell ordered. "So far so good."

"They're about half way, Mother," Henry said from the shore. "Looks pretty simple. Double check inside our wagon. Ken will probably be comin' back soon to lead us over."

"Hot damn, Pa. This'll be fun. I can't wait for Charlie and me to take ol' Betsy and Biscuit through this river. We'll for sure give these stinky old horses a bath," Bob said. "Just like Jeremy Dwyer there. Look at that clownin' fool. He's got ol' Diamond Nose off to the left, playin' with her for sure!"

Henry's glance shot up, "What the hell, Tamsen, look at that boy. What in God's name is he doing?"

The middle Dwyer boy, Jeremy, was thirteen, Bob's age. Jeremy was big for his age and a terrific horseman. Henry couldn't imagine why the boy had broken ranks and moved out to his left. Then he saw the reason. A straw bonnet festooned with yellow ribbons was bobbing, ducking and dancing across Jeremy's path. One of his little sisters, riding beside her mother on the front bench

Bleeding Kansas—Life and Death in Bourbon County

seat, had lost her hat. She was on the starboard side, so when the hat dropped in the drink it went shooting under the wagon, popping out on the downstream side in front of Jeremy.

Being an excellent master of horseflesh, he was extremely confident on Diamond Nose. And being almost fourteen, and therefore invincible, Jeremy took action. His sister's hat was escaping and he had a captured audience. Out he went, twenty feet or so, into the perfect position to intercept the bonnet. Littrell was still out front poling, with his back to the action. As the rapidly moving hat was shooting by, Jeremy leaned to his left and bent all the way down to water level. With right hand firmly grasping Diamond Nose's thick mane, he swooped down, grabbed the hat and let out a piercing, "Yahoo!"

Then instantly, everything seemed to the spectators to proceed in slow motion.

"Oh, sweet Jesus," Tamsen whispered, almost breathing the words. Henry thought he said something, but no sound escaped his lips.

"Mama," Bob said, slowly turning to stone.

Gretta Dwyer was just now responding to her daughter about a lost hat and had no idea tragedy was being spelled out on the other side of her wagon. Harlan's eyes and ears were ahead on Ken Littrell, so he neither saw nor heard anything else.

Henry responded in a somnambulant state, enough to shout out to the MacNaughtens and LeClercs. With the roaring river in their ears, and all other participants

Wolves at the Door

including the Dwyers behind them, they were totally unaware of what was unfolding.

In a flash, Henry inexplicably was back at the battle of Westport fourteen years earlier, looking at Frank Banks stumbling forward with his sliced off arm. Henry saw that long gone dead man staring back at him as if to say, "Look, Hank, I'll die again for you. We'll all die for you, Hank, Just you watch and see!" Henry covered his eyes and started to shake uncontrollably.

Just as Jeremy grasped the bonnet, with all his weight keeled over to the left, Diamond Nose's front left leg hit quicksand. He instantly quartered head under heels to his forward port side, rolling full over Jeremy in the now only two-foot depth of riled river. The terrified horse bucked and kicked into the boy, driving him under a snag that protruded from the sandy bottom. The horse bolted upright, frantically high stepping. He then righted himself and careened through and out of the Fall on the far bank.

All eyes from the shore bound wagons locked onto Jeremy. His legs were hopelessly fixed into the tangle of branches. With great effort against the oncoming current he sat upright, so that from his chin up, his head seemed to be sitting on a table of water. His position from the horse tumble had him staring back at the onlookers on shore.

"Father! Pa! Pa!" Bob screamed at the top of his lungs, "help him, he's ... help him!"

As in times past, some other entity entered Henry's body. He started dashing through the moving water into the

Bleeding Kansas—Life and Death in Bourbon County

main torrent. Then at fifty yards, forty yards, he began to hear, "Go, go, fire, load! Go, go ..." again as though it were yesterday. He was stepping over bodies. To his right was a running man with his brains oozing out, a huge dent in the back of his skull. He jumped over a laughing man trying to put a boot on the remaining stump above his missing knee. They were all laughing. "C'mon, Henry, come run with us again."

He snapped back to the present reality. Jeremy was staring at him, panic in his gaze, when a gush of blood poured from his mouth. The horse must have gotten him right in the lungs or heart. Henry could see the spirit exit the boy's eyes, as he slowly reclined backward beneath the racing stream. The boy had blue eyes. *God damn it,* Henry thought, *do they all have to have blue eyes?*

As Henry got to the rushing but stationery death scene and picked Jeremy free of the tangle, he held him in his arms and stood up. There on the far bank stood Harlan and Gretta Dwyer, looking back at him. They were in complete confusion as to what was going on. Ken Littrell, the LeClercs and the MacNaughtens were standing beside the Dwyers. All the children of these families were hooting and hollering, shouting across the water to those who had stayed behind. "Hooray, we made it!" "Hoopity doo, we're high and dry!" "We got here afore you all, slowpokes!"

"Hey, Daddy," said one of the Dwyer children, "there's Diamond Nose, but where's Jeremy?"

Gretta Dwyer looked around both sides of their wagon, then followed her husband and Littrell's stares out into the river. Slowly and quietly, and one by one, all the folks on both sides of the river locked eyes onto Henry. There he stood, now only calf deep in the slowing stream, with the limp body of Jeremy in his arms. He was looking with a blank gaze toward the west bank at nobody in particular, until he saw the face of the boy's mother. A gruesome bond of understanding flashed between them. Gretta fainted but was caught by Littrell on her way down.

Through the remainder of the day, chaos and confusion reigned. Littrell rushed out with Harlan to retrieve Jeremy. They got him over to the west bank and tried to resuscitate him, but it was clear that drowning was not the cause of death. The horse had kicked Jeremy's life away. Another man might have, in a rage, illogically shot Diamond Nose, but Harlan did not react that way. He stood up from his prostrate son, walked over and stroked the horse's face without saying a word.

"Dick," he finally said to another son, "unsaddle him and tie him to the wagon. Feed him some oats. He's been through trauma not of his making. Try to calm him down."

This day ended transporting the remaining families on across the now serene Fall to the incredulous families awaiting them. Henry returned to his family and helped them across; then he and Tamsen approached the Dwyers.

"Harlan, Gretta, I am so sorry. We just don't know what to say," Henry whispered as Tamsen took Gretta's hand in hers.

Bleeding Kansas—Life and Death in Bourbon County

"You done the best you could, Henry, and we appreciate that. We'll never forget how hard you tried to get to him," answered Harlan. The formality of the Mr. and Mrs. disappeared forever at this moment. These two families were now permanently bound by the joy of marriage and the pain of tragedy. It would forever be.

The next morning, their fifteenth, May 26, dawned on sorrow. All the wagons were safely on the west shore, and a decision had been made. Since Eureka was less than a mile back, the Dwyers decided to have a small service here among their friends and then take Jeremy back to the small cemetery near that town. Most casualties of these trips resulted in burials right beside the remote and desolate wagon ruts. But Gretta couldn't bear that.

"I want him to be with people, not alone over here. Is that all right, Mr. Littrell?"

"Yes, of course," answered the guide. "While you all attend to him here, I'll ride on over to town and make arrangements. Then those that's goin' can accompany him over tomorrow."

"No, Ken," interrupted Harlan, "no sense delayin' these good folks any longer than necessary. This here awful thing was my doin'. If we, I, hadn't been so blasted impatient, if we had just waited a day … well, anyway, we'll dress him right and these his friends can say their goodbyes here, today, now. Then Gretta and I and the kids will take him over in the small wagon this afternoon. No point in draggin' it out. And I want us all to rid ourselves of this goddamn river once and for all."

Wolves at the Door

By one o'clock the Dwyer family was somberly retracing their route over the now almost dry Fall River bed to the Eureka cemetery, and the others were equally somberly pulling out and heading west. By nightfall all were rejoined in camp a dozen miles out. No one said much; suppers were subdued. The Dwyers kept to themselves.

"I know you're hurting, Henry. I'm so sorry it had to be you in that river. You've been through so much death, I just wish it could've fallen to somebody else," said Tamsen as she tucked little Tommy under his blanket. Bob and Charlie were trying to sleep under the wagon, the others, in the wagon.

"No, if it had to happen I wouldn't want it to have been you or these children. I guess no one else, neither. And you've been through it too, Mother. I know I've seen the war killin's and all, but we've both together put our little babies in the ground. You've been through it as much as me. Poor Harlan and Gretta, though. This is their first. And them kids is in shock," he said. Henry and Tamsen lay silently for a while. The night was quite clear and comfortable, and rather noisy with chirping crickets, howling coyotes and snoring emigrants.

"Can you sleep?" Henry asked.

"Not a lick. Let's take a walk."

They quietly rose and slipped out of the wagon.

"Where ya goin', Pa?" Charlie whispered. "I'm comin' with you."

"Me, too," added Bob. "We can't sleep neither!"

Bleeding Kansas—Life and Death in Bourbon County

What Is, Is

It was between eleven and midnight as the four of them strode an imaginary path ringing the camp. They could see horses, oxen and wagons silhouetted against the firelight as they walked.

"Why'd it happen, Pa? Why was it Jeremy and not, say, me?" Charlie asked.

"Son, if I knew that ... well, I dunno. I don't know if I ever told you boys about my battles, but I had the same thoughts back then. A friend of mine got his arm blowed off and was kilt right aside me. Coulda been me. I can only say I don't know, son. Nobody does."

"Will it happen again, Pa?" asked Bob.

Henry and Tamsen walked hand in hand between the two boys. Henry pensively tried to think of an answer. Tamsen, in an effort to relieve him, jumped in.

"Bobby, you see those stars up there?" Both boys looked up at the billions and trillions of flickering lights. "You pick one out and Charlie pick another one out. What're the chances you both picked the same star? Who knows why you pick one, Bob, and you another, Charlie. This universe has only one engineer decidin' which stars flicker or fade, and that's God!"

"But why did he pick on Jeremy, Pa? Why not some Injun, or old man, or some Chinaman?" Charlie asked.

"First of all, son, I don't know why," Henry said. "I know your ma is better at explainin' about God, Jesus,

Wolves at the Door

and the Bible 'n' all. But just let me say, I don't think God picked on Jeremy in that sense. I think it kinda comes down to, what is, is! Our job is to do all we can to do what's right, to try to figure stuff in advance. But I guess I'd have to allow, there's somethin' a whole lot bigger 'n us up there. Just look at those stars. Your ma mentioned an 'engineer' runnin' things. Well, neither George Washington nor Mr. Lincoln theirselves could keep all those stars in runnin' order. The head engineer is who we call God." He paused for breath, and curiously awaited whatever was going to come out of his mouth next.

"And another thing, look at those stars, again. Millions of 'em. Now again, pick one out, now a second one, now a third. OK, both of you look at me. Can either of you tell me if one of your stars is better than the other two?" No answer. "What I mean, Bob, do you see any up there better than the other million? Or Charlie, are your stars better 'n Bob's? They all look about the same to me. You boys agree?" They both nodded, trying to figure where this was leading.

"Then why on God's green earth do you two cusses think that poor boy in the river should've been an Injun, or a Chinaman, or an old geezer like me?"

"Well, we just thought, Pa—"

"No you didn't think," interrupted Henry. "It's too late of the evenin' now, but remind me sometime to fully explain what I saw of Osages on a buffalo hunt years back. Believe me, no Injun or Chinaman or whoever shoulda been in that river. They all got lives and families, just like Jeremy. Just like you. You'll figure it out someday yerselves, but remember I told you, we's all like those stars. That God your momma loves, or sure as hell somebody, put us all here. We all got the same value and right as everyone else. You make damn sure you live your lives believin' that. You hear me?"

"Yes, Pa, we do," Charlie whispered. Bob nodded.

Tamsen squeezed Henry's hand tighter and thought, *Yes, Father, they do!*

May 27, their sixteenth day out of Fort Scott, as well as the next three days, brought them slowly to the outskirts of Wichita. They had gotten into a regular routine of travel, which was much more sober than before the Fall River calamity. Conversation among and between the families had fallen to quiet and necessary comments. Even over the creaking of the wheels and groaning of the wagons, Gretta Dwyer's sobs could occasionally be heard. The other ladies had cooked for and watched over the Dwyer family. As the group set up camp on the evening of May 30, Harlan and Gretta approached the Deteau fireside, around which most of the folks were sitting.

"Hello, everyone. Gretta and I got something to say," Harlan began. "We been dying these last few days over Jeremy. You all know that, and we know you been walkin' and talkin' easy to spare us. Well, it's over. Not our pain, I don't mean that. It'll never be. But Henry, you and your family, in fact most of you, I think, have lost someone. We thank you from the bottom of our hearts for ..." Harlan broke up. He went into convulsive sobbing.

"... for loving us and our boy so much," Greta continued. "We just want to say please go on like normal now. We'll keep up. If we don't speak for a while or we kinda drift off, you'll know why." She and Harlan moved on slowly to the other fires, and their kids fanned out and mingled with the other children.

I guess Pa's right, thought Bob. *What is, is.*

Drunk as a Robin on a Berry Bush

They arrived at the outskirts of Wichita in late morning, May 31, 1878, the twentieth day out. All the horses needed to be shod, and everyone needed supplies. No problems occurred in crossing the Arkansas River. They could have chosen to be shuttled over wagon by wagon on an available ferry boat, but the river was low and the bottom, firm.

As soon as they eased up on the west bank, Littrell pointed out the way into town. "We'll head a bit north and you'll see the railroad. You'll also see thousands of head of cattle in the pens. And it'll stink like all gitout! We're gonna hole up well to the south of 'em 'cause you don't want your stock to get no disease from them longhorns. And there's more. Y'all have most likely never seen a town like this. These ol' boys get in here, get paid, and get drunker 'n robins on a berry bush. And I don't want to be indelicate, but some of 'em's pretty stoved up for a woman, if you

Bleeding Kansas—Life and Death in Bourbon County

catch my drift. Don't you dare let any of your ladies or girls wander off. We'll take two of our smaller wagons for supplies. And I know these horses need to be shod, so we'll ride and walk 'em all in. We'll get water back out at the railroad. We'll also have to start pickin' up wood or cow chips where we find 'em. I'll tell you now we'll have to be burning sage pretty soon, which is all right. It's woody and burns pretty good. Now tie down what stock ain't goin'. Who's gonna stand watch back here?"

"We will," said Red LeClerc. "Cob will pick up what we need, mostly horse feed and some flour. Me and the missus will keep an eye back here if you don't mind our kids goin' in town with you."

"C'mon you two, hop in the wagon with our kids," Walli Stamler said to the LeClerc children. Those who wanted to ride horseback did so, leading the other horses on tethers.

As they eased into town and crossed the Santa Fe tracks, they were mesmerized by the landscape. Except for a few scrubby cottonwoods along the Arkansas, there wasn't a tree in sight. Partly by nature, trees were scarce. And partly because any little old tree that dared poke its nose out of the ground was long ago picked off by the thousands of cowboys and emigrants who had passed this way. It was a true moonscape.

"Boy, was Littrell right!" Henry said. "Do these cows ever stink!"

The odor literally burned the eyes and nostrils of everyone. And the dust made a choking sensation even more pronounced.

"Henry, this is plain terrible!" Tamsen said.

"It shore is. We'll get in and get out as quick as possible. Let's go to the smithy first thing."

There were three streets in Wichita running north and south, with the railroad tracks bisecting them east and west. Up from the river, the first street held the blacksmith shops and the liveries—lots of them. Henry and Littrell ushered their party into the first one they came to and spoke to the proprietor. "We got about twenty horses here need shod," Henry said. "How long you figure and what'll it cost?"

"Well, we can spread 'em on down the street and probably have 'em in two hours, maybe three. And as to cost"—he grinned— "I 'magine it'll cost about what it costs. What're ya gonna do, traipse 'em on back to Emporia to get a better deal?"

"We didn't come through Emporia," Henry said, "but I get your point. I guess we'll just hope you'll treat us fair."

Henry, for some reason, liked this man and didn't doubt he'd treat them right.

"Listen here," warned the 'smith. "I assume you all are headin' up to Main Street. Go to Dinkins' Hardware for equipment supplies, Massenelli General Store for groceries, and John Bain & Son livery for horse feed. He's the best, and he'd just send you down to me for the shoein' anyway."

"Thanks for the advice," Henry said as he extended his hand. "I'm Henry Devon. Our group here is all together. We come this far from Bourbon County, Fort Scott."

Bleeding Kansas—Life and Death in Bourbon County

"Good to meet ya," the blacksmith replied. "I'm James Bain, the son in John Bain & Son. Where you folks headin'?"

"Barber County, Kiowa. Ever hear of it?" Henry asked.

"Sort of. We get folks streamin' through here from all points back east to hell and gone on westward. Kiowa, down toward Medicine Lodge?

"That's it," Henry said as Tamsen walked up. "Mother, this here is James Bain. He'll be shoddin' our mounts. James has given me some pointers on this Main Street. My wife, Tamsen." Henry gestured and Bain shook her hand.

"Can you suggest a good dentist, Mr. Bain?" She turned to her husband. "Hooz Deteau has a bugger of a toothache, Henry."

"Several of 'em up on Main Street or the next street. None of 'em any good. Two to really avoid is Dr. Fielding and Dr. Rikehurt. Both torturers. Fielding will pull the wrong tooth and Rikehurt won't even find your mouth. I sent a cowboy to Rikehurt last year. The man told me later Rikehurt filled him up with whiskey, finished the bottle himself, then went to work. Somehow he missed the poor wretch's tooth altogether, but did manage to extract a hemorrhoid! And then had the nerve to charge three dollars. Highway robbery!"

Noticing the conversation, Littrell walked over. "What's so all fired funny here?"

"Never mind, Ken. It's a long story," Henry said. "Mr. Bain here was just telling us where to go uptown, and where not to go."

Wolves at the Door

"Seriously, Mrs. Devon, if you need a dentist, look for Dr. Holliday's office up on the corner. Strange character, coughs a lot, but when the chips are down, a real steady hand. Tell him Jim Bain sent you."

So up they went, past rough looking saloons and bawdy houses, over muddy streets and uneven plank sidewalks to Main Street. They brought up one wagon pulled by a horse that would have to wait until the return trip to be shod. Dinkins was well stocked with rope, grease, canvas, thread and other sundry items. Massenelli had any and all food items at a fairly stiff price.

"You Eyetalian or vut?" Inga Korzack asked Dominic Massenelli.

"Vut!" Dominic answered.

"I said, you Eyetalian or vut?" repeated the voluptuous Swede.

"Vut!" Dominic said again. "I'm from the little country of Vut. It's off the coast of Smillvopia, just above the Commonwealth of Plingmirth, you know, just to the left of the equator."

"I'll be svitched, dear," Inga said to Boney as they left the market. "I'd a svore that guy vas Eyetalian!"

Henry was walking by at that moment and started to inquire.

"Don't even ask," Boney said as he held his hand up. "Ingaism!"

Don't Hurt His Mouphy

They pretty well got all they came up the hill to get. It neatly stacked into the wagon, except for a few bags of the horse feed, which they simply balanced on the back of the horse. They stopped by Dr. Holliday's office to pick up Hooz Deteau. He was sitting out front on a bench, jaw bandaged, holding his head in both hands.

"You all finished, son?" Jane Deteau asked her son.

"Mmrrt!" he answered.

"What'd he say?" asked Frank Stamler, who was a tad hard of hearing.

"Mm godmn toof, rts," Hooz said, attempting to explain.

"What the hell is he trying to say?" Stamler said to anyone who would listen.

"Muh gdmn snfbn toof z klinme!! Tht gdmn kwk tur mwy jwa off!"

"I think he's experiencing a bit of pain," said Jane, his doting mother. "Don't worry, boy, we'll stop in the hotel restaurant in the next block and get us a nice steak. I'll even cut it up into teeny weeny pieces for you so it won't hurt your mouphy." She gently kissed his cheek to make it feel better.

Hooz was somewhere north of six feet six inches tall and way north of 250 pounds. He was a fun loving guy who liked his barley and hops, just as his father, Timothy, did. As the group was walking to the restaurant they passed a saloon, the Golden Bear. It had a lifelike stuffed bear out front on which somebody had somehow attached some elk antlers. While Hooz himself could dish it out pretty well when inebriated, he didn't suffer a drunken fool very well. As the Deteaus passed a group of cowboys loitering in front of the establishment, one of them yelled out at Renee, one of Tim and Jane's daughters, Hooz's sister.

"Hoohee, look at that little filly! And me being as horny as that big ol' bear," the cowboy wailed as he pointed at the stuffed bear with the elk horns. "I'm of a mind to mount that sweet little mare and ride her down the street!"

His only miscue was he didn't really point at the bear or at Renee. His timing was off due to either low quality or high quantity whiskey, and he was somehow pointing at Hooz when he added, "I'd like a little piece of that honey chile."

Hooz never missed his stride. He just kept moving straight ahead with his left arm coming up like a bronc out of a chute. His fist balled with all the pinpoint timing the cowboy's comments had lacked. At about eight inches from his face the poor stumblebum saw the five-fingered ham about to enter his cerebellum. From the inside of his skull, the show was pretty much over. He didn't really stick around to enjoy it, but his friends gave him a good rendition of it three days later.

From the outside, however, the event played out almost as a comedy. Hooz hit him so hard a spray of blood and flying teeth momentarily diverted everyone's gaze. But when all eyes snapped back, the limp buckeroo had flipped right over the boardwalk railing and landed belly up and

Bleeding Kansas—Life and Death in Bourbon County

spread eagled across the water trough. He was legs up, facing the onlookers, out colder than Milwaukee in March. Which was bad enough. But to add insult to injury, his pants were split stem to stern. With legs spread as they were, his long johns, which hadn't been changed since before Kansas got statehood, were fully exposed. Which was bad enough.

But the real coup de grâce, the situation that caused this old boy to eventually have to leave town, was the colorful state of those long johns. There appeared to be a brownish stripe about six inches long right along the path of the rip, permanently imbedded in his under drawers. Everyone gasped.

"Holy moly, Dagmar, look at that!" Cob MacNaughten said.

"Gee, Ma, Pa, it looks like a mule done slammed on his brakes on those pantaloons!" said one of the kids

Even the cowboy's cronies stepped in front of their comatose comrade for a peek at the sight. "Ye gads, Spike, so that's what we been smellin' for the last month. And here I thought it was the cowpens!"

As the amazed little group of travelers paused in wonderment, some in awed shock and others in stifled mirth, Hooz had the presence of mind to say, "Kmon dmnt, lts get owfta hre afor the lau shus up. Mufer, gif hm a whidle kwisz on thu mouphy to muake it fill bwetter, nn lez gow!"

They skipped dinner, went back down the hill to reclaim their now well shod horses, and headed back through the

Wolves at the Door

cowpens toward camp. Before they left, Jim Bain asked Henry how everything had gone up town.

"Quite nicely, Jim, we appreciate your help. We got our supplies, and our young man even got his tooth pulled by your Dr. Holliday. Oh, by the way, there was a small disturbance up on the main street. Should the law or anyone else happen to inquire after us, we was never here!"

With that, everyone in their group hopped into wagons or remounted the horses, some riding double. In a short while they were back at camp marveling at how some of these everyday missions seemed to turn into adventures.

Ken Littrell gathered them together at his campfire that evening. "Just so you all know, we will now be angling down southwest to Medicine Lodge. Up till now we've been in somewhat well traveled territory. I know we haven't seen a lot of other folks along the way, but we've had Eureka 'n' El Dorado, and of course Wichita to rely on. I know you're all gettin' antsy and want to get there. Our most direct route, now, is to head straight for Medicine Lodge. It means crossin' two more rivers."

"Jesus Christ, Ken," Frank Stamler said, "no matter where the hell we go we either just crossed, are crossing, or are about to cross another river!"

"Frank, must you use the Lord's name and blaspheme so much?" Wallace whispered.

"Well, God da—er, gosh darnit, Walli, there must be some other way."

Bleeding Kansas—Life and Death in Bourbon County

"There's not, Frank," Henry said. "I'm sure Ken is right, unless we keep weaving way up and around headsprings of these streams. In which case we'll never get there."

"Look, folks," said the guide, "you don't want to be dilly dallyin' all over the place forever. And quite frankly, I don't have the time neither. These two rivers, the Ninnessa or Nindesha or something like that, and then the Chikaskia, I think it is, I've crossed 'em both. They're pretty much like all the ones we've already gotten through. And with all my respects to you and your missus, Harlan"—he nodded toward the Dwyer family—"they aren't that bad. We gotta plan the timing and place of entry, and we'll get through 'em just fine. Let's be up and ready to roll by eight bells tomorrow."

Peering Eyes

June 1, their twenty-first day, arrived to the cadence and creaking of the wagons and teams in motion toward the promised land. They passed to the north of Haysville but didn't stop. The mood was one of "let's get goin' while the getting's good." The day had dawned clear, and it stayed that way. If no weather, breakdowns or other problems arose, they could sometimes make twenty miles in a day. This day they were all exuberant and pushed on until dark, about eight o'clock. They had done twenty-seven miles.

"Boy, Tim," Hank said to Deteau. "That was some day. I'm bushed! Let's roll 'em in and tie up."

Wolves at the Door

They had passed through the Ninnescah River with little effort, its water very low. All the livestock got a good drink, and those folks who so desired got a quick swim or bath. They camped ten miles short of the Chikaskia River, which they would ford the following day.

"I am just about gettin' the hang of this, Father," Tamsen said. "I see how folks can go all the way out to Oregon or Californy, once they get their minds set."

"Yeah, Pa," added Charlie. "Let's just keep headin' on till we get to Californy. I like this."

"Let me point out a couple of things to you would-be explorers," Henry said. "First, we just had a fine beautiful day with no problems and we made, probably, our best distance yet. Have you forgotten all the rain, cold and miserable hail? Have you forgotten all the cow pies you've had to collect for firewood, Charlie? And allow me to point out one little thing we haven't had. Mountains! I don't know what they're like, but to hear some folks that's seen 'em up close, they're hellacious. Let's just hope the rest of the way is as nice as today was."

"Father, did you share the telegraph cost with Harlan back near Wichita?" Tamsen asked.

"No, Mother, he wanted to do it. I think he wants to support James as the man of the house. Jim and Libby will be leavin' Fort Scott tomorrow and should arrive in Medicine Lodge by evenin' day after tomorrow. Don't know the route or changeovers. Whichever of us gets there first will just wait."

Bleeding Kansas—Life and Death in Bourbon County

As everyone finished locking down the wagons, releasing and feeding the teams, and getting the supper supplies out, Hooz Deteau came riding in yahooing to beat the band. He had a gutted antelope hung over his horse just ahead of the saddle. He had ridden out with one of the other boys earlier and, for the first time, struck pay dirt.

"How do ya like them apples, Ma?" he said as he dropped the carcass to the ground in front of one and all.

"Hot damn, boy, where'd you get that?" his father asked.

"Two ridges over in cottonwood by a real little creek. We spooked him up and I got off one lucky shot. Right through the lungs and out his side. I swear he didn't run ten more paces."

"Two ridges? What ridges?" Red LeClerc asked. "This here is the flattest prairie land I ever seed. It's dead level 'bout as far as a body can see."

"I know it seems that way, Mr. LeClerc, but there is some very slight rise 'n' roll to it on horseback. Anyways, we got him field gutted. I'll tie up my pony and we'll dress him out."

They enjoyed the fresh meat, the warm weather, the starlit sky and the friendly camaraderie of likeminded people after a day of accomplishment. They valued the good feeling that comes with well-earned fatigue.

"Good night Ma and Pa," Bob called up to the wagon.

"Night, Frank," whispered Ollie.

"Night to you, too, Boogernose," Frank responded. Ollie smiled and drifted off.

Wolves at the Door

Everyone in the vicinity felt comfortable, well-fed and secure as sleep overtook the campground. All except the owners of nine pairs of eyes peering on from outside the ring of fire light.

Neva, Neva

"Who the hell are they?" Cob MacNaughten wondered aloud as the gray mist of morning slowly allowed the shadowy outlines of several people to become apparent.

"Oh, my God," Dagmar said, shuddering. She reflexively dropped her coffee pot to the ground and watched the fresh brew disappear into the sand. "Who are they, Cob? What do they want? Where are the kids?"

"Hold up, folks. Let's not panic," LeClerc said. "Real easy like, get a hold of your weapons, but let's not point 'em yet. Guide man, what do you make of this?"

"Not sure yet. I make out four or five of 'em. Those to my best guess are Injuns. Thank God they ain't renegade whites. There's some real mean sonsabitches out here on the lam from society. But I think I'm seein' three men, those on the left is women in skirts, two of 'em. Is that what you're seein' Red?"

"Look, there's several little kids behind them," said Deborah LeClerc.

"I think that's a family of Injuns," Tamsen said.

"Should I shoot 'em, Pa?" Bob said.

"What the hell's the matter with you, boy? Just everybody stand still. Or better, I suggest everyone just slowly go about doin' what you were doin'. Dagmar, go ahead and start another coffee pot. Cob, you add a couple of chips onto that fire. Everyone, don't pay 'em a whole lot of lookin' at. Just take it easy. I'm going to … Ken, you come with me … we'll just sorta saunter over to 'em and, well, kinda say hello."

"Oh, Henry, should you? You take your pistol!" Tamsen said.

"Pa, any funny business and I'll plug 'em from here," Bob added.

"Will you hush up and put that thing down, you young fool. We don't need you makin' a harmless situation into a calamity!"

By now the morning fog was clearing enough to display the campsite scene at the start of June 2, the twenty-second day. Everyone in the group, almost four dozen emigrants, was now fully attentive, well-armed and ready to face this threatening band of dangerous savages. Until they got a good look at them.

About forty feet on the far side of the morning fire, stood a pretty sorry looking excuse for a Kiowa war party, or whatever tribe they belonged to. There was one very old, leather skinned man, noticeably stooped, displaying some kind of palsy. Even at that distance, his rheumy eyes suggested he was blind. Beside him was an equally ancient woman holding his hand, seemingly in an effort to steady him.

Along with them were three middle aged men and two women. The men appeared to be in their forties or fifties, although one may have been in his thirties. He was missing one arm below the elbow. The two women were both middle aged, hard to tell. All were raggedly dressed in a mixture of deerskin outer garments and a few items of white man's clothing. The ancient woman had on the remaining ruins of an old stovepipe black hat. Several had woven rug or old saddle blanket type shawls draped over for warmth. Two of the men wore patched and ragged Union Cavalry jackets. And it seemed their entire armament was the very beat up Winchester one of the middle aged men was carrying, muzzle down. It was beaded the way the Indians often decorated these cavalry cast-off rifles.

There were at least four, maybe six, small kids behind them. Henry couldn't tell, but he was sure of one thing—this was no band of warriors. This was a starved and disoriented looking family, probably in search of a handout.

As Henry and Littrell slowly approached, one of the men stepped forward with both hands extended slightly forward and open, palms up. He spoke three or four words, which neither of the whites understood. The three men just looked at each other. Henry pointed at his group and made a circular swirling arc with his right arm to indicate his entire party. He then pointed at the wagons and made a tight little rolling action to indicate wheels in motion. Then he pointed west by southwest and said, "Chikaskia."

The Indian nodded and raised ten fingers. Henry assumed this meant miles, but wondered if this red man knew what a mile was.

Ken Littrell pointed at the man in front of him, then a slow extension of his finger to encompass the whole Indian family and asked, "Kiowa? Comanche? Osage?"

"Humpph!" The man nodded.

Then the three of them just looked at each other for what to Henry seemed to be several minutes without speaking. Henry couldn't take it any longer. He pointed at each adult and as best he could, made an inquisitive gesture rocking his arms as if holding a baby. "Family?"

"Aarumph." The man nodded again. He pointed at himself and one of the women. After drawing his finger back and forth between the two of them he then pointed at the ancient pair. Then he made a series of other hand indications criss-crossing between all members of the band.

"I think I'm catchin' on here, Hank," Littrell said. "That there's his sister and the two old 'uns is their parents. The other man 'n' that woman is their mates. I'm guessin' the younger man with the arm gone is either a young brother, or a son, or just a friend who needed help. The other woman is probably a widder needin' help."

"Or maybe a sister. Oh hell, Ken, whatever they are, they sure look sorry. Look at the hollow look in these kids' eyes."

The lone speaker cleared his throat, but without speaking, rubbed his stomach, then bent over and rubbed a little boy's stomach. He then pointed way off to the east and put two fingers up to each side of his head, like antlers. He gently removed his knife and made a mock incision up his entire front, from lower abdomen to neck. Replacing the knife, he demonstrated a charade of digging out and dumping his innards on the ground.

"I got it, Ken," Henry said. "They found the antelope guts Hooz cleaned out back on the prairie. They're starvin'. They know we had meat, and they followed us here last night. We gotta help 'em. You got any problem with that?"

"Hell no, Hank. You go on over and explain to the folks what's goin' on. No threatening moves. And no offense, Hank, but tell Bobby and all the other kids, this ain't no time for a scalpin' party. These is just hurtin' and harmless folks. The shoe could certainly be on the other foot."

"No offense taken, Ken," Henry said with a laugh. "Bobby is my son, and I love him, but he can be a bonehead."

Henry strolled over and explained to the anxious group what was happening, while Littrell tried to assure the small, disheveled family they would be welcome to come in and get something to eat.

"Please, come."

"Unkuh, odik," answered the Indian. At least, that's what it sounded like to Littrell.

As the sheepish, small group approached the larger, curious group, arms were extended, little black-haired heads were patted, and extra ham and biscuits plus a few eggs were conjured up. Every shred of antelope left over from the previous night was quickly devoured. Lots of coffee was consumed, a treat for the red people. Within an hour they were all making frequent trips out behind the bushes.

Most of the emigrant children were playing with the Indian kids with great animation. Bob, Charlie and the other older boys were taking turns racing the horses in circles around the camp, with Indian boys hanging on behind them. Sadie was playing patty cake with two of the little Indians. One of the red women spied Tommy hiding behind Olive's skirt. She realized he belonged to Tamsen and made a "May I hold him?" motion with her arms.

"Sure, ma'am, or missus," said Tamsen as she swooped Master Thomas up and into the woman's waiting arms. The woman smiled and said some soothing words to little Tom. Both Tamsen and Tommy and all within earshot fully understood the meaning of the words, although no one actually knew the definitions.

The kindly woman motioned to Tom's blond hair and blue eyes, then to Tamsen's similar features. "Neva, Neva," she cooed, or something that sounded like that. Tamsen then pointed at the lady's eyes and hair followed by stroking the hair of a little girl standing beside them. "Neva, Neva," Tamsen said as both she and the woman laughed.

"Chikaskia?" one of the visitors asked Littrell. "Chikaskia?" he repeated as he made a flowing water hand motion.

"Yes," answered the guide as he made the rolling wheel motion, "Chikaskia." He pointed due west.

Wolves at the Door

"Behya, iska behya," scolded the Indian as he shook his finger. He stood still for a few seconds, getting his bearings as he looked west. He then slowly and very deliberately pointed a bit south of Ken's outstretched finger. As the Indian gently pushed Littrell's arm and emphatically gestured with his own, the guide realized he was getting a free recalculation of direction. No common language was necessary, although the man did keep muttering to himself, trying to get Littrell to understand these more accurate directions.

"But he doesn't know where we're headed. So how's he know where to send us?" Hooz said. He was at the age at which, though not a fully accepted adult, he wasn't a kid anymore either. So in order to underscore his newly developing seniority, he hung with the adult decision makers as much as possible.

"He does know, son," Timothy said. "I mentioned Medicine Lodge to him a moment ago and he clearly understood."

"Aarumph, Medicine Lodge," the Indian said as he held his directional signal out. He then squatted down and with his finger drew a diagram in the dirt. He drew a long wavy river line, and again deliberately pointed at it. He drew what was obviously a clump of trees on the near side of the river. To the northwest of the indicated trees he drew some squiggly lines and made rolling waves with his hand, all the while shaking his head.

"Rapids, Hank. He means rapids," Deteau said.

Bleeding Kansas—Life and Death in Bourbon County

He then pointed to the dirt diagram a bit southeast of the trees and made slow sinking motion.

"Quicksand," Hooz said, "he must mean quicksand, Mr. Devon."

Henry thought to himself with humor, *I either see this kid with a wicked hangover and a bad toothache, or with a fresh shot antelope and an enthusiastic comment. He's a fireball of a good kid. Hope my lunkhead of an oldest son tends like him in a few years.*

"You're right, Hooz, and you too, Tim. This man is leadin' us to where to cross over. Probably saving us some time and possibly some problems. And speakin' of time, folks, don't you all think we better get on with it?" Henry said.

They gave the Indians what food they could and also some fresher items of clothing. Some of the white children coughed up a few toys and a couple of dolls to the red children. One young Indian boy gave a pretty impressive arrowhead to Frank. One young girl took off a beaded string necklace and draped it over Bob's head. He blushed.

"Hoo, boy, Bobby's in love," teased one of the Stamler kids. Now Bobby really blushed.

"You shut up, you cowpie," was Bob's emphatic retort.

All the white adults gave something to the red adults. The Indians had virtually nothing to give in return, except the two ancients. The old man took a very old, extremely mangy looking clump of something off his rope belt and handed it to Boney Korzack. It looked like a wad of fur or hairball some coyote had coughed up. Some sort of a dried-up leathery and bloody artifact.

Wolves at the Door

"Thank you very much, Mister, er, Indian, sir," Boney formally stated as the old man stumbled away. As the old lady firmly held the man's hand with her left hand, she removed her old stovepipe hat with her right. She handed it to Inga, who proudly put it on. Boney and Inga had quietly conversed with grunts, groans and sign language with the old couple throughout the morning.

"I guess like all old couples, they appreciate the attention," Inga said knowingly to her husband. "I'll keep this old stovepipe forever most likely, as a remembrance of this event," the voluptuous Swede said. "I vonder vut that old furball chunk is he gave you?"

"A scalp!" said Littrell. "Most likely another Injun's scalp he took in his youth!"

Inga went whiter than usual. "Oh my! Oh my goodness! Oh my," she said, gasping between her comments.

They bid their visitors farewell and headed south by west in the direction they had been told. About a dozen miles later they saw a dark clump sitting on the horizon.

"It's the cottonwood clump, I believe," Dan Traisley said.

Then they heard a faint rushing, rumbling sound.

"It's the rapids," Harlan Dwyer said.

Then they pulled up to the east bank of the Chikaskia.

"Hooz, ride on over right here," Littrell instructed. "I imagine it's good, like he said. Everything else he told us is right."

Bleeding Kansas—Life and Death in Bourbon County

Hooz took off across the river and was back in a heart beat. "It's all good, Mr. Littrell, good 'n' firm, about a foot deep, two at the most."

"OK, folks," bellowed the guide. "Don't even pause. Let's stay in this order and ramble on over like it wasn't even there. I say let's pause on the other side and take a little rest. Let's see, it's just past three o'clock. If we let the stock drink, refill our water, take a dip, wash if anyone wants, we can probably still get in about three more hours afore dark. Or we can hold up here for the night. Whatever you all want."

"Let's keep it moving, friends," Stamler said. "I figure if we push it on through today, with a continuance of good weather, maybe we can push hard to Medicine Lodge by tomorrow of the evenin'."

Neither the LeClercs nor the MacNaughtens felt they could encourage speeding ahead after the disaster back at the Fall River, but they were all for pushing hard. While everyone had to some degree or another valued this trip as a meaningful life experience, all of them were ready to get to the end of it.

"We agree," Traisley said, and it was echoed by the others.

Then Harlan Dwyer spoke. "Again, Gretta and I and the kids know you've all been pussyfootin' around us about pushin' hard. Well, don't. We agree with you all. Let's make this a race to the finish line." And with that he loudly clucked his team and snapped the whip behind their ears. "Last one across is a polecat!" he shouted as his wagon eased into the stream.

Wolves at the Door

"God bless them, Mother, they're back," Henry said. "That man, both those Dwyers, they got the courage that'll make this whole idea work. Let's follow 'em across. Yahoo!"

Stone Dead of a Heart Attack

That night in camp, after eating supper and stowing livestock, two fiddles and a guitar were taken out. The sky had clouded over, but it was a still, pleasant night. The fiddles squealed and scratched out enough recognizable tunes to turn the evening into a full-fledged frolic. Tamsen danced once or twice with Harlan, and Henry with Gretta. Boney let it rip with Inga. She said for all to hear how coincidental it was there was a song called Red River Valley and she had heard there really was a Red River Valley.

"That couldn't happen again in a million years," she said.

As all the youngsters hippity hopped to music around the prairie, trying not to step on the prickly pear, the oldsters relished what they felt sure was their last evening meal of the trip. Several of the men had shot another antelope in a comedic encounter. The poor animal must have been asleep, because they nearly ran over it. Up it jumped in a startled attempt at escape. Luckily, four men had loaded shotguns or rifles right beside them. Two blasted shots at the escapee from less than fifty yards, and missed. One man drew down and fired from about seventy yards and the other from just under a hundred yards. Both thought they had missed. But at about a hundred-fifty yards out, the antelope crumpled up and dropped dead.

Bleeding Kansas—Life and Death in Bourbon County

They led a mule out, loaded up the antelope and brought it back to the wagons. Upon further inspection, they could find no evidence of buckshot or bullet. But still, Cob MacNaughten felt his quick 12-gauge blast surely had made a hit.

"Nope," said Timothy Deteau. "I'm positive I got him with my Winchester."

They all laid claim to the kill, but no entry wound was found.

"Not to be indelicate, ladies, but I think I know what happened," Frank Stamler said. As you can see here as we open him up, his heart area seems all burst apart. I am sure one of these fine marksmen sent a pellet right up his, uh, backdoor, so to speak. I think that deadly missile followed right up his intestinal tract to his heart, and killed him."

That evening, after the antelope meat had been grilled up, portioned out and sampled, everyone had the same reaction.

"Pitouiee!" "My Lordy that's awful" "Get outta my way, I'm gonna upchuck this rotten meat," and other like opinions were freely voiced. The meat was so tough and rangy it couldn't be eaten.

As all the adults tried to figure the mysterious cause of this phenomenon, Tamsen started laughing. "You dead-eyes, you fine marksmen!" She laughed harder. "I know exactly what happened here. This here antelope is so gosh danged old it could hardly get out of your way. You darn near ran over it with yer wagon, Red. And then you chased the poor ol' critter, shootin' at it, probably farther

Wolves at the Door

than it walked all last month. It was so tired and so disbelievin' all that lead could be flying by with nary a scratch, it just said the heck with it and dropped over dead!"

Silence.

"By God, boys, I think she's right!" Henry said. "Yessir, she's absolutely keerect! No other way possible." He was laughing so hard now he could hardly speak. "You pioneerin', pistol packin' potshot artists all missed him."

All but the four shooters were doubling up with glee as Henry continued. "Holy gee willikers, you sharpshootin' sonsabitches—"

"You hush up, Father," Tamsen ordered.

Henry continued. "You caused this poor elderly gentleman to exhaust hisself sprintin' across the prairie like that and, it's clear as a bell, drop stone dead of a heart attack! You should all four be ashamed of yourselves." Henry stopped his discourse with a question: "Anybody got any prairie hen eggs left?"

Most families had enough vittles to tide them over. The antelope carcass and steaks were ignominiously dragged well out away from the camp. At least the coyotes tonight and vultures tomorrow wouldn't be so picky.

As a parting shot, Henry solemnly announced, "Services for the dearly departed will be held at sunrise tomorrow morning."

So ended the twenty-second day, with laughter and hopes that this night would be their last one on the trail to Medicine Lodge.

Bleeding Kansas—Life and Death in Bourbon County

If Anyone Says "My Lordy"

Those hopes remained alive the following morning, June 3, 1878, their twenty-third day. Although the ultimate destination was Kiowa, they considered Medicine Lodge to be the end of this trail. It had been the target Littrell had signed on for. They had pushed hard enough the day before to leave only about two dozen miles.

At sunup everybody was raring to get on with this final day. A slight drizzle had started about three A.M. and was continuing now. As the procession of trail worn wagons and people inched forward, Henry enthusiastically proclaimed, "Well, children, this is our last day before Medicine Lodge. Master Thomas," he said as he grabbed the baby's finger, "you'll be able to tell your grandkids you pioneered through Kansas in a wagon, even though you won't remember a single minute of it! How 'bout you others? Have you enjoyed it? What's your favorite story of it, Frankie?"

Before Frank could even begin to answer, there was a loud crack. In one quick instant the whole back half of the Devons' wagon dropped almost to the ground. Everybody and everything suddenly was thrown to the rear. Two of the kids, Ollie and Charlie, flew right out the back flap opening and splatted into the mud. They were instantly joined by a box of flour, which split and emptied its contents all over them. At the same time, the rear cargo box hit the ground with enough force to dislodge it from the wagon. Their water barrel toppled out before anyone thought to grab it,

Wolves at the Door

and it soaked the two kids, but so did the rain, which was now coming down in sheets.

"What in the Sam Hill blazes was that? Whoa up, whoaaa," Henry shouted as he reared back on the team. Tamsen, who would have been sitting beside him on the bench seat, was not there to answer him. She had tumbled straight back, rolling right over Raisin and coming to rest on Sadie, before they both landed on a large sack of oats.

"My Lordy," she blurted out.

Bob had been riding Biscuit and was right beside the rear of the wagon when the loud crack scared the daylights out of him. He almost fell off the horse. "Ma, Pa," he yelled as he quickly dismounted, "the axle done broke right in two. My Lordy, is everyone OK?"

"You watch yer mouth, son," Tamsen said. "If anyone says 'My Lordy' around here it's gonna be me. And, no, I'd say we ain't OK, wouldn't you, Father?"

Danny Traisley had seen the mishap, and he now sprinted forward in the downpour to help out. "Geez, Hank, yer axle snapped right as I was lookin' at it. No big hole or rock, just all of a sudden, bang!"

Henry, Bob and Danny were soon behind the broken down wagon, hats pulled down and collars pulled up against the rain. Just as Henry stooped to help Ollie and Charlie, Raisin tumbled out, instantly joining the two kids in the mud and flour broth. With the wagon bed tilted down, bow to stern, the rest of the family came popping out one by one, like eggs from a tortoise. In ten seconds they were all in a heap in

Bleeding Kansas—Life and Death in Bourbon County

the flour caked mud. As a final coup de grâce, Frank did a kind of flying belly flop out the back, yelling, "Yahoooo", until his mouth hit the mud. "This is it, Pa, my favorite part of the trip!"

The entire procession came to a halt. Most of the folks braved the rain to get an up close look at this unexpected mess. By now it was hard to pick out any specific Devon with certainty, all caked in the paste as they were.

"Vell, sweet Jesus, Tamsen," said Inga, "you ain't exactly a vision, but you sure is a sight!"

Boney thought that was a pretty funny and well-thought comment. He guessed it could count as an "Ingaism," even though its wit was, most likely, unintentional.

But once the initial humor dimmed, the seriousness of the situation set in.

"What happened, Hank?" "Let us help you all up." "Geez, Hank, what're you all gonna do?" and other like comments were flying around.

Several men examined the broken axle. "What do you suppose caused it to snap?" "Must've been a weak spot." "Looks like a knot right at the break, Hank." Everyone had an expert opinion.

"Look, I have no idea what caused it to go, though it does look like some kind of flaw in the wood. Wish I had noticed it before," Henry said. "But now, this is a most unfortunate problem. I don't want to hold you all up, but this ain't going to be a real quick fix. Ken, you think one of the spare axles will fit my rig?"

Wolves at the Door

"I think so, Hank," the guide replied. "We'll have to whittle on it some. Man, I expected a wheel maybe breakin', but not this. I guess that's why we bring a couple of spares. Well, we might as well get at it."

With that comment, the rain suddenly stopped, as though somebody turned off the spigot. All the women and some men helped Tamsen and the children out of the road pudding. They all had to change clothing, most of the wagon contents had to be cleaned, and some supplies had to be reboxed.

Four or five of the men assigned themselves to blocking up the wagon bed, removing the two wheels and procuring a spare axle.

"It'll fit better than I thought, Henry. The length's easy to cut back a few inches, but it'll take a while to reduce the diameter to fit your wheel hubs," Littrell said. "We'll get it done, but it may take an hour or two."

So that's the way the supposed last day started. By noon they were barely a hundred yards from where they had started, but they were about to start up again. The axle had been replaced and greased. Their clothing was fresh. Wagon contents were as rearranged as possible. On they plodded.

"Oh my, Harlan. Look at the depth of mud those mules are sinking into. They must be pulling through a six-inch mess!" Gretta Dwyer said.

"I know, Mother. That soaking downpour wrecked the road. I can feel the drag on the wheels. It ain't quicksand, but it might as well be."

Bleeding Kansas—Life and Death in Bourbon County

"This is pitiful, Deb," said Red LeClerc. "These poor mules just can't get through this mud. Worse 'n' any we've had the whole trip. I don't think they can last in it!"

The rain had turned the ground surface into a quagmire. By two P.M. the rains came again. The wagon train was running right along a railroad track. Earlier, the tracks had seemed to disappear straight ahead into the distant horizon, but now visibility was down to one or two wagons ahead. Conditions were truly miserable, worse than the big storm early in the trip. Everyone was wet to the bone. Most of the duck canvas had lost any waterproofing it originally had. The rawness of the day seemed to permeate all bedding and clothing. And worst of all, they were slowly realizing this wasn't going to be the last day after all.

"How much farther, Pa?" Sadie asked. "You still think we'll make it?"

"Of course we'll make it, honey pot, only not today, I'm afraid. These animals will be plumb wore out soon with this mud."

Although he couldn't have known it, his timing was perfect. At the very moment he uttered those words, Korzack's other lead mule dropped dead. When Henry went to Korzack's wagon to help dislodge the animal from the span, he couldn't help smiling as he thought to himself, *At least this ol' gal never had to suffer the humiliation of wearing a yellow dress!*"

After the hour delay caused by Korzack's mule, another problem arose. When the emergency stop for the mule occurred, the LeClercs' wagon was in a dip in the terrain. The delay and the ensuing rain allowed a small lake to form under their wagon. When the call to proceed was issued, they couldn't. They had mired into the muddy morass and were stuck. The thought of unloading the contents in the rejuvenated downpour to lighten the load caused Deborah to break down and weep.

"I just can't stand anymore," she cried. "This is too much for a woman to endure," she whimpered as she flailed her fists against Red's chest. "I just can't, I can't," Her crying devolved into shoulder-shaking sobs.

To make matters worse, they all heard a faint whistle and a distant rumble. "Wheeou, wheeou," spoke the train whistle as the engine came into view. With visibility so limited, nobody had noticed it coming. By the time they heard the lonesome wail and felt the vibration, it was almost on them. As this limping little expedition of cold, wet and angry travelers looked up, the passenger cars were whizzing by with dry, warm and happy people gazing out the windows and waving at them.

"God damn 'em, if that don't pour salt in the wound!" Frank Stamler said.

"Look at them sonsabitches, all happy, dry and well-fed," added Tim Deteau.

Hooz Deteau squinted and saw several very comely young ladies spiriting by, wine glasses in hand, smiling at him and waving. *Well if that don't beat all,* he thought, *them pretty pansies flyin' by in style and me out here rollin' in the mud with my folks and these other old farts!*

Bleeding Kansas—Life and Death in Bourbon County

"God dang it!" he bellowed loudly, to his own surprise as well as everybody else's. "Quit yer bellyaching Mrs. LeClerc, you ain't unloading no wagon. Pa, why don't you and me help tie Mr. Devon's two oxen to this mess and just hoist 'em on out?"

"That's exactly what I was thinkin', Hooz," Henry said. "Burr and Bon are strong as oxes. Well, er, of course, they are oxes, heh, heh. But, you're right. Red, help us tie up ahead of your mules. Together I'm sure we'll have you up on drier land real quick."

Which is what they did. The wagon eased out, Deborah's wailing simmered to merely spasmodic sniffles, and the party proceeded on. It was about nine o'clock when they stopped that night. All the teams were totally worn out. They could graze some or be fed horse feed, oats, whatever.

"Let's hope, Mother, they all have at least one more day left in 'em tomorrow," Henry said as he and Tamsen went through their normal routine, buttoning up for the night.

All the families were dog tired. Even Raisin was fittingly dog tired. So much water and mud had splashed up on his platform throughout the day he had to laboriously trudge along off to the side. Sadie prevailed to let him in the wagon a few times, but he was so sloppy he fouled everything. After half an hour in the wagon, they'd toss him out again.

As they bundled in for a damp and dreary night, Bob said, "Geez, Pa, it's a downright swamp down here. Charlie ain't said a word for sometime, now, I think he went ahead and died!"

"I didn't die," came Charlie's reply, "I jest wish I had!"

"Did you smell those vittles, Ma?" Frank asked. "That train smelled like fresh bread, beef and vegetables all rolled up in one. And it all just whizzed by us! I'm so danged hungry I'd eat what they threw out as garbage!"

"I'm so hungry I'd eat the south end of a northbound skunk," added Bob.

"Hush yer mouths," Tamsen said.

But as Hooz Deteau lay awake under his wagon, he wasn't thinking of beef, bread, skunks or dry bed sheets. He just couldn't rid himself of the sight of those pretty girls smiling at him, and the caboose lights fading into the distance as that train disappeared toward Medicine Lodge.

"I knew it!" Sadie said as she sat bolt upright in the wagon at about three A.M. "Ma, Ma! It just now comes to me! I knew somethin' about those dry and smilin' faces shootin' by seemed familiar. I seen some people in one of the middle cars, they's been stickin' in my mind and it just come to me. They was Libby and James! I swear it, Ma. It was Libby. She was lookin' out the window like the others. And Ma," she whispered, "it's comin' to me kinda clear now. She was holdin' one of those … wine glasses!"

Growin' After Yer Dead

The first light of day spread enough illumination on this sorry bunch to cause grown men to weep, or laugh. There were eight covered wagons, about as many smaller road wagons, several dozen animals and more than a dozen people beginning to stir. Everybody and everything was caked with mud. It was June 4, 1878, the twenty-fourth day of this joyride.

"This better be it, Henry, or we're going to have to lash Deb LeClerc to a pack horse. She's about to go loony on us, and quite frankly, so are some others, including me," Tamsen said.

Bob had stumbled out about thirty yards to relieve himself in the dark gray mist. He sauntered up beside Hooz, who was likewise employed.

"Mornin', Hooz," he mumbled. "Wonderful night wasn't it?"

Hooz just grunted and kept urinating, still half asleep.

"Geez, Hooz, what's that board yer wettin' on?" asked Bob.

"Huh? What board?" Hooz asked as he squinted through the dark.

"That, that's a cross, Hooz. Fer Chrissake, you're pissin' on a cross. Holy Geez, Hooz, that's a grave marker!"

Hooz jumped so suddenly he almost tore off his willy. He spun around fast and shot a stream of urine out in an arc that was really quite pretty. With barely the first glow of sunlight glinting on it, each molecule glistened like a pearl in a maiden's necklace.

"Wow, Hooz. Yer kinda an artist with that thing. But doncha think we better tell our folks about this here marker?"

Wolves at the Door

They both reholstered their weapons and high tailed back to the wagons. As they approached the entourage, they noticed another strange thing. Clearly becoming visible through the morning mist, there were three, no four, dead mules lying beside their respective wagons.

"Geez, Hooz, what do we tell the folks first? 'Bout these here dead mules or you peein' on a grave?"

"You listen up, you little shit. You shet yer goddamn mouth about me peein'. That don't enter in nohow. One word about that outa you and I'll make sure you don't ever make a similar mistake. I'll rip off that little bitty pisser of yours and stick it up yer—"

"Boys!" Tamsen said. "That you, Bob? Oh, howdy, Hooz. Could hardly make you out in this mornin' fog. Everything OK?"

"Yes'm. Hooz 'n' me were just out inspectin' the perimeter, makin' sure everything was in order. And, well, it's not!"

"What do you mean, son? What's the problem?"

"Well, ma'am, it appears you all's animals is OK," Hooz said as he squinted through the haze, "but come here with us and take a gander around camp. We got us a few dead mules."

"Oh, Lordy! Don't tell me …" Tamsen said as the scene began to clear in front of her. Sure enough, the other folks were arising and milling around the stiffening hulks of five carcasses.

"Oh, how horrible, Jane, they must have just given it up during the night," Tamsen said, commiserating with the Deteaus.

"I guess yesterday was too much for 'em," Littrell said as he wandered from wagon to wagon. "We'll just have to make do with what's left."

"Ma, Pa, come quick," Ollie shouted as she ran up to her parents at the Deteaus' wagon. "I was climbin' down from our wagon and Luke just sunk to the ground. He's just layin' back there."

They rushed back and saw the mule pathetically twitching in the mud with his eyes bugged out.

"Oh no, Father, look at him," Tamsen said.

Luke quieted down and lay still except for his labored breathing. "He's done for, Mother. We just wore him out. Maybe didn't get enough water. The others seem OK, but Luke's finished. Ollie, you go on up to the MacNaughtens' wagon. Tamsen, take Tommy on up. You know what I gotta do."

Tamsen complied. She knew what had to be done was the most merciful kindness they could bestow on Luke. Ollie started crying the moment the shot rang out.

"Why'd he have to do that, Ma? Luke mighta got better. Why'd Pa hafta shoot him?"

"Honey, old Luke was too far gone, and he was hurtin' bad. Pa did a kind thing for him. We'll pray for him tonight to go to animal heaven. He won't have to pull through mud no more. All right? You understand?"

Ollie nodded.

"Now you stop your cryin', honey. We don't want to make your Pa feel even worse 'bout what he had to do."

Wolves at the Door

Ken Littrell orchestrated a realignment of animals so everyone had an adequate team for the final leg. After yesterday's miserable delays, he figured they had about ten or fifteen miles left. He thought, *Boy, will I be glad to get these folks to Medicine Lodge more or less in one piece.*

"What do you think, Ken?" Stamler asked. "Do you think we can do it?"

"I sure as hell hope so, Frank. I know we're all at the end of our patience. Deb LeClerc is about to pee up a rope."

Stamler tried to picture that but was drawing a blank.

"These roads, this ground, seems a bit drier and firmer today don't it, Ken?" Walli Stamler said.

As everyone discussed getting started and the conditions of the day, Bob sauntered up to Tamsen and said, "Er, Ma, there is one other thing. Me'n Hooz, mostly Hooz, sort of accidentally ran up on something out there you may oughta see. I think it's a grave, a grave marker, a wood cross. It was pretty dark but I think it was, you know, what I said."

Tamsen followed Bob out and sure enough, there it was. "Henry!" she shouted. "Danny, Cob, Frank, go find Henry and you all bring him here. We got us a grave!"

Several people were soon standing in front of the marker. In a fairly clear hand, carved on a plank attached to the cross was a poem of sorts. To the amazement and amusement of all it read:

Bleeding Kansas—Life and Death in Bourbon County

> James McGreevey
> Here's Big Jim, a thief by heck,
> He's taller now, since we stretched his neck!
> (Hung by yonder telegraph pole 5/18/1875)

"Wow!" said Boney Korzack as he pointed a finger. "That 'yonder' pole must be that one over there."

"How can he be taller after he's dead?" Inga asked. "Can you grow when yer dead, Boney?"

Boney just stood still, eyes closed, while he appeared to say a prayer.

A few others silently wondered why one arm of the cross was soaking wet.

That's Medicine Lodge, Shore Is

As the day wore on, the weather greatly improved. The underfooting firmed up considerably, and they made good time. They stopped briefly at a small stream for a light mid-day dinner. A couple of the boys brought in some very large, long-eared rabbits, which were fried up, and the families pretty much finished off the last remnants of their food supply.

Commenting on the extra meat, Littrell said to Dagmar MacNaughten, "Jack rabbits're kinda silly lookin', but when you're good and hungry, they eat out passable!"

Wolves at the Door

As they continued their journey, they passed a couple of sights they thought were somewhat bizarre. In one stretch they counted seven telegraph poles in a line about a mile long that had been struck by lightning during the previous day's storms. All had been hit, snapped off about ten feet up, still smoldering.

"That is something, Frank," Walli Stamler said to her husband. "It's really scary. What could have caused that, so much lightning?"

"I don't know, dear. Maybe they get storms out here the likes of which we ain't never seen! But don't you worry 'bout that now. This is today, that was yesterday. With this gorgeous dry day, well, don't you worry your pretty little head. We'll make it into Medicine Lodge smooth as silk, I guarantee!"

"Really, Frank? You really guarantee it, that we'll make it today?"

"I guar ... on ... tee it, love blossom. A piece of cake, an absolute piece of cake," he asserted with perfect certainty.

Another thing they saw over the latter part of the afternoon was a growing number of sod houses. With few creeks nearby, there were very few trees.

"We must be gettin' close to a village or town, or these soddies wouldn't be mountin' up like they are," said Henry.

"Is that what we'll have, Pa? A sod house?" Charlie asked.

"Maybe, son. Don't know for sure if any lumber or logs is down in Kiowa. But if it's built right, probably nothin' wrong with a soddie."

Along the way they had seen only a few head of cattle, but in this one day they had already seen four large herds.

"Look at them off to the northwest, Mother. Must be close to a thousand cows 'n' ponies movin' up there," Henry said.

"That's unbelievable, Father, Why so many, now?"

"Well, we're about halfway below Wichita and Dodge City here. Kiowa is really 'bout exactly between 'em. All those Texas and Mexican cowboys is movin' tons of 'em. I really do mean millions of those goddamn rangy longhorns up to the railheads. Someday I suppose they'll run out of 'em, but they sure do seem endless."

"Look up there, Pa," Sadie said. "Look at that building! A steeple? Isn't that some kind of a church?"

They all peered toward the horizon.

"Can't tell for sure," Henry said. "Bob, you got the best eyes, what is it?"

"It's a school, a school house. That's a bell, I think. But maybe it's a church."

"Well, whatever that particular building is, folks," interrupted the guide, "I can assure you that's Medicine Lodge. See those tracks anglin' in from the south? I think that may be the new bed headin' down toward Kioway. Can't quite make it all out, yet, but, yessir, that's Medicine Lodge, shore is."

Did You Get Any Rain?

As the energized little band of pioneers got closer, some of their old social concerns came back to life.

"Hold up a minute, Red," ordered Deborah.

"Father, why not clean up just a tad?" Tamsen said.

"Harlan, with Libby and James just ahead, shouldn't we tidy up a bit?" said Gretta.

The women in general prevailed upon the men to take just an hour before dark to try to clean and rearrange this sorry looking caravan. With the last of their water, and knowing plenty of water lay ahead, they splashed down the wagons and spritzed off themselves as well as they could. They straightened the wagon contents. And every one of the ladies changed clothes for their grand entry into town.

Then they headed on in. Littrell had been here before and knew who to see. He had telegraphed ahead that they were coming, but they were a couple of days late. He had arranged rooms, each with a private bathtub, at one of the hotels. Nothing fancy. Medicine Lodge was no Wichita. But clean beds and a hot meal following a bath would seem like a great luxury to these wanderers. So in they rolled, not sparkling clean but at least with the big chunks of mud knocked off.

And who was waiting on a small platform sidewalk to greet them as they arrived? None other than Libby and James.

"Well, Mother, yahoo! Look at you and Pa 'n' everyone. You all look wonderful!" Libby said. "We were so afraid you mighta had a rough time, but you look splendid! Jim and I are so sorry we missed it. We had to stay in that boring hotel and then make that long wretched train ride all day yesterday out from Fort Scott. It was awful. How we wished we could have enjoyed the great outdoors and fun with you all. Did you get any rain?"

Tamsen could have slapped her silly.

Everybody who left Fort Scott had finally arrived in Medicine Lodge with the exception, of course, of poor Jeremy. Everyone was bone tired but ecstatic, with the understandable exception of the Dwyers. Everyone buttoned up their rigs, tethered and fed their animals, and headed over to the hotel to bathe and settle in. The hotel, called Pioneer Palace, was rightly and wrongly named. Its guests were mostly pioneers, but it wasn't a palace. It was, however, the most welcome abode any of these folks had ever seen, given their current condition.

One by one the Devon family, upon entering their assigned room, peeled down to their under clothes and sunk into the bathtub. Clean, hot water was substituted after every third bather. Tommy first, then up the ladder by age and sex. Except for Tamsen, in last place was Henry. Technically, that wasn't true. The absolute last one in that bath water would be Raisin, who undoubtedly would repay the gift of such luxury by shaking water all over the room. But Tamsen was the last human to ease into serendipity, in her own fresh hot water.

"OK now, Father, you take this spit 'n' polished bunch of renegades on down to the dining room for dinner. I'll be along in a while. Go ahead and order. And please lock the door on yer way out. I aim to just bask in this here tub until about 1890. And don't any of you come back in here and bother me, on pain of death."

They did as she said.

Tamsen totally stripped down and got into the tub. She dunked her head under and lathered up her hair. She kept throwing water in her face and rubbing her closed eyes. The small towel on the tub edge helped wipe soapy water from her eyes before they started burning. Then she lay back and went into a kind of suspended animation. A bath never felt so good. She leaned over and picked up a hand mirror someone had left on the floor and gazed into it.

I'm 45 years old, my hair is turning white, I'm getting old, she thought. She recalled the younger women flying past on the train cars in their pretty dresses and plumed hats. *I'll never again look like that.* She laughed the instant she had the thought. *But of course… I never did.*

Again she closed her eyes and leaned back. She thought of her parents back in Illinois. They had come out from Indiana. Why had they done that? And their parents had for some reason gone to Indiana from Pennsylvania and Kentucky. Why do people keep doing this? She unexpectedly started crying. She was completely exhausted and was releasing all the pent up emotion of the last month, or maybe of the last year, or of the last five or ten years. Her venting was intense but short.

Just as she was getting herself back under control she heard a key in the door. Henry poked his head in and said, "Ready or not, here I come."

She laughed as he came over in his shirt sleeves, his thinning hair all slicked down. He sat on the edge of the tub.

"Well don't you look fetching, Mr. Devon. Where's yer coat?" she asked.

"I left it on the back of my chair. It's kinda warm in the dining room. Jim and Libby joined us. They're in shock about Jeremy. We ordered lobster if you can believe it. I came up to check on you. They're watchin' the kids." He paused. "And may I return the compliment and say you look rather fetching yerself, all naked and dripping wet like that!"

They both laughed, then slowly locked eyes. Without a word she was out of the tub and in his arms. There was a mad scramble of love making amidst wet clothes, splashing water and soapy flooring. It was over in only a few minutes, and when some semblance of decorum returned to the arena, Tamsen blurted out, "My Lord, Mr. Devon, yer kind of an Apache when you get riled up, ain't cha?"

"May I point out, Mrs. Devon, that you were the one jumpin' out of the tub all naked 'n' all!" And although he couldn't say it in so many words, Raisin just glared at them both as if to say, *Would you two uncouth dolts mind stepping aside to let a feller take his bath?*

As she quickly dressed and dried her hair as well as she could, he tried to dab at the water splashed all over the room. "We'll blame the wet floor on Raisin. We'd best get down pretty quick or the whole dining room is gonna suspect something's wrong.

"OK, I'm about ready," she answered as she adjusted her collar and brushed at her hair. "How do I look, Henry?"

As he gave some vague and fumbling answer to that question that all husbands know is never the right answer, she stooped and picked up the hand mirror. Upon gazing into it for the second time, she thought maybe she wasn't so old and washed out after all.

"You are truly a restorer of life and passion, Henry, you truly are!"

He had no idea what she was talking about, but he took her lightly by the elbow as they descended the stairway and entered the dining room.

Libby, You'll Never Know

"Well, folks," Ken Littrell said as he raised a coffee cup of champagne, there being no goblets available. "Unbeknownst to any of you, I've been totin' these couple of bottles of bubbly since we left Fort Scott, twenty-four days ago! I got 'em from Cecil Goodlander, the undertaker, but don't let that put ya off. And you mothers, let all the little ones have jest a tiny taste of it to celebrate."

"Folks, I just want to say it has been my pleasure to know you all and lend whatever hand I could in gettin' you out here to Medicine Lodge. A trip like we just done ain't never easy. Even under the best conditions, and as we all know, these wasn't the best conditions, a trip across this prairie can be a killer."

He gave a knowing glance toward the Dwyer tables and Harlan nodded back. Libby and James were still reeling from the news.

"You all, and me, too, we'll all go our separate ways now. I'm headin' on to Dodge, then I have a mind to go on out to Californy. I've about had it with these prairie crossin's and think I'll quit while I'm ahead. Plus, you all know I ain't caught a fish yet. I think mebbe I'll try a little salt water fishin' offa the Pacific. Maybe my luck'll change."

They all laughed as Hooz yelled out, "Mr. Littrell, my Pa says you couldn't catch a fish if someone tossed it to you!"

The guide winced but continued. "After that cruel comment, I'll wind up by wishing you all the best, whether you end up down in Kiowa, or somewheres else. Here's to you all."

And they all raised their glasses and took a tiny sip.

Then Henry stood. "Ken, and really all of you, I want to add my two cents. I know we all have great respect and appreciation for what you done for us, Ken. Your advice and guidance is what got us through. Those storms, the sleet, the mud, especially our beloved Jeremy's tragedy … Well, we all jest been through one helluva episode. And, Ken, I'm truly not sure we would've made it without you. Tamsen and me, well, we thank you from the bottom of our hearts, as do all the others."

Henry paused, scratched his whiskers, took a deep breath and continued. "And as to you others, we been good friends back in Bourbon County, and far as I know, nobody's had

Wolves at the Door

any fallin' out on this trip. We've all seen each other in bad times. Some good times, too, let's not forget that. But we just been through some stuff that would kill a mule. In fact, it did—five or six of 'em to be exact. Whether we all stay in Kiowa, or even go to Kiowa, is uncertain. But I don't think any of us will ever forget this here trip, or each other."

To lighten the mood, Cob MacNaughten announced with gusto, "Yer darn tootin' about that, Hank. Why, from now on every time I see a mule walkin' down the road sportin' a purty yeller dress, I'll think of Zilly!"

Everyone laughed except James and Libby and, of course, Zilly, who got more confused with each additional comment.

"What on earth happened out there, Mother?" Libby asked. "Was it a much harder journey than it appeared to me and Jim? Everyone seems so, so, battle-weary!"

"You'll never know, Libby, and we will never be able to fully explain it. We suffered like we never thought we could. As yer father just said, though, it wasn't all bad. We had some sunsets 'n' starry nights that defied description, and some sunrises, too, for that matter. We had spirited good humor, both as a group and within just our family. But the miserable cold and wet and"—she spoke very low as she added—"the dyin' of Jeremy in that Fall River. You'll hear more of it from Bobby and the Dwyers and others. But it hit your Pa real hard. It took him back to his killin' days a long time ago. I never seen him like that." She stopped and bit her lip to compose herself.

Bleeding Kansas—Life and Death in Bourbon County

"Libby, you know my little wood butter box, the one out in the wagon?" Libby nodded as Tamsen continued. "Look, I can't ever tell you what we went through as a family and how close it brought us together. You're our family, too, you and your Jim. You wasn't out there with us, so I'm givin' you that little butter mold box 'cause it was with us. I know it's nothin', but let's jest pretend it soaked up the whole trip and it's all sort of invisible like, stored in that little square box. You keep that as a remembrance of your family's wagon trip across Kansas back in 1878, goin' to Kioway. All our love and spirit will be in that box. And ever' time you use it, or even hold it in yer hand, it'll remind you who you came from. All right, honey girl?"

Libby was crying. She had had no idea the depth of emotion this trip had engendered or what stresses they had all endured. She was ashamed of her flippant comments at the sidewalk earlier. "Oh, Mama, I'm so sorry. I didn't know."

"No, no, darlin' girl. Don't you be sorry. You done nothin' to be sorry about. You jest take that little butter box and know it's full of your family's love. Both families, us and the Dwyers."

She suddenly became aware that Henry, Harlan and Gretta were listening on in agreement with her sentiments.

She added her final comments. "You give that small gift to one of your children someday, and then to their child. Whoever has that silly little butter box in the future will know their people, one time, way back, went west. We crossed our part of America. And maybe it'll give them the courage and strength to keep carryin' on. You do that for me, child!"

With that she sat back and relaxed. She caught Harlan and Gretta's approving glances as Henry squeezed her hand. She felt wonderful.

"OK, folks," she said as she rose from the table, after everyone had finished polishing off an ocean full of lobsters, "it's time to turn in. We got us a big day comin' up. In fact, a bunch of big days iffen we ever plan to get to Kioway."

Red turned to Deborah and said, "My gosh, she's a stout-hearted woman. But ya know what, sweet? So are you!"

Zilly whispered to Danny, "I lugged my trunk up to the room and quickly went through it. All my dresses are there except the yeller one, 'n' Cob said somethin' about a yeller dress. What the devil is goin' on here? You know you know, c'mon, out with it."

Hooz drank his third beer as he was finishing off his third steak, all three of which Jane had lovingly cut up for him.

"Weren't all those sentiments lovely, son?"

"Huh? What? Oh, sure, Ma, what comments? Er yeah, lovely, just lovely," he absentmindedly mumbled as his eyes scanned the dining room for those fine lookin' fillies he had seen on the train.

Finally they all slowly ascended the stairway to their separate rooms. Each family had run the gauntlet of a

Bleeding Kansas—Life and Death in Bourbon County

once in a lifetime endeavor, and each person would be forever changed. Even baby Tommy seemed to carry a look as though he knew something he hadn't known a month ago.

PART-II

II

Wagon Ho!

New Beginning in Kiowa

Dawn broke on June 5, 1878, in Medicine Lodge, Kansas, to reveal the start of a calm and sunny day. As the first few rays of light warmed the Pioneer Palace, most of this tired party of travelers remained comatose in their beds. Even the kids, mostly scattered around on the floor in each room, were still out cold under blankets. In the Devons' room, however, not everyone remained locked in slumber. Raisin, who had had to sneak in past the proprietor, began to stir. He was the first to hear a rooster crow. He hopped off Henry and Tamsen's bed, where he had spent the night as a stow away, and slowly edged between some of the sleepers who lay on the floor. Agile as a cat, with curiosity to match, he jumped up on a dresser and peered out the open window.

    The lace curtains were barely moving in a gentle breeze, and he rather enjoyed the sensation of them softly stroking his right ear. As he looked out upon the slow illumination of this little town, an intelligible feeling of contentment washed over him. He looked back into the room at the prostrate forms of what was truly the bosom of his family. That was all well and good, but it was time to get the ball rolling on this fine day. Raisin didn't have

Wolves at the Door

enough intellectual fire power to know exactly what was in store for the day, but after all, the rooster had crowed.

He lept down off the chest and back up on the bed. Since Tamsen's face was closest to him and exposed, he gave it a big wet tongue swab.

"My Lord, Henry," Tamsen moaned as she was yanked from a very deep sleep, "What the devil are you doing? Wasn't yesterday enough?" Then she abruptly realized it was Raisin, not Henry, breathing down on her. "Oh, my gosh," she sheepishly said, hoping no one else had heard her comment. No one had.

"What's up, Mother?" Henry asked as he, too, surfaced to the new day. "What's that you said?"

"No, never mind, Father. Raisin startled me with a big old lick across my face. Thought it was you. But now I know it was the dog, cause his breath's a might more tolerable than yours."

"And top of the mornin' to you, too, Mrs. Devon," he said as a few of the kids began to stir. The only two still totally lights out were Tommy and Ollie, both wedged comfortably between Henry and Tamsen in the bed. The others were desperately trying to bend out the kinks from a night spent on the hard plank floor of the Pioneer Palace.

"Man, I feel like I fell off the top of a water tank and landed on the tracks," Bob began, then was startled into silence as a shot-like roar emanated from the adjoining room.

Wagon Ho!—New Beginning in Kiowa

"What in the ... did you hear that?" Charlie said as he tried to stifle his laughter. "That was a fart! A big old bell ringer that almost knocked the building down! Pa, did you hear that?"

"Charles! You be quiet. They can hear you," Tamsen said.

"Well, I guess they can, Ma, seeing as how that blast about singed my eyebrows over here in our room. Holy smokes! Who's in that room? We better send in a doctor."

Tamsen knew the Traisleys were in the adjoining room. "No way of telling who actually let that slip, but I'm sure it was an accident. Zill would be mortified if she knew we heard it."

"Let it slip? My Lord, Mother, that sounded like the last cannon fired at Gettysburg," Henry said.

As Tamsen tried to hush up her own howling children, she could hear other renditions of stifled mirth coming from the room across the hall, as well as from the room on the other side of the Traisleys.

"These walls are paper thin, Henry. I'm sure everyone awake heard it."

"You can say that again, Mother. Kinda like 'the shot heard 'round the world' wasn't it? Oh well, we might as well get the day started on that note!" he said, overwhelmed by his own wit.

With Sad Feelings

At breakfast the conversation slowly turned to a more serious discussion of everyone's plans. Ken Littrell had received his due pay from all, exchanged last pleasantries and departed into his own private future. The Dwyers hadn't surfaced yet, but everyone knew they were having a sober and sad meeting with James and Libby, bringing them more up to date on their tragedy. The other seven families were all present and scattered at tables throughout the dining room.

After breakfast the younger kids were permitted to run free while the adults and older children settled in at just a couple of tables.

"Well, we all had quite a journey together didn't we?" Henry said. "I guess it's time we reshuffle the cards as to what we do now. I know I've heard a lot of different mumblings over the last day or two, but what're we all really gonna do? Frank, how 'bout you and Walli? Goin' on to Kiowa or somethin' else?"

Frank Stamler fidgeted in his seat for a moment or two, then calmly said, "Don't rightly know for sure, Henry. Walli and I and our three here feel like you all are family. After this trip we just done together, well, you surely know how we all feel about each other. None of us here will ever forget each other. We all know that." As he spoke, his wife dabbed at a tear in her eye.

"But Walli and I can't seem to get a handle on what to do from here. We've decided to stay over here in Medicine

Wagon Ho!—New Beginning in Kiowa

Lodge for a while. After experiencing the desolation we've seen so far out here, well, we think Kiowa may be just too remote for us. Walli's sister LaRue said iffen we found a spot out here we liked, they may follow on out. We think they'd maybe like a little more developed town. And so would we. Maybe right here, or Dodge City, or back to Wichita. But for now, not Kiowa. Our good wishes will, of course, go with you all, and we'll stay in touch as to what we do. Hope you all understand." With that he sighed and leaned back in his chair.

"Of course we understand," Henry said. "I 'magine we all got a little uncertainty as to what to do. How 'bout you and Zill, Danny?"

Zill Traisley had positioned herself with her back to the other tables to avoid all eye contact. Even though the morning's attention-demanding trumpet blast had, in fact, come from one of her kids, she knew everyone suspected it was her. She was still royally embarrassed.

Danny's only comment assigning blame to the offending child had been, "That just proves the biggest presents come in the smallest packages." He moved on and left his wife to deal with her agonizing humiliation.

"I think we're in it to Kiowa, Henry," he said. "In our mind, that was our intended target to begin with. Don't know what Kiowa will be like, and if it's somethin' not good, well, I guess we could always move on. But we ain't got no reason not to proceed there, so we figure we might as well. Isn't that so, Zilly?"

Wolves at the Door

Zill didn't turn around, and she kept her mouth fully loaded with grits so she wouldn't have to utter a single word. She just nodded.

"I might as well say we feel about the same as Danny," said Boney Korzack. "We also thought of Kiowa as our final goal. Of course, none of us really has much idea what's there, but with no other better idea, for now, count us in."

"Red, Cob, what do you folks think?" Henry asked.

"Well, Henry, you know Cob 'n Dagmar and us, and all our kids, has always kinda hung together," Red replied as he pushed back his chair and stood. "We've bounced it around, really, the whole way out. I got to laugh at myself about draggin' along those pool cues and balls. Can you imagine trying to ship my old pool table out here? What the hell was I thinkin'? We brung that ol' thing from Bellefontaine, Ohio, when we headed to Bourbon County. Never actually had room to put it together back there, I guess luggin' it to Kiowa would really be 'Red's folly,' wouldn't it?" He shook his head, chuckling at himself.

"No, we've all four of us, Deborah and I and Cob 'n' Dagmar, pretty well decided to keep movin' west. Or at least like Frank said, try to find a little bigger town. Don't know if Californy is in the cards, but we've kinda discussed maybe goin' on the big trail on out to Santa Fe. I guess the bottom line for both families is we won't be goin' on to Kiowa with you good folks. But we'll hold you in our hearts forever."

Wagon Ho!—New Beginning in Kiowa

With that, Red LeClerc sat down and a hush fell over the room. Everyone realized what a momentous discussion they had just witnessed. Devons, Dwyers, Deteaus, Korzacks and Traisleys were in, LeClercs, MacNaughtens and Stamlers were out. No bad feelings, but very sad feelings. Long time dear friends choosing different life paths that could and probably would separate them forever. Just like the friends they had left in Fort Scott.

"Well, OK, I guess that's it then," Henry said. "Phew, this will be hard leavin' our dear friends. But we're all agreed on what we all just said, then, right? Any other comments?"

Everyone just nodded and stared at the floor. They all slowly stood, mingled together and hugged. Tears were shed. Finally, the non-Kiowa families edged out of the lobby into the street.

"Well, folks," Henry said to those who remained, "we might as well start figurin' out where Kiowa is and how to get there."

New York, Rome, Paris and Kiowa

It took the families more than a week to prepare to disembark. The first thing they did in Medicine Lodge was sell any of the wagons they would no longer need and switch out provisions. Some of the food, both for humans or animals, didn't quite make sense now. They would eat in the restaurants in Medicine Lodge while in town, and their livestock was either at a corral or temporarily pastured out.

Wolves at the Door

Henry figured he would be building a small herd down in Kiowa, but he could surely use the three mules he still had. Same with Burr and Bon, the oxen. He'd need more horses, but Betsy and Biscuit, although getting well up in years, were holding their own. He did, however, sell off Victoria, their one cow. She had stumbled across Kansas, giving them needed milk at first, but then pretty much drying up. The trip had simply been too much. She wasn't about to die, but she had lost a lot of weight along the way. What she really needed was to not take one more step for quite a while and just be left to graze. Henry sold her for ten dollars to a young couple on a small farm just out of Medicine Lodge. There she would gain back her weight and health. He hoped she'd serve them well.

The Dwyers were continuing to Kiowa. They had intended to from the start, and Jim and Libby's union cemented it. Also, the unspoken bond formed between Gretta and Henry back at the Fall River was further glue to the relationship. Both families kept their wagons. So did the Deteaus. But the Traisleys and Korzacks sold theirs. It was decided they would simply take what they really wanted to keep and piggyback it on the remaining wagons. With some of their provisions being thinned out, the Devons and Deteaus each had some extra space for the twenty-mile trip down to Kiowa. Since they could pick good weather, there was no doubt it would be a fairly easy one-day trip.

"I'll be glad to unpack my dresses and let them air out," Zill said. "They must be terribly wrinkled."

Wagon Ho!—New Beginning in Kiowa

Danny could only imagine what some future wagon train would think passing by an Indian encampment and seeing two or three squaws running around, each in a section of Zilly's yellow dress.

They all engaged in conversations with local folks who might be able to tell them something about Kiowa.

"Where exactly is it?" Boney asked a town constable.

"It's twenty or so miles down in the southeast corner of Barber County, right on the west side of this here Medicine River. You can't miss it."

"Why is it named Kiowa? That an Injun name?" Jim Dwyer asked a mercantile clerk.

"I'm told it's like our town of Medicine Lodge. I guess Kiowa was, or is, some Indian word meaning *big medicine.* Supposedly there was, or is, a medicine lodge of sorts down that away. Ain't never been there myself, so don't really know fer sure."

Henry and his friends would learn later that a Captain John Mosley was reported to have started a small trading post in the Kiowa area in or around 1867. It served Osage Indians as well as buffalo hunters. The same Captain Mosley got his thanks by being killed in an Osage attack in 1874. Then a man named Hegwer and another named Rumsey opened a post office and general store there in 1876. Kiowa was on the map and starting to grow by the time Henry and Tamsen and friends showed up in 1878. Families such as the Rumsey clan, C.N. Vaultier, A.J. Crewdson and others were already there.

Wolves at the Door

Those families were about to get some newly arrived neighbors.

Mr. Ricardo Hazen, an attorney in Medicine Lodge, told Danny Traisley, "One man you'll probably meet quick if you buy any property will be Aleck Hopkins. He's the only lawyer down there. Nice man. He'll help you buy in on the up and up."

Oh, great, Danny mused with a chuckle, *and here I'm already tardy on my promise to Ken Littrell to keep all the damn lawyers out of the territory!*

"Another man you'll want to know for your horses will be Clarence Stowell, a pretty fair blacksmith down there."

Baxter Corzilius, owner of the Palace, knew practically all other innkeepers in the area. Tamsen and Jane Deteau asked his advice. "Where we gonna stay until we settle? Got any suggestions?"

Baxter yelled to his wife, who was cleaning up the kitchen, "Hey Martha! What's the name of the new boarding house down in Kiowa? I heard it, but I forgot."

"Well, that's understandable, Bax, cause it's a real tricky name, it's called the Kiowa House." Martha came out, drying her hands on her apron. "No wonder you couldn't figger it out!"

Baxter glared at his wife and then continued, "Right, that's it. It was just built last year by a man named Davis. Go see him and tell him I sent you."

"No," Martha said. "Go see his wife, Mrs. Davis. As is always the case, the mister just promenades around and

Wagon Ho!—New Beginning in Kiowa

doesn't do a damn thing. The missus is the doer. She manages the place. I hear it's a clean, decent roomin' house. Forget the old man. Tell her I sent you."

Tamsen and Jane laughed and were glad to get a lead on housing—from a woman.

So off they went. These tightly connected friends were equally tightly packed into several wagons. Just about every horse had a kid or two mounted on it. Just about every mule or ox not hitched to a wagon had a trunk or box or implement tied on. They departed at about eight A.M., June 12. After a nice leisurely picnic lunch and an enjoyable swim in the clear river for the kids, they turned slightly to the east and pulled into Kiowa at about six P.M. As they came to a halt in a field just down from the Kiowa House, a confidant and friendly looking man approached them from across Main Street, just south of the hotel.

He greeted the Devons, whose wagon was the first in line. "Hello, sir! Hello, ma'am." He extended his hand to Tamsen in a warm welcome. "Please allow me to introduce myself. I am A.W. Rumsey. I own the mercantile there across the street. We received your telegram two days ago and have anxiously awaited your arrival today. I hope the trip was easy and pleasant. Others will be along shortly to welcome you to our fair city and offer help in any way we can. Are you, perchance, Mr. Devon?"

"That I am, Mr. Rumsey, and this here's my wife, Tamsen, and our children are scattered around here somewheres."

"Well, welcome folks. I know you're bookin' in at the Kiowa House. Let's take you in to meet Mrs. Davis so she can get you all set up. We're really glad to see you. We're building us a whiz-bang of a little town here that we expect to rival New York, Rome and Paris someday. And we are thrilled you all are here to help us do it!"

What Kinda Name is IBar?

After boarding arrangements had been made at the Kiowa House with Mrs. Davis, the Devons, as well as all the other families, began spreading out in all directions. Henry followed up his acquaintance with A.W. Rumsey by inquiring about permanent housing.

"Well, sir, it's done two ways. Those without kids sometimes throw up a little cabin, usually a sod house, out where they're ranchin'. You folks with your, what, five or six children, will want to be in town for the school. Our little school was built just two years ago. That's my home down that street over there. Then just a little south of that is the school. Just south of that, I'm sure you know, is Indian Territory, the I.T. We all, that is those in the cattle business, make full use of the I.T. to graze our cows. Are you planning on ranchin', Mr. Devon?"

"Yes, and please call me Henry."

"Fine, Henry, and please call me A.W. I've got brothers, sons and nephews all over the county. We mostly just go by our initials."

Wagon Ho!—New Beginning in Kiowa

"I do plan on buying a quarter section or so," Henry said as Tamsen rejoined them. "I reckon it would have to be a little ways out of town, so I see your point about living in close for the school."

"Hello again, Mr. Rumsey," Tamsen said. "I just met Mrs. Remer at their store and also Mrs. Umbarger. They were telling me what you just said. Their husbands are both cattlemen, but they both live in town. I guess that makes sense. Henry, we've never lived in a town proper. It would be nice to be so close to folks who will become our friends. But for now, the Kiowa House is a godsend."

Bobby and Charlie came running up. "Hey Pa," Bob said, "we just met some local kids. And a couple of real purty girls! One kid's name is IBar. Can you believe that? What a name! I Bar, IBar Johnson. I didn't laugh or anything. He seems nice enough, and funny. Full of stories of this here town."

"Bob, Charlie, this is Mr. Rumsey," Henry said. "That's his store over there."

The boys politely shook hands with A.W.

"Mr. Rumsey was tellin' your mother and me about the Kiowa school."

"How old are you, Bob?" Rumsey asked.

"I'm fifteen, and Charlie here is fourteen. Where is the school house, sir?"

A.W. Rumsey pointed to the south and explained that they had a brand new teacher, a Mrs. Florence Horton.

"We've also got a brand new school bell. Just delivered and installed last month. We had us a very successful school play last year to raise the money. Folks came in from all over. Had the bell brought down from Wichita. You'll hear it tomorrow."

He Had Only Three Legs

For the first week or so, the new immigrants took the time to relax and investigate Kiowa at their leisure. Fortunately, most of the families had enough savings with them so that this was not a financial hardship.

"What do you think so far, Harlan?" Henry asked of his daughter's father-in-law.

"I like it. Gretta and I and our three younger ones are going to try to buy that little frame house behind the Kiowa House. I guess you heard that Mrs. Davis has been feeling poorly and her husband isn't really up to runnin' it. We'd like to buy it and run it with help from Jim and Libby. What do you think of that?"

"Yes, Libby mentioned that to us. Sounds good. Folks will keep coming out and they have to have a place to stay for a while."

People tend to do what they know how to do. Boney Korzack announced he would offer himself as a jack-of-all-trades contractor. He knew his own skills and was confident he could help build Kiowa, regardless of what those meadow muffins back in Fort Scott thought.

Wagon Ho!—New Beginning in Kiowa

Inga agreed. Declaring that Boney had always been competent and honest and would reap just benefits for that, she loudly proclaimed he was living proof that, "He who sow shall, so shall he who!" Somehow this declaration made perfect sense to her. Everyone stood with their mouths agape. Nothing more needed to be said in Boney's defense.

Tim and Jane Deteau were equally enthusiastic. "We'll probably start with a few cows. Maybe run 'em on the I.T. and stay in town. Renee seems to like it. She's met a boy named Ibear, or Y Bear, somethin' really odd. He's showed her around a little. Hooz plans to help us build a herd. Says we'll have a thousand head in ten years." Tim laughed and shook his head. "In any event, this here town seems a place to make a go of it. Plus, Hank, you folks hear of the Santa Fe runnin' track down here? Wouldn't that be something?"

"How 'bout you, Danny, you and Zilly? Whatta you and your kids make of it so far?" Harlan asked.

"Well, so far it seems promising. As you know, we was into pigs back home. And as they say, pigs is pigs. I don't know if folks is raising 'em much out here, but don't know why not. If cows, horses and sheep can make it here, I s'pose pigs can, too. We'll probably give that a try."

"That reminds me of an interesting story," Henry said, "back in Bourbon County. Any of you ever meet ol' man Mazzola, out on the south end of Fort Scott? Not near where any of us farmed. He was a big, pleasant Eyetalian man. Ran a place down there, little of everything. Cows, ponies, sheep, lots of vegetables. And one solitary pig. And

Wolves at the Door

of all things, it was a three-legged pig." Henry was just getting warmed up.

"Three-legged pig? How'd it come to only have three legs, Mr. Devon?" asked Hooz Deteau. Tim, Harlan, Traisley and all the others had been had-one at time-by Henry, but Hooz had not been initiated.

"Well, Hooz, glad you asked, 'cause that's the same question I put to Mr. Tomaso Mazzola. 'Mr. Mazzola,' I asked, 'all these other animals around your farm seem in fit fettle. Them ducks and geese all have one bill and two wings like they's supposed to. Those sheep have curly wool and four legs like they should. Same with your horses, mules and cows. Everything seems as it should be 'cept that ol' sow. She has only three legs. In fact, I now see she's even missin' a few inches off her foot on another leg. What gives?'"

"Yeah, what was the deal?" Hooz asked, as he bit hard on Henry's hook.

"Well, son, that kindly old Eyetalian said to me, 'that there is a real special pig. She has saved exactly three lives of family members on our farm, includin' mine. Once I got bit by a rattler out beside the outhouse and passed out. That ol' girl saw it and came out and dragged me back to be doctored. Another time, my missus, the ravishing Mrs. Mazzola, was hangin' our laundry on a real windy day. The sleeves of my shirts and legs of my overalls was dancin' a storm on the line 'cause of the wind. The missus tried to do a two-step with my overalls, got caught in 'em around her windpipe and was slowly stranglin' in and amongst the laun-

Wagon Ho!—New Beginning in Kiowa

dry. That blessed old sow ran over, pulled her down and restored her breathing apparatus to workability.'"

"Holy moly!" Hooz said, gasping. "What was the third one?"

"Well, son, you're not gonna believe it. I know I found it incredible. That Eyetalian swore it was true. He had a pond beside his road 'bout the size of that Kiowa House building over there. Not quite as big, and maybe one or two feet deep. His four-year-old son waded in after a duck, fell down and commenced to drown. Nobody saw it except the pig. Since the pig couldn't swim, and was in fact terrified of water, he couldn't jump in. So he did the only thing he could. He started drinkin' the pond faster than a fire wagon pump. Within thirty seconds the pond was down six inches. Within sixty seconds the pond dropped six more and the pig started pissin'. She was suckin' it up in front and firin' it out the back like that Niagary Falls deal. Within two minutes the boy was saved and the pond was transplanted to the other side of the road, where it is to this day! Isn't that amazin'?"

Just then Tamsen walked by and rolled her eyes. She had heard this story a hundred times before, and feared she'd hear it a hundred times more.

"Wow, what a story! What a pig!" exclaimed Hooz. "But tell me, Mr. Devon, as terrific and heroic as that pig was, what's all that got to do with it only havin' three legs?"

"Well, Hooz, think about it. If you yerself had such a high quality sow as that one, you sure as hell wouldn't eat it all in one sitting, now, would you?"

Everyone erupted with groans. Even Hooz immediately knew he'd been bamboozled, and he joined in the glee. Only Inga remained stoic.

"I don't get it, Boney, why couldn't the pig just walk out and get the boy? The water was only a foot or two deep. Oh that's right, he only had three legs."

A Million Cows is Comin'

Now that everybody more or less had a plan, it was easier to make some progress. Everyone had formed an early impression of Kiowa, but realization of the true state of affairs began to set in after a month or so. Just prior to the Bourbon County contingent's arrival, several incidents had occurred that were a bit sobering.

First, wolves started running in such great numbers they made venturing out on Main Street at night hazardous to life and limb. Wolves, it seemed, were, both figuratively and literally at everybody's door. In addition, rumor of Indians "on the warpath" got so strong lots of folks boarded up and assumed a fortress-like existence for a while. Nothing actually happened, but Henry and Tamsen were beginning to understand that although well-meaning folks like A.W. could paint a rosy picture, Kiowa in the late 1870s was still a very primitive piece of the American frontier.

Scott Cummins, an early buffalo hunter in the area around 1870, later described Kiowa as "abounding in game of every description, bison by the tens of thousands, and deer, antelope, bear, wolves and coyotes everywhere."

Wagon Ho!—New Beginning in Kiowa

He described flocks of wild turkeys flying in to roost at night as sounding "as loud as thunder."

"That may sound a bit idyllic, Hank," A.W. Rumsey said as he and the Devons met for a noontime meal at the Kiowa House one day, "but it wasn't far off. In fact, it still isn't."

"But what about the other stories, A.W.? What truly is the Osage situation? What and when was this uprising we keep hearing about?"

"I can't deny that, folks. I wasn't here, but the truth is on August 7, 1872, the Osage really did attack the budding little Kiowa settlement. Old Captain Ed Mosley had just come to the Kiowa settlement with only a few other families, the Leonards and the Lockwoods, I believe. Mosley was reputed to be one tough son of a gun to his enemies, which you'd of had to be back then. Somehow he got crossways with local Osage, probably over buffalo killin'. Anyways, yes, they sure as hell attacked and killed Ed. And for what it's worth, it's pretty well accepted that Mosley's son John got revenge later by killin' a few Osage in return. But, Hank and Tamsen, it's important you folks and others like you know that them days is over. Oh, sure, we hear about some big deal Injun rumor every now and again, but it's over. We simply outnumber them. They was beat from the start in this country by sheer numbers. I tell you, and I really mean this, I not only don't have reason to fear the Osage or Comanche or Kiowas, or any of 'em, but I do have cause to pity 'em. What we done to them, mostly by killin' so many buffalo, is awful. It had to be done 'cause our cattle can't compete with a prairie full of buffs, but we've finished 'em off for good. We'll hear of a few more clashes, but the poor starvin' red man is gonna be history. Can't match our numbers, can't match our machines. He's done!"

Henry leaned back and sighed.

"You're surely right," Tamsen said. "We ran into what we thought were Kiowa back past the Chikaskia River. We was scared at first, till we saw what a miserable shape they was in. Sorry! They was really a sorry outfit."

"Now let me bring up a more realistic situation than Indians for our town. I'm talkin' about the railroad. It's either gonna be a blessing or a curse, our true birth or our death. If we get it, prosperity comes with it. If we don't, we may as well pack up and leave."

"Why is the railroad so all important A.W.?" Tamsen asked.

"Cows, Mrs. Devon, cows. Thousands, tens of thousands, shoot, probably hundreds of thousands of 'em. In fact, over the next few years ... why I'll bet a million cows get driven by here on their way up to Dodge City or Wichita. They go there for the train ride back east. But they don't have to go that far north if we could just put 'em onto the cars right here, in Kiowa. If we can just get a main line or even a branch to come right here ..." He stopped speaking, lost in thought.

After a moment's silence, Rumsey continued. "See that man eatin' over across the room?" Henry and Tamsen turned and looked. "The rough lookin' fella with the full black beard? That's Wilbur Campbell. About ten or twelve years ago he was farmin' somewhere over near Wichita, barely twenty years old at the time. He then got into drivin' cows up from Texas and hit on the idea of fattening them up with corn and hay before drivin' them to a shipping point. He saw, as did others, the potential of the Indian lands, the I.T., as a grazing source for cattle. 'Bout five years ago he began developing a bunch of good Injun prairie between Barber and Harper counties, about twenty miles southeast of here, as a pretty big cattle ranch. I hear tell he's at 20,000 acres, probably headed to 50,000 acres. And look at him, can't be more than thirty, thirty-five years old."

Henry and Tamsen were finishing up dinner as A.W. got up to leave. "Folks, you and me is both older than thirty, right? No offense, Tamsen," he said as Tamsen laughed.

"Yes, Mr. Rumsey. Both Henry and I saw age thirty come and go, and now forty has done skedaddled, too. No offense taken."

"My point being, if you look around this town you'll notice some very adventuresome but thoughtful risk takers hoppin' on board. And they're young, mostly under forty. You're gonna see more and more young families arriving. The cows is the main thing, though we raise sheep, pigs and about any other dang thing pretty well, too. But the cows is being brought in from Texas and Mexico. And those cowboys need all their cowboyin' equipment. So some blacksmith provides 'em, so does some hardware store owner. And those men have wives who need some flour 'n' sugar, and a dress or two plus a new bonnet. And their kids

Wolves at the Door

need some schoolin' paper or a whittlin' knife or some cough remedy at a drugstore. Doncha see? This here little town is just barely sproutin', but it's headed for great things if, and I repeat, if, we can get all those cows to come and stop here because it's a closer railhead than Dodge City, Wichita, Abilene or wherever."

They bade good day to A.W. and wandered out on the street. It was now autumn of 1878. Henry and Tamsen had not only made it to the mythical and mystical Kiowa, Kansas, along with a few friends and their families, but they had also established a very small but identifiable beginning point. They had comfortable, if temporary, lodging and had gotten to know their way around the tiny burg. And most important, they had met people. More accurately, the right people.

"A.W.'s correct, Mother. Things are just startin' to bud out here, and by sheer luck we're arrivin' in the nick of time. We got to get a move on. We need to get us a quarter section, or at least be lookin' into it while we start building us a small herd. I think we need to see if Kiowa is gettin' a train spur like A.W. says. We need to see about the kids' schoolin', too. Before we know it, '79 will have flown by and the 1880s will be out of the chute and gettin' a jump on us."

Buffalo Bones ... and Wolves

By 1879 Kiowa had about fifty inhabitants, not counting the many folks passing through or working in the surrounding areas. Drought had hampered the cattle efforts of recent

Wagon Ho!—New Beginning in Kiowa

arrivals, such as the Devons. They, along with the Dwyers, Traisleys, Deteaus and Korzacks, all had to scramble to make a go of Kiowa. They all still had some savings from selling out in Bourbon County, but that couldn't last forever. In the case of the Devons and the Traisleys, they found a little bounty in bones. Buffalo bones, that is. With literally tens, maybe hundreds of thousands of buffs gunned down and stripped of fur over the previous decade, the plains in some spots was almost knee deep in bleached bones. The bones had fertilizer uses, plus ornamental use, too. In 1879, they were fetching on average about $10 per ton.

"I read in the paper a man killed a buffalo nearby here last month. Probably one of the last ones anyone will ever see alive out here," Henry said to Danny Traisley as they huffed and puffed loading bones into a wagon.

"I guess so. We sure got a helluva lot of deer, antelope and other game. I heard what's his name, Mr. Champion, got sixty-seven turkeys in one day's hunt last year. But you're right, the days of the buffs is gone, other than a few strays now and again."

"How have you and Zill been makin' out, Dan? You still into this venture?"

"I think so," Dan said as he hoisted an armful of rib bones over the side of the wagon. "I guess I told you we're about to set up a little farm just out of town. We'd like to go big like a quarter, but don't think that's prudent quite yet. You know that abandoned soddie a mile northwest? Up along the river? A.W. told us the family that built it just

Wolves at the Door

up and took off. He says nobody will bother us if we just squat on it and start some pigs on a couple of acres. Not directly on the Medicine, but close enough to carry water afore we get a well dug. It's close enough to school for Ron and Millie. Zilly is for it. In fact, she seems surprisingly enthusiastic. I think just finally gettin' started at puttin' down some roots appeals to us all."

They had Henry's wagon almost full and were about to start on Traisley's. It was actually the Deteaus' wagon, which Danny had borrowed for the day. They had started out before first light to get several miles out of Kiowa where the bones were still in abundance.

"Geez, Hank, look over there at the edge of that ravine."

Henry casually glanced over and then stiffened a little.

"Lordy, Dan, are those all wolves? There must be at least a couple dozen of 'em."

"Yeah, and I don't like that at all. Vautier told me some cowboys up from the I.T. were reporting lots of 'em wandering around, pretty hungry and aggressive. Says the lack of buffalo is hard on them, too! These here horses must look like dinner to them."

"Well, it may not just be the horses, Danny. They may also like to dine on us two-legged fooljacks pickin' up bones beside the horses! We probably look like easy prey, and goddamn, I'm not too sure we ain't. You got your Winchester in the wagon?"

"No, I don't, Hank. It's Deteau's wagon. I didn't think to bring my rifle. I just got my Colt."

"Shit, Dan, this could be bad. I got my shotgun but only a half dozen or so shells in the box, and my Colt. I sure wish we could put one or two of 'em down from this distance."

"What do you suggest?"

"I don't know quite yet, but they're definitely onto us now. Look at 'em. They're all turning toward us and those ears are all peaked up. They're riveted on us for shore."

The two men stood and watched more than thirty gray wolves lower their heads and slowly approach the wagons. As though somebody pushed a button in their brains, the two horses were instantly going crazy.

"Jesus, Dan, we got to unhitch these horses fast, now!" Henry said as both men jumped into action. Within a minute or less, both mounts were free of the wagons and both men had made a decision.

"I think we have no choice but to try to run for it, Hank."

"I agree, but I'm sure that pack can outrun these nags. Have that Colt at the ready. Lemme grab my shotgun and shells and let's git, straight back to town." *God, I hope we can make it,* he prayed.

They mounted and wheeled the horses around. The race was on. At most, two hundred yards separated the wolves from the men.

"These horses will keep the distance for a half mile out of fear and adrenalin, but they just won't be able to stay ahead," screamed Hank.

"Maybe we oughtn't push 'em to the limit!"

Wolves at the Door

"OK, you're right, even 'em out, maybe get a little farther. But they're still gonna go down well before town. Those sonsabitches will be on us in a few minutes Danny, I'm sure of it!"

The wolves began to close the gap. Slowly at first, then quite rapidly. In short order they were only twenty yards behind. Then two or three charged up, lightening fast, and nipped at Biscuit's heels. Another took a slashing bite out of Deteau's horse's exposed belly. The horse jumped in panic, stumbled and fell. She rolled partially over Danny, who miraculously didn't break anything. Henry pulled around and placed himself and Biscuit between Dan and the wolves. He then blew one of their heads off with his double barrel. His second blast missed completely, but the noise and the dirt explosion caused the pack to howl off in temporary retreat.

"Jesus, sonsabitchin' Christ, Dan, you OK?" Henry asked.

"I guess so, Hank, but that there horse ain't. He's squirmin' in agony. His front leg is hangin' on by a thread."

The wolves regrouped and were again approaching. Henry reloaded and delivered one blast into them, then a second shot about ten yards to the right of the first in hopes of scaring a larger number of them.

"Hank, it's good to scare 'em and maybe disable a few, but they'll be back quick. I think you're shootin' the wrong animal!"

Henry and his friend locked eyes, and without further discussion Dan Traisley stood up, pulled out his pistol and

Wagon Ho!—New Beginning in Kiowa

shot the disabled Deteau horse just behind the ear. Mercifully, it barely twitched, dying instantly.

"Hurry, get on here, Dan," Henry said, extending one arm down. Traisley swung up on Biscuit and off they went.

"I hope to God this ol' girl can take double the weight. At least if we can put some distance between us and Tim's horse ... look back, Dan, are they comin' after us?"

"Yes, well, no, well, a few of 'em are, but most is turnin' back to the dead horse. Just keep Biscuit goin', Hank."

As one mile turned into two, the last three wolves stopped, howled maliciously at the two mounted men and totally exhausted horse and turned back to rejoin the pack in devouring Deteau's horse.

"There's town, Dan. Just about a mile or so ahead. They all gone now?"

"Yeah, thank the Lord. Let's stop. They ain't comin' back. I'll bet that poor horse looks like the buffalo skeletons by now. And poor Biscuit's about dead, too. Stop, and let me off."

Hank let Danny drop off and then he dismounted also. They slowly walked Biscuit back to town. They hardly spoke, but both men were clearly shaken by their near brush.

As they entered the outskirts of Kiowa, Boney happened to see them. He was tearing apart an old abandoned wood plank building. There were several of these outbuildings made from disassembled wagons scattered around town.

Wolves at the Door

"Howdy, fellas!" called Boney, innocently adding, "Whatcha been up to? Keepin' the wolves away from the door?" Without pausing for an answer, he continued, "I'm fixin' up this ol' outhouse for me and Inga and Darlynne to live in. I guess we all should have brung along our wagons and as much plank boards as we could carry. At least they make a barely passable cabin for a real small family. Say, you two look a little tuckered, and ol' Biscuit looks totally whipped! And come to think of it, Danny ... where the hell's yer horse?"

See a Man About a Horse!

As news of the near tragedy spread around town, it was accepted by the "old timers" as just another calamity that could befall anyone living in frontier Kansas at any time. The newer folks weren't so casual about it.

"Saints in Heaven, Henry," Tamsen said, "don't go off half cocked like that again. I ain't too keen on raisin' this passel of hooligans you gave me all by myself. Especially here at the edge of the earth where you decided to bring us."

"Very interesting, dear," Zilly said as Dan sat glassy eyed on a stool, putting back a glass of some very questionable corn whiskey. "By the way, you haven't seen my good black dress have you? I'd hate to think you'd get eaten by wolves and me with nothing to wear to the funeral."

"Gee, Dan, that's an awful story," said an obviously concerned Timothy Deteau. I can only imagine the fear and trepidation going through your mind through all that. And

Wagon Ho!—New Beginning in Kiowa

you still have to go back out there, with a well-armed posse of course, to retrieve our wagons and your buff bones. But when Jane asked why I was walking out the door so fast when she told me what happened, why, all I could think of to say was, 'I've got to go see a man about a horse!'"

When Boney related the story to Inga, she didn't see the big deal. "Go avay, volf, shoo boy, go on, git! That's vhat I vould've said. You men make such a big palaver about everything."

The wolf problem was truly serious, and getting worse. It very well could have been from the lack of either old or very young buffalos that were easy to prey upon. But whatever the reason, local cattlemen, as well as drovers, didn't take kindly to finding beef carcasses picked clean by wolves. If some yahoo wanted to venture out unarmed or under armed and get picked off, well, that was his business. But cattle was money, and nobody wanted to feed money to the wolves.

Poison bait worked somewhat. It was mostly used to get one specific lobo, one problem canine who was known to be pestering the cattle in one locale.

But the better way to try to corner and kill a larger number of wolves was circle hunts. A group of hunters would fan out along the perimeter of a large circle, maybe a few miles in circumference. They would then converge on a pre-determined center spot, driving wolves and coyotes in. For the sake of safety, no rifles were allowed; wolves caught in the circle were killed with shotguns, clubbed to death by hand or torn apart by dogs.

Wolves at the Door

"This may be a pretty grisly scene, Bobby. You sure you and Charlie want in?" Henry asked his eldest son.

"Yeah, Pa, it'll be fun. I'll get those mangy critters back for almost gettin' you and Mr. Traisley," Bob said with his usual bravado.

"I'd drop the swagger, son. Those poor critters was only tryin' to eat. Today's hunt isn't about revenge or being a tough man. It is necessary to protect some cattle. Now, go get Charlie and let's go."

The day went as planned. Being mid-winter, 1880, the ground cover had died off some, making the prey easier to see and flush. By the time over a hundred fathers and sons, as well as a few mothers and daughters, formed the circle and closed it in, at least a dozen wolves were trapped. Shotguns blasted, and most of the animals fell dead. The hunt was deemed a success.

"C'mon in, Father, how'd it go?" Tamsen asked at the end of the day as her three menfolk came through the door of their Kiowa House rooms. "Did you get yourselves any critters?"

Henry and Charlie entered first and were obviously tickled about something. They were a bit grimy from the day's hunt and immediately went to the washbowl.

"Sure did, Mother. I shot one big gray, and believe it or not, ol' Charlie here got hisself two. By the way, what was that we all had for early breakfast? I forgot."

Puzzled, she said, "Eggs 'n' gravy 'n' grits, why?"

"Oh, no reason, it's just that—"

Wagon Ho!—New Beginning in Kiowa

"Bobby! Bob Devon!" Tamsen shrieked as number one son skulked through the door. "What on earth is that awful lookin' mess all over your coat and pants? And phewie, awful smellin', too. Henry, what did you allow that boy to get into?"

"Don't look at me, Mother," he said. "The Big White Hunter here and his crazy friend IBar Johnson had the last already shot-up wolf hunkered down right in front of 'em. These brave boys were movin' in to club the poor critter, who already had the whole top of his head blowed off. Ol' IBar swung first with a pretty stout fence post and really caught that dying gray smack on."

Henry was chuckling, but Charlie was laughing so hard he had tears in his eyes.

"Well, what's so all fired funny?" Tamsen asked as Bob just glared at the other two.

"Them's brains, Ma, wolf brains," roared Charlie with delight.

Tamsen gasped and swung her gaze back to son Robert's coat and pants. "Oh my word. Henry, how could you?"

"Mother, I had nothing to do with this." Henry said with his two hands up over his head in surrender. "I was two hunters away. How was I to know IBar would splatter wolf brains all over Bob?"

"Well for the love of Pete, son. Come here and let me look at that mess. Just look at that. Well, get out of that coat and take off those pants. We'll soak 'em in the tub."

She then squinted and looked a little closer. "What in the ... Father, I never saw anything like this. What could that wolf have been carrying inside his skull? What on earth is that yellow stuff, and look at all that brownish mess. What is all this? This ain't just brain material."

"No it isn't, Mother," Henry said. "I think if you look real close you'll find a pretty big load of eggs, gravy, and grits!"

Charlie let loose with howls of glee as the situation came into focus for Tamsen. As Bob got one more whiff of his coat and reacted, Charlie ran out the door yelling to anyone who would listen, "Bobby barfed up his guts all over some wolf brains ... and he's doin' it again right now!"

Wild and Wooly Western Town

"We picked a helluva time to show up here, Hank," said Tim Deteau.

"Yeah," Dan Traisley echoed. "This here drought isn't making pig raisin' much easier, either. Seventy-nine was bad for rain, and seems we haven't gotten a drop so far in '80."

The two-year drought and resulting crop failure were very real. This type thing had happened now and then back in Bourbon County, but it seemed more painful here.

"Have you fellas heard of the new Drought Relief Act just passed? Sounds like some of our friends may get help gettin' through this," Henry said. "Maybe even you, Dan."

Wagon Ho!—New Beginning in Kiowa

"Why? It only applies to leavin' your homestead for a while doesn't it? That don't help me none. Zill and I are stayin' put. We just ain't having an easy time keepin' the pork fed and watered. Same as everyone else."

"I guess that's so," Henry said. "But I know several fellows are gettin' off their spreads for a while, till the rains come back. Ol' Uncle Sam must think lettin' them take a little time off the prove-up years will encourage 'em to stick it out. But I guess it don't apply to Tamsen and me neither. We ain't going nowhere. And of course we don't have a homestead anyway."

Tamsen and Henry had for some reason dragged their feet in applying for a Preemption or Homestead grant. They had begun to build a small herd on land they leased to graze. Henry and Bob, now seventeen, had built up to almost three-dozen head of cattle. They just let their cattle join a couple of other herds. They paid a little to do it, but not much. Life at the Kiowa House had been pleasant, and Tamsen thought they should live in town for the kids' schooling.

"I agree with that part of it," Henry said, "but we shouldn't waste too much more time before we start buyin' our own ranch. 'Fore long, the herd will be big enough to justify a quarter section. There's land still available over in Harper County, not as much left here in Barber. Most of what was available near town is already bought up."

Throughout 1880 and most of 1881, the Devons bided their time. They and their friends' primary goal was to just hang on. The rains finally did come back, and the cows got to eat, drink and grow fat again.

Wolves at the Door

"Did you see that fancy saddle the Medicine Sand boys gave Wilson?" Dan Traisley asked Tim Deteau. Dan was referring to Abner Wilson, who headed the well-run Medicine River and Sand Creek Cattle Pool. They had just had an extremely successful round-up to close out 1881, and everyone was elated.

"Sure did. Ol' Tom Miller told me it cost a hundred smackers. Says it is a humdinger of a saddle. Miller is so old he's had his ass on about a thousand saddles. That old Texas trail bum shore enough knows good leather. If he says it's a top rate saddle, I'd bet it is."

"I was there when A.W. presented it to Abner," Henry said. "The damn thing is breathtaking. Zinc covered leather-lined taps, bearskin covered saddle, monogrammed with Abner's initials and brand, and a silver plate engraving 'to Ab Wilson from his friends.' The whole shootin' match. Absolutely gorgeous. So when A.W. gets up to present it, everyone expects a flowery speech."

"Well, I 'spect so, what'd he say?" Deteau asked.

"You wouldn't believe it. He puffs up like he's gonna deliver the Gettysburg Address and says, 'Abner, there's your saddle. I wish you'd take it away. I ain't got room for it!' And he sits down."

"Yer kidding, that's all he said?"

"Yeah. Abner looked flummoxed and everyone else was lockjawed. About ten seconds went by, then the whole room, including Wilson, totally erupted in howls. Best speech any of 'em ever heered."

Wagon Ho!—New Beginning in Kiowa

Kiowa was by some measure booming through 1881. New buildings were going up, while existing ones were being painted. The Kiowa House was always busy, and the stable connected to it was enlarged. Marshal Mike O'Shea never had a dull moment. Just as fast as the cowpokes would get out of line, he'd throw them in the pokey. Kiowa was turning into a prototype wild and woolly western town.

A desperado named Jim Talbot was reputed to lead a gang of horse thieves working out of Kiowa. They went over to Caldwell and killed a former Wichita chief of police. This led to an unsuccessful posse chase into the I.T., which served only to get the local hotshots all lathered up.

"Maybe I should go with 'em to get the sonsabitches," young Bob suggested to his father.

"You stay put, son. No sense runnin' all over the countryside when we got cattle and horses to tend to here. 'Sides, you already got your name in the paper real good lately!" Henry was kidding about an article in the paper identifying Bob Devon and IBar Johnson as the "ugliest and laziest men in Barber County." It was referring to a story about a lyceum or debate contest, all in fun.

"Yer boy there didn't come out quite as good as our girl," Harlan Dwyer said. Little Belle Dwyer had been voted "the handsomest baby." Everyone except Bob and IBar thought this was all very funny.

A Citizen of These United States?

In these years, the important players in the birth of Kiowa slowly filtered into the old town. Not the least of whom was Mr. Dennis T. Flynn. He showed up in 1882.

"Thought I was coming to the land of shootouts 'n' rattlers, of Injuns and rustlers, which I was," said the young lawyer some years later. "I expected the worst of danger and pestilence when I first rolled into town. But what I got was measles."

He told of leaving Kiowa to go visit his folks in Chautauqua County in December of that year, 1882. He had gotten about a dozen miles up Sand Creek to the cabin recently built by Henry and Tamsen, who had finally gotten moving on some permanency where they were grazing their cows. Flynn had ridden out to their ranch by nightfall, in time for supper.

"I noticed several of their kids, Frank and Ollie, and maybe young Tom, had red spots on 'em," Dennis would say, giving his account. "I didn't think much of it, but I sure did a couple of days or week later at my parents' home. I came down with the measles in spades. And I'd druther have had a gunshot wound or snake bite any ol' day! I've been thankin' Hank and Tamsen for that ever since."

The Medicine River and Sand Creek Cattle Pool, formed in 1881, became an integral part of the Devon family's life. Through it, they met several people who were extremely important to their course of action. One was J.L.B. Ellis, known as Jesse.

Wagon Ho!—New Beginning in Kiowa

"Jess, Tamsen and I consider you one of our most trusted friends," Henry said as the two men sat at a table at the Kiowa House. "Let me buy you a beer."

"Uh oh, Hank. I know I'm about to be had when an old coyote like you gets generous with his beer buyin'. What's up?"

"Jess, you 'n' me both came to this here metropolis in '78, but you got more to show for it than me. We've been comfortable here at the hotel, but we gotta do two things. One is buy or build a respectable house right here in town. That can wait a bit longer till we see about the train business. But train or no train, my other necessary task is to get my name on a quarter section. Most likely up where we're grazin' now, in the Medicine Sand Pool. I know you got plenty of land up there already. What do you think of that, Jesse?"

"I been surprised you haven't done it by now, Hank. I probably was lucky enough to come in here from Massachusetts with a bit more backing than a lot of you fellas, so I got a jump on buying up some grazin' acreage. I guess it's no secret I now have my ol' John Hancock on a couple thousand acres up there. Hank, I not only don't need it all, but I'd also feel real good about havin' you and Tamsen as neighbors. And so would Ella. What you lack in brains and beauty, your handsome and well-bred wife more than makes up for." He snorted a laugh and rapped his knuckles on the table, making the beer in their glasses jump.

"I have a pretty nice quarter that just nips at the edge of the Medicine. I'm sure Beyersdorf and Whittenburg would carve off a little of theirs, too, if need be. You just say the word and we'll work it out, Hank. But 'fore you decide, I got maybe a better idea for you. We all, of course, homesteaded that land, or bought real cheap. I'd surely sell at a good price, 'specially to you and Tamsen and those unruly kids of yours. 'Specially to ol' 'ugly and lazy Bob,'" he added, winking. "But first listen to this."

Henry held up two fingers to his son-in-law, Jim Dwyer, the proud new owner of the Kiowa House. Jim brought over a couple of fresh brews and set them on the table.

"Uh oh, if this is turning into a two-bottle discussion, should I go tell Mother Devon to bolt the doors and padlock the safe?" Jim said.

The young man had turned out to be a wonderful son-in-law for the Devons and husband for Libby. The birth of Belle, Kiowa's "handsome baby", had further cemented the Dwyer/Devon family.

"No, but Mr. Ellis and I are talkin' about money issues, so it could soon turn into a three-bottle negotiation," Henry said.

"Hank," continued J.L.B., "why don't you first look into applying, like I first did, for a Homestead. I know there's none left right near Kiowa in Barber County, but there is up yonder aways in Harper. I, for a fact, know of a quarter, a right good section, that I was gonna buy myself. It actually does touch the Sand Creek, at least a corner does. It's a real nice quarter. I can't no longer qualify as a homestead, but I'm sure you can. Hank, lemme ask, are you a citizen of these here United States?"

Wagon Ho!—New Beginning in Kiowa

Henry was a little dismayed. Harper County? Homestead Pre-Emption? U.S. Citizen? "Well, no, not exactly. I mean, yes, I like the idea, but no, I ain't a citizen yet. Just never applied."

"That's what I figured. You was born in England, wasn't you?"

"Yeah, I was, in eighteen and thirty-two. Been here since a baby. Canada that is, then into Illinois in the late '40s. Actually, my father went and got hisself naturalized. He was on me to do the same but I just ain't never done it. I did homestead a quarter back in Bourbon County, out of Fort Scott, back in the '60s."

"Yes, but you told me you soldiered, didn't you?"

"I was in the Sixth Militia. Just about got my ass shot off at Westport in '64. Maybe us militia fellas got to bypass the citizen thing but could still get the homestead. I can't rightly remember how it all worked, but I had the deed, signed by President Grant hisself."

"Well, that could be, but I don't think it is a real big problem. Just may be a few more forms to fill out. Why don't you ask Dennis Flynn or Alec? Some lawyer will surely know what to do. Meanwhile, don't you think that may be the way to start your 'land baron' career, then come back to me, or anyone else, a little later to add to your ranch land?" Jesse asked.

"Yes, I do Jess. I knew you'd have some good thoughts. I know this rumor of a train comin' has got to pan out somehow. Don't see where Harper County wouldn't be goodly affected by a track as much as here in ol' Kiowa itself. You're right, and I appreciate your friendship," he said as he held up another two fingers in the direction of his son-in-law.

Right in Front of the Antelopes

"It's the southwest corner of section four in township thirty-four, and some other legal gobbledy gook, up in Harper. That's the piece Jess told me about," Henry said to Tamsen. "I rode out with Flynn today. To me it looks pretty good, and you know why? It's the same quarter we already threw up the little cabin on. Unbeknownst to us, 'cause we were just runnin' cows at random out there, we can actually prove up the land we're already more or less squattin' on. Don't that beat all?"

"Is it good enough to go through five years to homestead?"

"I believe it is. Never looked at it as a permanent ranch, but don't know why not. Why don't we run out there in the morning? Maybe take the kids in the wagon, see what they think."

"Not on your life, Henry. We can do nicely only dealin' with two opinions, yours and mine, not another six. Let's just you and me ride out without the wagon. Leave the kids in school, and Gretta will watch Tommy and Olive if we're late gettin' back."

"You're on, Mother. Let's leave at first light to get a jump on it. Shouldn't take more 'n' a couple of hours at a leisurely pace. That'll leave us time to scout out the

Wagon Ho!—New Beginning in Kiowa

property more than I have in the past. I'll also look to see whatever cows we find with our CX on 'em."

So up they were, just past six A.M. with two horses saddled and a picnic basket neatly tied on behind Tamsen.

"You and Bob at least check in with Sadie and Frank," Tamsen said to Charlie as she mounted up with Henry's helping hand. "Be sure the little ones are over to school before you go in yourselves. After school, we may be back, but keep yer eyes on 'em just in case."

And up the road they went. By eight o'clock they were just approaching the cobbled-together cabin. They had spent a few nights there with the kids, including the time of the measles episode.

"I hope that measles bug is plumb gone from here by now," Henry said. "Let's just head east down what I think should be the south line. I believe Jess says it goes on over to Sand Creek."

"You're my leader, captain."

They gently rode the horses side by side, and so peaceful was the setting that Henry reached over and took Tamsen's hand in his.

"This is really nice, dear. I never thought we'd be lookin' this far out of town for land, but that wasn't so much of a ride. And it's quite lovely out here," he said as he momentarily had a flashback to the wolves episode. That wasn't a concern this time. He had enough firepower on him to stop a whole pack of the critters if need be. But they didn't see a single wolf all day. As they approached the creek they did flush out some grouse. And on the other side of the creek a few antelope were lying down in the scrub while a couple of others were drinking the crystal clear creek water.

"What a paradise this is, Henry. I have a real good feeling about this. We ain't as young as we were buildin' the homesite back in Bourbon. What were we then, barely thirty? Fifty feels a little different than thirty don't it?"

"You throw that picnic blanket down on that sandy bar right over there and I'll show you exactly what fifty feels like," he teased.

"Now don't you go gettin' sparky with me, Mr. Devon, 'specially if you go to startin' somethin' you can't finish!"

"I think you'd be hard pressed to remember a time I didn't finish what I started, Mrs. Devon. And I sure as hell would hate to say we were out here all alone in our new-found Garden of Eden, and let the opportunity slip through our fingers."

They laughed as they dismounted. She took down the picnic basket while he spread out the blanket on the very spot he had indicated. They flopped down, stretched out and looked up at the sky.

"You know what, dear," Henry said, "iffen I had a chance to start out all over again, and follow exactly the same path we been on these last almost twenty-five years, I'd do it all again. I'd do it even if I knew we'd have to bury John and Mary. I'd do it and accept every hard bump along the way. Our first homestead, the Westport fight and all the killin' before it, the wagon ride out here, everything. I'd do it all again, but only if you was at my side. My father once told me, referring to my ma, that nothing in life was any fun without a good woman, yer own woman, by yer side. He was right. I know I don't remember to tell you very often how much I love you, but I do. I'm tellin' you now."

She soaked his words in and answered. "We been blessed, Henry. Not everyone could say what you just said. And you know I feel the same. Layin' here with you, in this beautiful countryside, lookin' up at the sky—"

Before she could finish he rolled over on his side, put his arm over her and kissed her. Then he kissed her again. And then, by God, he went right ahead and got sparky. Right in front of the antelopes, who didn't seem to give a damn one way or the other.

"Well, sir," she said a little while later, "I guess you sure enough can finish what you start."

"Thank you, ma'am. I aim to please," he said as he pulled up his jeans and she readjusted her skirt. "Now that my stud service is complete, how 'bout that picnic lunch? A man can't work hisself to death just pleasurin' every dang female he passes without some culinary repast. Serve it up, woman!"

She chuckled, and as she told him he was like one of Dan Traisley's pigs, she was opening the basket and getting out food and drink.

They finished in short order, took a brief snooze and then waded in the creek.

"It's past noon. Let's ride the circuit of this quarter so we can say we actually did something out here other than love nestin'."

"As I said this mornin', you're my leader, captain."

They got enough of a purposeful look at the quarter section to agree it was a fine spread and that they wanted to proceed with it.

"Let's get back to town and I'll rustle up Flynn to see about making it legal." They were back rounding up their children by four o'clock.

You, Sir, Are a Dead Man!

"Good mornin', Tamsen!" said Dennis Flynn. "Fine day to fill out these homestead papers, ain't it? Let's just sit here in the lobby, Henry. Unless you folks would rather go up to your room. You know, for privacy's sake."

"This here is fine, Dennis. How 'bout that table and chairs in the far corner?"

The three of them strode over to the quiet corner and sat down. Mr. Flynn got out his Pre-Emption Proof/Testimony of Claimant form, spread it out on the table and cleared his throat.

"OK, Hank, I ask these questions and you answer 'em. Ready?"

"Shoot!"

"OK, this is, let's see … southwest quarter, section four, township thirty-four, south-range nine west. Correct?"

"Keerect!"

"And your name is William Henry Devon?"

"Yessiree! Except I never use the William."

"That's OK, but I got to put down your legal name. Now, let's see, uh … how old are you, Hank? Tamsen looks about thirty-eight, and you look about ninety-eight. That about right?"

"Close, Dennis, but Tamsen's fifty and I'm fifty-one."

"And you're the head of a family of six?"

"Yes, I'm absolutely the head of it. That OK for me to say that, Mother?"

Tamsen nodded and they both grinned.

"OK, now here's the question. You're not a native born citizen, right?" asked Flynn.

"Right. Born 1832 in Sidbury, England. That's in Devonshire. Came across as a kid with my parents. We came in at Chicago in 1849 from Canada. He is a naturalized citizen. I just never got around to it. Is that a serious problem?"

"I hope not," said the attorney. "It really shouldn't be. But we need you to apply for citizenship pronto. Your Union soldierin' will help. Let's move on here. You ever file for Pre-Emption before?"

"Well, I don't remember filing on a form like this. We did get a homestead on a quarter section back in Bourbon County. We were on it during the war years, '61 or '63. I know we were on it by '64 at the time of my militia battle up at Westport. Somehow I ended up with the patent deed from U.S. Grant hisself. Sold out and came here in '78."

"Well," Flynn said, "that may have been a different thing. If being a citizen didn't come up, maybe it was given to Union militiamen. Anyway, let's just say no."

"Whatever you think, I can't rightly remember."

"Can that get us in trouble, Dennis?" Tamsen asked.

"Naw, they never check this stuff out anyway. I think you could say you had a homestead on Mars signed by Julius Caesar and it'd sail on through. Now, let's see … when did you first make any kind of settlement on this property you're applying for now?"

"Well, we've been sorta squattin' on a little makeshift cabin since June of last year, 1882. We've just been slowly adding to it, not really knowin' we was gonna apply for it," said Henry.

"What is it, the cabin? How big, any other out buildings?"

"It's a log cabin. We was lucky to find logs. Got 'em from Boney Korzack when he tore down the old Jennings cat house in town. Lots of folks thought we was gettin' too civilized for that ratty old whorehouse right on Main Street, so Boney got the job and gave me the old logs. Other'n that it would've been a soddie."

Tamsen harrumphed and looked straight ahead while she lectured, "Well, good riddance! No loss, that den of evil gettin' tore down."

"You might want to ask your son Bob about that, Mother," Henry said. "I think he and IBar was just about planning a trip into that establishment. Said something

Wagon Ho!—New Beginning in Kiowa

about taking Charlie with him, too," he added to the lie, just to get her goat.

"Father! You hush your mouth. If that boy even thinks about—"

"Folks! Folks! Let's get back to the matters at hand. OK, how big is the cabin?"

"It's sixteen-by-eighteen with a twelve-by-twelve kitchen we've just added on. We got a stock corral, a branding pen and, of course, a well. That's about it," Henry said.

"Value?" asked Flynn.

"Somewheres between four and five hundred if we'd paid for the whorehouse logs."

"Henry!" Tamsen shrieked. "Must you so crudely tarnish our legal dealings with Mr. Flynn? And if Bob ever goes into—"

"OK folks." Flynn again interrupted. He held up his hand as if refereeing a prize fight. "Let's not get sidetracked. Use…what are you doing with the place now?"

"We graze cows," Henry said. "We also cut hay out there. And we use it as a weekend home sometime, like when you visited and got the measles."

Henry was now chuckling at his own wit, and he really didn't know if it was over the measles or the whorehouse comments, but both Tamsen and the lawyer looked piqued. "That's what we'll always do out there, Dennis, just run cows. It's way too sandy to grow anything. No good for plantin', just grazing cattle."

Flynn filled out the rest of the form, signed it and had Henry sign it.

"That's it, folks. Now the hard part. Let's see if you can prove up on it over the next five years. As you know, you may get a little interference from locusts, grasshoppers, wind, drought, snakes, blizzards and what all. But just keep addin' to your CX herd, and by 1888 you may just have another patent deed with another president's name on it, whoever he may be!"

"Or we may fail out," Henry admitted. "Who knows, we may have to give it up and return those old logs back to Boney so he can put 'em back into service in their previous employment. That'd make Bob and IBar and Charlie happy."

Tamsen just glared.

"By the way, Hank, did you fill out the personal property form for Harper County? I've got one here. You may as well get off on the right foot," Flynn said.

"Yeah? Oh OK, what is it? Go ahead and ask us what they need."

"How many horses?" Flynn asked.

"How many, dear?" Henry asked Tamsen.

"Fifteen."

"What're they worth?" Flynn asked.

"What do you think, dear?" Henry asked.

"Three-fifty, maybe four hundred. Put three-seventy-five!"

Wagon Ho!—New Beginning in Kiowa

"OK." Flynn wrote the information on the form. "How many head with the CX on 'em now?"

"Seventy-five," Henry said. "We just branded last week."

"Value?"

"About seven hundred, give or take."

"Any other material items, your wagon?"

"Still the same old one we made the trip out in. Falling apart. Not hardly worth nothin'. Put down ten dollars. Almost worth more as firewood."

"Well, that should do it," Flynn said. "Grazin' cows and cuttin' hay. No other activity? You two never use the land for any other purpose?"

"Well, to tell the truth," Henry said, "my love here and I did go out the other day, and we did engage in a rather frolicking adventure!"

Tamsen's eyes bugged out, her breath caught short and she began to see her whole life pass before her eyes.

"Really, folks," asked the uncomprehending attorney, "and what was that?"

"Bare backing!" Henry said.

Tamsen didn't know whether to post bail or shuck corn. She was struck dumb.

"We took the saddles off our mounts for a few minutes just to see how they'd react. They've never been ridden without saddles. They didn't seem to care one way or the other. I enjoyed the naturalness of it, though. Like man and animal together. What did you think of it, Mother?"

She couldn't speak and was considering just passing out on the floor. She just waved her hand in front of her face and nodded, saying, "Warm … isn't it very warm in here?"

"Well, anyway, Dennis, if that's it we may as well call it a day. Tamsen is a little lightheaded as you can see and may want to go lay down."

They shook hands and in parting the lawyer said, "You should sooner or later get around to applying for U.S. citizenship, Hank. I know Tamsen's got it, and you'll have to by the time you prove up in five years."

"I'll do it, Dennis, and thanks for your help." As Flynn departed, Henry called after him, "See you soon!" While trying to stifle his mirth at his wife's distress, he added, "I've got to get my sweetheart here back to rest."

"You, sir, are a dead man," she said. "You just wait till I get you back to our room!"

"Well, if yer gonna be so all fired threatenin' about it, I ain't goin'!"

No Train, No Town

By May of 1883, Dennis Flynn was launching himself as Kiowa's first actual newspaper editor. He had dabbled at his lawyering and had, in fact, gotten the Devons' Pre-Emption

Wagon Ho!—New Beginning in Kiowa

paperwork on track. But his passion for starting a real Kiowa paper was consuming him.

"Know what is just about to happen to make this place absolutely explode?" he rhetorically asked the five or six men at the dinner table. "The train's a comin'!"

"Well, if that's true," Harlan Dwyer said as he and Gretta helped clean off tables, "we all better do something to make sure it goes right by the front door of this hotel."

"Oh, don't worry about that," said Hooz Deteau, now fully grown into a comfortable position with his father's friends. "Where the hell else would they run it?"

"You're most likely right, son, but shouldn't someone from Kiowa be in contact with the railroad boys? You heard anything about anybody talking to 'em, Dennis?" Tim Deteau asked.

"Yes, in fact, that's why I wanted to join you fellas for noon meal today. We got a bit of a committee rounded up—A.W., Augie Hegwer and maybe George Male. They're willing to present our case for Kiowa."

"To who?" Boney Korzack asked. "I hear several lines mentioned. The G.C. and Santa Fe, the Southern Kansas, and the K.C.L. & S. Do we have any idea who we should be talkin' to? And isn't this a sure thing?"

"No, not necessarily, Boney," said Flynn. "Those fellas we're talkin' about, Rumsey, Hegwer and Male, are, as you know, all the landowners here in town that would be sellin' right of way to the railroad. And the railroad may want them to just donate the acreage. I mean, it's a negotiation and anything can happen."

Wolves at the Door

What happened next, to the amazement of all, set the course for Kiowa's biggest occurrence in its storied history. A general conclusion formed that the railroad, whichever one or ones happened to lay track here, would be forced to come right through the old town. This conclusion was wrong. The Santa Fe officials met with the three men from Kiowa and made their offer. Nobody exactly knew which of the three held out for better terms, but for whatever reason, no deal was made. The Kiowa contingent had been a little too smug.

"They did what?" a mystified Tamsen asked Henry as he was explaining the turn of events. They were strolling over to the Kiowa House on a fine September morning.

"I know, I know, no one can believe it. But that's what Flynn is sayin'. They went over to near Campbell's ranch about five miles south of here and somehow struck a deal there. It's over, Mother. We lost out. Damn them guys. I don't think it would have been A.W. who squelched it. I bet it was Hegwer or Male. But how stupid. Poor Harlan, or really poor James 'n' Libby. They was about to buy the hotel, but hell, we're all finished here now."

Several reactionary meetings were held around town. Everybody got their two cents in.

"How the hell did that happen?" Danny Traisley asked. "Jesus, we can't be trottin' these pigs over five miles every time to get 'em on the cars!"

Henry wasn't verbal yet. He was just starting to formulate a plan based on a comment Tamsen had made to him in private. She had said, "It ain't maybe directly out of my

Wagon Ho!—New Beginning in Kiowa

Bible, Father, but there is a quote that I've heard that may apply here. You ever hear anybody say, 'If you can't take Mohammed to the mountain, bring the mountain to Mohammed'?"

Yes he had heard that, but he didn't think her quote would help much in this current dilemma.

"I was just beginning to think we was buildin' a nice little town here," said Tim Deteau, with a moan. "But if all the train folks, the ones travelin' through, and the cattle drovers, and other new folks don't come here, I mean, won't our little town here just up and die?"

"I'm afraid it will," Dennis Flynn said. "It's clear as a bell out here in Kansas and everywhere. No train, no town."

"Here's a plumb loco idea I just conjured up," said a somewhat hesitant Boney Korzack. "You know, I've torn apart about six of the original plank buildings here and moved 'em around the corner. Two of 'em I didn't even tear apart. You know that, Hooz. We just jacked and moved your little house. Now this may set you all into a full gale hoot and holler, but why don't we just move the whole damn town of Kiowa? Just jack it up and move it to wherever the train's goin' by. I've done it before and I can do it again. Regardless of what them sonsabitches back in Fort Scott say, I really ain't all that dumb."

Nobody said a word, dead silence, for almost two minutes.

"Jesus, fellas," Henry said, "you're not gonna believe this. Tamsen said the same thing to me. She said, 'If you can't bring Mohammed to the mountain, take the mountain to Mohammed'! I'm not sure she knew what she was saying, but isn't Boney's idea exactly that? Could we really do that, Boney?"

New Kiowa. I Knew From the Start

On January 1, 1884, the newly organized Kiowa Building Association held its first meeting. The declared purpose was to refurbish some of the main structures in the old town and generally improve its appearance. Now that was beginning to be a questionable endeavor. Henry Devon was elected president; A.T. Wilson, vice president; C.H Vautier, secretary; and Henry's good friend A.W. Rumsey, treasurer.

"We don't really know what we're doin', Mother," Henry said. "A.W.'s got another meeting lined up with the Santa Fe. But this time it's for real. It's going to be near Campbell's ranch. A depot will go in. They got to exactly figure out and survey the track bed, then we got to figure out and lay out lots. I mean, an actual planned town. The streets, school, businesses, home lots, everything. You're a genius, Mother, you and Boney. Why didn't we all think of the idea sooner? And, merciful Lord, if a new town does come to be, my job as president of this old Kiowa Building Association is over before it even starts. Hallelujah!"

"The answer to your question, Father, is … because you're all men, and as such, yer all a trifle slow-witted." She was enjoying this. "I'm surprised Boney caught on, but now and again, one of you is capable of activating a brain cell! And as to the second point, I agree. Hallelujah!"

Wagon Ho!—New Beginning in Kiowa

"Speaking of Boney," he said, "we gave him the honor of submitting the first candidate for a name for the new town. I was thinking Plainsview or Pleasant Valley or Tumbleweed, you know, something descriptive and pretty. You know what he comes up with? New Kiowa! You ever hear of anything sillier than that? New Kiowa." He laughed. "Like we move old Kiowa five miles and call it New Kiowa. How unimaginative is that?"

She paused for a moment and then said, "I like it. It conjures up progress. The word "new" indicates new and better improvements and leaving Kiowa in it kinda suggests permanence or stability, don't ya think?" She excused herself to the privy, leaving Henry standing with a blank stare and a dropped jaw.

By the next meeting of the building association, Henry had recovered. "Ladies and Gentlemen! Hush up and let's get this here meetin' going. My first and probably last order of business is to congratulate our good friend Boney Korzack on, first, his wonderful idea to simply move our town to the train. And second," Henry cleared his throat, "on his name of New Kiowa being selected by you all. I knew from the start that was a most fittin' name." He glanced at Tamsen, whereupon she ostentatiously rolled her eyes. "I have a little news. Of course, you know that Mr. Campbell went up to Topeka to meet with Mr. Robinson, the Santa Fe man. As of the telegram I hold in my hand here, we now know the deal's been made." Everybody applauded. "Now that we're all on the right track,", he paused waiting for further applause for his intended pun, but none came, "it is now our job to, well, finish our job here. I move we disband this here building association committee of old Kiowa. We got to take the first steps to start layin' out New Kiowa. I hereby quit ... and you're all fired." Again, everybody applauded

Dropped Like a Tomato Off the Vine

The very first business to be moved to New Kiowa was the Kiowa House. As much lodging space as possible would be needed quickly. However, one odd occurrence happened in the hotel at its original spot in the old town shortly before it was moved.

"A bank robber?" Gretta Dwyer said. "Here? He stayed here with us last night?"

"Actually, two nights ago," Libby said to her mother-in-law. Ate supper right at the window table. Jim says he did remember the man constantly looking out the window like he was expectin' someone. Seems the feller slept here, then went up to Medicine Lodge and robbed a bank."

"Which one?" asked Harlan.

"Don't rightly know, yet," Jim said, walking in the door. "But Flynn just got this telegram with an update. The man left here and joined two others in Medicine Lodge yesterday. Robbed the bank and made their escape on three very slow horses. The posse got 'em within five miles. They'd a hung 'em a few years ago, but now with all our hidy-tidy weeping hearts in this state, they'll probably just end up in the state penitentiary."

Wagon Ho!—New Beginning in Kiowa

"I miss the hangings," said A.W. Rumsey, who came striding through the front door. "God, they were good for business. Folks would come for miles to see one, kids 'n' all. They were a nice family event. Lots of folks would spend the night, eat and sleep in this hotel, maybe shop a bit at my mercantile."

"Wasn't that just a tad barbaric, A.W.?" Jim said.

"Yes, Mr. Rumsey," added Libby, "kids, young children, would watch, too?"

"Oh mercy, yes. Most folks thought it was a good lesson for 'em. I'll tell you this, after a good hanging, 'specially if the desperado peed himself—'scuse me ladies—we had very good behavior around town for a week or two. In fact, the most entertaining one was a huge Mexican feller who got strung up for rustling some cows off Andy Drumm's range. Back about '77 or '78, I forget. Don't you remember this, Harlan, or weren't you folks here yet? The man must have weighed near to three hundred pounds, absolutely huge. They'd been using the one big cottonwood at the river ford for hangin's. Oh, c'mon, you must remember this, Harlan. It was such a big event, and this bad man was so dramatically, well, bad lookin'. We knew it would be great for business if we could get a real big turnout. It was about June 28, 29, 30, late June anyway. We talked O'Shea into keepin' him jailed till the July Fourth festivities. The hombre was so big and dumb he didn't seem to mind. The more steaks and beans and corn muffins O'Shea fed him, the more he seemed to like jail. God, he was ugly, scars all over his face."

Wolves at the Door

A.W. paused for a breather. Harlan began to smell a rat in this story, but nobody else did.

"You mean they purposely held the poor man, almost like fattenin' him up for the kill? That is abominable, Mr. Rumsey," Libby said.

"You had to understand the times, Libby. We really weren't real civilized and all like now. And men like Campbell and Drumm and most other big ranchers sorta looked unkindly at rustlers. As you know, our Mike O'Shea is a pretty tough customer hisself, but he couldn't patrol the whole prairie for these bandits. Had to make a pretty stiff example when they did catch one."

"Well, what happened, A.W.?" Jim Dwyer asked.

"Well, as I was saying, we figured to hold it right here in town so's more folks might shop more. Y'know, no self-respectin' well-groomed lady is gonna be caught dead at a holiday hangin' without a new bonnet at least. Lot of 'em came in the day before and bought a new dress! So we built us a scaffold. Nothing fancy. If Boney had been here it could of had a nice platform, trapdoor, the works. But we just did the best we could. Figurin' a little platform would be OK to drop this feller from and could also be used that night to shoot off some fireworks, we threw a six-by-six beam roof to roof from this hotel to the livery next door. Spanned the alley, what, twenty feet or so? Spectators could stand in the street or on the sidewalk across the street. Some young boys even climbed up on the roofs across the street to see better.

"I can't believe we never heard of this, Mr. Rumsey," Gretta said.

Wagon Ho!—New Beginning in Kiowa

"The ol' cottonwood had always had a little bounce to it when a hangee hit the end of the rope." A.W. further explained. "They'd bob up and down for a while. The boys used to bet how many bobs until the corpse came to rest. But this solid beam had absolutely no give."

"This is awful, I don't want to listen to no more," Libby said.

Totally ignoring her, the merchant continued.

"They brought ol' Pancho out, blinkin' his eyes and finishing off a chicken bone. I remember he smelled like an outhouse, had grease, chicken chunks and beans all matted in his beard. Up the makeshift ladder they led him to the small platform. He was so big the man attending him could hardly squeeze beside him to fit the noose. Boy, I can still see the look in that Mexican's eyes as the awful reality of his immediate future slowly dawned on him. 'Course he was handcuffed and his legs were tied together right before the hood went on, but boy did he squirm when the darkness enveloped him. You could hear his pathetic gurgles under the hood."

"Please, Mr. Rumsey, no more. I can't stand no more," Libby pleaded as she and the others hung on every word.

"Well, the henchman didn't take long. Just about simultaneous with the giant relievin' hisself out of both ends—'scuse me ladies—the attendant stepped back onto the ladder and gently booted the man into thin air. The minute gravity was employed, he took the fastest plunge south I ever saw. I guess cause he was so heavy, he dropped like he'd been shot from a cannon." A.W. paused and closed his eyes in deep contemplation. "It was a scene to behold. And the kids loved it."

"Well, A.W., don't leave us hangin' in mid-air like that Mexican," Harlan said, now convinced this was a well-delivered put on. "What in God's name happened?"

"Folks, that man's head snapped off like a tomato from the vine. And just as much red sauce came a shootin' out. His huge body, now free of any rope, simply dropped straight down in a heap. But that head, well it hit the ground a spinnin' and rolled and bounced right through the crowd over to the hotel here's steps. We picked it up, and as God is my witness, Libby, it sat right on that table you're sittin' at now for at least two weeks."

Libby gasped and jumped away from the table.

"It was a wonderful thing, a civic betterment," he continued. "Mrs. Davis charged a nickel for folks to come in and see it, unless of course they was hotel guests or already eatin' a meal here. In which case they got a free peek. Kept it up till it finally got too gamey to put up with."

Mrs. Davis was quietly sweeping over in the corner, but she still grinned and shook her head. She had heard A.W. pull this prank before. Though most of the others had by now caught on, Libby was still in the dark until she glanced at her father-in-law, Harlan, who could no longer hide his laughing countenance. Then it hit her.

"Oh, Mr. Rumsey, you mean man, you awful prevaricator. How could you? I believed the whole story," she said as she pounded the table with her fists. "There wasn't a headless hanging?"

"Libby, there wasn't even a Mexican." He chuckled as everyone else howled. "But I will say this, dear. Every time I've told that story to our local boys, even though they suspect my veracity, they are models of good behavior for at least a few days. Now, Mrs. Davis, I actually came in to inquire on your plans for the Kiowa House."

Thirty Rooms and All New Carpet

"Kiowa House will be moved to the new town," said Mrs. Davis, "but if you want more specific information than that, you better inquire of the new owners." She smiled as she gestured toward the Dwyers. "They'll be taking over soon."

"Really? Well, congratulations, Harlan," A.W. said as he moved to shake Harlan's and Gretta's hands. "No kidding? That's great!"

"We accept your good wishes, Mr. Rumsey," Gretta said, "but they'd be better directed at the actual new owners." She gestured toward James and Elizabeth.

"Well, I'll be darned. This is gettin' confusing!" said a smiling A.W. "And me standing here deliberately pulling the legs of the new Kiowa House owners. Hope you'll still allow me to take a meal and a drink in this esteemed establishment."

"That we will, A.W., that we will. We'll need all the help we can get in the new town," Jim said.

The old building was carefully removed to New Kiowa in September of 1884. The new town had been incorporated on August 6 of that year. On August 12, the name of New Kiowa was officially voted in, and on August 14, lot prices were agreed upon. Main Street lots ranged from $200 to $300; Campbell Street from $75 to $150; other street lots were somewhere in between. After moving the hotel in wagons to a town site, Jim and Libby set about a serious remodeling effort. After a dozen years at the old place, the new Kiowa House was to be a showplace.

"Thirty rooms," Tamsen told Zill Traisley. "That's what they're tellin' us. And all new carpet and furnishings. I just hope they aren't biting off more than they can chew."

"They'll be fine, Tamsen. Everyone agrees the new town is bustin' out all over, and it ain't even built yet. Danny and I are buying a lot on Hopkins Street, so are Boney and Inga. What about you folks and the Deteaus? You stayin' out at the ranch or at the remodeled Kiowa House?"

"We haven't decided on a street or lot yet. Haven't heard from the Deteaus, either. But I feel sure both families gotta have a house in town for the schools. I doubt we'll stay at the hotel anymore. Libby and Jim will need all the rooms for full paying customers."

"Campbell Street, Mother." Tamsen turned to see Henry coming into the mercantile where she and Zill were standing. "I just came from signing up. I apologize for not gettin' your OK, but I was afraid somebody else would snatch it up before you and I conferred. Nice corner lot for a hundred and fifty."

Tamsen momentarily wished he hadn't mentioned the price out loud, but quickly realized the whole agenda, prices and all, were common knowledge. There was no secret about it.

"Well good for you two, and ain't you some uppity rich folks," Zill kiddingly said as she hugged Tamsen.

"Thanks, Zilly," Henry said. "This new place is gonna bust loose from all appearances. Down at the brickyard they're fixin' to make a hundred thousand bricks by year's end. Can you believe that? I think the Deteaus are gonna buy in town, but I haven't seen them."

Activity throughout the balance of 1884 was feverish. Although there was some enterprise in the old town and a few people lingered behind, all direction over the next three years was toward the new settlement. By 1887, old Kiowa virtually ceased to exist. The liveries moved, as did the feed store, as did Vautier's stagebarn. The stagecoach line was the arterial lifeline between towns. People coming and going to and from New Kiowa saw a new metamorphosis each time they returned.

There's Double the Saloons.

"We're mighty impressed with your little town, Mr. Devon," said Arthur Gregory and his fellow Missourian, Mike Woodworth. "We're here only temporarily, but I'm buying a home lot and another one to build a hardware store on. Came in on the stage almost by accident

Wolves at the Door

from Attica. We was on our way to Hazleton and got snowed in here."

"Well, glad to meet you," Henry said as they shook hands in A.W.'s new mercantile store. "The more the merrier."

"Exactly how many buildings are up now, Mr. Devon, by the first of '85?" Woodworth asked.

"Well, I know almost exactly," Henry said, relying on a conversation he had had with Rumsey at the end of January. "It's about forty-five, counting residences. One hotel, our Kiowa House, and three restaurants, a furniture store, three groceries, two drug stores, four saloons, three lumber yards, four livery barns and, of course, this here mercantile outfitter. And saving the best for last, two hardwares. But we can always use a third!"

By the time Gregory had left to get his wife and daughter back east and then returned to New Kiowa a month later, things had changed.

"Holy Saints! "There's double the saloons now. And one, the White Elephant, is built plumb up against my new hardware store, Henry. What's going on?"

"Progress, Mr. Gregory," said Hooz Deteau. "It's a sight to behold. The cowboys comin' in here to deliver their herds are the wildest I ever saw. The White Elephant is like all the others. You can buy beer or whiskey in a glass or one of yer boots! Card games at every table, revolvers at every table. They cornered a tenderfoot from Cincinnati in there yesterday and made him dance a jig with their six-shooters. Two of 'em rode right into Rumsey's store last week, all the way to the back, shootin' holes in the floor and ceiling. Let

Wagon Ho!—New Beginning in Kiowa

their horses drink out of A.W.'s water bucket, then marched 'em out. And then they dismounted, came back and paid A.W. double for the damage. He loved it."

"But your alarm is well founded, Arthur," Henry said. "For the sake of the women and kids, we got to tone this down a bit. We want to keep the cowpokes' good will and business, but got to have some peace 'n' order, too."

At a March 18 town meeting this problem was addressed. Mike O'Shea was again hired to keep the peace. He had been a druggist and a saloon keeper in old Kiowa. He also had been sheriff. Now he was hired as the town marshal.

O'Shea wasn't a big man, but he had absolutely piercing black eyes and ice water in his veins. He was a plucky Irishman—some people called him Black Irish—who was afraid of absolutely no one. But he did succumb to the charms of Miss Gerri Lucas and married her in July of 1885. Theirs was the first wedding on record in New Kiowa.

"Well, congratulations, Mike," said Bob Devon, now almost twenty-two years old and friendly with O'Shea. "You finally found a woman with absolutely no taste in men."

"That's about it, Bob. The only way she could've dipped further into the barrel would be to end up with you! Now you gonna just stand there spoutin' drivel or are you gonna sweep those cells and earn yer pay?"

"Well, for the lousy little bit you pay me, Mike, I think I'm of a mind to lay down on one of these bunks for a nap."

Wolves at the Door

William Robert Devon was now a man. He still lived at home, as did his brother Charlie. But at twenty-two and twenty-one respectively, they were hardly ever there. Both ate some meals and slept at the house in town for the next couple of years, and Tamsen still helped with their wash and other needs. But they were very close to leaving the nest. Marshal Mike allowed them both to help around the jail for a paltry pay. Bob, particularly, was drawn to law enforcement, not due to any excitement, for there was little of that. He just liked the camaraderie. Both Bob and Charlie still worked either the CX brand or the 23, which was another of their father's brands. They also hired out when needed to friends like the Deteaus or big ranchers like Mr. Drumm. But in off-seasons Bob could usually be found at O'Shea's pokey.

A Nekkid Lady at the White Elephant

Bob and the marshal were strolling down the street near the White Elephant on a Saturday night in late summer.

"Look up yonder, Mike. Ain't that Mack Jones on that appaloosa?"

O'Shea squinted and said, "Believe yer right, Bobby. Let's just keep on at this pace towards him. Don't make no eye contact with him, just keep talkin' and laughin' the way we was."

Mack Jones was one of many hard cowboys who would come into New Kiowa now and then, get all drunked up and raise hell. They'd usually do some minor property damage and maybe scare some of the town folks.

Wagon Ho!—New Beginning in Kiowa

On a visit about a month earlier, Jones had purposely embarrassed a smallish man from Ohio out visiting his brother. The fellow was an eye doctor and had expressed an interest in relocating to New Kiowa, which the residents of the new town were happy to hear. All looked promising, until he met Mr. Jones.

The Ohioan and his brother had quietly enjoyed dinner at the Kiowa House and then stepped out onto Main Street. Mack Jones and a half dozen cronies were sauntering by. Mack grabbed the optometrist's bowler off his head and flung it into the air, whereupon the whole entourage of cowboys commenced to shoot it full of holes. By the time it hit the dirt it wouldn't have held shelled peanuts. That part was all right, not much more orneriness than any other Saturday night in New Kiowa. But the Ohioan talked back. He called this behavior an outrage and wanted Jones to pay for the hat. Jones was well liquored and in a bullying mood. He slapped the man across the face and split his lip, causing blood to splatter all over his white shirt. The victim was furious. His brother was livid. The Jones gang thought it quite funny.

Upon arrival of the next morning's stage to Medicine Lodge, a small contingent of town leaders had been on hand to try to dissuade the man from leaving.

"No, thanks, Mr. Rumsey. If these are the conditions you people want to live with, be my guest. Dick, you're my brother and I love you. But I'm not going to live in fear, wondering what the next Neanderthal is going to do to me. Come see me next time you're back in the buckeye state."

Wolves at the Door

And he got on the stagecoach and left. Preventing incidents like that one was precisely why Mike O'Shea had been hired.

As O'Shea and Bob got closer to the mounted Mack Jones, Bob began to get nervous. He knew he had a ringside seat to whatever was going to happen. Bob talked a big game but rarely delivered. From his earliest boyhood his bark had always been worse than his bite.

"What're you gonna do, Mike ... 'er, what should I do?" he whispered.

"Bobby, as soon as we are kissin' distance from Jones' leg, you yell 'Lordy, Lordy, Marshal, ain't that lady on the sidewalk at the White Elephant bare nekkid?' and yell it loud and point over there. Got it?"

"I guess so, Mike, but-"

"Just yell it loud and point, Bob."

As they got within six or eight feet of the cantankerous cowboy on his horse, Jones noticed who was approaching. He immediately fingered his revolver and prepared to draw it.

"You halt right there, O'Shea. Don't you come no closer, 'cause I ain't goin' with you."

"Lordy, Lordy, Marshal!" bellowed Bobby Devon. "Ain't that a bare nekkid lady right there at the White Elephant?" He didn't need to point. Not only did Mack Jones immediately swing around in his saddle to see, so did his six friends and every other man within earshot.

Even A.W. Rumsey came running out the front door of his mercantile shouting, "What? Where? Where the devil is she?"

Wagon Ho!—New Beginning in Kiowa

All but Marshal O'Shea. He leapt forward, cat-like, at the momentary diversion and grabbed Jones by his belt and pants. With one Herculean jerk of his left hand, he propelled the cowboy out of his saddle into thin air. With his right hand he drew his Colt. As soon as Jones hit the street in a stumbling display of confusion, turning toward O'Shea in speechless protest, the marshal swung the two and a half pound metal mass with all the force he could muster.

Years later, Mack Jones, who eventually saw the light and became a pretty good citizen was heard to say, "That little mick was a damned good marshal. I'm lucky and grateful to have left his esteemed company with my life. And he was gentleman enough I'm told—'cause I was out cold at the time—to pick up this purty right ear and put it in my pocket so's Doc Tyler could sew it back on as best as possible."

This event enhanced the marshal's reputation in New Kiowa and surrounding towns.

"He is truly one tough and incredibly brave man," Henry said around the supper table. "And your speech, Bob, will go right along with 'Four score and seven years ago' and 'Give me liberty or give me death.' I can just see it now carved in a stone monument up at the state house ... 'There she is, a nekkid lady',"

"And the best part," Charlie added, "is that Bobby missed the whole thing. He kept watching for a nekkid lady over at the saloon. He yelled it so loud he believed it hisself!"

Tamsen looked at her men with a disapproving scowl. "What do we pay Mike to be marshal, Father?"

"One hundred dollars a month. And keep this under your hat, but we got a surprise for him. The town's paying for a solid gold police badge for him as thanks for his doing such a good job."

"I wouldn't mind goin' into police work myself," Bob said. "I mean, sorta like Mike. I'd keep ranchin', but as part-time here or some other town, or even full time. I like it."

Assuming You're Their Father

The Devon family had been in Barber County for seven years. "Unbelievable," Henry said when discussing the subject at a Sunday picnic with Tamsen. They had gone with several other families to a favorite grassy meadow abutting the Medicine River, barely a half-mile north of town. The riverbank gently sloped down to a sandbar on which a dozen or more kids fished, swam and splashed around.

"Look at 'em, Mother. I absolutely can't believe Libby there is holdin' her own little baby. Where on earth has the time gone? And look at ol' Hooz over there with that beautiful gal of his. Eliza? That her name? She's a beauty! He's a full bloomed man now and becomin' a fella to deal with. He'll probably be mayor here someday. They gotta be proud of him." Henry lay on his side and chewed on a long grass stem.

Wagon Ho!—New Beginning in Kiowa

Tamsen took off her sunbonnet and leaned back against the picnic basket. "I know, dear, and I can almost get more used to our older children growin' up than the babies. Sadie and Frank is almost becomin' growed. And Ollie and Tommy, look there at Tommy."

Young Thomas Albert Devon, Tommy, Tom was now nine years old. He had been at Tamsen's breast years ago on the wagon trip to Kiowa. Now he was hardly "the baby" anymore.

"He's runnin' the show with those friends of his as far as I can see," Henry said. "Look at 'em over on the other bank there. Who was the first boy to wade and swim across? Who's always the king of the mountain champ? He seems to have a confidence about him, don't he? Maybe 'cause he seems just a little taller 'n' stronger than the others."

"And maybe 'cause he's had to survive against six older brothers and sisters. He's like a puppy fightin' for a bone in the litter. But he's still my baby boy," Tamsen said.

"And then there's ol' Bob. What is he now, Mother, twenty-one?"

"Lordy, Henry. You got no more accounting for these children than a father polecat. Do you not remember giving him a pocket watch over a year ago on his twenty-first birthday? My goodness, you are a forgetful man!"

"Well, dang, Mother, you done dropped so many of 'em, how's a fella supposed to keep track? Yeah, I guess you're right, he must be twenty-two by now. You think he's on the right track?"

"I'm his mother, Henry. I think they're all perfect. What do you think?"

"I think he's doin' OK. He is showing more spunk than I would've guessed a few years ago. I'm told he puts in a full day when he hires out to Andy Drumm. And if I keep an eye on him he does all right for me. He seems to be talkin' about applyin' for his homestead, which is a good sign. And a little marshalin' part time with O'Shea ain't bad, if he don't get himself kilt doin' it."

"Don't even say that."

"He's OK for now I guess, and Charlie's doin' good, too. Don't you think he's just a more natural go-getter than Bob? Too early to really tell on Frank, but both he and Tommy seem pretty well focused for their ages. And both of 'em damn good lookin' fellas. Of course they get that from me don't ya think?" he said with a straight face.

"That would assume you are actually their father," she said with an equally straight face.

Noah's Ark, Har, Har, Har

The impetus for the very existence of New Kiowa rolled into town on August 4, 1885.

"My Lord and hot damn, Hank, thar she blows!" Boney Korzack said as Engine Number 245 chugged to a stop. The Southern Kansas, formerly the Harper and Western Railroad Company, had kept its side of the bargain. An entourage of town notables, several of whom were the Devons' friends and neighbors, had boarded the first passenger train up in Hazelton for its maiden voyage into town. Off stepped Charles Vautier, Crate Justis and Henry's fellow grangers north of town, Messers Hickle, Stranathan and Noah.

"Hey, Mr. Noah," yelled Hooz Deteau, quite full of himself with his keen humor. "Bet you ain't been so glad to step off a conveyance since yer ark came to rest on dry ground! Har, har, har." He was becoming alarmingly like his father.

The whole town realized what an incredible day this was.

"Thank God we tied up our quarter when we did, Mother," Henry said. "Word has it the minute that train pulled in those ranchers are all adding five dollars an acre to part with any of their spreads. This town is surely on the map now, ain't it?"

As everyone applauded their friends and the dignitaries who were debarking the train, Charles Vautier approached Henry and Tamsen.

"Greetings Hank, and to you, Mrs. Devon. It's good to see you two welcoming us in on this beautiful day. I'm sure you'll be using this train, as we all will."

"Right you are, Charlie," said Henry. "I just can't believe our good fortune. Sure as hell this will give us an advantage loadin' up our stock here rather than havin' to run 'em up to Dodge and into those goddamn diseased longhorns. I know its a train, but it looks from here like our ship just came in."

"I hear you, Hank, I sure do!" the exultant Vautier said. "Oh, and by the way, I haven't seen you since that river incident in January."

Wolves at the Door

Lane and Vautier was the main stagecoach line entering New Kiowa. In January, the Medicine River had bogged down crossings due to rotten ice. Too thin to run over, too thick to boat. Passengers had been forced to hole up in Hazelton until it went one way or the other. On a Saturday morning, the stage finally made a try at crossing the ice. It had overturned half way across.

"I've heard other renditions, but I'd be interested in your version, Hank. I know you came up right behind 'em. In fact, I sure thank you for helpin' that poor woman and child out safely."

"No, you got that wrong. My son Charlie and I did, sure enough, come up on the scene, but other folks had already drug 'em out. I don't want to take credit where it ain't due."

"Did you see anything that would suggest our driver was at fault?"

"No, surely not. I took my team on across at a different spot, which looked about the same. I'm sure it's hard to decide to go or stay put when you got payin' passengers urging you to get movin'. Yer damned if you do or don't. But I'll say one thing that you more'n anyone else must agree with. We sure as hell need a bridge over that river!"

Vautier whole-heartedly agreed. "That lady is lucky to be alive. Forget that we've made that same run hundreds of times in winter. That same driver, Jimmy Van Hook, has even taken it over the ice many times himself. But one mishap can really throw a wrench in our reputation."

Wagon Ho!—New Beginning in Kiowa

"What about this here train, Mr. Vautier?" Tamsen asked. "Will it knock out the need for the stageline?"

"I'm sure not, Tamsen. The train's main benefit is, of course, for the cattle. Human passengers in no hurry can wait for the scheduled train runs. I can't deny they're a sight more comfortable, but they're also more expensive. And if you need to get over to Attica, or Caldwell, or up to Medicine Lodge today or tomorrow, you're probably still going to hop on with Lane and Vautier aren't you?"

The Woman on the Roof

Not too long after this conversation a tragedy involving the river played out before the eyes of the Devons and the Deteaus. For a change of pace, the two couples had planned a day's excursion over in Harper. They booked on the Lane and Vautier stage, and Jimmy Van Hook gave them a nice ride over early on a peaceful summer morning. No sooner did they get to Harper than the sky turned gray and rain came down in sheets. The storm was bad enough there, but the sky was pitch black to the north.

"Folks," Van Hook said, "I sure hate to rush you, but I'm a bit worried about gettin' back home. Unless you all want to stay here overnight, I suggest we get on back. I think the road'll be OK, but I'm worried about the river. That dang stream runs high quicker than any river I cross after a hard rain. And judgin' by the looks to the north, well, I think we'd be wise to hot foot back."

Wolves at the Door

The foursome finished their noon meal in Harper and reboarded the stage.

"Shoot, Henry, Jane and I were discussing all the money we planned to spend here in Lynch's Lace Emporium today," Tamsen said as they settled in for the return ride. "You and Tim are gettin' off Scott free just 'cause of a little sprinkle."

"I know, dear. Tim and I were just discussing how we loved seeing our two lovebirds spend our money. Drat the luck!" Henry winked at Deteau.

The rain slacked off on the trip back, but on approaching the Medicine it was clear a lot of rain must have fallen upriver. It was rolling by in a torrent.

"It's up to you folks, but if we're going across it'd better be now," Van Hook said. "In just a few minutes we'll be stuck on this side for several hours or more. I think we can safely make it, but you're the bosses. What's the verdict?"

"Let's go. I gotta get back for a meetin' with the pastor," Tim said.

"I agree," added Tamsen. "I got no provisions for the children past supper."

"Go, Jimmy," Henry said. "Hit it!"

Off they went. They could feel the pressure against the wheel rims, and a couple of times the wave surge rolled high enough to wet the undercarriage. At about two thirds across, Jim Van Hook yelled out, "Sweet Jesus!" and really lashed the team. "Haurgh, haurgh, haurgh!" he bellowed as he kicked the horses into high gear to the other shore.

"What's up Jimmy?" Henry asked the driver. "Why the panic?"

They all got out on the high slope and looked up river. The problem that Van Hook had been able to see from up top was a huge wall of water rushing down river like a tidal wave. It was a repeat of the Fall River conditions so common to these flash floods.

"Oh my God, Hank. What the hell is that comin' up past the bend?" Deteau asked. "I'd swear that's a roof stickin' out above those bushes 'n' cottonwoods."

"It sure as hell is, Tim. And it's bobbin' along pretty fast. You ever see the likes of this before, Jimmy?"

"Not like this. I swear this is unbelievable. A whole house torn loose from somewhere."

"Oh goodness, oh no!" Jane screamed, pointing at the floating house. "A woman, look!"

"She just crawled out that window onto the roof. What can we do, Father?" Tamsen asked.

Nothing. There was absolutely nothing anyone could do. The house slowly but steadily moved on by. At one point the entire roof with the poor woman clinging on for dear life ripped apart from the house itself. As it carried her by they could hear her muffled, pitiful screams, but they could not distinguish her words over the river's roar. Nobody spoke as the roof progressed another fifty or a hundred yards past them, caught up momentarily on some unseen obstacle, and then disintegrated. It and the woman disappeared beneath the roiled surface and did not come back up.

"She's gone, Tamsen," said Jane as they hugged each other. "I mean, she's gone under. Does anyone see her?"

All were mesmerized. Finally after what must have been a full minute, Henry asked Van Hook, "Jimmy, any way to get downriver to where she was?"

"No, Hank. And the way that current is runnin', she's way past that now. Or jammed under a snag along the way. We can't do a thing."

A few days later the body of Mrs. Frank Shepler was found in the river debris four miles downstream. Another young woman and her five young children were also found caked in mud, all dead. The father and three other children survived.

"How on earth can that happen, Henry?" Tamsen said. They were sitting with a pitcher of iced tea and reflecting on the horrific event.

"I don't know, Mother. But the older I get the more focused I'm becoming on one main reality. The time to zero in on is now! Right now. I don't know why this thought is creepin' into me stronger than it used to—I mean with the war, and Mariah and John and Jeremy, and now this."

"I know, I have the same sensation. That poor woman was probably just tendin' her house only minutes afore that wave swept her away. And as Bobby asked after Jeremy died, why her and not some other woman, or me?"

Wagon Ho!—New Beginning in Kiowa

"But that's not exactly what I'm sayin'. I think I mean, forget all the 'why this or that' questions, and forget the heaven 'n' hell stuff, and forget the 'what ifs.' I think the time to appreciate and concentrate on is now, today, the present. That poor man had a wife and eight kids a few days ago. Now what does he do?"

"Well, for one thing, he has to trust in the Lord. He has to know that Jesus will—"

"Oh, that's pure poppycock, Tamsen." Henry interrupted, surprising even himself. "Look, I don't mean to insult you and a whole lot of other good folks' beliefs, Mother. That's what we fought for. To make this country open so anybody can say or believe or preach whatever they want."

He was clearly worked up, and Tamsen could see he needed to unload something.

"But it should be just as allowed for people who don't go along with all the Jesus stuff to say that, too. I mean, I've thought on this for years and years. I'm truly glad for the comfort you get from your Bible. And I hope the kids get it from you, but look at it this way for a minute. Suppose when we die, well, say it's like a wall that is infinitely thick, deep, wide and high. We can't possibly know what's on the other side can we? Why all this heaven and hell baloney? No man who ever lived and died ever came back to tell us what's on the other side. We can conjecture, we can guess, but the feeling I'm gettin' more and more is, who gives a damn anyway?"

Tamsen was a bit dismayed but couldn't think of a retort. So she simply remained still while he continued.

Wolves at the Door

"Where'd we come from? I mean before this life, where was we? I sure don't know, but it couldn't have been too bad. Least ways, to my knowledge it don't have no bad effect on me here 'n' now. So why does every damn preacher from pastor to pope want to strike the fear of God into us 'bout the next life? If the reason is to cause everyone to be good 'n' honest 'n' charitable in this life, well, I can see that. But I try to do my best toward others, and you are surely an upstanding, honest woman. And our friends is all good folks tryin' to do what's right anyway."

Henry gazed into the distance as though he were looking for the answer out there somewhere, then he shook his head and took another sip of tea. "No. I'm about of a mind to say to hell with all that holier than thou'n stuff. I say let's forget about studyin' and worryin' so much about the next life that we somehow miss this one. I know I got today, this hour, this minute. So did that Mrs. Shepler up to the moment the wave hit her. She thought she had a bunch of tomorrows, too. But she didn't. Well, we may not have a bunch of tomorrows left, either. So I say we squeeze ever' bit of juice out of this here apple we possibly can, and let tomorrow take care of itself!"

He had finally spoken his mind on this subject. Although it had been simmering in him for decades, he hadn't intended to dump it all on the table in front of Tamsen. Well, at least no kids were in the room to hear his blasphemy, but he knew she'd take him apart as soon as she collected her thoughts.

She surprised him. "I'm not sure if yer right or wrong, Father, or if I am or anyone is. And by the way, don't think I haven't pretty well known your feelings for years. I've always appreciated your letting me raise the kids as church goin' Christians just to promote good behavior, and for family unity. But I sure don't know either. Bein' eye to eye with that poor Shepler lady does make you realize how we're all on borrowed time, don't it? Well, I got washin' to do," she said as she left him standing there with his thumb in his ear.

The finality of this entire calamity appeared in the paper about a week later. The article stated the wall of water was caused by a waterspout. About two dozen people were thought to have been killed by the five-foot wave as it rolled from Medicine Lodge to New Kiowa. Eighteen bodies were recovered.

A couple of months later a bridge was built over the Medicine River. The stage-coach lines continued until about 1904. With their passing into history, a colorful era would end.

Both the Devons and the Deteaus had an enhanced appreciation and awareness of everyday life from that catastrophic day in 1885 forward.

Thirteen Ain't an Unlucky Number.

"Hooray, boys, look at them sweet faces lookin' back at us!" Danny Traisley said to the others in the crowd on a hot August day in 1885. "Got any room on that train for some pork?" he yelled as the first trainload of cattle departed New Kiowa.

"Hey, Hank, how are you doin' today?" inquired A.W. Rumsey. "I been out of town a couple of weeks and just heard that today's the day. Whose herd we got loaded up?"

"Wilson filled two cars, Major Lemont three and Frank Waters four. Terrific, huh? This will have poor ol' Dodge City quiverin' in her boots, won't it?"

"Not to mention little piss-ant Caldwell," Tim Deteau added, to everyone's amusement. "And its Engine Number 13, which just proves thirteen being an unlucky number is bullshit."

The very next day, Monday, August 10, the cork really blew the bottle. J.V. Andrews shipped sixteen cars and Andy Drumm forty. Well over sixty thousand head of beef were shipped from New Kiowa by year's end.

"You were sure on the money A.W., back when you sang the benefits of us gettin' the railroad here," said a beaming Boney Korzack at a celebratory luncheon. A few dozen town men had gathered to wallow in their good fortune. "It's just heaven sent for all of us, even us folks not directly shippin' cows."

"I guess I did spout the railroad so much I come to believe it myself," Rumsey said. "We damn near got us a town here now. That 'iron horse,' as they call it, will connect us to the outside world, and for a whole lot more things than cattle. We'll be able to bring in building material for you, Boney. But a whole lot of other stuff, too. Hell, Hooz Deteau may just want to order hisself a spinet from Philadelphia. Or somebody may need some fancy doctorin' to save a life."

Wagon Ho!—New Beginning in Kiowa

At that comment, Henry stared at the floor, glassy-eyed, remembering John's death back in Fort Scott. How ironic that A.W. would hit on the same example he himself had used to cajole Tamsen into the move to Kiowa.

Danny Traisley was sitting beside Henry and winced when he heard A.W.'s comment. He saw that Henry's eyes had teared up a bit and that he had reached for his handkerchief. Danny put his hand at the back of Henry's neck and gave a little squeeze.

"He didn't mean nothin' by that Hank. He don't even know about Johnny," Traisley said.

"Oh, hell, Dan, I know that. I'm just a sorry ol' sonovabitch who can't help gettin' a little choked now and agin 'bout days gone by. And the pisser is I never know when it's gonna hit me. Plus, he's right. Sure, it's all too late for my two kids, but I'm truly happy for this here railroad. I truly am. I know in my heart somebody else's kid's life will be saved someday. Hell, that's progress and that's terrific. And in the meantime," Henry said as he rose to shout above the other voices, "I want to make a toast with this here mug of beer to A.W., Dennis Flynn, Andy and all you other ugly sonsabitches that were responsible for the train comin' to New Kiowa! Here's to ya!"

With that, all applauded with a general clinking of glasses and a hearty, "Hear, hear!" except for Boney Korzack, who said with feigned disgust, "I hate to continually have to remind you all, but the train didn't come to New Kiowa. Old Kiowa went to the train!"

Wolves at the Door

Life Was Good For a Lucky Family

Everything looked good. The Devons had, in fact, built their home in town on Campbell Street. It was a modest but adequate brick structure, and the family seemed to revel in being "towners" for the first time. And the quarter section ranch house was, although also quite small, equally adequate. Henry and the older sons could work the herd from it for days at a time, depending on the school situation. Bob and Charlie were finished with school. Frank at age 15 was still enrolled and did quite well. He liked school, and some talk around the dinner table had begun about his future.

"Your ma and I know you to be a good student, son. Any thoughts on continuin' with it past high school?" "Not really, Pa. I like the mathematics. And I like to read. We just finished up Melville's *Moby Dick*. Now there's a story for you! But I can't see much benefit to go on. The future in the cattle business here in New Kiowa seems unlimited. I'll be followin' Bob and Charlie out of the house in a couple of years. We've talked about our own spread some day. Course we'd all always be here to help you whenever needed."

Henry felt like the luckiest man alive—a king. Along with his whimsical musings about where the years had gone, he increasingly was aware of his abundant blessings. On the one hand, his herd, which had started from practically nothing, was now several hundred. And the market for them due to the train had such promise that Henry didn't doubt they'd hit a thousand head eventually.

Wagon Ho!—New Beginning in Kiowa

He was also aware and pleased the Devon family had arrived just at the right time and was recognized as a fairly prominent New Kiowa family. Not so much in terms of riches, but certainly a well-liked and well-respected family.

And there, on the other hand, was his family. He was truly a blessed man. Tamsen had been a wonderful wife for more than twenty-seven years. He didn't know what he'd do if he ever lost her, as Frank Shepler had lost his wife. As for their children, none of them had ever given him and Tamsen any serious problem. The boys were all hard-working, ambitious young fellows. Bob, Charlie, Frank, well, who knew about any of them? But he was sure they'd be all right. Tom was going on ten and sharp as a tack. He was a real good horseman and was already putting in full days when he worked the herd. And it was beginning to look like he was the best student of the bunch, especially in mathematics.

The girls were different, at least to Henry. Tamsen had done very well by Libby. As a wife and mother herself now, she and Jim seemed quite happy. They would probably be in the hotel business forever. Which was fine with Henry, because New Kiowa was growing and he figured they'd keep growing with it.

His mind drifted back to the day Tamsen gave Libby the butter mold box. That was what Tamsen was good at. She could dream up something like giving that little wooden box, insignificant in and of itself, and make it seem very significant. He hadn't heard much about it in recent years, but he had overheard Libby telling Belle about it one time.

"This comes from Grandma Devon, sweetie," she had explained. "It's a special little treasure box of our family's love, hopes and dreams. I'll tell you all about it someday."

Henry smiled as he recollected the box's history and felt confident that not only Libby, but Sadie and Ollie would end up just fine, also. Yes, he concluded, they were a lucky family, and life was good for the Devons in 1885 New Kiowa. Then it all began to change.

The Blizzard of '86

"Last winter sure weren't no walk in the park, Hank, but this is gettin' serious," Dan Traisley said as the two men had coffee at the Kiowa House. The latest gale had howled in during the night on almost hurricane strength wind, dumping nearly a foot of snow. With what was already on the ground, the herds would have a tough time grazing.

"Did you hear that telegraph feller's comment on it being an electrical storm?" Henry said. "Really unusual, the lines and instruments all fidgety just like in a lightning storm. He also said a lot of cattlemen out with their stock ended up frostbit last night."

"Geez, Hank, this really ain't good. That SK train still sittin' over there ain't good either. Wonder why it ain't pulled out yet?"

"Too much snow, Dan. Here we are in the first week of January, and the train's damn near frozen to the track. Yer right, it sure ain't good. I rode over my spread day before yesterday. The cows 're searchin' for what grass they can get at, and now this! We all gotta get some hay out to 'em. Your pigs OK?"

"So far. I guess as long as I can feed 'em. The barn's a little warmer than outside. So far so good."

The blizzard was really a series of storms, one upon the other. The blast of early January was quickly followed by another on January 21 and another on the twenty-eighth. The latter of these provided some thrills for New Kiowa rail passengers.

"This is hard to believe, Mother," said a fascinated Tom Devon as a crowd of onlookers gathered at the tracks near Hazelton. "Both those trains are snowbound. How they gonna move 'em, Pa?"

"The freighter ain't too serious. It can just sit there till they can dig it out. But those folks on the other one got to get going. I'm told a bunch of witnesses for a trial up in Medicine Lodge are on that train. They'll be wantin' to bust that one through those drifts."

Sure enough, an effort was made to reinforce the passenger train engine with a second engine to push the snow off the track. That idea doubled their trouble.

"Oh, Lordy, Tamsen, look at her jump the track. What a mess now," Henry said with chagrin.

The rear engine had overpowered the lead one and pushed it off the rails and across the track. Now a major effort commenced to re-right the engine and still get the snow removed. Just to be of some help, Henry and sons, including young Tom, joined with other men in shoveling snow off the tracks. Although Tom was enthralled with the trains, Henry realized this winter was harsher than anything they had ever seen. And it was just getting started.

January 31 brought another tragic event related to the blizzard of '86. Gus Hegwer and young Dave Freemyer departed into the I.T. in shirtsleeve weather on a hunting trip. They were so elated by the unexpected thaw and so stir crazy they both reveled at getting out on a pleasant camping sojourn for a couple of days.

"I guess they were camped at Driftwood and Mule Creek and it hit 'em in late afternoon," Hooz told Bob and Charlie. "I got the story from Dad. The temperature must have dropped forty degrees in three hours, or at least it seemed that way here. Dad says, according to Dave, the snow 'n' wind knocked out their fire. They could hardly stand up. Had to set loose their horses and try to get to Streeter's camp on foot. Apparently poor Mr. Hegwer tired out too much and couldn't make it. Dave—what is he, thirteen or fourteen?—went on but didn't make it either till the next morning, yesterday. I guess he finally stumbled into Streeter's just after sunup, 'bout half froze!"

"What about Mr. Hegwer?" asked Charlie. "Did he come on in later?"

"No, that's why I'm here. I gotta round up you fellas and your pa to go look for him. Dave's in real bad shape. My dad says they had to cut his foot off cause it froze. He's been dreamin' and rantin' and just now rememberin' about Mr. Hegwer. Can you fellows help in a search for him?"

"We can, but we'll never get to Pa in time to help. He's out at the ranch ... who knows where. But we'll come."

Wagon Ho!—New Beginning in Kiowa

"Me, too," Tom yelped. "I'm coming, too."

"The hell you are, squirt. You ain't goin' nowhere. Ma, tell him he ain't goin' with us," Bob said.

Tamsen could hardly believe her own words. She was an excellent judge of people and a good decision maker. Before she could really think about it, she heard herself say, "Why not? He's as good a horseman as any of you, and if that was your pa out there I'd want every possible pair of eyes and ears out lookin' for him. Tommy, you sure you want to go?"

"Yes'm, I'll be saddled up in fifteen minutes, Bob," he said as he ran out the door.

Gus Hegwer was a well-known and highly respected pioneer of both old and New Kiowa. He and his wife and children had been among the first to settle in the area. He was one of the three men who had engaged with the railroad representatives in discussing tracks coming to Kiowa. Nobody knew if his refusal to cooperate, or one of the other two men, had doomed the old town, and nobody cared. He was a beloved old cuss whom everyone held in high esteem. When word got out that Gus Hegwer was lost in the blizzard, the whole town went on high alert. Several of the wives took food to the Hegwer home, and about a dozen men were soon mobilizing at the Streeter ranch to go find him.

"Snow's totally covered young Dave's tracks," Boney Korzack said. "But the story is they was down at Mule Creek near Driftwood. I say we head that way. We'll fan out there and find him!"

Wolves at the Door

Young Tom didn't say a word. He rode along behind his brothers, just glad to be included with the men in a man's job. For not quite ten years of age, he had a sense of purpose that far surpassed his brothers'. They arrived in the desired area and, as agreed, took positions about forty or fifty yards apart. The terrain was somewhat rolling and jagged with small ravines. In spots, snow had drifted to a couple of feet. They slowly and quietly rode along Mule Creek, in and out of the cottonwoods. Nothing,

"Hello, Gus! Gus Hegwer! Hello!" individual men shouted every few minutes.

Dan Traisley fired his revolver five or six times over the course of an hour. They came upon two steers over a two-mile stretch, both freshly frozen and both freshly chawed on by wolves. The critters didn't do so well in these conditions either.

Then Tommy, who was riding out on the end of the line, saw another dead animal. He edged farther out to inspect and discovered it was a wolf with most of its chest cavity blown away. The snow in front of it was crimson red. That sight unnerved him, but when he glanced a few dozen feet to the left of the dead wolf, there was Gus Hegwer sitting on his haunches, observing his handiwork. Tommy jumped enough that he almost came out of his saddle.

"Holy Jesus, Mr. Hegwer! You 'bout scared me to death!" said young Tom as his wide eyes met Gus's clear gaze. "I never even heard you shoot, but you sure blew a hole in that there lobo! He must have been just about on you, too. Did you just now fire on him?"

When Mr. Hegwer didn't answer, Tommy walked his horse on over to him.

"Mr. Hegwer? Sir? You OK?"

Gus didn't move. He just rested in total comfort down on his heels, knees bent, starin' straight ahead. Eyes wide open as if calmly studying the carcass of the wolf.

"Jumpin' jehosophat! Yer dead ain't ya, Mr. Hegwer? Yer just sittin' there dead, ain't ya?"

Tom yelled at the top of his lungs for the others. Quickly his brothers, Mr. Traisley, Mr. Korzack, all of them were surrounding the frozen corpse of their friend.

"He won't unbend, Hooz, and we can't take him back all squatted down like that. Specially not to town where Mrs. Hegwer will see him," Frank said.

"Tommy, you done good to spot him, so we're gonna reward you by tying him to your horse so's you can bring him on in," Bob said in a bit of black humor.

"The hell you are, brother. I ain't gettin one inch closer to Mr. Hegwer. He done give me the shakes as it is."

Dan Traisley ended the foolishness by devising a plan.

"Cut it out boys and show some respect. Go get us some branches and we'll get enough fire going to thaw him out. We'll get him limber enough to at least get into the undertaker. He can get him presentable before he starts turnin' black. We can't let his missus see him like this."

On the way back, Bob, Charlie and Tommy conjectured about Gus's last moments.

"He must of been hunkered down just to try to stay warm," Charlie said.

"Or to stay out of the wind," suggested Bob.

"I don't think so," said their youngest brother. "He looked so peaceful and pleased, I bet he knew that wolf was closin' in on him. I bet he just squatted down, lured that critter right up to him and blew a load right through him. Probably was so pleased with hisself, and figured he was gonna freeze anyway, I think he just enjoyed his last hunt and went to sleep with a smile on his face."

The big blizzard played out all over the southwest. The Dodge City papers argued over the number of deaths, but agreed it was between twenty-five and one hundred people, and between twenty-five thousand and one hundred thousand head of cattle.

One odd incident involved a Mr. Mills' sheep. The snow completely covered his sheep shed for more than twenty-four hours and all were presumed dead. Upon eventual inspection, smoke was seen coming from a crevice in the snowdrift. It was the breath of all his sheep, who when uncovered were found happily chewing their cud.

Another oddity was that most of the cows that perished in the blizzard were not from local herds. They were through cows up from Texas, not accustomed to the extreme cold and wind.

"Regardless where they come from, Henry, get your boys out and skin 'em out. We may be facin' some bad times comin' up. Those thousands of carcasses should yield something in skins and bones," instructed A.W. Rumsey. "Like another buffalo bones business, don't you imagine?"

And Then Came the Summer

"How about Wyoming?" Henry asked Tamsen as they discussed the next calamity, drought. "Major Drumm and several other ranchers are shippin' their herds north to get at some grass. Or how 'bout over to Colorado? I'm told it ain't as bad there, maybe because of mountain water tricklin' on down in the streams. But boy, it's sure dry as a bone here!"

"I hope you're joshing, Father, cause I got absolutely no plans to uproot again!"

"Oh, hell, Tamsen, I'm just kidding. Our herd really ain't big enough to fret real bad over. We've sold down to a point where we'll just wait for rain and then rebuild. But it is interesting to listen to some folks' plans on lookin' at other places. I mean, I don't know that you fully appreciate the pickle a lot of the big overhead ranches is in with this drought, on the heels of that godawful winter."

The irony of the situation was that rail shipments of cattle out of New Kiowa were huge in the late 1880s. In 1886, '87 and '88 the highest numbers of them ever, were shipped. But a large share of the number were "sea lions." That was the slang term for Texas longhorns because they swam so many rivers on the way up to the Kansas cow towns.

"I'll whip any man in the house who says his cows are prettier 'n my sea lions," bellowed Shanghai Pierce, smiling jovially. "Or, I'll buy drinks for the house if ever'one of you cow pokin' sons-of-guns admits I got the damn handsomest cows around!"

All present laughed, applauded the sentiment, and bellyed up to the bar.

"He's one audacious gentleman ain't he?" Hooz Deteau said to those at his table in the Riled Rooster Saloon. "Who is he?"

"That's ol' Abel Pierce, son," Tim Deteau said. "Everyone calls him Shanghai. Don't know why. He runs lots of longhorns up from his Matagorda ranch down on the Texas gulf coast. And I mean lots. Over the years he's drove a hundred thousand of them rangy critters up through these Kansas towns. He's a real colorful buckaroo. I've never actually met him. By reputation he's a good man, but not to be trifled with."

"Yeah, I've heard of him. Jest didn't ever see him before. Big sonovabitch ain't he? I'm not tiny, and he and I would go about nose to nose."

"That appears about right son, but I suspect his beak has been in a few more scrapes over the years than yours has. The papers have written about him every now and then. I think I remember he's a good friend of Wyatt Earp up in Dodge. Supposedly he keeps a good watch on his cowboys when they hit Dodge City. Makes Earp's job easier. O'Shea says the same thing here. Let's go get us one of his free drinks."

As they worked through the crowd toward the bar they happened to pass behind Pierce. He turned just as Hooz was beside him and they did, in fact, come "nose to nose."

"Well, whoa, boy! You're sure a tall drink of water ain't ya? I do believe you got me by an inch or two. And you

Wagon Ho!—New Beginning in Kiowa

must be his dad," Pierce said as he extended his hand to Tim and then Hooz. "I'm Shanghai Pierce, and I'd like to buy you both a drink."

"Hello, Mr. Pierce. I'm Timothy Deteau and this here is my son, Hooz. Glad to meet you, sir."

"Well, it ain't Mr. Pierce. That was my dear old departed daddy. It's Shanghai. Pleased to make yer acquaintance."

Just then the crowd surged between them, and Pierce was swept to the other side of the room to another bunch of adoring cowhands.

"Holy Joseph, Dad," Hooz said. "I may never talk to him again, but I can say I once met the great Shanghai Pierce. And even better, I can forever say I shook the hand that shook the hand of Wyatt Earp. Hot damn!"

"And even better than that, son, you can even say you met him fair 'n' square, nose to nose, in the Riled Rooster, and you best'd him!"

"Bested him? How's that, Dad?"

"Well think on it, Hooz, yer drinkin' his beer ain't ya?"

In spite of blizzards and droughts, in that month of 1887 alone, Shanghai Pierce delivered more than 7,000 of his Texas sea lions to some of the big New Kiowa ranchers. The Deteaus ended up buying about a dozen, largely out of sentiment over their meeting him. The Devons didn't buy any because Henry wanted to keep his herd down. He just wasn't sure what the future had in store.

Wolves at the Door

Voices From the Past

"I'll be horsewhipped, look at this, Ma," Charlie yelled across Main Street. As they converged in front of A.W.'s store, he said, "This letter is posted to us from Colorado. Who on earth could it be?"

Tamsen took the letter from her son and hastily opened it. "Henry, come on over here. We got us a letter from Dagmar MacNaughten! Can you believe that?"

"I'll be damned, what are they up to?"

"Well, I'll be, they're in La Junta … Colorado" she reported as she read. Her expression went dark, "Oh no, Cob died! Says here he died last winter, heart failure." She read some more. "Dagmar and the children moved to La Junta from Medicine Lodge with the LeClercs early this year. I thought they was out in Californy, didn't you?"

"Didn't rightly know, Mother. We haven't heard from them, but, yes, I guess I did think they were going to go on to California. So they stayed in Medicine Lodge?"

"That poor woman. Cob always looked after her so well. What a shame." Tamsen kept on reading.

"Wonder why La Junta?" Henry said.

Tamsen read a while more and then handed the letter to her husband. "You can read it, but she says the LeClercs are sold on La Junta. Red and Reg think it's a bigger town, and they want to try opening a haberdashery together. She's gone with them 'cause they're such good friends. I'm sure

Wagon Ho!—New Beginning in Kiowa

Deborah is like a sister to Dagmar. This is terrible, Henry. How old was Cob?"

"I believe my age, about fifty-five. I guess we're all gettin' up there, dear. Losin' friends will probably start happenin'. At least she's got her kids, but I guess just like ours, they're growing up and scattering, too. Well, she's got the LeClercs." He continued to glance at the letter. "La Junta must be a bigger town than Medicine Lodge, a helluva lot bigger than New Kiowa. And its smack on the Arkansas River. That must come right down from the mountains, and I know it carries pretty near across southern Kansas. La Junta's always been a main stop on the big trail. Don't you remember readin' about Bent's Fort? That goes back to the earliest Santa Fe days. If Red is settlin' in there, he must see something in it."

Tamsen could see the wanderlust in her husband's eyes, but she decided to ignore it. "We've all been at fault for not keepin' in touch," she replied. "I'll write and tell her what we've done here. Maybe she'll keep us posted on life in La Junta. After they're there awhile it would be interesting to hear from them."

All Good Things Come To An End.

The year 1887 came and went, and 1888 burst on the scene. Henry Devon couldn't shake the uneasy feeling of discontent. Over the previous three years he had added to his Harper County ranch by taking Jesse Ellis up on his offer to sell him a Barber County quarter. Jesse had been correct in their early conversation about Dave Whittenburg and Bill Beyersdorfer being willing to sell a little land to the Devons. So Henry had acquired enough grazing range for his hoped-for thousand-head. He was sitting on the sofa in their parlor showing Tamsen the official papers.

"Look here, Mother. Our good buddy and esteemed leader Grover Cleveland says that we now are the proud owners of our Harper spread. I'm glad I went and got my citizenship. We done proved up. I guess he don't even know how I personally proved up on the banks of Sand Creek that day," Henry said with a smirk.

She just shook her head and said, "Iffen the government knew what a naughty boy you've been, they'd kick us off that land pronto!"

"And this fancy lookin' deed to it is almost as sentimental to me as the first one back in Bourbon by Grant. I loved that man."

"Then what are you so all fired down-in-the-mouth about?"

"I don't know why, but I just have a strange feelin' my days here are waning. For one thing, I'm fifty-six, and at times I feel seventy-six. I've spent the last twenty-five or so years bendin', liftin', pullin', pushin', diggin', choppin', sweatin' and freezin'. Tamsen, I hate to admit it, but at times I'm just plain tired. Maybe we should think about moving where life would be a bit easier. I notice a lot of the smaller ranchers like me, those not really big enough to hire it all out, are much younger fellas. With the boys growin' up, and Bob buyin' his own quarter ... well, I can't expect them to ignore their own futures to help me. Bob's told me he wants to grow his own herd and also keep marshalin'. Charlie is about to apply for his quarter. Looks like Sadie is about to marry young Stonefield. Frank is now age, uh, he must be about, uh ..."

"You don't know, do you Henry? His own father, and you have no idea how old he is, do you?" She glared.

"Well, sure I do, dagnabbit. I know he's more than ten and under twenty ... well, ain't he?"

"He is eighteen, you old fool, and Ollie is fifteen, nearly sixteen, almost a complete woman! Tell me, Father, how old is your precious youngest and last child? That is if you know which one that is."

"Well, of course I know, it's Tommy! And I ain't seen him around the house for a while. He didn't up and get married and move out did he?"

"He's twelve, Henry, twelve years old! Just in case anyone asks. You are beyond hope!"

From Queen Victoria to Bat Masterson

Late in 1888, a group of eastern businessmen made an attempt to outright buy the I.T. from the Indians at $3 per acre. Actually, they were a syndicate of New York and Colorado ranchers. The benevolent government of the United States of America, in its ever-enduring objective to screw the Indians, squelched the deal and forced a sale to the government at $1.25 per acre. The Indians got scalped again.

President Benjamin Harrison would eventually sign an order to remove all cattle from the Cherokee Outlet. This doomed most of the ranchers with leases to run cattle in the I.T. With the leases outlawed, the Indians were forced to sell out to the government. With the ensuing glut of cattle and not enough space to graze them, the ranchers had to sell off quickly. Prices for beef plummeted. The era of the large cattle ranches was over.

The Devons and Traisleys had become extremely good friends over the years. They met for either dinner or supper every couple of weeks, usually at the Kiowa House. On one of those occasions, Danny Traisley commented on the move the Devons had decided to make. Taking a slice off his supper steak, he said, "I guess you were right, Hank," Danny Traisley said. "You're doing the right thing in tryin' to get a start in Colorado this year."

"I'm not sure it's a question of bein' right, Dan. We'll keep a foot in here. I ain't sellin' my ranges right away. Who knows how long Jim and Libby will stay in the area? This place has been real good for them to raise their own family. Bob ain't rushin' out immediately, neither. New Kiowa will always be a wonderful area to call home. We all came out in, what, '78? That's ten years. I'd say we all—you 'n' us and especially the Dwyers—we were all kinda like founding fathers here." He paused to chew a bite and flag down Jim Dwyer to have a seat.

Wagon Ho!—New Beginning in Kiowa

"Can't right now, Dad. I'm deep into the orderin' for next week's supplies. No rest for the weary! Yer dang daughter and grandkids keep me hoppin'!"

"Then before you disappear, fill up these mugs again and put 'em on Danny's bill." He spoke with a perfectly straight face as he turned his attention back to the table.

"Look at A.W., at Scott Cummins, at Flynn and all the other old timers here who have some connection elsewhere now. I think Tamsen 'n' I would like the comforts of a little bigger town. Dan, you two have your pork business going good. Both your kids are close to growed. In fact, with Ron out and Millie getting' hitched, and both probably leavin' the area, don't you ever get an urge to start over somewhere else?"

"I guess now and then the grass looks greener," Zilly said. "Our stock don't take so much land and lookin' after as your cows. And I love New Kiowa, as I think Danny does. But yes, we both probably get a bit itchy for some new excitement now and then. Tell us again, exactly what did you buy in La Junta?"

"Didn't buy, gonna rent a house in town. We'll go on over this year or next."

"We told you the LeClercs are there and Dagmar, too," Tamsen said. "Dagmar's letters are very encouraging. She says a lot of nice, decent homes are going up, a lot of stores and shopping. Sounds like the ease of livin' is stronger than here."

"You know, we're a bit longer in the tooth than you two," Henry added. "I want us to just go over with no expectations and set up strictly in town. They got some huge ranches there, but I just may throw in the towel on cattle, or at least on ownin' my own spread. We'll keep our sections here and maybe help the boys get started on something over there. Pass over that gravy, will you Zill? Thanks. O'Shea has written their marshal for Bob. Claims the man says he can use him."

"What does Charlie think? He excited about movin'?" Traisley asked.

"It's a problem," Tamsen responded, "for all of the kids, really. They've all got good friends here. IBar Johnson's been cowboyin' for the major for years, but with that dryin' up, he swears he's coming to La Junta with Bobby. Charlie's twenty-four now. He's got friends, too, but honestly they all seem inclined to jump at new adventure. Henry's filled 'em full of poop about being closer to the mountains and about Santa Fe Trail lore. Bent's Fort is right there, y'know."

"What about the girls, Tamsen?" Zill asked.

"Jim and Libby and the Dwyers are open to move, but just not right now. This hotel gets more saleable with each passing month. They've had quite a few offers on it already. Sadie is so hot to marry young Stonefield, who knows? And little Ollie ... little? Can you believe she's goin' on fifteen? 'Member that little squirt on our wagon trip out? Lordy, where do the years go? Both she and Frank are at the age they hate to leave friends. He's eighteen and ready to light out anyway. But she is like peas in a pod with her girlfriends, Doreen 'n' Nancy 'n' Sharon. It'll be hard on

Wagon Ho!—New Beginning in Kiowa

her for shore, but she'll manage. Fork over a little more of them potatoes, please."

"Tom's the one," Henry said. "We don't know exactly what to make of him. He's as loony and spirited as the others, but he has a certain focus 'n' seriousness, too. We think La Junta being bigger, he may get better schoolin'. And with the AT&SF runnin' through it, he may have a chance to hook up later with the Santa Fe."

"What's the deal with the Santa Fe there in La Junta?" Traisley asked. "Bigger 'n here?"

"Oh, hell yes, Dan. To the best of my knowledge that railroad's been in there for about ten years. It's the headquarters for the AT&SF for a large part of the Colorado, New Mexico and Kansas territories."

"It got a depot?"

"Yes, and I hear it's been enlarged."

"You ever hear of a Harvey House, Zilly?" Tamsen asked, anxious to spill out her new-found knowledge.

"No, can't say I have. Is it like this here Kiowa House?"

"Sort of, I guess. La Junta has had one for the last couple of years. It's somehow connected to the railroad. Dagmar says its real nice. It's a restaurant and maybe a few rooms for Santa Fe passengers comin' west, or east for that matter. Some feller in Topeka had a lunch counter beside the train depot. His name's Harvey. He struck some kind of deal with the Santa Fe to run a string of restaurants all along their routes, you know, to give the folks a meal. Well, there's one in La Junta. Dagmar says there's talk of expanding it to a real nice full-blown hotel. I guess they got 'em from Chicago to

Kansas … all the way to Galveston, Texas … and out to San Francisco. Seems they make an extended train ride not only possible, but a downright pleasure!"

"Ain't that something, Tamsen? Gee, I'll come visit you and we'll take a trip just like those fancy duded-up folks on the train that passed us back on our wagon trip!" Zilly chuckled until she remembered that Libby and Jim had been among those "duded-up folks."

"Another interesting thing, guess who the city marshal over there is, or was," Henry said.

"Hell if I know, Hank," responded Dan, "Johnny Appleseed? Queen Victoria?"

"Bat Masterson!"

"The hell you say! Ain't he up in Dodge?"

"He was, and may be back there now. O'Shea told Bob that the mayor of La Junta hired him especially to knock some heads into line. He must of got the job done and left town."

"Speaking of the Queen, Father, do you realize we completely missed her Golden Jubilee last year? Fifty years on the throne! And our own son Tom named after her!"

Henry cringed as Danny said, "Yer boy is named after the Queen? Ain't that a might odd?"

"No, dammit," Henry said. "Tamsen, you need to be a little more clear on that or you're gonna get that boy in a lot of fights. His middle name is Albert, Dan, after Prince Albert. Hell, that's bad enough. But back to missing the Jubilee, Mother, I forgot to tell you we did get an invitation

Wagon Ho!—New Beginning in Kiowa

in the mail. But it was at branding time and I knew we couldn't go. I threw it away."

The subject of another major move had snuck up on the Devons. It seemed to be a natural breaking point for several of the early families. A lot of them had aged to a point at which they began to be attracted to a less remote area. Not that La Junta wasn't remote, but its future seemed brighter due to the Santa Fe Railroad location. And the hardships of weather over the last few years had worn out folks. No guarantees, but the hope was that eastern Colorado might be a tad milder, more mountain sheltered.

In addition, the demise of the Cherokee Strip had a big effect-psychologically as well as in reality. New Kiowa would always be a passing-through shipping point town for the Texas herds, but the perception was that the glory days might be over for the local ranchers. And perception can be reality. Henry had somehow sensed all this.

"You know what, Mother? What the hell, let's give it one last shot! You got one more adventure left in ya?"

"You ain't steered us wrong yet, Father. And I told you years ago, we'll all sail to wherever you point the ship. Lead on, Captain!"

PART-III

III

On to La Junta

The Baton is Passed in Colorado

"I can't believe we're doing this again," Tamsen said. "This'll be the third big chapter of our life together, Henry. I hope it works out well and lasts a long time, 'cause I have to think it'll be our last one."

Henry didn't articulately answer. He merely grunted an uh huh. He was finishing packing his suitcase for a weeklong visit—maybe a little longer—to La Junta.

"The ride over shouldn't be much more than seven or eight hours, not countin' stops. If Bob's ready we may as well go on over to the depot," he said.

The plan was for Henry and Bob to take a brief sojourn to their new hometown for a closer look. Similar to their entry into Kiowa ten years earlier, they planned to make the transition simple. They would just rent a house until they got a feel for the place. On this short visit it would be easier for the two men to travel alone and just check into a hotel or rooming house for several days. It was mid-January of 1889, and Henry's duties at home and out at the ranch could be covered easily by his other sons. Tamsen and the girls would, literally, keep the home fires lit.

Wolves at the Door

"We'll be pullin' into Dodge soon, Pa," Bob said. "I'm hungry. Why don't we get off an' get a bite. Conductor says we got about half 'n hour."

As the two men were getting off the train, to Bob's total astonishment, a familiar looking man with a prominent handlebar mustache accidentally bumped into him while getting on.

"Oh my heavens, I'm so sorry," the man said.

Henry just laughed and said, "Don't think a thing of it, mister. I guess we're both in a hurry to either get to or away from Dodge. Be our guest." He and Bob politely stepped aside to let the pleasant looking man enter the car. "Oh, one question if you don't mind. My son here and I was lookin' for some quick vittles before we re-board. Any suggestions?"

"Well, there are a couple of beaneries up town ain't too bad, but if you're in a hurry, may I recommend Lulu's just around the corner. Where are you boys off to?"

"La Junta, we got us a long day, startin' from Kiowa," Bob said.

"La Junta? I'm going that way myself, back to San Diego. Friend of mine worked over there several years ago as a police officer. Rough town!"

"I'm Henry Devon and this is my son Bob. Who may I tell Lulu was kind enough to send us her way?"

"Oh, my name's Earp, Wyatt Earp," the man said as he held out his hand. "Nice to meet you fellas. If you don't mind, I've had an exhausting couple of days over here

On to La Junta—The Baton is Passed in Colorado

hootin' it up with old friends. I used to live and work in Dodge. I'm in bad need of crawlin' into my berth now for a little shuteye. You men have a good trip to La Junta, and I hope your business there is successful!"

With that he disappeared into a closed compartment, not to be seen again. Henry stepped onto the station platform toward Lulu's. Noticing that Bob wasn't keeping step, he turned to find him still in place. Bob was in a stupor, staring glassy-eyed into space.

"Earp, Wyatt Earp ..." he was mumbling.

"C'mon boy, what's gotten into you? We ain't got all day to eat, get movin' son."

"Pa, you do realize who we just met don't you? That was Wyatt Earp."

"Yeah, and I'm Henry Devon. And for all I know, that lady over there on that white horse may be Joan of Arc. Now c'mon!"

"Pa!" Bob said as he finally started walking to Lulu's lunch counter. "That man is the meanest lawdog in the west! I have a copy of *Police Gazette* from a couple of years ago. You wouldn't believe his exploits. You know about Tombstone and the OK Corral?"

Throughout their meal at Lulu's, Bob could not shut up about what he had read about Wyatt Earp and his friends. Henry was tired of listening to it. "Look, Bob, I know about all that shootout stuff, or at least the gist of it. But that don't help us brand 'n' feed cows, does it? You got to focus on the task at hand, boy."

Wolves at the Door

"Pa! It just dawned on me who his friend in La Junta police work was. It had to be Bat Masterson! Wait till I tell O'Shea about this!"

"Oh, hell, why don't we just sit here and wait for ol' Doc Holliday to show up?"

"'Cause he's dead, Pa. Died of consumption in Glenwood Springs back in '87. And he weren't old, only thirty-six if I'm rememberin' right. I'm tellin' you, I read up on all this."

Henry could have told Bob that Hooz had had his tooth pulled by the very same Doc Holliday years ago during the wagon trek west. He decided, however, to stay mum and not prolong this conversation. He paid for the meal and walked out of the restaurant, figuring Bob would follow.

On the train, Bob was beside himself. As the Santa Fe cars rolled easily along the western Kansas tracks, Henry drifted off to sleep to the clickety, clickety, clickety cadence. Bob, on the other hand, was too fired up to doze.

Jesus Christ, he thought, *here I'm on the same train as Wyatt Earp and ain't nobody around to tell it to. Wish I could sit in his compartment and talk to him.*

As Bob stared out the window he began to notice how absolutely dead flat the terrain was.

"Gee, Pa," he said, waking his father, "this here countryside looks like a pool table it's so flat!"

Henry didn't answer, but the passing conductor did.

"That's right, young man. The wagon trains movin' by here had no idea how easy they had it compared to what was

On to La Junta—The Baton is Passed in Colorado

comin' in a few hundred miles. It sure enough is flat as a pancake out there, ain't it?"

"I wonder how far a feller can see just standin' up, or sittin' on a horse." Bob said.

"Don't know exactly," returned the conductor, "but I know a man who lives around these parts, says he had a dog once who ran away from home. Claims they could see him for three days!"

As the conductor grinned and moved on down the isle, Bob quietly said to himself, "Wonder if that's true. Wonder if they could really see him for three days."

Even though Henry's eyes were closed, he nevertheless rolled them in their sockets and thought, *He's a good boy, but I sure as hell hope he can find a guv'ment job.*

The train stopped briefly in Granada, then again in Lamar, finally pulling into the La Junta station at about supper time. Father and son stood and stretched, trying to get the kinks out, and then shuffled down the steps onto the platform.

"Well, there's the Harvey House that Dagmar mentioned, and look, there's Dagmar and the LeClerks' boy!" Henry said.

"Bob!" yelled Reg, "Mr. Devon!"

"Hello, Knothead … er, Reg, and hello to you, Dagmar!" Henry said as he gave Cob's widow a heartfelt hug. "It's so nice to see you. Tamsen sends her best. We're both so saddened about Cob. You look wonderful!"

"I am, Henry! Me 'n' the LeClercs are so tickled to be joinin' up with you folks again. Let's get your bags in Reg's rig and amble over to their house for a good supper. I'll bet it was a long, long day!"

"You're right on that, Dagmar. I swear it's easier to mow hay for a day than sit still on that train."

"And Reg, Mrs. MacNaughten," interrupted Bob, "you'll never guess who we met on that train!"

You Got Yer Mexicans, Farmers, Cowmen, Railroaders

La Junta in 1889 was a town in transition. Kansas was to some degree filling up with homesteaders, and good, cheap land was becoming scarce. The Devons were not alone in edging over to Colorado. And although the railroads had certainly been a boon to New Kiowa, even to the point of justifying its existence, they were the soul of La Junta. Over the coming years it would become a major division office for the AT&SF, but even upon the Devons' arrival in 1889, the railroad's impact was evident.

"You didn't really see it, Hank," Red said after Deborah's delicious chicken dinner. "In full daylight tomorrow morning you'll get the picture that this here's a railroad town! The Santa Fe is the engine that's drivin' growth here. Not to say cattle 'n' farmin' ain't a big thing, 'cause they are. In fact, you may want to take a look see at buyin' a quarter from the standpoint of ranchin' again, Hank, or farmin'. There's talk that the Arkansas River may be tapped for irrigation. May be better than the Medicine for that."

On to La Junta—The Baton is Passed in Colorado

"I'm done, Red. That's fine for Bob here, or Charlie 'n' Frank if they come over. But, hell, I'm bushed. Tamsen and I plan to live in town. Don't know exactly what I'll do, but it may involve a rockin' chair more'n branding irons."

After breakfast the next day, Red took Henry and Bob for a short tour.

"This is the second depot here for the Santa Fe. Actually it's a remodel of the last one built about ten years ago. The general feeling is a bigger and much more serious depot can't be more'n a few years off. And that there is the Harvey House. I think Dagmar wrote Tamsen about it. You get a pretty dang good meal there. That'll probably be enlarged soon, too, maybe as an actual hotel."

Henry glanced around at the obvious building growth. "What're those down that street, Red?"

"That's Trinidad Plaza, Hank, and those particular establishments yer pointin' at are saloons—thirteen of 'em!"

"Lord, Mr. LeClerc, this place is lookin' more 'n' more like New Kiowa," Bob said.

"How old are you now, Bob?"

"I'm twenty-six, Mr. LeClerc, why?"

"Then quit callin' me Mr. LeClerc, or I'll be forced to slap you silly. It's Red, goddammit!"

"Yes, sir, Mr. LeClerc, it's Red from now on. How 'bout lawlessness and crime over here, Mr. Le— er, Red?" inquired Bob.

Wolves at the Door

"It's pretty rampant, truth be told. I sure want you 'n' Tamsen to come join us, Hank, but I ain't gonna lie to you fellas. You probably already know they brought Bat Masterson here several years ago to clean it up. He did some good, but it's just too much of a mixed crowd to rightly control. You got yer Mezzigans, farmers, cowmen, railroad men, town folks, speckerlators, I mean just about every description of hombre you can think of, and the thirteen saloons. It may come to sort itself out, but for now—"

"Morning, Red!" a voice boomed from across the street.

As all three men turned to look, LeClerc spoke back, "Oh, howdy, Ty. Come over here! I want you to meet some old friends about to become neighbors again. Ty, meet Henry Devon and his son, Bob. Fellas, this is Mr. Tyson Woodruff, Mr. Know-it-all in La Junta. Ty has been here about a hundred years. He's a dadburned lawyer, so watch what ya say."

They all shook hands, and as they were chatting, Henry couldn't help remembering back a decade when he met A.W. Rumsey in such similar circumstances.

"We were just discussing our occasional fights, hangings, knifings, shootouts and whatall in our fair city, TY.

You ever hear of such goings on?" Red said.

"How far back would you like me to begin?" said Woodruff. "How 'bout just three years ago in '86? Let's start off with the critters first. In one kill-off we dispatched over two hundred mongrel dogs in one day ... in town! Then we

On to La Junta—The Baton is Passed in Colorado

went to work on the skunks, about the same number. That thinned 'em out a bit, but we still got 'em around."

"Let's not give these boys a bad first impression of La Junta, Ty. Let's just tell 'em about our two-legged critters."

"OK, August of the same year, '86. How 'bout them dimwit drunken cowboys wanderin' around town shootin' holes in practically every building they saw, even Mayor Dalton's abode! We had to stash twenty-six of 'em in the Black Hole."

"That's our pet name for the town lock-up," Red explained.

"Then, we got us our lovely population of sportin' ladies, our soiled doves! They do their damnedest to keep all that cowboy money right here in town. Them and the professional gamblers. Where you all from, Henry? Is my rendition a shock to you?"

"Not at all, Ty. We've been over in Kiowa, Kansas, for ten years. I do believe we've seen all this before."

"Red may have already told you that we're about to get our own county here. La Junta will soon be in the new Otero County, broken off from Bent County. You know about Bent?"

"Old Bent's Fort on the old Santa Fe Trail," Bob said. "I even had to do a report on it for a high school history class. Back to law problems, Mr. Woodruff. Who is your marshal now?"

"Hickman. Marshal Alex Hickman," but he's havin' some problems. Folks ain't too happy with the job he's doin'.

The town's still too rowdy. I got a feelin' he'll be out soon. We got a pretty good fella named A.J. Rock might get appointed this year, we'll see. Why? You interested in the job?"

"Well, probably not the marshal job, but I've been doin' some deputyin' over in Kiowa, along with my ranchin'. I'd sure like to be considered for a deputy when I move here."

Henry noticed Bob said "when," not "if," he moved to La Junta. The excitement of the town was obviously getting to number one son.

Plunky and Bob and the Big Shootout

Back in New Kiowa two things were on Tamsen's mind, and both involved her men. One was the realization that in more than thirty years of marriage to Henry, they had spent, at the most, ten nights apart. And most of those were long ago in his militia days. In New Kiowa, Henry now and then was out overnight rounding up stray cattle. But his being gone to another town, in this case La Junta, and her not by his side was a rare occurrence. *Well, you silly old fool. She laughed to herself. What the devil trouble can he get hisself into at his age?*

Her second concern was Tom. She worried about moving him at age thirteen. He was just about to sprout. She knew within a couple of years he'd be her biggest and probably brightest son. He was included in most family discussions now, no matter how serious. She hoped uprooting him just before he became a man wouldn't

On to La Junta—The Baton is Passed in Colorado

somehow knock him off kilter. But she let the thought pass in deference to the self-confidence he exuded. *Oh fiddle, he seems to be able to look about anyone in the eye now and not blink. He'll be fine.*

She had no way of knowing, however, that her first concern, her husband getting into trouble, was a premonition. Back in La Junta, the four men standing in peaceful discussion as they gazed across Trinidad Plaza were about to have a little excitement.

Thunk! A stray bullet hit the wooden framework of a town drinking well not eight feet from Woodruff. Pong! Another bullet clanged off a metal bucket sitting on the side of the well. Henry, as well as Red and Ty, merely looked around to determine the direction the shots came from.

Red said, "What in the hell were those, Ty?"

Before Woodruff could venture a guess, Bob pointed at a person sitting in a chair on the boardwalk a couple of doors down from the Bearded Buckaroo.

"That sonovabitch took those shots at us, Pa," Bob said as he took off across the plaza toward the villain.

Woodruff squinted in the direction of the offender and blurted out, "Shit, Red, that ain't no purposeful shooter, that's Plunky Rasmussen. He's the slow-thinkin' nephew of Trent Rasmussen, who owns that shop. He's one of our gunsmiths. Plunky must have gotten into a firearm case without Trent knowin' it. You better stop yer boy, Henry, afore somebody gets hurt."

Wolves at the Door

Henry was off like a greyhound, although a somewhat old and lame greyhound. *Jesus Christ*, he thought, *I'm a tired old fart runnin' down a street in a strange town trying to stop my nitwit son from pluggin' another nitwit over a mistake. And on our very first morning here.*

"Bob! Bobby! Hold up son, he's just a—"

Plang! Bob hit the dirt just as another shot hit a shovel blade out front of Sternheimer's Hardware.

"Why, you goddamn..." Bob said as he fired back at the hapless Plunky Rasmussen. The bullet found its way directly through the heart of one of Miss Candy's Dress Shop mannequins. Had she been a real person she'd have been dead as a doornail. Bob very professionally rose to one knee, aimed his pistol with both hands and let loose his second shot. This one only missed Plunky by about twenty feet, but it did put a glancing sting on the rump of Lawrence Clark's mule, Elvira, still tied up at the Beardless Buckaroo from the night before. Had Lawrence not been lying comatose under a blackjack table, he would have been quite perturbed. Elvira, however, was upset at the rude treatment she had received and proceeded to kick out four railings as she careened down the boardwalk.

"Plunky still don't know anyone's shot at him, Ty!" Red said.

"And he sure as hell don't know he's shot at someone hisself. His banjo just don't have all the strings tuned, does it? But you better help your friend get his son back here before one of those two desperados accidentally hits what they're aimin' at!"

On to La Junta—The Baton is Passed in Colorado

Henry was petrified that exactly that would happen. He had to divert both gunslingers' attention before another shot was fired. Before he even consciously planned it, he heard his own voice barrel out, "Hey, fellas, ain't that a nekkid lady on the front porch of the Bearded Buckaroo? Look, right there! Look at the size of them tits!"

To Henry's mild surprise, Plunky put down the Colt he had been innocently playing with and shouted, "Where? Where's she at?"

But to his total amazement, bordering on astonishment, Bob also turned and squinted over at the saloon.

As Henry arrived panting and out of breath to remove the pistol from Bob's hand, he heard his not-so-perspicacious lawdog son ask, "What? What the hell're you talkin' about, Pa? There ain't no lady over—"

Smack! Henry slapped Bob's hat right off his head. "Jesus Keerist, son! That's yer own trick fer God's sake, and you've now fallen for it twice yerself. What the hell's the matter with you, boy?"

Red approached to calm Henry down, and Tyson ambled on up to disarm Plunky, just as Trent Rasmussen came out the front door of his shop.

"What's all the excitement, Ty?"

"Oh, nothin', Trent, Plunky just set off another mini Gettysburg here. You might want to keep a little distance between him and loaded weapons. I'm afraid we may have us another loose cannon movin' into town," he whispered, as he gestured with his head toward Bob.

Wolves at the Door

Back in New Kiowa, Tamsen just kept rocking gently as she finished darning up some of Henry's socks. She again laughed at herself and thought, *Yep, he's too old and harmless to get into trouble, but what about Bob?*

Who Goes and Who Stays?

Over the next few days Henry casually surveyed the town. He got information on a couple of new housing additions being developed. He met friends and business folks, mostly shopkeepers, through Dagmar and the LeClercs. All would be helpful, he was sure, when the family actually made the move. He and Tamsen would wait until school ended in late spring. He felt certain the initial entourage would consist of himself, Tamsen, Bob, Ollie and Tom. Charlie and Frank would stay back in New Kiowa to look after the family's interests for a while. Henry and Tamsen's ranges would be leased out to other ranchers, then most likely eventually sold. Same with Bob's. Libby and James would decide at their leisure when and how to best sell off the Kiowa House and move to La Junta. Harlan and Gretta were very family oriented and would follow along, bringing their other children.

The decision to leave some children behind had not been an easy one for Henry and Tamsen, but the children staying in New Kiowa were adults with plans of their own. Frank and Charlie had made plans to open a meat market in New Kiowa. They had such good contacts with local ranchers, a well-run meat market seemed to be a natural.

On to La Junta—The Baton is Passed in Colorado

They had already leased a brick building suitable for an ice house, sent out flyers, put an ad in the paper, and bought their first inventory order. Not only were they eager to proceed, they were hesitant to walk away from a good opportunity in a town where they were known. They'd just play it by ear as to a future move to La Junta.

Sadie was now twenty-one years old and much in love with Simon Stonefield, a twenty-three-year-old rancher. Si was a solid young man well known to the Devon family. Bob, Charlie and Frank all gave him high marks as a possible brother-in-law. They, of course, didn't tell Sadie that.

"He's the ugliest cowpoke I ever saw." Bob said to his sister. "You have kids with him, they're all gonna look like mules."

"And them ears!" Charlie said. "He better keep them glued to his head or on windy days he'll be in Caldwell 'fore we can catch up with him."

"Well, he can't be too bad accordin' to a couple of my rowdy friends," added Frank. "They see him comin' out of Priscilla's House of Pleasure 'bout every night. The ladies there seem to love him!"

"Mother, would you please make your uncouth sons shut their pie holes!" Sadie said. "You saddle bums wouldn't know a refined gentleman if he stepped on yer danged foot!"

"Refined, my butt!" Charlie said. "Why we could tell you things about ol' Mr. Simon Stonefield that'd make a Frenchman blush!"

Wolves at the Door

In reality, they all liked the young man and would welcome him into the family if things went that way.

"We can't interfere at all, Father," Tamsen said. "She'll do what she thinks is best."

"I know. Or more truthfully, I don't know," admitted Henry. "I could never figger you out, let alone any of those daughters of yours. But if Stonefield is going to come aboard, I wish he'd propose or somethin'. You know, let's poop or get off the pot!"

"Henry, that's why I'm so attracted to you. You're such a romantic!"

And then there was Raisin. He had been only a few years old when he happily flopped his way alongside the wagon on the way out a decade ago. Now at age fourteen or so, he was a tired old pup.

"I know I should put him down," Henry said, "but I just can't. I love that old bag of fleas so much,"

"I know, Father, me too. But he ain't too stoved up, yet. We can take him on the train, I'm sure. 'Les he starts messin' himself, he'll be all right. I guess the question of who goes and who stays will just work itself out." What do Traisleys 'n' Korzacks 'n' Deteaus say now?" she asked.

"Same as our family, I reckon. Except Korzacks. I'm sure they're stayin' in New Kiowa. Boney's done real well in his construction business. There's so many houses and buildings goin' up, he'll be busy forever. And folks know him and like him. He has a real good reputation no matter

On to La Junta—The Baton is Passed in Colorado

how much we remind him of his Fort Scott incarceration," Henry said with a chuckle.

"Traisleys are comin' as soon as possible, I'm almost sure. Deteaus may come, depending on Hooz. If he wants to throw in with his folks here in Kiowa, they'll probably stay. Like Charlie and Frank, Hooz knows everyone here and may not want to throw that away. Tim and him may run their brand for a while here. But Tim ain't a spring chicken, either. I imagine they'll eventually get too tired and drift on over to La Junta. At least we and Dagmar and Red 'n' Deborah will have set up a Bourbon County contingent over there. Whoever follows, follows."

Tom Was a Different Matter

"I just signed off on the land and the stock last week! No more pigs for me! Zilly and I will find us a nice little house in La Junta and relax," Dan told Henry as they lifted storage trunks onto the platform at the station.

It was June 10, 1889. All who were going were going, or, as the conductor yelled, "All aboard who's goin' aboard!"

The ride over was pleasant. Settling in was relatively easy. Expectations were high. The balance of the year was exciting for all, as most new adventures are. Henry and Tamsen had rented a small home on Belmont Avenue. In Henry's previous visit he had met Ronald Graves, an agent for the Ohio Syndicate Company. The company had laid out the Ohio Addition on the west side of La Junta only a year earlier.

"You should consider buying a homesite now at our discounted introductory prices, Mr. Devon," Mr. Graves had said. "We've got seventy-four acres there to develop, and I imagine it will be bought up fast. Then you will have to go farther out of town, less convenient."

Henry had had no objection to the Ohio Addition, but he doubted all the lots would be snapped up before they arrived. Since he had essentially bought their New Kiowa town lot prior to discussion with Tamsen, he wanted to include her this time.

"Thanks for the suggestion, Ron, but I'll get back to you when we're permanently in La Junta. I would like to go ahead and rent a home starting early June." Thus the house on Belmont.

"This look OK, kids?" Henry asked Ollie and Tom. "The Lincoln School is where you'll go, over on Second Street. I'm told our friend Woodruff gave the land for it."

"I wonder how big it is, compared to New Kiowa," Ollie said.

"Three hundred or so," Tamsen said, "according to Dagmar. She volunteers to help out there. But she says it's outgrowing itself. A new, bigger school is due to go up in a couple of years."

Olive's interest was unenthusiastic and almost a moot point. She had recently turned seventeen, and it was questionable if she would even bother to attend school.

"I wish I could've just finished with my class in New Kiowa," she muttered.

On to La Junta—The Baton is Passed in Colorado

With no plan for further education, she was more interested in getting a job than finishing her senior year of high school in an unknown environment.

"Can I write back to New Kiowa, maybe do some courses by mail and get a diploma from them?"

"Oh, go ahead and go here, Ollie. You'll meet kids your age. Besides, you won't meet a future husband working at the bakery or the millinery," Libby said while helping Tamsen move in.

"No, but I might working over at that Harvey House!"

Tom was a different matter. He'd be going to the Lincoln School as a high school freshman starting in September. There were supposedly more than four hundred students enrolled for the coming year, about half boys. He figured there would be maybe thirty or forty in the ninth grade alone. He knew what was going to happen, and he knew how to handle it.

On his first day in the ninth grade, Tom walked over to the school. Tamsen had packed a sandwich, an apple and a few cookies in a paper sack, which he carried in a canvas bag along with a few books he had brought from New Kiowa. He really liked math and looked forward to geometry, which he had studied a little on his own. Just before he got to the school, he beheld exactly what he had expected, a group of six or eight boys waiting for him.

Henry had advised him on what would probably happen, explaining it as the usual orientation of a new kid on his first day at a new school. Henry had also told him the two possible ways to deal with it.

"Hi, shitface," a fairly small boy said to Tom as he attempted to pass by. "Where do you think yer going?"

A much larger boy, probably about fifteen, stood silently beside the small boy. He was six to eight inches taller and twenty pounds heavier than Tom.

"To school, get out of my way," Tom said.

"How tough are ya, kiddo?" the small boy asked.

"You don't want to find out. Move!" Tom said as he strode forward.

Just as his chest met the little fellow's chest, he could see the big guy's fist moving at him. Instinctively, Tom pushed his book bag into the big boy's face, blocking his vision. Then with his left hand he hit the boy in the solar plexus with pinpoint accuracy. He heard the air rush from his adversary's stomach and knew the fight was over. But that didn't complete his father's instructions.

"The first thing you can do, son, is nothing. If you are set upon by a bigger fellow or a group of boys, wisdom would say to smile, bow down to 'em, give them your apple or whatever they want and avoid a fight, which you figure you'll probably lose anyway. That'd be the smart thing to do."

"Yeah? And what's the other way to handle it?"

"The other way is the way we Devons have always done it, the stupid way. Let me explain, and don't you dare tell your mother I ever said this. If it's one man, bigger or

On to La Junta—The Baton is Passed in Colorado

smaller don't matter, and you did nothing to bring it on, then you've got to be the first one with the goods. Too often you get lulled into a pushing match. First thing is decide quickly if you are somehow in the wrong. I mean, did you someway, maybe accidentally, offend this fellow. If so, its your fault so you apologize. You don't want no fight that don't have to be," Henry had said.

"But that's not the case we're talkin' about here, is it?" Henry had continued. "We're talkin' about some wacked out yahoo trying to impress someone, or he's drunk, or just nuts. So as I say, don't get in a pushin' match. Try to avoid it, but the very first time he lays a hand on you, even a finger, blast him. Lemme see you make a proper fist, that's good, thumb up tight to those first two fingers. Don't ever put it inside yer fingers or it'll break."

"I know that, Pa, you think I ain't never been in a fight? I been in a hundred with my own goddamn brothers!"

"Watch yer language, you might slip and say that to your ma, and then there'd really be hell to pay. No, I know you can handle yourself, but this is a new school. This ain't yer brothers. You got only one chance to set the tone for the next several years,"

"OK, so I blast him first. That it?"

"No, son, that ain't it. There's never just one fight. There's always three. You hit him once, first and hardest, for this fight. Then even if he's out cold, hit him again for any thought he may have of a second fight. Then hit him once more, just as hard, to serve notice to any lookers on who may have plans against you. And don't ever forget what I say. A one-punch fella will pay for it later. If you gotta strike once, strike three times. Got it?"

Tom did. It had made sense. "But what if it's a bunch of men, not just one?"

"Same rules apply, except one," Henry said. "If it's a gang, a little guy will always do the talkin. A big coward will be standin' beside or behind him just waitin' to sucker punch you while you're jabberin' with the midget. Again, don't push. When it's time to strike, forget everybody but the big guy. Don't make no move whatsoever at Tiny, just quick as a cat deliver your fist to the chin or gut of Mr. Big, and always follow it with two more. He'll be so surprised he'll pee himself, and the rest of the crowd will disappear like snow in July."

And that's what Tom remembered. So after he heard the air whoosh from the bigger boy and felt him double up in pain, Tom came up with another shot to the chin, standing the boy up like a cigar store Indian. As all the others stood motionless, as though they were watching their Pa's prize mare fall off a cliff, Tom delivered his third missile. This one caught the boy's beak as he was already falling and produced the geyser of blood so appreciated in these schoolyard tangles. The boy was down, out and bloody. And to the general delight of all, he did in fact, pee himself.

"Anybody else have a comment or opinion?" Tom asked.

For as long as Tom lived in La Junta, nobody did.

On to La Junta—The Baton is Passed in Colorado

From Selling Bricks to Milking Cows

The 1890s were galloping upon La Junta. The approximate population when the Devons arrived was just under fifteen hundred souls. In the very next year, it grew by a thousand, and by 1895, it had grown by two thousand. That year the Devons were experiencing not only normal geographic change, but also something of a cultural change brought about by progress. All within the first few years of their arrival came electricity, a telephone exchange, even city sewer lines, things they wouldn't have imagined in their wildest dreams back in New Kiowa.

"Mercy, Hank," Danny Traisley said, "this is amazing. What do we have now, four or five brickyards? That way outdoes New Kiowa."

"I guess so … Brown Yards, Norcross & Holland, and I 'speck more will pop up. The new McNeen Yard is supposed to make a high heat brick, good for the steel furnaces," Henry said as he slumped into an overstuffed chair in the parlor of the Belmont Avenue house. He appreciated a comfortable chair now, more than he ever could have expected ten years ago.

Bob, walking in through the front door, added, "Yep, McNeen is the top-notch outfit for the furnaces. And guess who just got himself hired on with them?"

"You?" said a surprised but hopeful Henry.

"Not just me, but ol' IBar Johnson hisself."

"IBar! You're kidding. He's here in La Junta?" Tamsen asked.

Wolves at the Door

"In the flesh. He just got in last night, and I ran into him this mornin' at the Harvey House. Haven't seen him for over five years. We had coffee and breakfast and laughed over old times. The hiring agent for McNeen was at the table beside us. Got talkin' to him and next thing we got hired on as salesmen. IBar will cover east of here back to Dodge City. I'll go west to towns all the way down into New Mexico. They pay a commission on all we sell!"

"Can you sell enough bricks to make a living, son?" Tamsen asked.

"It ain't just bricks. It is both building bricks and furnace bricks, but it's also building tile, silo brick, sewer pipe, all kinds of stuff. Heck, yes, Ma! I know I can sell. Plus I'm still single and don't need a whole lot right yet. And ol' IBar is a born salesman. Hell, he could sell scales to a snake!"

Tamsen winced. She didn't doubt Bob's salesmanship. She just wished he wouldn't say hell so much.

The brick business boomed in and around La Junta. So did light colored limestone and the darker sandstone. Many of the buildings put up in the 1890s of these local materials were to stand proudly more than a hundred years later.

"You ain't the only one with a new job, brother," Tom said. "I just got hired on to run the town herd for the summer. Mr. Huber's going back to Illinois for a couple of months to visit family. He said I could fill in with the herd when school's out at the same pay he gets, a dollar a cow per day."

On to La Junta—The Baton is Passed in Colorado

La Junta in the mid 1890s had a lot of folks wanting milk, but as yet no dairy existed. The routine of folks turning a cow or two over to Mr. Jack Huber had worked pretty well for everyone. Huber would come by each subscribing household every morning and add their animal to his wandering herd. He would then walk them just out of town to available grass and water. After a full day's grazing, he would lead them back into town and drop each one off at the appropriate house for the night. Come morning, the homeowner would milk them and tie them out by the gate for Huber to again pick up.

One time Huber, who had befriended the Devons, tapped on their door at about 7:30 A.M.

"Hope I ain't disturbin' you and the missus, Mr. Devon. I got me an idea and want yer opinion on it. Mind if I come in for a minute?"

"No, no, Jack, c'mon in and have a cup of coffee," Henry said, as Tamsen got out another cup. "What's on your mind?"

"Well, this herdin' service I got is doin' all right, but I'd like more customers. Since it's the ladies who most likely handles the kitchen stuff, like having good fresh milk every day, I got an idea for a business flyer to hand out all over town. What do you all think of this, 'specially you, Mrs. Devon?" Jack Huber asked as he handed Henry the rough draft.

Henry glanced at it, smiled slightly, read it again and then quickly handed it to Tamsen as he garbled a muffled excuse of having to go to the outhouse. Tamsen could hear Henry laughing as he ducked down the side alley toward the backyard. Her eyes fell on the card, which read, "Jack Huber, Cow Herder, 412 Eighth Ave." That line was followed by, "Ladies, if you got full udders that need tending to each morning, and your husband ain't up to it, why not put 'em in the reliable hands of Mr. Jack Huber?"

Huber stood there with a deadpan look of innocent earnestness, waiting for Tamsen's reply.

"Whadya think, Mrs. Devon? Think that'll churn me up some business?"

Tamsen looked into his hopeful countenance deeply enough to be satisfied he was serious. She then politely answered. "It's a fine idea, Mr. Huber. May I suggest a very slight rewording of your thought, to avoid any possible confusion on the service you actually perform?"

From a stifled voice outside the alley window had come an addition: "And to avoid being shot by a very un-understanding husband!"

That's it: Barnes Avenue. I Ain't Movin' Again!

January 1, 1896, was an invigorating blue skied and crisp day. Henry and Tamsen were walking hand in hand down Belmont Avenue, Tamsen's other hand holding the leash of their new pup, Rascal. They headed north. They got to Hancock and turned east. Then to Warren, where they again turned north.

On to La Junta—The Baton is Passed in Colorado

"This whole Ohio Addition is being re-plotted," Henry said. "I'm pretty sure this next street is going to be called Barnes Avenue, or one of these is. I read it or heard it somewhere. And they're changing the side streets from Main and Hancock and all to numbers—like Third, Fourth or Fifth."

"Anyway," he continued as they approached a particular lot on the street he thought would be Barnes, "I think this lot right here may be the one Ron Graves told me about. This and several others are still available. The others are closer to the school, but we don't need that anymore. How do you like this?"

Henry had never had a strong desire to own the home he lived in. Back in his farming and ranching days he did want ownership. That came out of his father's English phobia of the problems the lords of the manor could inflict on tenant farmers. The European system had resulted in an almost fanatical desire on the part of first and second generation Americans to own their farmland. But Henry had no farmland anymore. He was a balding, sixty-four-year-old man who was aging to the point of wanting as little hassle as he could get by with. That included the inherent stresses of property ownership. It was Tamsen who was pressing to buy their own house.

"I know what you're thinking, my dear," Henry said. "You figure I'm going to that Great Ranch in the Sky any day now, and you want to be nestled into your own place, don't you? You think these little outgrowths on my bald dome are my brains poppin' out don't you? Well, let's go ahead and build us a comfortable place, but don't count on me goin' to Fiddler's Green too soon. I'm stickin' around just to annoy you!"

She laughed and looked at the lot. Rascal proceeded to stroll over and pee on the dirt at the building site. Raisin had wandered off to die a couple of years back, or so Tamsen thought. In reality Henry, who couldn't stand to see Raisin suffer anymore but couldn't shoot him either, had told Bob to take care of it.

"Your mother has a church meetin' Tuesday night and I'm playin' cards with Harlan, Dan and Red. Just come get him and take care of it," Henry had said as he teared up. "I don't want to know what happened, and I'll tell your Ma he just wandered away to die."

So that's what had happened. They never saw their old friend again. It was heart-breaking for them for a few weeks. They never wanted another dog. Then at Christmas of 1895, off the train and totally unexpected, stepped Charlie and Frank.

Henry and Tamsen were delighted when Tom came whooping up the street, yelling, "Ma! Pa! Come out quick! Look who's here!"

They all hugged and slapped backs, then Frank handed his mother a hatbox all wrapped up with Christmas bows. "Go ahead, Ma, open it up!"

"Lordy, this is heavy," Tamsen said as she pried off the lid. And there was a little multicolor mutt that immediately began licking at her fingers.

"Oh my gosh, he's adorable," Ollie said. "What's his name?"

On to La Junta—The Baton is Passed in Colorado

"Rascal!" Charlie said, "'cause there's no reason to think he'll be any different than any of yer other sons, Ma!"

This was the Rascal who was now piddling on the Barnes Avenue lot that would be his home for the rest of his life, as well as Henry and Tamsen's. "Barnes Avenue," Henry said. "That's it, and I ain't never movin' again."

The Devons were living in their Barnes Avenue house in 1896 when all the Dwyers visited to scout out La Junta. Henry had mentioned Tom's temporary job with the town herd a while back and pointed out a need for a dairy. Like Henry and Tamsen, Harlan and Gretta wanted only a small house in town, but they were quite willing to help James and Libby start a Dwyer family dairy. They were all looking for land on the north side of the Arkansas River.

Sadie had also come to La Junta with the party from New Kiowa, and she brought her intended. Simon Stonefield finally had "gotten off the pot" and proposed. The young couple had come to tell her folks in person. And Simon wanted to formally ask Henry for his blessing. Even though it was technically after the fact, Henry graciously gave it.

"Where you two gonna live?" he asked.

"I believe we would be wise to stay in New Kiowa, sir," answered Simon. "I know you all are here now, and Sadie misses you powerfully, but I got my ranchin' contacts over there, and my family's all there, and I've assured her she can jump on the train for a visit as often as she likes."

"You two have our sincerest blessing, Simon," Tamsen said. "You know this here girl is our pride and joy, and sure, we'd like her right next door. But I married this old fool some thirty-eight years ago, and he's drug me all over hell's half acre. So I guess you two ought to be able to light where you want."

Tom had graduated from Otero Union High School in its second graduating class, in 1884. He had earned honors in science and was quite interested in mathematics, possibly engineering. He had been working at the Santa Fe since grade school, as many La Junta boys did, starting off sweeping floors. In Tom's case, as soon as he got out of high school, he quickly rose to fireman and then engineer. He was a bright fellow, and he retained the leadership qualities he had displayed since his youth. Plus he was a cool customer. Emergencies and accidents frequently occurred in running the trains. Where a lot of the young men panicked, Tom didn't. He was running the route over to Las Vegas and Santa Fe, New Mexico, which he enjoyed. By the time of the Dwyers' visit he was twenty. He was now a full-size man of six feet and a couple of inches, about one hundred eighty pounds.

After walking around the town and getting acquainted, one of the first conversations Libby had with Tamsen had to do with Tom. "And he is, by all accounts, the most handsome man in town!" she said about her baby brother. "You wouldn't believe the way the girls are throwing themselves at him, Mother. It's shameful, but funny, too. I don't think he knows what to make of it yet."

"He'll figure it out real quick, or he ain't a Devon!" Henry said.

On to La Junta—The Baton is Passed in Colorado

"Well, Devon or no Devon," Jim, said, "from what I observe, he seems to do quite well with the ladies. He drops names of girls in every town from here to Santa Fe. I don't think he needs your help Lib, or yours, Mother. And by the way, we got us a buyer for the hotel. In fact, we've had several offers. This one came in out of the blue, and it's too much money to turn down. We should have it done and be over here by Easter."

"Howdy folks," Tom said as he barged in the front door. His route brought him back to La Junta about every eight or nine days. He'd have three or four days in town, then head back out.

"Well, hello, my handsome boy!" Tamsen said.

"Yeah, lady killer ... How are the señoritas?" asked Libby.

Tom looked puzzled and started to question, but Jim interrupted him with, "Don't even ask. Yer mother and sister have been tellin' tales about your romancin' the young ladies!"

"Don't pay 'em no never mind, son. How was this week's trip?" Henry asked.

"Great, Pa. And look what came in the mail for me. It's the application for Kansas Mining and Manufacturing School. I aim to go get the courses for engineering. The railroad will pay for it. Get to know boilers better. It's called combustion engineering."

Sadie looked at her brother, saying, "Now don't go getting' too smart for your britches, buster."

Wolves at the Door

Poof, and They Were Caught for Eternity

"Listen," Henry said, "this here family seems to be blowin' to the four winds, so I got an idea. Before I lose the very last hair on my head, or your mother's hair turns any whiter, let's get us a family photograph, taken in an actual picture-takin' studio. I mean suits on, all gussied up. We may never be all together again. No offense, Jim, or you either, Si, but I mean just us original Devons. Whadya think, Mother?"

"Sounds like a good idea. We'll set it up for Easter if you'll be back here Libby. Sadie, will you be able to come over with the Dwyers? And Bob 'n' Charlie and Frank, and of course Ollie and Tom. That'll be wonderful."

The week following Easter 1896 seemed to work for everyone. Hunt and Haberkorn Studio scheduled the photo shoot. The morning it was to come together, a damper was thrown over the event. Ollie awoke with a screaming toothache and a badly swollen jaw. Even if they could somehow disguise her temporary disfigurement, she simply felt too awful. She was out. Then a telegram arrived from Frank. He was back in New Kiowa overseeing the books of the meat market he and Charlie still owned. They were living in La Junta but took turns returning once a month to check on the manager.

The manager had the gall to drop dead of a heart attack the very morning Frank planned to return for the photo. He had an hysterical young widow and her three youngsters on his hands, not to mention a serious business problem. He simply couldn't leave for several days. And the others couldn't stay in La Junta that long. Frank was out.

On to La Junta—The Baton is Passed in Colorado

"Well, we'll just go with what we got," Henry said. "That right, Mother? We'll do it again sometime later when the others is here. Or maybe we'll do one with spouses, grandkids, dogs, cats and chickens in the future. But the studio is all set up now, so let's march on over."

"Poof!" went the shutter as Christopher Haberkorn squeezed the bulb. Seated in front was Henry on the viewer's left, and Tamsen to the right. Henry had on his good three-piece suit and a rather flamboyant tie he bought for this photo and never wore again, actually that's not true. It was the tie he wore years later to a funeral—his. Because he had a totally bald pate, he combed up his snow white beard as fluffy as possible for the photograph. He put his right arm on the side of his wicker chair, looked straight at the camera, and relaxed.

Tamsen had washed her luxuriant white hair and combed it straight back to reveal her peaceful and motherly face. She was proud of this family, but it didn't show in her smile because nobody, on pain of death, smiled. The exposure took too long to hold a smile steady. She wore a lovely dark blue dress, but nobody would ever know it because all pictures for the first fifty or so years of photography were black and white. Future generations just assumed everybody wore black. And because nobody smiled in nineteenth century photos, their descendants naturally assumed they all must have had painful heartburn or hemorrhoids!

In the top row, left to right, were Bob, Sadie, Charlie and Tom. The backdrop to this photograph was a whimsical fake studio scene that included hazy wrought iron arches, fences, and palm trees. Only the viewer's imagination put limits on where this gathering might be.

Bob stood with his hands behind his back, his handlebar mustache nicely brushed. He looked a little like Wyatt Earp. He hoped future generations would notice that.

Beside Bob stood Sadie. Not that it ever was mentioned, but she was clearly the best looking of the Devon daughters. Clear and pleasant facial features, pretty eyes, attractive mouth. Fairly tall with an hourglass figure. Henry hoped Stonefield knew what he was getting, but he avoided any thought pattern about their coming union beyond that. He remembered a few of the action scenes on his own honeymoon of sorts with Tamsen, then tried to fight off the thought of any such activities involving Sadie and that goddamn Stonefield.

Next was Charlie, a bit more dapper and less rumpled than slovenly Bob. Nicely pressed three-piece suit, coat properly opened to reveal a watch fob, perfectly tied neck tie. He was cleanshaven, with attractive, wavy hair. Along with his other interests, Charlie was the tax assessor over in Saquache County. He looked like what he was, a sharp young go-getter.

Then came Elizabeth, Libby. She was and always remained a family favorite. Shorter and plainer than Sadie, and maybe a tad round shouldered, she looked like the kindly mother, daughter, wife and sister that she was. Being the oldest and first to leave the nest, she felt a certain responsibility to the others. Although it was almost never mentioned in those years, she had come to treasure the

On to La Junta—The Baton is Passed in Colorado

meaning of the butter mold box Tamsen had given her so many years ago. To Libby it would forever embody the essence of, and her love for, this family.

"You can't imagine the almost mystical aura that little box has for me, Pa," she had told Henry once. "Ever since Mother gave it to me in such an eloquent fashion, it has somehow become the tangible symbol of the love and decency and strength of our family. Every now and then I explain your wagon trip to my kids. I don't know that they understand what powerful souls they spring from, but that box will help, I'm sure." She had become the assistant mother hen of the family, destined to eventually take over from Tamsen.

And then, Tom. As stated, he was the tallest of the Devon men, by one or two inches. In the photograph, he would seem to be the most imposing. But at the same time, he had something of an innocent, youthful gaze. Of course, that's all in the eyes of the beholder. One thing certain, however, he was the only one of the children who still presented a mystery to his parents.

"It's interesting, Mother, to look at this picture," Henry said in midsummer after they had the finished product for more than a month. "We pretty much know the direction life is taking for Bob, and Charlie, the girls, all of 'em. Tom is the only one I can't seem to put a saddle on quite yet. Seems like he has a lifelong career with the Santa Fe starin' at him. But he's off to Topeka for several months or more over those courses he wants. What the hell is a 'combustion engineer' anyway? And then who's he gonna end up with as a wife? I'm sure he's got his pick from around here, or up and down the tracks, but far as I can tell, no gal yet seems to interest him."

"Someone will, Father. Some pretty gal will give him enough resistance to overwhelm him. That's how I got you!"

Henry made no comment. His courting of Tamsen had been a totally confusing blur to him back then and still was. May as well have been Romeo and Juliet it was so long ago.

Hell, Dear, I'm Still in My Prime

The next couple of years seemed to evaporate for Henry and Tamsen, as is the nature of aging. Their friends the LeClercs, the Traisleys, Harlan and Gretta, even old friends still back in New Kiowa, still saw each other or at least communicated. They all finally had put in party line telephones, so in addition to writing, they occasionally got to hear each other's voice. Plus, Henry and Tamsen took the train back now and then to see Sadie and her family.

"Boney, I sure hoped the years would have made you a little better looking, but I see they took you the other way!" Henry said to Korzack on one of those return trips. "Thank God Inga is still in full blossom."

"Bosom? Vhat'd he say about my bosom, Boney?" Her hearing was by now pretty much gone.

"Nothing, dear, he was just saying how nice you still look," Boney said as he whispered "Ingaism" to the Devons. "She still has 'em."

On to La Junta—The Baton is Passed in Colorado

"Tim, is that you? Hell you're gettin' almost as bald as I am! How are you two?" Henry said, struggling up from his chair at the Kiowa House to greet the Deteaus.

"Jane," added Tamsen, as she rushed to embrace her old friend, "you look wonderful."

"Well, so do you, Tamsen. La Junta must agree with you."

"Oh, phooey, you liar. I'm just a white-haired and wrinkled old fat lady, and you know it. If this old fool weren't half blind, he'd a throwed me out by now."

They had a great visit. Mayor Hooz Deteau came into the room with great fanfare and read an "honorary and perpetual citizenship" citation welcoming back two of New Kiowa's "leading and most respected founding fathers." He had, of course, just typed it up himself only an hour earlier and forged the governor's name on it.

"How vonderful, Boney, but vhy didn't you tell me the governor vas in town?" Inga said to her husband, who took a deep breath and said nothing.

On the way back to La Junta, Henry and Tamsen mused over the visit.

"I just can't come to grips with so much time going by," she said. "They all look all right, but they've clearly aged. Tim's cough is terrible. Boney can hardly move he's so stiff. Both Jane and Inga are holdin' up OK, but I guess none of us is a spring chicken anymore. What about you, Father, how do you feel in general?"

"Oh, hell, dear, I'm still in my prime. I'd still be chasin' you around the bedroom if I could only remember what to do if I caught you!"

Wolves at the Door

Looking up at him as the sage and tumbleweed swept by the window, she laughingly but coyly answered, "Well, Henry, I'll run a little slower if you'd like. And if you catch me, I'll remind you."

As she was looking at him she noticed an irregularity along his jawline, just below his left ear.

"What the devil is that, Father?" she asked as she reached up and touched it.

He winced. "Oh, that's nothing, just a bump. I might have a bad tooth or something."

"Well, do you have a bad tooth, Henry?" she persisted.

"No, I guess not really. This 's been comin' on about a week or two now. Don't rightly know what it is."

"You've got a cancer, Hank," Doc Briggs said after examining Henry. "A skin cancer, a tumor of sorts. Probably from more than forty or so years of plowin', plantin', and runnin' cows in the hot sun. It ain't gonna kill you tomorrow, but I'd get rid of it if I was you."

"How do you do that, Warren? Is it a big deal?"

"Nope, I just tie yer head to a tree an' lop it off with a pole ax. I only miss two or three out of ten. And if I kill you, it's half price."

The small surgery was simple and successful. Henry's jaw area was a bit sore for a few days and remained scarred, but three instead of two shots of bourbon per evening smoothed it over.

"Doc Briggs says I'm good as new, Mother."

"Doc Briggs tells me to keep a close watch on you, Father. He says where there's one of those things, they'll be more."

On to La Junta—The Baton is Passed in Colorado

War, Rough Riders and Train Wrecks

In spite of the passing years and oncoming aches, pains and maladies, Henry enjoyed simply sitting back and whiling the time away. A racetrack of sorts had opened in La Junta back in 1896 for horses and bicycles. Everybody from townfolk to ranchers to railroad men enjoyed racing something. The Santa Fe put a temporary end to it by taking over the track for more storage room they badly needed. And what was good for the Santa Fe was good for the town. But very quickly another trotting track was opened out near the Anderson Arroyo, not far from the Devons' Barnes Avenue home. They enjoyed the races and all the resulting hullabaloo, frequently attending with Dagmar, the LeClercs and other friends.

"The colors those jockeys wear are beautiful," Tamsen said to Deborah. "The racing flags or whatever you call them, it's all exciting."

"Speaking of colors, or colored, we got us a few extra colored folks around town. Have you noticed?" Deborah said.

"Oh goodness, Deb, we got so many whites, Injuns, Mexicans, Poles and Russians going by, I guess it don't matter. I think the railroad employs some, and maybe they are comin' in to work with these trotters. Plus, according to Tom, there's a whole lot of every color, including Negroes, streamin' into the coal mines over near Walsenburg. I guess I don't give a hoot long as they all behave theirselves like everybody else."

Another thrill for La Junta was the oncoming Spanish American War. Some of the local young men joined the army out of whooped-up patriotism. Henry wasn't sure what that was all about.

"Even our own War of Rebellion was a strange one to figure out, but at least we had it on our own doorstep. This dang thing makes no sense. I don't really give a damn who does what in Cuba. I just hope Tom doesn't get sucked into it."

"I won't, Pa," Tom said, coming up on the front porch. He sat down beside his parents. "The engineering course I took seems to put me in a category of necessary people. The railroad don't want their investment in me gettin' shot in Cuba. They put me on their 'do not take list.' Seems I'm one of many needed to keep the war supplies movin'."

A side event of the war that gained more attention in the southwest than the war itself was the use of Las Vegas, New Mexico, as a training base for the army. The Rough Riders under Teddy Roosevelt found glory in Cuba at San Juan Hill. They had achieved notoriety when they trained in Las Vegas before the action, but they got much more when they started having reunions there in 1899. It was a heightened experience for Henry and Tamsen because Tom actually had a room on Grand Avenue in Las Vegas at that time. He was an active train engineer by then, over in the Santa Fe area, and he lived in Las Vegas. He was now coming back to La Junta for brief visits only every month or so.

Just before the very first Rough Rider reunion was to be held, June 24, 1899, Tom had an experience that increased his

On to La Junta—The Baton is Passed in Colorado

aura in the eyes of railroad people, his family and the public. He didn't say a word about it to his parents. Tamsen came into the house one day in late June with a letter from Tom.

"Oh, good," Henry said. "I wonder what he's up to? What's he say?"

Tamsen sat down, put on her reading specs, and opened the letter. "It's a newspaper clipping from Las Vegas. He attached a little note saying we might be interested in the article, that's all."

"Well, what's the article? Go ahead and read it out loud. I don't want to go in for my glasses."

"It says, 'Engineer Proves Hero. Tom Devon prevents disabled locomotive from colliding with Limited—'"

"What! Holy Smoke! Well don't just sit there, go on!"

"'Bravery on the part of Thomas Devon, a Santa Fe engineer residing at 317 Grand Avenue, probably averted a serious accident on the Santa Fe near Watrous last night. As a result of self sacrifice and devotion to duty, Devon, badly burned from escaping steam, is confined to his bed at his home—'"

"What!" Henry again interrupted. "Oh, Christ, I hope he's OK. Well don't just sit there, goddammit, read!"

"Listen you old goat, I'm gonna read the rest of this to myself. Then you can read it or roll it up and smoke it for all I care. And you interrupt me one more time and you can roll it up and stick it up yer bee-hind. Now be quiet."

He sat still for a moment, properly chastised, before saying, "Well then, if yer gonna get all huffy about it, at least hurry up with it!" He got up with effort to go get his glasses. His pains at times were beginning to sour his moods, and his lifelong benevolent regard for all mankind was occasionally replaced with rancor.

The article went on to explain how the train had been on a siding to Shoemaker with the engine uncoupled to take on water. A pipe broke, allowing escaping steam to fill the cab. The fireman had jumped, but Tom stayed with the engine. He got out of the cab and reached his arm back in to the throttle. He got burned, but he eventually stopped the engine. The article said if Tom Devon hadn't been so brave and quick thinking, the train would have hit the oncoming Chicago Limited.

"My God!" Henry said when he finally got the article. "It says he got bad burns on his arms, legs and head. I wonder how bad!"

"Oh my beautiful baby boy!" cried Tamsen with her face buried in her hands. "How could this happen?"

"Now, now, Mother. It says he'll be on his feet in several days. And this article must've been back in mid-June, 'cause the article below it mentions Teddy Roosevelt comin' in for the Rough Rider reunion. That was the twenty-fourth. This must've been well before that. I'm sure he's OK, or we'd have heard from him by now."

Four days later Tom walked in the front door, still scalded red, but no worse for wear.

On to La Junta—The Baton is Passed in Colorado

A Tragedy, A Heartbreak

Tom's train incident had further convinced Tamsen and Henry that the torch had been passed to the next generation. Bob had finally gotten married to Etta, a local girl. Frank married Winifred, whose family lived over in La Veta, a town on the eastern edge of the mountains. They had met on the train. Everybody met on the train.

An oddity occurred with Ollie. She met and married a young fellow name Dwyer, Jack Dwyer, but no relation to Harlan, Gretta, Jim and Libby, which was a constant point of confusion. It was somewhat resolved when Ollie and Jack moved to Pittsburgh, Pennsylvania.

All the children were now married except Tom, who remained Henry and Tamsen's golden boy. Everywhere they went, everyone asked about Tom. If they went to the race track, "Hi, Hank, whadya hear from our hero?"

When they went to the new Rourke Theatre to see *Browns in Town* on September 19, 1901, Tom also happened to be in town. Since his twenty-fifth birthday had been only two days earlier, they took him along as a celebration. Tamsen burst with pride when she saw all the mothers who had marriage-age daughters mumbling and pointing at Tom.

"You see that, son," she whispered, "You c'mon home and you got the pick of the litter!"

"Not interested, Mother, now hush up and watch the play."

Bob had joined the newly formed La Junta Elks Club #701. He confided to his father, "I get the same thing, Pa.

Wolves at the Door

Everyone at our Elks meetings wants to know about Tom Devon, hero of the Santa Fe. And they all got a daughter or a sister. God, I wish I had his problem. Don't tell Etta I said that!" Both men chuckled.

The La Junta population in 1901 was right at four thousand and growing fast. All the progress and optimism was only slightly tinged with the ongoing problem of crime and lawlessness. Bob repeated his Kiowa activity of being a part-time deputy. He reported to Marshal John Lewis. Same old stuff, mostly bar fights, noise disturbance, pilfered cooling apple pies, bar fights, shoplifting, bar fights and more bar fights. No big deal. Then it happened, an event that changed Tom's life as well as Henry and Tamsen's lives forever.

In late May, 1902, Henry, Tamsen, Dagmar and Deborah were walking home after the trotter races, enjoying the unseasonably warm evening. Red LeClerc had died in his sleep the year before, and this was one of Deborah's first fun outings. As they passed the entrance to an alley easement running behind a row of houses, they were startled when a young woman burst out of the alley not ten yards in front of them. She appeared to be about sixteen or seventeen years old and was crying hysterically. Most of her lower clothing was torn off, and she was bleeding through what was left of her underpants. Her eyes were wide, bulging and very red; they would be swollen and black by morning.

"What in the …?" cried Tamsen, as Henry hobbled forward to catch the girl before she fell. Since they were

On to La Junta—The Baton is Passed in Colorado

almost at their home, they took her there to help clean her up and try to understand what had happened.

"Go call Bobby quick, Henry. Maybe he should bring Marshal Lewis to see this."

Bob was at the house within thirty minutes. "Marshal's gone for a few days, Miss. Care to tell me what happened? And for the record I'm Bob Devon, deputy. These nice folks who helped you just happen to be my parents."

The girl stared at the floor and began crying. She shook her head. "He was awful, what he did … I can't tell you,"

"Ma'am, you'll have to tell me if—"

"Bob, why don't you and Father go out on the porch for a while. I think maybe this young lady would rather just talk to us ladies," Tamsen said. "Understand?"

"Well, no, Ma, I have to—"

"Son, let's do what your mother says," Henry said, cutting him off. "Let's go have us a glass of buttermilk."

The girl's basic story was that she was going to a friend's house and cut through the alley to save time. Somebody grabbed her, threw her behind a row of overgrown bushes, and beat her about the face. He then tore at her clothes, very roughly ripped her underpants off, and proceeded to rape her.

"What time was it?" Tamsen asked.

"Did you see his face?" asked Deborah.

"Did he have a shirt or coat you'd recognize?" added Dagmar.

"Dark, it was dark," the girl said before lapsing into full hysteria.

Wolves at the Door

They did their best to calm her down, but she was totally out of control. She started screaming, which drew Henry and Bob back into the house.

"It's no good, Father," Tamsen said. "We got to get her to the hospital 'fore she hurts herself. She may be bad hurt inside. Bring around the buggy."

So off they went. By midnight a Mennonite nurse was seated in front of them after examining the girl. "First of all, her name is Susannah Frakes. Family lives in the Ohio Addition."

"That's Daniel Frakes' little sister, I bet," Bob said. "They live four or five blocks from you, Pa. Dan is a real good friend of Tom's. I'll bet Tom knows this girl."

"She's been badly beaten and she has, in fact, been raped," continued the nurse. "Her beating bruises will heal up. Her emotional ones may not. This man was needlessly rough. She's permanently hurt inside. It won't kill her, but she'll most likely never be able to have children. I'm very sorry. If you know her parents, would you be so kind as to inform them? We're quite busy and can't spare anyone."

Bob said he'd go as the deputy on duty, but he was tremendously relieved when Tamsen offered to go with him.

"Girls, you two go on home. We don't want to overwhelm these people," Tamsen said to Dagmar and Deborah. "Go on, go home. Come over to the house tomorrow. Come around nine o'clock and we'll hash this out. Henry, you go on home, too. Bob and I will go tell Susannah's folks. I'll be home soon."

On to La Junta—The Baton is Passed in Colorado

They all went separate directions into the night, having no idea what repercussions this tragedy would produce.

"Bob was right about the family bein' friends of Tom," Tamsen said to Dagmar and Deborah the next morning. "Henry and I never met them before. They moved in only a year ago. The mister is with the railroad accounting department, and so is their son Daniel. They say Tom has stopped by a few times. Seems he was chummy with the girl, too. Very nice folks. They was all torn up over the news. I'm sure they stayed at the hospital last night."

The three ladies sat in Tamsen's kitchen, drinking coffee and nibbling on biscuits.

"Well, what happens now?" Deborah said as Henry scooted up a fourth chair. "Is Bob involved until Lewis gets back?"

"He is back. He was just visiting his folks over in Pueblo," Henry replied. "Bob called him. He's probably at the hospital now."

"Hello, anybody home?" boomed Bob's voice from the porch.

"C'mon in, son! We're in the kitchen."

In strolled Bob with Marshal Lewis right behind him.

"Mornin' folks," said the Marshal.

"Ma, Pa, ladies, Mr. Lewis here just got a quick look at Susannah at the hospital. She's so sedated she's knocked out," explained Bob.

Wolves at the Door

The marshal shook his head and sighed. "I can't believe this would happen right here in town, just a couple of blocks from here. Would you all mind if I got a feel of what happened by asking exactly what you saw?"

"We really didn't see anything," Henry said. "She just stumbled out of the alley in front of us, all beat up and hysterical."

"You didn't see anybody in the alley? Did you hear anything?"

"No," Deborah said, "but we couldn't see the nigger who done this in that black alleyway at night anyway."

"Nigger?" Lewis said, with raised eyebrows. "Why do you say that?"

Tamsen was shocked at Deborah's comment and wondered the same thing.

"'Cause she told us a nigger did it to her!"

Tamsen caught Dagmar's eye and saw surprise on her face, too.

"When did she say that, Deb?" Dagmar asked.

"Last night. You was sittin' right there when she said it!" Deborah replied defensively. "You, or, heck I don't know, maybe Tamsen. One of us asked who did it and she said a nigger. Well, I think she actually said 'a darky'."

Tamsen was stunned. "I can't believe I missed that, Deb. I remember I asked what time it happened and she said it was dark."

"And I asked the color of his coat and she said she thought it was dark," added Dagmar.

On to La Junta—The Baton is Passed in Colorado

The marshal again raised his eyebrows and looked at Bob, then Henry. "Any clarification on this, fellas?"

"No sir, 'fraid not," Bob said. "My father and I were out on the porch. We have no idea."

"Well, I absolutely can't believe this," Deb LeClerc said with obvious irritation. "Are you girls deaf? That poor girl sat right in that chair, Tamsen, and said it clear as a bell, said a damned darky done raped her. Now that's positive, I heard it, and so did you!"

By the time different versions of this interview got around town it became common knowledge that a Negro was the culprit.

"Maybe I'm going deaf, Father, or tetched in the head, but I swear I didn't hear it that way," Tamsen said later as she tried to recollect the conversation.

"Well, that's the way it is now, Mother. Deborah is sure as hell about it, and Dagmar says she just ain't sure. The whole town is tryin' to round up the right colored man."

"Or any colored man," she said.

Bob came back to the house the next day to bring his folks up to date. "We got her story this afternoon. Lewis and I went back to the hospital. Her parents and brother were in the room when we arrived. Marshal asked her point blank who raped her, and she answered, point blank, 'a nigger.' I saw her exchange glances with her mother, and they both nodded at each other."

"You think the parents had told her Deborah's opinion?" Henry asked

"Oh, hell yes, I'm sure they did. They need and want to pin blame on somebody. Might as well be a nigger. That's sure better than finding it was the mayor's son, or someone like that."

You Sure? She's Sure!

Washington Wallace had been born and raised in Louisville, Kentucky. He was twenty-eight years old, and he was a Negro. He had drifted out of Kentucky in the early 1890s hoping to find a more hospitable political climate for those of his hue. He wasn't a real good boy, but no devil, either. He had committed a small burglary or two and had decided to head west to escape his past and turn over a new leaf. He hooked up with the AT&SF and had spent the previous ten years with a more or less clean nose. He did have one chronic vice, which caused him to lose his job a few times, whiskey. Each time he got fired he just moved a hundred miles or so down the tracks and hired on again, always as a low end, totally dispensable scut laborer. He had arrived in La Junta in February of this year, 1902.

"Yeah, we know him," the personnel manager told Marshal Lewis. "Been around doin' odd jobs for a couple of months, I figure. Don't even have him on the books. We just pay him cash when he does some work."

"Where's he live?" Lewis asked.

"Hell, I don't know. I guess where most of the niggers live, a little south of town. But if you need to see him, he's over in the machine shop right now, sweepin' up shavins'," said the manager.

On to La Junta—The Baton is Passed in Colorado

"He been around the last day or two?" asked the marshal.

"Can't really say. I haven't seen him. He goes off on a bender now and then, sleeps it off for a day and then shows up hungover for a couple days' work. He don't seem to bother nobody. Go on over to the shop and talk to him."

Marshal Lewis took Bob and another part-time deputy with him as witnesses to the conversation. There wasn't much to witness. Yes, Wallace had been in town the last two days. No, he had not been to work. Yes, he drank a little and couldn't exactly remember his precise whereabouts on the night in question. And "No suh, as God is my witness" he had not been in the vicinity of the horse tracks, never had heard of any Ohio Addition, "wasn't in no alley," and "please suh, please believe me, I didn't see no young white girl. I ain't never put myself on no white girl, not her, not no white girl ever!"

"Wash, I got to take you into the jail," Lewis said. "You're the only colored man new to town right now. The girl says it was a nigger. We got to take you in and see if she recognizes you."

Two days later Washington Wallace was asked to stand up in his cell because the young lady was coming in. He had been fed, but not allowed to wash or change clothes since arrested. He had about a three-day beard, looked dirty and smelled awful. Standing beside him, two other colored men, volunteers, had been brought in as other choices in this line up. One was Rev. Hosiah Smith, a well dressed and clean-shaven black man from South River Baptist.

Wolves at the Door

The other was a thirteen-year-old Negro Mexican boy. Nobody knew his name. He was just thrown in to make it three.

"That's him, there in the middle," the Frakes girl said, pointing at Washington Wallace.

"You sure?" asked Marshal Lewis.

"She's sure," Susannah's mother said as she grabbed her daughter's elbow and led her out of the jail.

That was pretty much it. The court convened, the witnesses spoke, the jury listened, and promptly convicted Mr. Washington Wallace, described in court proceedings as "the 28-year-old Negro man, employed by the Santa Fe," for "assaulting and raping Miss Susannah Frakes, a 17-year-old Caucasian girl on the night of ..." and so forth. He would be held for sentencing, which could be life in the state penitentiary or death. His attorney was outraged and insisted on appealing the case in Denver. So there sat a terrified and very sober Mr. Wallace in a rather flimsy jail cell, awaiting his fate.

And Back Comes a Furious Tom.

Bob had sent a telegram to Tom in Las Vegas, briefly explaining what had happened. Although Tom wasn't in any way connected to Susannah Frakes other than through her brother, he was enraged. He was scheduled to return to La Junta in just a few days anyway. For reasons even he couldn't explain, his anger over the assault grew and grew the closer he got to La Junta.

On to La Junta—The Baton is Passed in Colorado

"Can they really just give this bastard a jail term?" he asked Bob.

"I'm just goin' by what Lewis tells me. Washingon's lawyer wants to get him up to Denver for a retrial. He doesn't think this jury was fair. And, yes, he'd probably just go to the pen, or maybe get off Scott free!"

"You're kidding!" Tom was amazed. "Are you serious?"

"Again, Tom, this is just what I hear Lewis say. Who the hell knows what'll really happen?"

"Well I sure know one thing, brother. That sonovabitch ain't gettin' off, not after what he done to Daniel's sister!"

Henry and Tamsen, even though they were two of the four people first on the scene, didn't know what to think of this episode.

"Listen to me, son," Tamsen said to Tom. "I was standin' right in front of her, and I'm still not at all sure what she said. Deborah swears she used the word 'dark' or 'darky' to refer to a colored man. I'm about as sure she didn't. At least at the moment, I took her to be talking about the darkness of the night in that alley. If Deb hadn't spit out what she did, I never in a million years would have come up with any opinion that a Negro did it."

"Well, there sure ain't no confusion from her family now. Dan's sure it was this colored drunk, and he's fearful that bastard'll get off," Tom said. He caught himself, thinking he should tone down his language in front of his mother. "Excuse me, Ma."

As the next two days went by, hysteria grew throughout the populace. "What if this nigger gets off, will they all start jumpin' our daughters and wives in alleys?" was a commonly spoken concern. Or, "What the hell do they know up in Denver about this? This is our town and we'll handle it."

As the younger men around town began gathering and ranting about Wallace going free, they began turning into what more and more resembled a mob. Standing with Dan Frakes to support his friend, Tom was getting swept up in the fever. It didn't help that with his two-fisted hero reputation, he was looked upon by most of the others as a leader and a doer.

"What can we do with this black bastard, Dan?" came one query.

"Dan, you and Tom go in and get that rapist and we'll follow you. Let's hang the sonovabitch right here. Them Denver pricks can go to hell!" came another.

Then everything just came apart. Marshal Lewis was at dinner with Wallace's lawyer and had no idea this thing was mushrooming into disaster. Bob was snoozing in Lewis' office, minding the jail cell. No prisoner had ever broken out or escaped, but the townspeople had never really given a damn before. Bob was completely out of his element when his own brother and about twenty or thirty other men showed up to get Wallace.

"Tom, what the hell are you—?" Bob began but was cut off when Tom gently but firmly pushed him aside.

"Don't make no resistance, Bob. I didn't instigate this, but it's probably the right thing to do, and these boys ain't backin' off."

On to La Junta—The Baton is Passed in Colorado

One of the men from the angry mob lifted the clearly visible key ring off the nail, fumbled with the lock and the three keys, finally inserting the correct one. Washington Wallace didn't say a single word. He couldn't help crying, for he clearly knew what was about to befall him. He covered his face with his hands, gurgled something and went stone rigid with fear.

"Tom, don't do this," Bob said. "I don't care about the nigger, but I'm responsible. At least go get Lewis and tell him what you all are doin'. If it's all on my head—"

Bam! Bam! Two shots rang out from the back of the crowd. It was Marshal Lewis trying to break up the mob. "You men, goddammit, hold up! Get away from this jail. You can't—" he yelled before the mob totally closed him off from Wallace and the ring leaders.

"I can't stop this, Bob, and I don't want to. This boy's gonna pay," Tom said.

Out they went, across from the Harvey House and Santa Fe Depot to a light pole on the corner of Kansas Street and Santa Fe Avenue. The scene was macabre, but not unusual in its rarity. It almost resulted in even greater tragedy because the lynch mob was spilling onto the railroad tracks, right in the path of an oncoming train. Luckily the Santa Fe engine had slowed almost to a stop as it pulled up to the platform.

An Ominous Meeting

One of the truly remarkable but unplanned side effects of the Harvey House phenomenon was the insertion of Harvey

Wolves at the Door

Girls into the American West. One such girl was Catherine Rodden, a twenty-four-year-old Wisconsin farm girl, born the thirteenth of sixteen children of Michael and Mary Rodden. She was an Irish Catholic girl anxious to get away from the tediousness of farm life and seek a life of adventure and travel. There had been no way, however, for a young girl to do that until Mr. Harvey opened his chain of restaurants. Then young girls such as Catherine finally had a safe and respectable way to at least see that part of the world visited by the Santa Fe Railroad. Harvey Girls had to be very clean, very pleasant and very attractive young ladies. Such a girl was Catherine.

"I hate this, Catherine," her mother had said as Catherine prepared to board a train headed for Milwaukee. They stood at the depot in Sheboygan in early spring 1902. "I know you don't feel a future on the farm, and I don't blame you. But I so fear for your safety. Go with God, my lovely girl."

They both cried, her mother much harder than Catherine, for Catherine was quite ready to step out on her own.

Her father, Michael, accompanied her as far as Milwaukee, where they had relatives, including a brother and two sisters of Catherine. They spent the night with the brother's family, who would put Catherine on the train to Chicago the next day.

Not until Michael had said goodbye to her and boarded his own train back to Sheboygan did he shed tears. *We'll never see her again,* he thought. *Please, God, look after her.*

On to La Junta—The Baton is Passed in Colorado

Catherine spent about a month in training in Topeka, then went on day trips serving rail passengers. After that she did a few weeklong stints in various local Harvey Houses. Finally in late May 1902, her supervisor, Miss Kegelmeir, called her into her office.

"Catherine, I'm pleased to tell you that you're being assigned. Your deportment has been excellent, and all associated with you during your training say the same thing—you're an absolutely delightful and pretty young woman. We all feel you'll be a credit to our Harvey family."

Oh, yes, thought Catherine. *I can't wait! Will it be San Diego, San Francisco, Santa Fe?* She quite politely said, "I am so happy, Miss Kegelmeir, and I'll do my best. May I ask where I'm to be placed?"

"La Junta!"

"Gesundheit!" Catherine said while looking for a handkerchief to offer the older woman.

"No. La Junta, Colorado. That's where you're going."

Catherine was stunned. She most certainly had seen the name La Junta on the Santa Fe schedules, but she didn't recognize it and honestly thought her mentor had sneezed. She was terribly embarrassed but had managed to choke out, "La Junta! Oh, yes, La Junta. Not San Diego, or—"

"No, my dear, La Junta. You'll love it. You will board early on June 1 and be out there that evening. Now go make what preparations you need, pack your belongings and be ready to leave on the first."

Wolves at the Door

The train pulled into the La Junta Depot on the evening of June 1 at about seven P.M. Catherine was excited, tired, frazzled and hungry. She knew her employer well enough to expect a good meal, hot bath and comfortable night's sleep in a clean bed, probably in a shared room or dormitory. With great enthusiasm she anticipated her introduction to her new life in a new town. And then the train slowly edged up to the platform and stopped.

"What on earth is the commotion out there, Cath?" said Miss Patricia Lee, another new Harvey Girl assigned to La Junta.

"I'm sure I don't know, but look! They're all over the track, both sides. Seems odd to have such a crowd right in the yard, doesn't it?"

Touched by a Comforting Angel

The angry and out-of-control men manhandled Washington Wallace around the corner of the depot to the light pole.

"You weren't whimperin' like a baby when you beat the hell out of that girl, were you, nigger?" came one voice.

"You sonovabitch, let's cut off his prick and stick it in his mouth."

These otherwise normal, if not exemplary, citizens had lost any semblance of civilized humanity. They had become animals, totally devoid of any self-control.

Tom, who had been marching along at the front and had himself shouted, "Clarence, grab that rope and toss it up

On to La Junta—The Baton is Passed in Colorado

over the lamp arm," now had a strange epiphany. *What the devil am I doing?* he thought. He looked to find Bob and finally spotted both his brother and the marshal off to the side in a state of bewilderment. *They've both thrown in the towel on this. It's up to me to stop it.*

But it wasn't. Nobody could stop this abomination. This poor, wretched and retching black man was slugged and kicked in the face, sides, back and stomach. The retching came when he was kicked multiple times in the crotch. His privates weren't cut off as originally called for. They were merely emulsified. By the time he was hoisted, his kicked-in face was unrecognizable.

Washington Wallace had made a poor decision in being a drinker. He shouldn't have decided to stop on the path of life in La Junta, shouldn't have worked in the Santa Fe Depot. But of all the unfortunate things he did, the worst was his coming into this vale of tears as a black man. That had put him in the direct path of Deborah's phobia, Tom's misguided position of leadership, Bob's cowardice, Marshal Lewis' incompetence, and America's racial hysteria. So there he hung, teeth and gums dangling down in a tangle of his lips, with an unbroken line of bloody spittle extending to his knees, head cocked severely to his left by the knot in the rope, and the one eye not kicked in almost humorously bugged out.

It was a proud day for, well, surely for someone. Maybe for the men in the mob. But no, they didn't look especially proud as they gaped at the corpse, said "Yahoo," and wandered off. Probably had to get on home because church services would come early the following morning. Maybe Bob or Marshal Lewis was proud. But no, neither of them really seemed so either. They cut Washington down, and while the marshal wrapped him in a blanket, Bob actually stood to the side whimpering. So no great pride there.

Then there was Tom. He hadn't moved a muscle since the victim's feet had left the ground. It was as though he was ever so slowly emerging from a deep, deep dream. Like coming up from the bottom of a lake and, just before using up the last bit of air, barely clearing the surface.

He just stood there now, practically alone, contemplating the chunk of raw and bleeding dark meat rolled in a blanket at his feet. He regained his consciousness when he heard approaching footsteps coming along the pathway from behind the depot. He turned to behold the most beautiful young woman he had ever seen. He was in no mood for beauty at the moment, but a feeling of awe descended over him, as if he were in the presence of Helen of Troy. Surely this must be an angel sent from above to rescue him from this horrific cesspool in which he was mired. *This must be an angel of goodness sent to lend me comfort,* he thought as she opened her mouth to speak.

"Are you responsible for this?" Catherine asked as she pointed at Wallace's corpse. "Are you the big brave man who, with the help of only about two dozen other cowards, beat and hanged this human being?"

She could say no more. She knelt by Wallace's head and stroked his temple and brow. His horrible disfigurement seemed not to bother her at all.

On to La Junta—The Baton is Passed in Colorado

Tom could not speak either. He could only wonder, What is this? Did I really do this to this man? Who is he? Who am I? Who the hell is she?

A terrible awareness enveloped him, and he clearly saw what he had been a part of. He realized he couldn't stop the world and get off. He'd have to stand before his parents. Then he totally and almost convulsively broke down. He sunk to one knee and started weeping, then shaking. It went on and on; he was unable to stop. Inexplicably he felt a consoling arm wrap around his shoulder and a hand stroke the back of his head repeatedly.

After several minutes of this a soft voice said, "You must change your heart. No man can do something so bad that Jesus can't forgive. But first you must acknowledge what you've done here ... and then you will have to forgive yourself."

He continued to breathe in gasps, then slowly calmed down. He finally dried his eyes, turned and looked up. No one was there. He now wasn't sure if anyone had been there at all.

The aftermath of this event, at least on a public scale, was almost non-existent. Since there had never been an actual witness to the crime, nobody really knew what had happened in that alley. The jury had convicted Wallace, therefore the state of Colorado felt it had far more important concerns than that of a convicted Negro who had simply received his justice a little early, and at no taxpayer expense. Townfolk argued a little against vigilante behavior, but they quickly forgot about the affair. Marshal

Wolves at the Door

Lewis shored up his jail somewhat and passed as much blame as possible to Bob in some circles, while keeping credit for himself in others. Some folks winked at the marshal and said he had been pretty shrewd in conveniently going to dinner at that time. And the Frakes family called it justice served.

"It don't help our little girl now, but at least that nigger won't jump on some other folks' daughter," said Mrs. Frakes.

If he did, in fact, ever jump on anyone at all, Tamsen thought.

One of the sad repercussions of the lynching was the reaction of both Henry and Tamsen, as well as the townspeople, toward Tom. The town was mixed. Some patted him on the back and loaded him up with praise, such as, "Atta boy, you done good, Tom. You hung that nigger high enough none of the rest of these black bastards will try a stunt like that." That was a common sentiment. Others who weren't so sure merely said a polite hello as they passed Tom on the street.

As to his parents, everything had changed. Tamsen had been sure from the start that Susannah had said nothing about a Negro that first night. *But that don't mean it wasn't a black man, even that black man,* she thought. But she knew there was no evidence of any sort on which to convict him. Therefore, she thought, *Tom, my baby boy, is guilty of ... what? Murder? Obstructing justice? What? And he didn't actually lay a finger on Wallace, according to Bob.*

On to La Junta—The Baton is Passed in Colorado

Henry had no idea what to think. He hadn't been privy to Susannah's first comments. Maybe Tamsen didn't hear it right. *Maybe Deborah was correct. Hell the jury found him guilty. We can't have a rapist going free! But then we have to give an awful lot of credence to Tamsen's opinion. She's rarely wrong.*

The one person Tom had to come to grips with was Tom. Within a week he had heard all possible opinions and renditions of the hanging. Most folks except himself, his parents and the Frakes family had already basically forgotten it. And both sets of parents, his and Susannah's, would eventually move past it also. He knew he would never forget it. Something had touched his soul that night. For the first time in his life, he was ashamed of himself.

What about Susannah, he wondered. *Is she convinced Wallace really did it? Does she feel justice was served? I can't ask her now.* Maybe years from now. But he had to admit to himself that in all likelihood that man had nothing to do with Susannah's rape. He thought perhaps she had let passion with some boyfriend lead to violence and then overrule judgment in that alley and couldn't admit it to her parents. Or even to herself.

"We'll never know," Tom said to Bob, "so I don't know what else to do but forget it and move on. But I'll never again act in unison with any crowd, ever, the rest of my life."

The Harvey House Dance

Later in the summer Tamsen mentioned to Henry that Tom had been away from La Junta longer than usual. "He went back early June, didn't he? Wasn't that terrible incident June 1 or so? So here it is late August. Isn't three months longer for him to be gone than usual?"

"I guess it is, Mother, but I don't think he feels too comfortable here anymore. And I can't blame him."

Charlie, Bob and Frank and their families were all in town at the Devons' for a Sunday dinner. The same subject came up about Tom.

"Oh, I'm sure that's true, Mother," Etta said. "Bob tells me they've talked, and Tom just can't get himself right about that hanging. Personally, I don't see the problem. If that man didn't do this rape, he's probably done others. But Bob says Tom is still all tore up."

"I don't think it's the Negro he frets over," Bob said. "In fact, I don't think Tom would care if the fella had been white, black, orange or purple. I think what is killin' Tom is he thinks he personally lost control, and maybe he acted before he was sure of the facts."

Frank nodded. "He just always felt he was a leader. We all know he has been a hero of sorts to friends his age, even back as a kid. Nobody ever got Tom Devon's goat. He's always been cool under fire, so to speak."

"Well, what is any different about this situation?" Winifred asked.

On to La Junta—The Baton is Passed in Colorado

"I'll tell you what's different," Henry said. "He came to grips in one instant with his own human frailty, his imperfection."

They all turned to their father. Henry had slowed down noticeably in the past year or two. He had begun to show the effects of arthritis in his general gait, and his several facial tumors had caused him to hang more to the side in family conversations. With his lower energy and confidence levels, he tended to speak less often, and mostly only when he had something significant to say.

"Bob, Charlie, do you boys remember years ago when Jeremy died in the river and we took a little walk that night? You two and your Ma 'n' me? Bob, I think it was you that said somebody else should have been killed—like some Chinaman, I think you said. Remember that night?"

"I sure do," Bob said.

"Me, too," added Charlie.

"I think in my poor way I tried to explain that nobody's any better or worse than anyone else. I think I added the one exception might be some damn Irishman," Henry said, laughing. "I asked you boys to remember that always, the part about each of us bein' of equal importance, remember that?"

"Yes, sir."

Henry rocked slowly in his chair, closing his eyes for a brief moment, then he asked, "Frank, you remember any similar discussion you and Ollie and me had way back when you was kids?"

"Yes, I do, Pa."

"Well, let me assure you that I, one way or the other, had that same discussion with all of you, includin' Tom. And to the best of my belief, it took with you all. I mean, I guess I don't have to remind you that I spent some dangerous and unpleasant days up in Westport as a young man, more or less risking my life to protect that very idea. So to whatever extent Tom absorbed that lesson about Negroes, or anybody, being equal under the same law we are, I'm sure he's sufferin' and ashamed of hisself, 'cause I know this wasn't a race thing with him. It was a 'that sonovabitch raped my friend's sister' thing. And he let it get out of control. He let himself get out of control. And that's what is eatin' at him. Bob's absolutely right."

They all sat quietly for a minute or so. It was obvious their folks were hurting because Tom was hurting.

Finally Frank broke the silence with, "He's comin' to town, you know, next Thursday, for about a week. He telegraphed me a few days ago."

"Oh, my gosh!" Etta said. "You know what's next Saturday night? The big Harvey House dance! We gotta make sure we all go to that and force him to go. Maybe that'll pep him up!"

Sure enough, Saturday rolled around and the Devons got ready for the dance. Daughter Sadie Stonefield and her family were bunking in with her folks for a week or so. They had just moved to La Junta, and the house they were buying wasn't available quite yet. Other than Ollie and her family in Pittsburgh, the whole family was now living in La

On to La Junta—The Baton is Passed in Colorado

Junta or nearby, that's if you counted Tom coming over from Las Vegas as nearby.

"I really don't feel like goin' to a damn foot stomp. And I ain't dancin' either, ya hear?" Henry said to Tamsen as she straightened his tie. "I'm seventy damn years old and I got no business going to a damn dance. That's for the young folks, you hear me?"

"Of course I hear you, you old toad. You been grousing about having to go to this all day. Well yer goin', so you may just as well shut yer yap. For Pete's sake, you'd think you was goin' to yer own funeral."

"Well, for about as good as I feel, I might as well be."

"Do you two bicker at each other like this all the time?" Sadie asked.

"Yes, dear," Tamsen said, "that's just how your father converses. After forty-four years, I now know that's how the old boy tells me he loves me. Kinda affectionate, isn't he?"

Sadie and a couple of the grandchildren laughed.

Henry could say only, "Harrumph!"

They finally got themselves into the surrey and trotted on down to Trinidad Plaza to the Harvey House. The band was already in full rip when they arrived. Nearly a hundred people of all ages were milling around, some eating, some dancing, all just enjoying the evening.

It was a beautiful, balmy evening with only the slightest hint that September was on the doorstep. The days were still fairly hot, but this evening the temperature in the mid-seventies was wonderfully comfortable. The full moon lit up the place so that dancers were spilling out on the street. Tom walked in with Frank, saw his parents and walked over to greet them.

"Oh, hello, son," Tamsen cooed as she rose to kiss him. "It's so good to have you back. When'd you get in?"

"Just an hour ago," Tom said as he hugged his father. "I didn't know about this here soiree. I see you got yer dancin' shoes on, Pa!"

Henry harrumphed again.

The Harvey House was, of course, not as big an influence in La Junta as the AT&SF itself. After all, the Santa Fe was a huge employer. But the Harvey House was, in most folks' eyes, definitely part and parcel of the railroad. And the Harvey people were smart enough to know that good relations with the townspeople made everybody's life easier. To promote fond feelings between all concerned, they occasionally had a dance, a picnic, a July Fourth parade or some other such thing for the townies.

Across the room from the Devon family, another reluctant participant was hearing a lecture. "C'mon, Cath," said Patricia Lee, "you can at least put on a smile even if it's fake. Heavens to Betsy, it's a dance! We don't have to dance, but it'll be fun to just hear the music and tap our toes."

"They probably don't know a jig from a polka out here," Catherine Rodden said.

Being Irish but having German friends in Milwaukee, she knew both jigs and polkas very well. She had enjoyed going to dances over the last few years. Whether back in Wisconsin or out here in no man's land, dances were attended by entire

On to La Junta—The Baton is Passed in Colorado

families, and everyone from the grandfolks to the youngsters participated.

At about age eighteen or so she had begun to pair off with several young men, and by twenty she had struck up a fairly strong friendship with a young farmer named Jack Corville. He was very nice, not bad looking and enthusiastic about taking over his father's farm some day. He had become quite serious in his affection for Catherine, and after being somewhat connected for a year or so, he proposed marriage. Being caught off guard and not knowing what to say, Catherine accepted, sort of. But she very quickly recanted her acceptance, told Jack she cared deeply for him but needed to go find herself first. She had explained the Harvey opportunity she was contemplating, kissed him tenderly and politely said goodbye.

Jack Corville may not have had enough high octane excitement in his demeanor or in his future plans to suit Catherine's fiery Irish temperament, but she really did care for him and respected him. And although she had left him standing hat-in-hand on her doorstep, she didn't necessarily rule out an eventual life with him.

But here she was, rather unenthusiastically, about to join her friend Patty and a dozen other young Harvey Girls in sashaying around the floor with some of these rough and rowdy La Junta cowboy clods. Mercy sakes!

Tom Devon bought a round of drinks for his whole family. They had pulled a few tables together and were, as always, enjoying each other's company.

Wolves at the Door

"C'mon over here and have a seat, Harlan," Henry said. "I don't want to be the only old fart at this table!"

"Well thanks a lot, you snake-in-the-grass!" said Gretta, who just happened to be three weeks older than her husband.

"Whoops, excuse me, darlin!" Henry said. "I forgot about your tender situation."

"OK, Etta," Bob said, "let's hit the hardwood so's I can show you a few new steps I've been workin' on."

"What's it called, Bob," said Charlie, "dance of the water buffalo?"

The general jabbering got pretty thick, with everyone in rare form. Spouses both paired and switched off on the dance floor. Even Henry was cajoled into treading the light fantastic.

"Hank, I'm gonna sashay my wife up there to this next waltz," Harlan said. "If you don't ante up yourself, I guess that'll make you the only no show in the family. And what's worse, I'm gonna ask your sweet wife for the following dance, so you'd better shake a leg." So goaded into it, Henry did.

Henry and Tamsen had been pretty good revelers in their younger years, but both now preferred sitting around and sipping a drink with friends and letting the young folks cut loose.

Tom leaned back in his chair, slowly bouncing a foot to the music and watching the bubbles in his beer. He was enjoying himself, but he was not too interested in seeking out anyone to dance. In sort of a daydreaming mood, he held his beer mug up in front of his face. With several dozen

On to La Junta—The Baton is Passed in Colorado

dancing couples rhythmically moving through the gold prism of his mug, the bubbles gave off an eerie effect. As he lowered the beer, his eyes fell on a girl across the room, and his heart pretty near stopped. His jaw dropped, and he almost let go of the mug.

"Holy Jesus!" he said to himself, but audible enough for Frank to hear, "Who in the world is that lovely creature? I've seen her somewhere, maybe in my dreams."

"I have no idea, little brother. Ever since I got hitched to my beautiful Winnie here, I haven't noticed a single other woman."

"You're full of road apples, too, Frank, but nice of you to say that," Winifred said. "Tom, since your lyin' brother can't help you out, why don't you get off your posterior and go ask that young woman for a dance? You may have to wait in line, 'cause she's the finest lookin' lady I've seen around here for a while."

Tom barely heard any of this. He was mesmerized. Slowly he stood up, straightened his tie, chugged down the last of his beer, and headed directly across the dance floor to this stunning young woman.

"Cath," whispered Patty Lee, "I hate to say anything, but one heck of a good lookin' fellow is heading your way. Brace yourself, 'cause I think the biggest ship in La Junta's armada is about to pull up to your dock."

Catherine Rodden felt a very light touch on her elbow and turned to face the perpetrator as he said, "Excuse me, Miss, I'm Tom Devon, and I would be honored if you would join me on the dance floor for this next waltz."

Wolves at the Door

For the next few seconds, two reactions were struggling within her for supremacy. One was her effort to control her breathing and to not simply pass out then and there. She had never heard a voice like his nor felt a touch like the one he so gently administered to her elbow. And now face to face, she had never gazed into eyes like his. At that moment, Jack Corville was history.

The other reaction was the certain feeling she had seen him before. She couldn't think where or when. In fact, for the first couple of minutes in his presence, she could hardly think at all.

As she stood in a near catatonic state, she heard a nearby voice say, "Yes, Mr. Devon, Catherine would be pleased to join you in this dance." She felt Patty Lee's hand push her gently toward Tom and the dance floor.

Tom took her in his arms as the beautiful music swept them along in the rhythm of the waltz. He vaguely recognized her. Their only previous meeting had been very dark, in more ways than one. It bore no resemblance to the enchanting circumstances they were now enjoying.

"Your name?" Tom asked for a second time before Catherine even heard him.

"My na—? Oh! My name! My name is Catherine Rodden. I work at the Harvey House. I've been here only a couple of months, I'm from Wisconsin, I'm Irish, yappy, yappy, yap." She went from struck dumb to can't shut up.

He started laughing.

"Miss Rodden, hold on for a minute and take a breath.

On to La Junta—The Baton is Passed in Colorado

You don't need to tell me everything in one sentence. We've got all night."

"Oh, I am so sorry. I don't know why I do that. I'll be quiet."

They finished that dance and the next and the next. He held her tighter in his arms with each successive waltz. They hardly spoke, but both felt an indescribable jolt pass between them. Then she stopped still and stepped back from him.

"I just realized who you are. You're the man I saw the night of that terrible hanging just outside here. It was dark, but it was you, wasn't it?"

He squinted at her face and tried unsuccessfully to pull it from his memory. But he now realized the comforting touch of her hand on his shoulder was the same touch he had felt that awful night.

"Yes, I guess that was you that evening. Yes, it was me."

They slowly held each other again at a distance to finish the dance. He took her back to her table, thanked her for the pleasant dances, and returned to his table.

"Who is she, son?" Tamsen asked. "She's quite pretty, even beautiful, I'd say. You haven't sat down for half a dozen dances. Did you two hit it off?"

Henry didn't say anything, possibly because he was sound asleep.

"Look at him, Mother, Mr. Excitement!" Tom said with a chuckle. Then, "Yeah, I guess we hit it off. But then she remembered she recognized me at the depot, you know, that night. So I thanked her and took her back to her table. I don't want to embarrass her."

Wolves at the Door

Just then Tom felt a tap on his shoulder and turned to see Patty Lee. Before he could stand to introduce her to anyone, she leaned over and put her lips close to his ear.

"Now, you listen to me, Jasper. Your conversation with Miss Catherine ain't over. It'll be over when she says it's over. She told me who you are and what happened. She also told me what she said to you that horrible night. Let me ask you somethin'. Have you forgiven yourself?"

Tom was flabbergasted. He looked around to see if anyone else, mainly his mother, could hear. Tamsen had discreetly poked Henry so as to have someone to appear to be talking to. Tom turned back to Patty.

"Well, yes, I guess I have. It ain't easy to forget what I was a part of, but … yes, I believe I have forgiven myself."

"Well then, I'm going back over to Cath, she didn't know I was coming over to speak to you. I'm gonna tell her you suggested you meet her out back, down on the depot platform, to iron this out. I'm gonna say she should go out the front door. I'll go with her, and then we'll duck around the building to the depot. When you see us leave, count to sixty, and you go out the side door. I'll leave you two alone down there so you can say what you got to say in private. Got it?"

Without waiting for his answer, Miss Lee turned on her heels and was gone.

"Holy saints, son, who was that?" Henry asked as he slowly regained his bearings. "She seemed all business didn't she?"

On to La Junta—The Baton is Passed in Colorado

"A friend, Pa, just a friend," Tom said as he watched Patty, with Catherine in tow, leaving the Harvey House via the front door. "It's not important," he continued as he nervously tried to count without anyone knowing what he was doing. ... *forty-eight ... fifty-nine ... sixty!* "Look, if ya don't mind, I gotta get some air." He jumped up and bolted for the side door.

"Mother, is it just me, or is that boy getting to be about as nuts as the rest of our kids? You got any inkling what he's up to?"

"Yes, dear, on both counts. He is about as nuts as the whole family, and yes, I might just have a slight inkling 'bout what he's up to." She smiled and gave him a wink, the purpose of which he had nary a clue.

But she didn't. Oh sure, she had a pretty good idea where Tom intended to go. But like Tom, she was very surprised to see where he actually wound up. When he cleared the side door in an unheeding state of anticipation, he totally forgot about the huge old apple tree that had been left only eight or ten feet outside that door. And in the dark, particularly with his eyes adjusting, he ran headlong into its lowest branch and knocked himself out, cold as a cucumber. His meeting with Catherine would have to wait a day or two, unless she wanted to visit him in the hospital surrounded by all those Mennonite nurses.

Several months later, Tom and Catherine were riding in a nice little buggy Frank had lent him for the day. They rode east of the Harvey House, turned north over the Arkansas River and then continued east to visit the old Bent's Fort, which Catherine had never seen. Tom filled her in on its history, but he had something else on his mind. He told her of its place in the route from Independence to Santa Fe, but his thoughts were elsewhere.

"You seem distant today, Tom. What's up?"

"Catherine, ever since I met you at that dance, I, well, I mean ... when I had to go back to Las Vegas, I, I mean I can't hold my job and keep comin' to La Junta, Catherine, and my mother really likes you. You know I've got all those brothers and sisters. Do you think you have to stay at this Harvey House? I took this engineering course. Anyway, I got to go back again on the late Sunday train. How's Patty? Well, that's about it ... Whadya think?

She looked at him in utter astonishment before saying, "Yes."

"Yes, what?" he hedged.

"I don't know if you have any idea what you just asked me. By the way, Patty is fine and I'm glad your mother likes me. You just asked me to marry you, and the answer is yes. You go on back to Las Vegas on Sunday. I'll give my notice here at work. Then next time you return in a couple of weeks, we'll get married in the Catholic Church on Second Street. Then I'll come with you wherever you want to go. Is that pretty much what you had in mind?"

Since it was a rhetorical question, and she expected no answer, she went ahead and kissed him hard on the lips right in the parking area in front of Bent's Fort.

On to La Junta—The Baton is Passed in Colorado

"Now turn this thing around and let's get back to Frank's place. I told Winnie what you were going to ask me today, and she's having your family over tonight for dinner to celebrate!"

In Looking Back and Ahead

"You know, for a guy who I used to think had his life under control, what the hell has happened to you?" an exasperated Henry asked his son.

"Pa, I've told you, I can't explain my actions that night. I let my emotions get ahead of my thinking. Don't think for a moment I wouldn't change it all if I could. But I can't take back what is," Tom said.

"What night are you talkin' about? And why can't you undo it, goddammit?"

Tom was confused about both his father's intent and his inexplicable surliness.. "Pa, the man is dead. I know I was wrong. I can't change it, so can we please just forget it? I'm lucky I didn't go to jail, damn lucky. Am I gonna have you breathin' down my neck about it forever?"

"Who's dead? Go to jail for what?"

"Pa, am I missing something here? You are still disappointed in me over Wallace, aren't you?"

"Wallace? God damn, the hell with Wallace. He's dead. He shouldn't have been around here anyway. And that's water over the dam. I ain't talkin' about Wallace. I'm talkin' about that Catholic yer fixin' to marry, son!"

Wolves at the Door

Tom's face went slack. He couldn't believe his ears, nor could his mother.

"Father, what are you saying?" Tamsen said. "Surely you can't mean—"

"I'll tell you exactly what I mean. I mean bad enough she's Catholic, but Irish, too! Them people is hot blooded, with no self control. Plus they can't hold their liquor. I'll bet her father, if she even knows who he is, is a goddamn Irish drunk. And a goddamn papist in the bargain. Tom, what are you thinkin', son, what the hell are you thinkin'?"

Tom and Tamsen sat on the davenport, speechless. This attitude from Henry was so out of the blue, it just didn't make sense.

"Father, we all know Catherine by now. She's a lovely girl. I couldn't hand-pick a better wife for our son, or mother for our grandchildren. How can you be so cruel?" Tamsen said.

"Yeah, our grandchildren! They'll most likely be a bunch of mackerel snappin', whiskey swillin' little hooligans, you can bet on that. What the hell is she doin' out here anyway? Why isn't she back where she belongs, in goddamn Ireland, the land of drunks and bums!" Henry said as he went to the bedroom to lie down.

"Tom, I'm so sorry you had to catch him like this. I don't know what is wrong with him lately. He suffers so with his rheumatism and cancers. I'm sure he don't really mean it. Please try to forgive him, son."

"Ma, I just can't believe it. Isn't this the same man who always preached everybody's equal? He gave me a big talk

On to La Junta—The Baton is Passed in Colorado

about the Mexicans. 'Don't belittle them, don't take advantage of them.' Well that's bullshit! Excuse me, Ma, but I can't take this about Catherine. I love her dearly, and this family, or any family, would be lucky to get her. And what's worse, I heard a couple of comments from Libby and Etta along the same lines. I'm not gonna have it, Ma."

The holidays came and went without a wedding. True, Tom had gotten a couple of schedule changes that ran him from Las Vegas all the way to Amarillo and back throughout October and November. But the unexpected hostility from some members of his family toward Catherine's heritage not only put him off, it put her off, too.

After a couple of very strained Christmas dinners, Tom made a decision. "Cath, I honestly can't explain this. You could have knocked me over with a feather before I'd ever have expected this. I guess my father's English parents built an Irish hatred in him that sets aside his overall fair-mindedness. I just can't believe it, and I can't abide it, neither. So here's what we're going to do. I'm scheduled to leave the first Monday in January for Las Vegas and then Amarillo. The hell with 'em. You just come with me, and we'll get married along the way. Your family ain't out here anyway, so what difference does it make? Can you live with that?"

She could and they did. She bid farewell to Patty and the others at the Harvey House. Her supervisor had given her a glowing letter of recommendation to present to the folks at any Harvey House she wanted. There was one in Amarillo and one in Santa Fe. They made the rounds to his brothers and sisters to say goodbye.

"Forget it, Tom," Frank said. "You know the old man. He'll forget he ever said anything. I just think age 'n' pain is gettin' the best of him. He don't mean it, Catherine."

Same with Bob. "You take care, little brother. I apologize for any comments Etta made. She's, well, she's just Etta. What can I do?"

Sadie, Charlie, Jim Dwyer, all of them wished them well. And Tamsen, of course, was dying inside. Like it or not, Tom was and would forever be her baby boy. And she genuinely liked Catherine. Maybe she wouldn't have picked a Catholic, but Tom did, so that was that. And she herself was Irish, which made this all the more nonsensical.

Tamsen stood at the depot with the young couple. "Go with God, or as they say out here, vaya con dios, son. I love you so much it hurts. Catherine, you take care of my boy, won't you?"

She hugged them both before they stepped onto the train, then turned and left quickly so they wouldn't see her crying. Henry did not go to the station to see them off.

As Tamsen got into the buggy that Bob had brought her in, she could hear the whistle and see the steam of the engine rise above the roof lines. The train was heading west, and she feared she might never see her son again.

Scale of Observation

Several months went by. Henry hardly ever mentioned Tom, and Tamsen kept her own counsel. No sense aggravating her husband. She knew that Tom—really all her

On to La Junta—The Baton is Passed in Colorado

children—had their own lives to live. Her life was in its twilight. She had had forty-five good, albeit not always easy, years with Henry. *Will we make it fifty years together?* She wondered.

Throughout the spring of 1903 she remained active around town. She loved buying and selling residential lots herself and also with a couple of her children. She and Winnie and Frank bought and sold a few in the new Orchard Place section of the Ohio Addition. Henry didn't participate in any of these deals. In spite of his strange behavior toward Catherine, however, he remained happy and helpful toward his other children and his friends, even though he was often in great pain from arthritis and frequent eruptions of facial tumors.

Once near the end of summer on a truly gorgeous night, he cajoled Tamsen into the buggy and they took a drive across the river, just before sunset, to look back at the town.

"Look at that, Mother. It's beautiful."

They sat silently for a while as the sun began to pool on the western horizon.

"You know we're within sight of the end of our trail, don't you?" he said.

"Yes, I guess I do, and it's been a wonderful ride hasn't it? Not always easy, but wonderful."

"I saw something in a magazine last week at Norm's barber shop. Kinda odd, but thought provoking. It was actually in a section on science, but I took it for philosophical, and at our ages, a philosophy is a pretty good thing to have."

Wolves at the Door

"What was it, Henry?"

"The scale of observation creates the phenomenon."

She stared blankly at him and said, "The who of what does what?"

"The scale ... of observation ... creates the phenomenon! Say it slowly to yourself a few times and think about it. I think it means nothin' is as it appears. Any phee—nom-onon, I think that just means anything—a horse, the weather, a ball game, a grandchild, whatever-ain't only one thing. 'It all depends' might actually be a simpler way to say it. It all depends on who, why, when and where the thing is being looked at from."

Tamsen was trying to home in on what Henry was getting at, but she was drawing a blank.

"We've had a long life, Mother. I find I'm looking' back a lot these days and wondering what I actually did or saw along the way. Here's an example. Do you remember Long Eyes?"

"Of course I do, and the day you saw him from afar in his buffalo hunt."

"Well, my scale of observation on that event is somehow different now as an old man. I didn't appreciate it so much then, but his raw, youthful physical power and endurance are so removed from our lives now that they glow brighter in my memory of that day than they did at the time."

As he paused to reflect, Tamsen was struck by his intensity in elaborating on his thoughts.

Henry continued. "Another difference in the scale of observation could be how Long Eyes was beheld by the

On to La Junta—The Baton is Passed in Colorado

young warrior on that day, and how that young Indian boy would probably think back on Long Eyes today. Or how his own grandkids might view Long Eyes now."

She was beginning to get his drift. "You mean nothing has an actual for sure meaning in and of itself. It all depends who's observing it, and when ... and from what angle."

"Something like that. It's like our life together was one thing when we was behind it lookin' forward, and now it takes a whole different cast at the end years lookin' back. I guess maybe what triggered me off on this is the situation with Tom and Catherine. As God as my witness, Mother, I ain't got nothin' in the world against that young girl. I have no earthly idea why her being an Irish Catholic steamed me so much. Oh, I sure as hell know why it may have steamed me thirty years ago. I know my own father had a dim view of 'em from his England days. But it's the scale of observation in that magazine. Here at age seventy-one, in the year 1903, out here in Colorado, I haven't got any idea why I care if she's Irish Catholic or a Bavarian Huguenot! I mean, if we could all just stop puttin' one meaning on things and grant that lots of different views might be more accurate, then maybe ... oh, hell, Tamsen, you got any idea what it is I'm tryin' to say?"

"Yes, Father, I think you may be tryin' to explain through a scientific statement you saw in a magazine at Norm's barber shop"—she paused for a breath—"why you have been such an all-fired ass to your son and his ladylove and, in so doing, buggering up the nice harmonious nature

375

of our whole family! Is it something along those lines, dear?"

On the way back to the house, and then on into the week, Tamsen found she couldn't purge herself of the "scale of observation creates the phenomenon" idea. "Does that little phrase seem to have more meaning after awhile, Dagmar, or is it just me and Henry?"

"I can see its meaning, Tamsen," her old friend said. "When I think of Cob now, I come at him from all directions. Without embarrassing you or me, I'll say I can still remember him as my lover in our youth. I can clearly remember his breath, his touch, everything. But he also calls on me in my dreams as the young father and farmer he also was. And I'll bet two or three times a month he sits in the rocker across from me on our porch, and we talk. Sounds silly doesn't it? Maybe that's the end of a long and fortunate life. We can finally see the forest for the trees. We can see many more sides to this human existence than we ever could have imagined in our youth. Things change, and we should change with 'em."

"Mother!" came Henry's voice booming into the kitchen from out on the front porch. "I just woke up from my nap, and damned if it ain't gettin' hungry out here! What's fer supper?"

"On the other hand," said Tamsen, chuckling, "as you can hear, some things never change, do they?"

On to La Junta—The Baton is Passed in Colorado

The Letter
December 1, 1903

Dear Mother and Father Devon,

Tom has no idea I am writing this, but I feel I must. He was, and remains, deeply wounded by the rift that exists. I'm still not sure what was said, but I know it somehow involves me. Not knowing how I may have offended you, I don't know how to apologize, but I do. For whatever I did to cause hurt, I am sincerely sorry.

Please know I care deeply for and truly love your son. It pains me greatly to see him sad in any way. But all is not sadness. As I write this letter, I see him across the room with a look of pure joy on his face, and with a tiny hand enveloped in his. He is holding our new baby son, your grandson.

Without meaning any rudeness toward you, I cannot and will not allow this handsome baby boy to be brought up not knowing his grandparents. My parents are too distant to be part of his life, but you are not.

As mentioned, Tom has no inkling of this letter yet. But please be informed that your new grandboy, Walter C. Devon, along with his parents, will be arriving in La Junta a few days before Christmas. He hasn't exactly said so, but I know he'd be right proud to meet his wonderful Grandpa and Grandma Devon, and his many aunts, uncles and cousins.

Yours with great love,
your daughter-in-law,
Catherine

Comin' Home

Well, I'll be. Good for you, young girl, good for you, Tamsen thought as she finished reading the letter to Henry. She was suddenly so delirious with joy she almost jumped out of her chair as she handed the letter to her husband. "'Baby boy,' she says. I know all about lovin' a baby boy, Father. Hallelujah and praise the Lord! They're comin' home!"

Henry held the letter limply in his left hand and covered his face as well as he could with his right hand. But he couldn't hide his tears. "Oh, my goodness, Mother. It's over. Maybe that Lord of yours is givin' me a second chance." He paused and dropped the letter, covering his badly scarred face with both hands.

Regaining some composure and dropping his hands, he continued slowly. "I am so sorry for what I done. I thought I caused us another loss, like Mary and John …" He began crying harder, now, and Tamsen took the few steps forward to cradle his head.

"No, Henry. You didn't cause—"

"Mother, I did! I almost cut us off from Tom, and now a baby Devon. Thank God for that girl. She's a bigger person than I am." He rested a moment and finally got himself under control. "Mother, you write them back and welcome them for Christmas. Let's tell all the family what's happening. We'll have us a wingding Christmas dinner. And you … No, I'll tell Bob to tell Etta to keep her big mouth shut. Not nobody better mention neither Irish or Catholic, includin' me! I swear it. Oh, think of it! He's comin' home!

On to La Junta—The Baton is Passed in Colorado

"*They're* comin' home, Father. *They're* comin' home. And this whole family you 'n' me started so long ago, or our folks 'n' grandfolks started, is gonna keep on goin' forward. You 'n' me won't see it forever, Henry, but we had a chance to guide it as we saw fit for a lotta years."

Henry would have answered, but he could not. He looked at Tamsen. There she stood, a plump, white-haired old lady, smiling like an angel. And there he sat, a broken down, bald-headed old man, bawling his eyes out.

And what tears of joy they were!

☆ ☆ ☆

Author's Note

This book is a novel—an historical novel. In the wanderings of the fictional Devons, I have intended to follow as closely as possible the adventures and misadventures of a real family in frontier Kansas, spilling over to Colorado in the second half of the 19th century.

The fictional Henry and Tamsen are, in reality, my great grandparents, William Henry and Mary Ellen Chown. The fictional children are patterned after their real children. Their youngest son, Thomas Albert—Tom—was in real life my grandfather. Although we never met, I am his namesake. Most of the personal friends depicted on these pages are totally fictional, but many of the local townspeople were real folks. As historical research often displays, truth can be more bizarre than fiction. This story is a blend of both, leaning heavily on researched facts. If the story strays from actual happenings in spots, it doesn't stray far. Anything portrayed as happening either actually did happen or certainly could have happened.

In case the reader developed a curiosity during the course of this story as to the fact and fiction involved, let me throw a little light on the two.

Henry's participation in the Battle of Westport, as well as his military pay drafting up the chimney, was factual. So were the U.S. Grant deed and the graves (and dates of death) of little Mary Mariah and John Enoch. The actual causes of their deaths are anybody's guess.

Henry (William H. Chown) really was the president of the Kiowa Building Association in 1884. The lady on the roof really did die in the flooded Medicine River. Mr. Hegwer really did freeze in the blizzard of 1886. Bob Devon didn't actually meet Wyatt Earp, but according to my father, his father Tom did! And sad to confess, according to family legend, Tom really was a ringleader in the hanging of Mr. Wallace in 1902. And it did happen just as Harvey Girl Catherine Rodden was arriving at the depot in La Junta. And Tom did run into the apple tree.

Tom and Catherine met again later and patched things up enough to enable me to exist today. The rift in the family was real; the description of the photograph taken the week after Easter in 1896 is that of the real photo, which at one time was torn in two, cutting Tom off from the rest of the family. For what it's worth, Raisin, the Devons' dog in the 1870s, was actually my dog in the 1970s. And a great dog he was!

I hope you have enjoyed this novel, in which fact informs fiction. And I am hopeful that it is equally as enjoyable for history buffs as for those who just like a good story.

Thomas Albert Chown II

P.S. I have in my possession the family Bible, the butter mold box, the .22 cal. rifle and the family photograph—one that was not torn in two! As to whatever happened to Tom and Catherine down in New Mexico? Well, that's another story for another day.

About The Author

Thomas A. Chown is originally from Columbus, Ohio, and graduated from Ohio State University with a degree in English literature. He put it to good use for the next three and a half decades by selling life and health insurance, bicycles, electric motors, lawn mowers and edgers, earrings, signs, and anything else he could get his hands on. After raising their children in Venice, Florida, Tom and his wife Barbara moved to Dunnellon, Florida, for the good life of playing golf and swinging in the hammock. It didn't work out. Tom was bitten by a latent literary bug that caused him to write a genealogical narrative of his family's wanderings from old England to the present day, which he self-published as *Our Chown Odyssey*. The study of his own family's history inspired him to create the fictionalized Devon family saga, a trilogy beginning in the pioneering days in 1860's Kansas and leading up to the present day. *Wolves At The Door* is the first volume of their story.

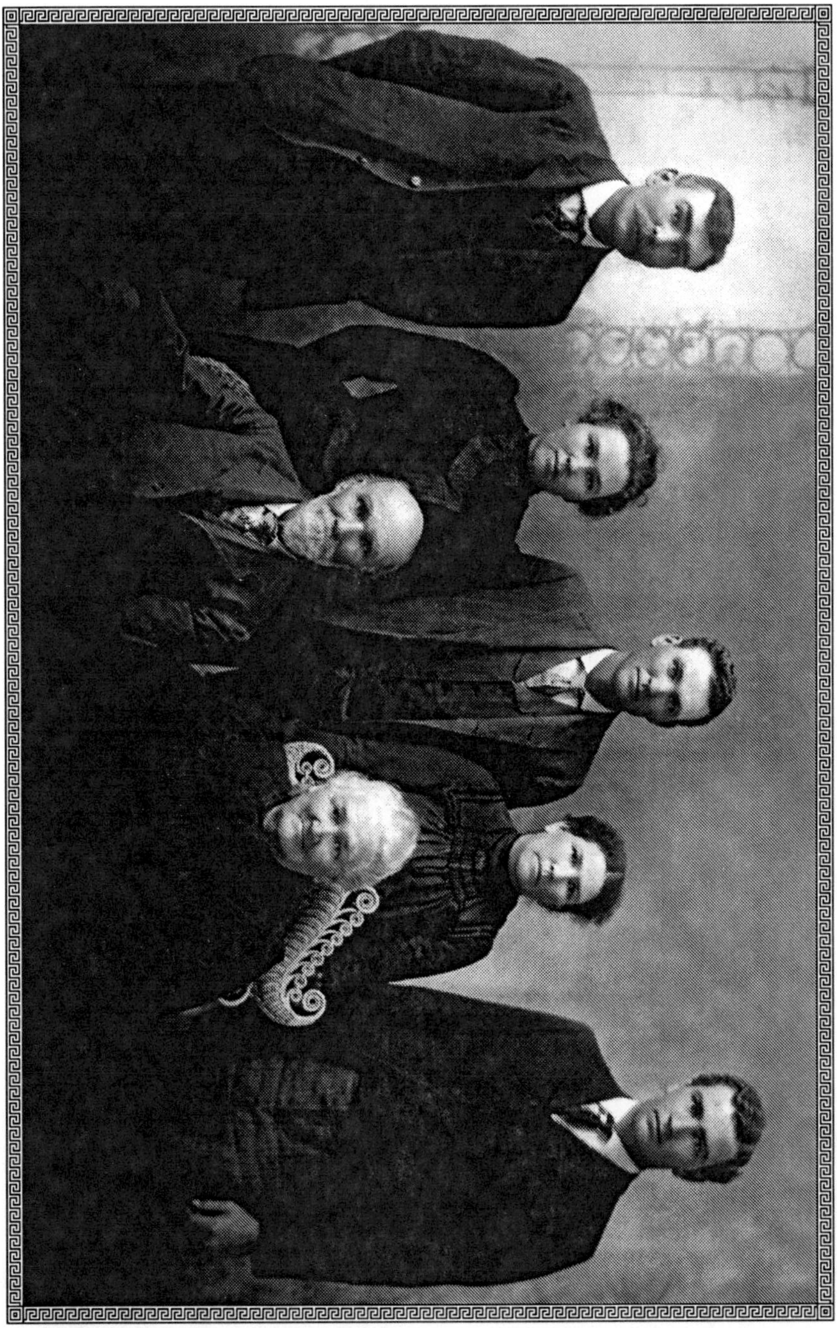

Printed in the United States
106366LV00001B/121/A